Billionaire BOSSES

MISTLETOE SEDUCTIONS

LUCY GORDON
SARA ORWIG
NICOLA MARSH

MILLS & BOON

Published in Great Britain 2015
by Mills & Boon, an imprint of Harlequin (UK) Limited,
Eton House, 18-24 Paradise Road, Richmond, Surrey, TW9 1SR

MISTLETOE SEDUCTIONS © 2015 Harlequin Books S.A.

A Mistletoe Proposal © 2010 Lucy Gordon
Midnight Under the Mistletoe © 2012 Sara Orwig
Wedding Date with Mr Wrong © 2012 Nicola Marsh

ISBN: 978-0-263-91574-7

24-1215

Harlequin (UK) Limited's policy is to use papers that are natural, renewable and recyclable products and made from wood grown in sustainable forests. The logging and manufacturing processes conform to the legal environmental regulations of the country of origin.

Printed and bound by
CPI Group (UK) Ltd, Croydon, CR0 4YY

A MISTLETOE
PROPOSAL
LUCY GORDON

Lucy Gordon cut her writing teeth on magazine journalism, interviewing many of the world's most interesting men. She's had many unusual experiences, which have often provided the background for her books. Once, while staying in Venice, she met a Venetian who proposed in two days and they've been married ever since. Naturally this has affected her writing, in which romantic Italian men tend to feature strongly.

Two of her books have won a Romance Writers of America RITA® Award.

You can visit her website at lucy-gordon.com

CHAPTER ONE

AFTER five years the gravestone was still as clean and well-tended as on the first day, a tribute to somebody's loving care. At the top it read:

MARK ANDREW SELLON,
9th April 1915—7th October 2003
A much loved husband and father

A space had been left below, filled three weeks later by the words:

DEIRDRE SELLON,
18th February 1921—28th October 2003
Beloved wife of the above
Together always

'I remember how you insisted on leaving that space,' Pippa murmured as she tidied away a few weeds. 'Even then you were planning for the day you'd lie beside him. And the pictures too. You had them all ready for your own time.'

A family friend had returned from a trip to Italy and mentioned how Italian gravestones usually contained a picture of the deceased. 'It really makes a difference to know what people looked like,' she'd enthused. 'I'm going to select my picture now.'

'So am I,' Dee had said instantly.

And she had, one for herself and one for her husband, taken when they were still in robust middle age. There, framed by the stone, was Dee, cheerful and ready to cope with anything life threw at her, and there was Mark, still bearing traces of the stunning good looks of his youth, when he'd been a daredevil pilot in the war.

Below them was a third photograph, taken at their sixtieth wedding anniversary party. It showed them standing close together, arms entwined, heads slightly leaning against each other, the very picture of two people who were one at heart.

Less than two months later, he had died. Dee had cherished the photograph, and when, three weeks after that, she had been laid beside him Pippa had insisted on adding it to the headstone.

Finishing with the weeds, she took out the flowers she'd brought with her and laid them carefully at the foot of the stone, murmuring, 'There, just how you like them.'

She rose and moved back, checking that everything looked right, and stood for a moment in the rich glow of the setting sun. A passer-by, happening to glance at her, would have stopped and gazed in wonder.

She was petite, with a slender, elegant figure and an air of confidence that depended on more than mere looks. Nature had given her beauty but also another quality, less easy to define. Her mother called her a saucy little so-and-so. Her father said, 'Watch it, lass. It's dangerous to drive fellers too far.'

Men were divided in expressing their opinion. The more refined simply sighed. The less refined murmured, 'Wow!' The completely unrefined wavered between, 'Get a load of that!' and '*Phwoar*!' Pippa shrugged, smiled and went on her way, happy with any of them.

Superficially, her attractions were easy to explain. The perfect face and body, the curled, honey-coloured hair, clearly luscious and extravagant, even now while it was pinned back in an unconvincing attempt at severity. But there was something else which no one had ever managed to describe: a knowing, amused look in her eyes; not exactly come-hither, but the teasing hint that come-hither might be lurking around the corner. *Something.*

A wooden seat had been placed conveniently nearby and Pippa settled onto it with the air of having come to stay.

'What a day I've had!' she sighed. 'Clients talking their heads off, paperwork up to here.' She indicated the top of her head.

'I blame you,' she told her grandmother, addressing the photograph. 'But for you, I'd never have become a lawyer. But you had to go and leave me that legacy on condition that I trained for a profession.'

'No training, no cash,' Lilian, Pippa's mother had pointed out. 'And she's named me your trustee to make sure you obey orders. I can almost hear her saying, "So get out of that, my girl."'

'That sounds like her,' Pippa had said wryly. 'Mum, what am I going to do?'

'You're going to do what your Gran says because, mark this, wherever she is, she'll be watching.'

'And you were,' Pippa observed now. 'You've always been there, just out of sight, over my shoulder, letting me know what you thought. Perhaps that was his influence.'

From her bag she produced a small toy bear, much of its fur worn away over time. Long ago he'd been won at a fair by Flight Lieutenant Mark Sellon, who'd solemnly presented him to Deirdre Parsons, the girl who later became his bride and lived with him for sixty years. To the last moment she'd treasured her 'Mad Bruin' as she called him.

'Why mad?' Pippa had asked her once.

'After your grandfather.'

'Was he mad?'

'Delightfully mad. Wonderfully, gloriously mad. That's why he was so successful as a fighter pilot. According to other airmen that I spoke to, he just went for everything, hell for leather.'

To the last moment, each had feared to lose the other. In the end Mark had died first, and after that, Dee had treasured the little bear more than ever, finally dying with him pressed against her face, and bequeathing him to Pippa, along with the money.

'I brought him along,' Pippa said, holding Bruin up as though Dee could see him. 'I'm taking good care of him. It's so nice to have him. It's almost like having you.

'I'm sorry it's been so long since my last visit, but it's chaos at work. I used to think solicitors' offices were sedate places, but that was before I joined one. The firm does a certain amount of the "bread and butter stuff", wills, property, that sort of thing. But it's the criminal cases that bring everyone alive. Me too, if I'm honest. David, my boss, says I should go in for criminal law because I've got just the right kind of wicked mind.' She gave a brief chuckle. 'They don't know how true that is.'

She stood for a moment, holding the little bear and smiling fondly at the photos of people she had loved, and still loved. Then she kissed him and replaced him in her bag.

'I've got to go. 'Bye, darling. And you, Grandpa. Don't let her bully you too much. Be firm. I know it's hard after a lifetime of saying, "Yes, dear, no, dear", but try.'

She planted a kiss on the tips of her fingers and laid them against the photograph of her grandparents. Then she stepped back. The movement brought something into the extreme edge of her vision and she turned quickly to see a man watching her. Or it might be more exact to say staring at her with the disapproval of one who couldn't understand such wacky behaviour. Wryly, she supposed she must look a little odd, and wondered how long he'd been there.

He was tall with a lean face that was firm almost to the point of grimness. Fortyish, she thought, but perhaps older with that unyielding look.

She gave him a polite smile and moved off. There was something about him that made her want to escape. She made her way to a place where there were other family graves.

It was strangely pleasant in these surroundings. Although part of a London suburb, the cemetery had a country air, with tall trees in which birds and squirrels made their homes. As the winter day faded, the red sun seemed to be sliding down between the tree trunks, accompanied by soft whistles and scampering among the leaves. Pippa had always enjoyed coming here, for its beauty almost as much as because it was now the home of people she had loved.

Just ahead were Dee's parents, Joe and Helen, their daughter Sylvia and her infant son Joey, and the baby Polly. She had never known any of them, yet she'd been raised in a climate of strong family unity and they were as mysteriously real to her as her living relatives.

She paused for a moment at Sylvia's grave, remembering her mother's words about the likeness. It was a physical likeness, Pippa knew, having seen old snapshots of Great-Aunt Sylvia. As a young woman in the nineteen-thirties she'd been a noted beauty, living an adventurous life, skipping from romance to romance. Everyone thought she would marry the dashing Mark Sellon, but she'd left him to run off with a married man just before the war broke out. He died at Dunkirk and she died in the Blitz.

Something of Sylvia's beauty had reappeared in Pippa. But the real likeness lay elsewhere, in the sparkling eyes and readiness to seek new horizons.

'In the genes,' Lilian had judged, perhaps correctly. 'Born to be a good time girl.'

'Nothing wrong with having a good time,' Pippa had often replied chirpily.

'There is if you don't think of anything else,' Lilian pointed out.

Pippa was indignant. 'I think of plenty else. I work like a slave at my job. It's just that now and then I like to enjoy myself.'

It sounded a rational answer, but they both knew that it was actually no answer at all. Pippa's flirtations were many but superficial. And there was a reason for it, one that few people knew.

Gran Dee had known. She'd been a close-up witness of Pippa's relationship with Jack Sothern, had seen how deeply the young girl was in love with him, how brilliantly happy when they became engaged, how devastated when he'd abandoned her a few weeks before Christmas.

That time still stood out fiercely in Pippa's mind. Jack had left town for a couple of days, which hadn't made her suspicious, as she now realised it should have. Wedding preparations, she'd thought; matters to be settled at work before he was free to go on their honeymoon. The idea of another woman had never crossed her mind.

When he returned she paid an unexpected visit to his apartment, heralding her arrival by singing a Christmas carol outside his door.

'New day, new hope, new life,' she yodelled merrily.

When he opened the door she flew into his arms, hoping to draw him into a kiss, but he moved stiffly away.

Then he dumped her.

For a while she'd been knocked sideways. Instead of the splendid career that should have been hers, she'd taken a job serving in the local supermarket, justifying this by saying that her grandparents, both in their eighties and frail, needed her. For the last two years of their lives she'd lived with them, watching over them, giving them every moment because, as she declared, she had no use for boyfriends.

It was then that the innocent beauty of her face had begun to be haunted with a look of determination so fierce as to be sometimes alarming. It would vanish quickly, driven away by her natural warmth, but it was still there, half hidden in the shadows, ready to return.

'Don't give in to it,' Dee had begged in her last year of life. 'I know you were treated cruelly, but don't become bitter, whatever you do.'

'Gran, honestly, you've got it all wrong. So a man let me down! So what? We rise above that these days!'

Dee had looked unconvinced, so Pippa brightened her smile, hoping to fool her, not very successfully, she knew.

Only after her death had Dee been able to put the situation right with a modest legacy, conditional on Pippa training for a proper career.

Pippa had changed from the quiet girl struggling to recover from heartbreak. Going back out into the world, starting a new life, had brought out a side she hadn't known she had. Her looks won her many admirers, and she'd gone to meet them, arms open but heart closed. Life was fun if you didn't expect too much, and she'd brought that down to a fine art.

'Aunt Sylvia would have been proud of you,' her mother told her, half critical, half admiring. 'Not that I knew her, she died before I was born, but the way she carried on was a family legend and you're heading in the same direction. Look at the way you're dressed!'

'I like to dress properly,' Pippa observed, looking down at

the short skirt that revealed her stunning legs, and the closely cut top that emphasised her delicate curves.

'That's not properly, that's improperly,' Lilian replied.

'They can be the same thing,' Pippa teased. 'Oh, Mum, don't look so shocked. I'm sure Aunt Sylvia would have said exactly that.'

'Very likely, from all I've heard. But you're supposed to be a lawyer.'

'What do you mean, "supposed"? I passed my exams with honours and they were fighting to hire me, so my boss said.'

'And doesn't he mind you floating about his office looking like a sexy siren?' Lilian demanded.

Pippa giggled.

'No, I guess he doesn't,' Lilian conceded. 'Well, I suppose if you've got the exam results to back you up you'll be all right.'

'Oh, yes,' Pippa murmured. 'I'll be all right.'

One man, speaking from the depths of his injured feelings, had called her a tease, but he did her an injustice. She embarked on a relationship in all honesty, always wondering if this one would be different. But it never was. When she backed off it was from fear, not heartlessness. The memory of her misery over Jack was still there in her heart. The time that had passed since had dimmed that misery, but nothing could ever free her from its shadow, and she was never going to let it happen again.

'I reckon you'd have understood that,' she told Sylvia. 'The things I've heard about you—I really wish we could have met. I bet you were fun.'

The thought of that fun made a smile break over her face. Sometimes she seemed to smile as she breathed.

But the smile faded as she turned to leave and saw the man she'd seen before, frowning at her.

Well, I suppose I must look pretty crazy, she thought wryly. *His generation probably thinks you should never smile in a graveyard. But why not, if you're fond of the people you come to see? And I'm very fond of Sylvia, even though we never met. So there!*

Her mood of cheerful defiance lasted until she reached her car, parked just outside the gate. Then it faded into exasperation.

'Oh, no, not again!' she breathed as the engine made futile noises. 'I'll take you to the garage tomorrow, but start just this once, *please*!'

But, deaf to entreaties, it merely whirred again.

'Grr!'

Getting out to look under the bonnet was a formality as she had only the vaguest idea what she was hoping to find. Whatever it was, she didn't find it.

'Grr!'

'Are you in trouble?'

It was him, the man who'd interrupted her pleasant reverie in the graveyard and practically driven her out by his grim disapproval. At least, in her present growling exasperation that was how it seemed to her.

Not that he was looking grim now, merely detached and efficient as he headed towards her and surveyed the car.

'Won't it start?'

'No. But this has happened before, and it usually starts after a while if I'm firm with it.'

His lips quirked slightly. 'How do you get firm with a car? Kick it?'

'Certainly not,' she said with dignity. 'I'm not living in the Dark Ages. I just—tap it a little and it comes right.'

'I've got a better idea. Suppose I tow you to the nearest garage, or have you got a special one where you normally go when this breaks down?'

'My brothers own a garage in Crimea Street,' she said with dignity.

'And do they approve of your "tapping" the car?'

'They don't approve of anything, starting with the fact that I bought it without consulting them. I just loved it on sight. It's got so much personality.'

'It's certainly got that. What it hasn't got is a reliable engine. You say you have brothers in the trade, and they let you buy this thing?'

'They did not "let" me because I didn't ask their permission,' she said indignantly.

'Nor their advice, it seems. I hope they gave you a piece of their minds.'

'They did.'

'So would I if you were my daughter.'

'But I'm not your daughter, I haven't asked for your help and I certainly haven't asked for your interference. Now, if you don't mind, I'd like to leave.'

'How?' he asked simply.

In her annoyance she'd forgotten that she was stranded. She glared.

'It's three miles to Crimea Street,' he pointed out. 'Are you going to walk it? In those heels? Or are you going to call them to rescue you? They'll love that.'

'Yes, and I'll never hear the end of it,' she sighed. 'Ah, well, I don't seem to have any choice.'

'Unless I give you a tow?' Seeing her suspicious look, he said, 'It's a genuine offer. I can't just leave you here.'

'Me being such a poor, helpless damsel in distress, you mean?'

His lips twitched. 'Well, there must be something of the damsel in distress about you, or you wouldn't have bought this ridiculous car.'

'Very funny. Thank you for your offer of help, but I'll manage without it. Good day to you.'

'Come off your high horse. Come to think of it, a horse would probably have served you better than this contraption. I'll fetch my car and connect them.' Starting to move off, he turned to add, 'Don't go away.'

She opened her mouth to reply, had second thoughts and closed it again. It was annoying that she couldn't help laughing at his jibe, but that was the fact. She was still smiling when he returned in an expensive vehicle that made her eyes open wide.

'Oh, wow! Are you sure you want that thing seen with my old jalopy?' she asked.

'I'll try to endure it.' He worked swiftly to connect the cars, then opened his door and indicated for her to get into the passenger seat.

She had to admire the smooth, purring movement of his vehicle, which spoke of expense and loving care, suggesting that this man had an affinity with cars. Since she loved them herself, she could feel some sympathy, even a faint amused appreciation of how she must look to him. He'd implied that she reminded him of a daughter, and she wondered how many daughters he actually had.

'I'm Roscoe Havering, by the way,' he said.

'Pippa Jenson—well, Philippa, actually.'

'Pippa's better: more like you.'

'I'm not even going to ask what is "like me". You have no idea.'

'Cheeky. Very young.'

'I'm not that young.'

'Twenty—twenty-one—' he hazarded.

'Twenty-seven,' she laughed.

It was as well that traffic lights had forced him to halt

because he turned quickly to stare at her in surprise. 'You're not serious.'

'I am.' She gave him a wicked smile. 'Sorry!'

'How can I believe you?' he said, starting up again. 'You look more like a student.'

'No, I'm a solicitor, a staid and serious representative of the law.' She assumed a deep voice. 'Strong men quake at my approach. Some of them flee to hide in the hills.'

He laughed. 'I think I'll get you home first. I won't ask who you work for. Obviously, you have your own practice which is driving everyone else into bankruptcy.'

'No, I'm with Farley & Son.'

She saw his eyebrows rise a little and his mouth twist into a shape that meant, 'Hmm!'

'Do you know them?'

'Quite well. I've used them in the past. They've got a big reputation. You must be impressive if they've taken you on. Aren't we nearing Crimea Street now?'

'Next one on the left.'

They saw the garage as soon as they turned into the street. The little business that Pippa's great-grandfather, Joe Parsons, had set up ninety years earlier had flourished and grown. It was now three times the size, and her brothers, Brian and Frank, had bought houses on the same street so that they could live close to their work.

They were just preparing to shut up shop when the little convoy rolled into view. At once they came out onto the pavement and stood watching with brotherly irony.

'Again!' Frank declared. 'Why aren't I surprised?'

'Because you're an old stick-in-the-mud,' Pippa informed him, kissing his cheek, then Brian's. 'And clearly you didn't mend it properly. This is Roscoe Havering, who came to my rescue.'

'Good of you,' Brian said, shaking Roscoe's hand. 'Of

course a better idea would have been to dump her in the nearest river, but I dare say that didn't occur to you.'

'Actually, it did,' Roscoe observed. 'But I resisted the temptation.'

The brothers laughed genially. They were both in their forties, heavily built and cheerful.

A few moments under the bonnet was enough to make Frank say, 'This'll take until tomorrow. And look, I'm afraid we can't invite you in. The family's away and we've sort of planned…well…'

'A night on the tiles,' Pippa chuckled. 'You devils! I'll bet Crimea Street is going to rock.'

'You'd better believe it!'

'OK, I'll come back tomorrow.'

'Don't you live here?' Roscoe asked.

'No, I've got my own little place a few miles away.'

'Where exactly?'

She gave him the address in the heart of London.

'I'll take you,' he said. 'Get in.'

Relieved, she did so, first retrieving two heavy bags from the back of her car.

'Thanks,' she said as she clicked the seat belt and slammed the door. 'I've got a heavy night's work ahead of me and I've got to give it everything.'

'No hungry man wanting his supper cooked?'

'Nope. I live alone. Free, independent, no distractions.'

'Except visiting your friends,' he observed.

'They're my brothers—oh, you mean in the graveyard. I suppose you thought I looked very odd.'

'No, you looked as if you were enjoying the company. It was nice.'

'I always did enjoy my grandparents' company. I adored them both. Especially Gran. I loved talking to her, and I guess I just can't stop.'

'Why should you want to?'

'Most people would say because she's dead.'

'But she isn't dead to you, and that's what matters. Besides, I don't think you worry too much about what other people say.'

'Well, I ought to. I'm a lawyer.'

'Ah, yes. Staid and serious.'

She made a comical face. 'I do my best.'

Outwardly, he showed nothing, but inside his expression was wry. Twenty-seven. Was he expected to believe that? Twenty-four, tops. And even that was stretching it. If she really worked for Farley she was probably little more than a pupil, but that was fine. She could still be useful to him.

A plan was forming in his mind. The details had to be fine-tuned but meeting her was like the working out of destiny. Somewhere, a kindly fate had planned this meeting and he was going to make the most of it.

'It's just there,' Pippa said, pointing through the window to a tall, expensive-looking apartment block.

'There doesn't seem anywhere to park,' he groaned.

'No need. Just slow down a little and I'll hop out. Just here where the lights are red.'

She reached for her bags, flashed him a dazzling smile and got out swiftly.

'Thank you,' she called, backing off.

He would have called her to wait but the lights changed and he had to move on.

Pippa hurried into the building and took the elevator to the third floor. Once in her apartment, she tossed the bags away and began to strip off.

'Shower, shower,' she muttered. 'Just let me get under the shower!'

When she was naked she hurried into the bathroom and got under the water, sighing with satisfaction. After relishing the cascade for a few minutes, she got out and dried herself off, thinking of the evening's work that lay ahead. She felt ready for it now.

But then something caught her eye. One of her bags lay open on its side, the contents spilling out, and she could see at once that one vital object was missing.

'Oh, heavens!' she groaned. 'It must have fallen out in his car and he drove off with it.'

The sound of the doorbell revived her hope. *Roscoe Havering. He's found it, brought it back to me. Thank heavens!*

Pulling a large towelling robe around her, she ran to the door. 'I'm so glad to see you—'

Then she stopped, stunned by the sight of the young man who stood there, his air a mixture of pleading and defiance.

'Oh, no,' she breathed. 'You promised not to do this again.'

CHAPTER TWO

For most of the journey Roscoe wore a frown. Things were falling into place nicely. Not that this was a surprise. He was an organised man, skilled at controlling his surroundings and making things happen as he wanted, but even he could hardly have arranged matters as neatly as this.

So his frown didn't imply problems, simply that there were still details to be sorted before he'd fixed everything to suit himself, and he was giving that desirable outcome the concentration it deserved.

Now he could see the large, comfortable house that had once been his home. These days it housed only his mother and younger brother Charlie, although Roscoe had kept his room and usually slept there a couple of nights a week to keep a protective eye on both of them. His mother was looking anxiously out of the window and came to the door as soon as she saw him. She was approaching sixty, nervously thin but still with the remnants of good looks.

'Is it all right?' she asked. 'Have you sorted it?'

He kissed her. 'Sorted what?'

'About Charlie. Have you arranged everything?'

For just the briefest moment he tensed, then smiled.

'Mother, it's too soon to arrange everything, but I'm working on it. Don't worry.'

'Oh, but I must worry. He's so frail and vulnerable.'

Luckily she wasn't looking directly at him, or she'd have seen the cynical twist of his mouth. Roscoe had an unsentimental, clear-eyed view of his younger brother. He knew Charlie's volatility, his ramshackle behaviour, his headlong craziness and his selfishness. All these he saw through a filter of brotherly affection, but he never fooled himself. Frail and vulnerable? No way!

But he knew his mother's perception was different and he always avoided hurting her, so he simply said, 'Leave it to me. You know you can trust me.'

'But you will make them drop those stupid charges, won't you? You'll make those horrid people admit that he's innocent.'

'Mother, he's not exactly innocent. He more or less admitted—'

'Oh, but he didn't know what he was saying. He was confused.'

'He's not a child. He's a young man of twenty-four.'

'He's a child in his heart, and he needs his big brother to defend him.'

'I'm doing my best. Just leave it to me.'

'Oh, yes, you always protect him, don't you? You're such a good brother. I don't know what I'd do without you.'

'Well, you don't have to,' he said gently. 'So it's all right.'

'Now come indoors and have your supper.'

'Fine, I'll just get my things.'

But, as he leaned into the car, he froze suddenly.

'Oh, Lord!' he groaned, seizing something from the floor at the back. 'How did that get there?' He straightened up, holding a large envelope. 'It must have fallen out of one of her bags and she rushed off without noticing. Perhaps I can call her.'

He pulled out the contents, all papers, and went through

them looking for her phone number. He didn't find it, but he did notice that these were serious papers. She'd spoken of a heavy night's work ahead, and would probably need them.

'I'm sorry,' he sighed. 'Can you hold supper? I'll be back in an hour.'

He was gone before his mother could complain.

'Jimmy, you promised to leave me alone.' As Pippa spoke she was backing off, one hand clutching the robe across her breast, the other held up defensively. 'We agreed it was over.'

'No, you said it was over,' he protested. 'I never said it. I couldn't say it, feeling the way I do. Oh, Pippa, I miss you so much, if you only knew. But you do know in your heart, don't you? I couldn't be so crazy about you if you didn't feel just a little something for me.'

'I do feel something for you,' she sighed.

'There, I knew it!'

'But it's not what you want. It's mostly pity and a sort of guilt that I let things go so far. Honestly, Jimmy, I didn't mean to. I thought we were just having a good time with no strings. If I'd known you were getting so serious I'd have discouraged you earlier.'

'But you didn't,' the young man pleaded. 'Doesn't that prove you feel something for me?'

'Yes, it means I feel like a kindly aunt, and that's not what you want.'

His face fell and she knew a pang over her heart. He was a nice boy, and he'd appeared on the scene just in time to discourage the one before him. She'd been grateful, and after that they'd shared many a laugh, some dinner engagements and a few kisses.

Then things had got out of hand. He'd grown serious, wanting to take her away for a weekend. Her refusal had increased his ardour. He'd spoken of his respect, and proposed marriage. Her rejection had cast him into despair.

'Couldn't we give it another try?' he begged now. 'You tell me what it is about me that annoys you and I'll be careful never to do that.'

Reluctantly, Pippa decided that only firmness would be any use now.

'When you talk like that it annoys me,' she said. 'When you haunt me, and telephone at all hours, sending me flowers which I don't want, bombarding me with text messages asking what I'm wearing, then I get very annoyed.

'You're a nice boy, Jimmy, but you're not for me. I'm sorry if I led you to believe otherwise. I didn't mean to. Now, please go.'

Something in his eyes made her pull the edges of her robe closer, clutching them firmly. His anguish was being replaced by the determination of a man who would no longer accept no for an answer.

'Please go,' she said, stepping back.

'Not without a kiss. You can grant me that, can't you?'

'I think not. Goodbye.'

Pippa tried to close the door but he forestalled her. Now his breathing was coming heavily, the arms that closed around her were strong, and she was no longer sure she could deal with him.

'Let me go, Jimmy.'

'Not until I'm ready.'

'Did you hear me? I said let me go and I meant it. Stop that. *Jimmy, no!*'

On the journey back to Pippa's apartment Roscoe was frowning again, but this time in confusion. On the one hand there was her appearance—young, dainty, vivacious. On the other hand there were the papers with their plethora of facts and figures that only a skilled, serious mind could understand. He tried to fit the two sides together, and couldn't.

This time he found a parking space and entered the building, going to study the list of residents by the elevator.

'Can I help?' A middle-aged man was passing by.

'I'm looking for Miss Jenson's address.'

'Blimey, another one. They pass through here like an army. Mind you, even she doesn't usually have two in one evening.'

'Indeed,' Roscoe said carefully.

'I tell you, it's pathetic. They come here with their flowers and their gifts, begging her, pleading with her, but it's no use. When she's bored with them she dumps them. I've tried to warn some of them but will they listen? You'd expect a man to have more dignity, wouldn't you?'

'You would indeed,' Roscoe said, still guarding his words.

'But they say she's magic and they can't help themselves.'

'You spoke of two.'

'Yes, the other one hasn't been here long so you'd better go carefully. Good-looking young fellow. Shouldn't think you'd stand a chance. She's got a pick of them, you know. Best of luck, though.'

He passed on out of the front door, leaving Roscoe wondering what he'd wandered into. But what he'd just heard was good news in that it made Pippa likely to be more useful to him, and nothing else mattered. He located the apartment and got into the elevator.

As soon as the doors parted he heard the noise coming from just around the corner, out of sight, a male voice crying out, 'You can't be so cruel—'

Then Pippa's voice. 'Can't I? Get out now or I'll show you how cruel I can be. I'm told I have very sharp knees.'

'But I only—*ow*!'

'Now go. And don't come back.'

Roscoe turned the corner just in time to see the young man stagger back, clutching himself, then collapse to the ground. Through the open door he could see a woman, or perhaps a goddess. She was completely naked, leaving no detail of her glorious figure to the imagination. The hourglass shape, the curved hips, the tiny waist, the breasts slightly too large, although his view of them was partly obscured by her glorious hair, not pinned back now but cascading down in a riot of curls.

After a moment he realised that the vision was Pippa, but not the light-hearted girl he'd met earlier. This was a very angry woman, standing triumphant over her defeated foe who was writhing on the ground. Literally.

The vision vanished at once, not in a puff of smoke but in a hasty movement to make herself decent by pulling on a robe as soon as she saw Roscoe. Only the fury on her face remained.

With the robe safely concealing her, she came to the door and addressed the young man. 'I'm sorry, Jimmy, but I warned you. Don't come back here, ever.'

Jimmy's face was sullen as he hauled himself to his feet, all good nature gone. 'You haven't heard the last of this,' he spat. '*Jezebel!*'

Incredibly, a smile flickered over her beautiful features. 'Oh, come on, you can do better than that. Who was Jezebel, after all? Now, if you'd said Mata Hari I'd have been insulted—or maybe flattered, one of the two.'

'Mata who?'

'Oh, go and look it up!' she said with the exasperation of a schoolmistress. 'But *go*!'

Scowling, he dragged himself to his feet and began to

limp away, but not before turning to Roscoe. 'You've been warned,' he spat. 'She won't treat you any better.'

Roscoe held up the envelope. 'I'm just the delivery man,' he said mildly.

Jimmy flung him a speaking look and limped away. Roscoe waited until he was out of sight before saying, 'I'm sorry to arrive unexpectedly, but you left this in my car.'

She made as if to take the envelope that he held out, but snatched her hand back as the robe fell open.

'I'll take it inside,' he said, moving past her.

She followed him, slamming the front door, hurrying into the bedroom and slamming that door too. Roscoe wondered at her agitation. After all, she'd been the victor, conquering and subduing her foe. He would have given a good deal to know the history behind that scene.

The apartment was what he would have expected, lush and decorative in a way he thought of as ultra-feminine. The furniture was expensive and tastefully chosen and the shelves bore ornaments that suggested a knowledge of antiques.

In one corner of the room was a desk with a computer and various accessories, all of which were the very latest, he noted with approval. It seemed to tell a different story to the rest of her. Ditzy dolly-bird on the one hand, technology expert on the other.

But probably the computer had been installed by her employers. That explained it.

She came whizzing back into the room, dressed in sweater and jeans. They were sturdy and workaday, unglamorous except that they answered all questions about her figure.

'Are you all right?' he asked.

'Certainly I'm all right. Why shouldn't I be?' She sounded a tad defiant.

'Just that he seemed rather overwrought—'

'And he called me Jezebel, implying that I'm a floozie, that's what you meant.'

'That's not what I meant at all.'

Even to herself, Pippa couldn't have explained why she was on edge, except that she liked to stay in control, and being discovered as she had been was definitely not being in control.

'Look, I just came back to return your papers,' he said hastily. 'Don't blame me for finding…well…what I found.' Too late, he saw the quagmire stretching before him.

'And just what do you think you found?' she demanded, folding her arms and looking up into his face. It was hard because he had a good six inches over her but what she lacked in height she made up in fury.

His own temper rose. After all, he'd done her a favour.

'Well, I found a girl who'd been a bit careless, didn't I?'

'Careless?'

'Careless with her own safety. What on earth possessed you to get undressed if you were going to knock him back?'

'Oh, I see. You think I'm a vulgar tease?'

'No, just that you weren't thinking straight—'

'Or maybe you're the one not thinking straight,' she snapped. 'You jump to the conclusion that I stripped off to allure him, and the true explanation never occurs to you. Too simple, I suppose. *He arrived after I had come out of the shower.*'

'Oh, heavens, I should have thought of that. I'm sorry, I—'

'I didn't get undressed for him,' she raged on, barely hearing him. 'I'm not interested in him and so I've told him again and again, but he wouldn't take no for an answer. Just like a man. You're all the same. You all think you're so madly attractive that a woman's no never really means no.'

'I didn't—'

'Conceited, arrogant, bullying, faithless, treacherous—'

'If you'd only—'

'Leave, now!'

'If I could just—'

'No, you can't "just". *Leave!*'

'I understand that—'

'Listen, the last man who came in here wouldn't go when I told him to, and you saw what happened to him.'

'All right,' Roscoe said hastily. 'I really only came to return your property.'

'Thank you, sir, for your consideration,' Pippa responded in a formal voice that was like ice, 'but if you don't leave of your free will you'll do so at *my* will and that—'

'I'm going, I'm going.'

He departed quickly. Whatever the rights and wrongs of the situation, this was no time to argue. For some reason, she was ready to do murder. It was unfair, but there was no understanding women.

From Pippa's window, a curve in the building made the front door visible. She stood there watching until she saw him get into his car. Then she turned and glared at the photograph of her grandparents on the sideboard.

'All right, all right. I behaved terribly. He came to return my things and I was rude to him. I didn't even thank him. Why? *Why?* I don't know why, but I was suddenly furious with him. How dare he see me naked! Yes, I know it wasn't his fault; you don't have to say it. But you should have seen the look on his face when he saw me on display. He didn't know whether to fancy me or despise me, and I could strangle him for it. Grandpa, stop laughing! It's not funny. Well, all right. Maybe just a bit. Oh, to blazes with him!'

Down below, Roscoe took a quick glance up, just in time to see her at the window before she backed off. He sat in his car for a moment, pondering.

He'd gained only a brief glimpse inside her bedroom, just enough to see a double bed and observe that it was neatly made and unused. He'd barely registered this but now it came back to him with all its implications.

So she really had refused him, which meant she was a lady of discrimination and taste as well as beauty and glowering temper. Excellent.

Later that night, before going to bed, he went online and looked up Mata Hari:

> Dutch, 1876-1917, exotic dancer, artist's model, circus rider, courtesan, double agent in World War One, executed by firing squad.

Hmm! he thought.

It was a word that occurred to him often in connection with Pippa. With every passing moment he became more convinced that she would fit his plans perfectly.

The two men regarded each other over the desk.

'Not again!' David Farley said in exasperation. 'Didn't he promise to reform last time?'

'And the time before,' Roscoe sighed. 'Charlie's not really a criminal, he just gets carried away by youthful high spirits.'

'That's your mother talking.'

'I'm afraid so.'

'Why can't she face the truth about Charlie?'

'Because she doesn't want to,' Roscoe said bluntly. 'He looks exactly like our father, and since Dad died fifteen years ago she's built everything on Charlie.'

The door opened and Roscoe tensed, but it was only a young woman with a tea tray.

'Thanks,' David Farley said gratefully.

He was a burly man in his late forties with a pleasant face and a kindly, slightly dull manner. He cultivated that dullness, knowing how useful it could be to conceal his powerful mind until the last moment. Now he poured tea with the casual skill of a waiter.

'Has your mother ever come to terms with the fact that your father committed suicide?' he asked carefully.

Roscoe shook his head. 'She won't admit it. The official story was that the car crash was an accident, and we stuck to that to discourage gossip. Now I think she's convinced herself that it really was an accident. A suicide would have been a rejection of her, you see.'

'Of all of you,' David ventured to say. He'd known Roscoe for years, right back to the time he'd been a young man who admired and loved his father. He too had suffered, but David doubted anyone had ever considered this.

Now, much as he'd expected, Roscoe shrugged aside the suggestion that he actually had feelings and hurried to say, 'If I can pull Charlie through this without a disaster I can get him onto the straight and narrow and stop her being hurt.'

'Do you know how often I've heard you say that?' David demanded. 'And it never works because Charlie knows he can always rely on you to rescue him from trouble. Just for once, don't save him. Then he'll learn his lesson.'

'He'll also end up with a criminal record, and my mother will have a broken heart,' Roscoe said harshly. 'Forget it. There has to be a way to deal with this, and I know what it is. It's important to put the right person on the case.'

'I shall naturally deal with this myself—'

'Of course, but you'll need a good assistant. I suggest Miss Philippa Jenson.'

'You know her?'

'I met her yesterday and was much impressed by her qualities,' Roscoe declared in a carefully colourless voice. 'I want you to assign her to Charlie with instructions to give him her full attention.'

'I can give Pippa this case, but I can't take her off other cases. She's much in demand. Don't be fooled by her looks. She's terrifyingly bright and one of the best in the business. She qualified with some of the highest marks that have ever been seen, and several firms were after her. I got her by playing on her sympathies. She did her pupillage here and I managed to persuade her that she owed me something.'

'So she really is qualified? She looks so young.'

'She's twenty-seven and already becoming well known in the profession. This lady is no mere assistant, but a formidable legal brain.'

The last three words affected Roscoe strangely. The world vanished, leaving only a young, perfect female body, glowing with life and vigour, dainty waist, generous breasts partly hidden by the luscious hair that tumbled about them, beautiful face glaring at him with disdain.

A formidable legal brain!

'What...what did you say?' he asked with an effort.

'Are you all right?'

The vision vanished. He was back in the prosaic offices of Farley & Son, facing David Farley across a prosaic desk, drinking a prosaic cup of tea towards the end of a prosaic afternoon.

'I'm fine,' he said quickly. 'I just need to settle things with Miss Jenson. Can I see her?'

'She's in court this afternoon, unless perhaps she's returned. Hang on.' He seized the phone, which had rung. 'Pippa! Speak of the devil! How did it go?... Good...good. So Renton's pleased. You made his enemies sorry they were born, eh? I knew you would. Look, could you hurry back? I've got a new client waiting for you. Apparently you already—'

He checked, alerted by Roscoe's violent shake of the head.

'You're already known to him by repute,' he amended hastily. 'See you in a minute.'

Hanging up, he stared, puzzled. 'Why didn't you want me to say you'd already met?'

'Best not. Start from scratch,' Roscoe said. Inwardly, he was musing about the name Renton, which he'd glimpsed on the papers he delivered last night, plus a mountain of figures.

'So she has a very satisfied client?' he mused.

'One of many. Lee Renton is a big man in the entertainment field, and getting bigger. There were some grim accusations hurled at him by someone who'd hoped to take advantage of him, and failed. Financial stuff, all lies. I knew Pippa would nail it.'

'So her adversary *is* sorry he was born?' Roscoe queried.

'Nasty character, up to every trick. But then, so is she. Great on detail, reads each paper through thoroughly. Nothing escapes her. She'll be here in a moment. The court is just around the corner.'

'Solicitors don't usually appear in court, do they? I thought that was the role of barristers.'

'The old division still exists,' David agreed, nodding, 'but its lines are getting blurred. These days, solicitors can act as advocates more often than in the past, and when they're as good as Miss Jenson we encourage it. You've made a good choice.'

'Yes,' Roscoe murmured. 'I have.'

'Luckily for you, she's a workaholic or she might be reluctant to add to her workload so close to Christmas.'

'Close to Christmas? It's only November.'

'Most people start planning their schedule now so that they can grab some extra days off when the time comes. Pippa does the opposite, comes in earlier, works later. The nearer to Christmas it gets, the more of a workaholic she becomes.

I could understand it if she was alone, but she's got plenty of family. It's as if she's trying to avoid Christmas altogether.'

'You make her sound like Scrooge.'

David grinned. 'Well, I think I really have detected a touch of "Bah! Humbug!" in her manner.'

His phone rang. He answered it and made a face. 'Don't send him in or I'll never get rid of him. I'll come out there.' Rising, he said, 'Stay there and I'll be back in a minute.' He hurried out.

While waiting, Roscoe went to stand by the window, looking down on a part of London that spoke of wealth and manipulation, people in control, sophistication—rather like one aspect of Pippa Jenson. But not all of her, he thought, remembering the unselfconscious way he'd seen her joking with the headstone yesterday.

The door opened. Somebody flew into the room, speaking breathlessly. 'Oh, my, what a day! But it was worth everything to see the look on Blakely's face when I had all the figures—'

She stopped as Roscoe turned from the window.

'Good afternoon, Miss Jenson,' he said.

CHAPTER THREE

FOR a moment Pippa's face was full of shock. 'You,' she murmured.

Then shock was swiftly replaced by a smile. 'So prayers do get answered after all,' she said.

'I'm the answer to your prayers?' he queried. 'Now that I wasn't expecting.'

'Meeting you again is the answer to prayer,' she said. 'It gives me the chance to say thank you, otherwise I'd have had to search for you all over London. You came to my rescue three times last night—towing me to the garage, taking me home, bringing my papers over—and then I was rotten to you. I can't forgive myself.'

'No, that's my job,' he agreed. 'Let's forget it now.'

'That's kinder than I deserve. When I think—'

The door opened. It was David with the man he'd been trying to get rid of, and who was now talking nineteen to the dozen, causing David to make a face of resignation.

'We're in the way,' Roscoe said. 'Let's have a bite to eat. Cavelli's is very good, and it's nearby.'

'Great. I'm famished.'

Cavelli's was a small restaurant over the road, just opening for the early evening. They found a table by the window.

'I'd toast you in champagne,' Roscoe said, 'but I'm driving. What about you?'

'I'm afraid my car's still on the sick list. I came in by taxi.'

'Champagne, then.'

'Not on my own. What I'm really dying for is a cup of tea.'

He placed the order and sat regarding her for a moment. Her hair was pinned back again, as he'd first seen it, but the rich honey colour still had a luxuriant appearance. She was dressed for business in a dark blue trouser suit of decidedly mannish cut. But if she thought for a moment that it masked her vibrant sexual allure, she was deceiving herself, Roscoe thought.

He pulled himself together. This was a time for business. The 'other' Pippa, the one he'd seen last night, must be firmly banished. He did his best to achieve that, but it was hard when all around them people were turning to look at her in admiration.

They toasted each other in hot tea, and Pippa sighed theatrically with relief.

'You don't know what I owe you,' she said. 'Those papers won the case for me. Without them, it would have been a disaster.'

'Yes, you couldn't have made Frank Blakely sorry he was born, which I gather you did.'

She gave a triumphant chuckle. 'I reported the figures, he disputed them, I produced the papers that proved them, he demanded to know how I came by those papers, I said my lips were sealed—'

'That sounds a bit dodgy,' Roscoe said, grinning, pleased.

'Do you mind?' she demanded, mock-offended. 'I am not "a bit dodgy".'

'I beg your pardon—'

'I'm *very* dodgy—when I have to be. It depends on the

client. Some need more dodginess than others. Some don't need any.' She added wickedly, 'They're the boring ones.'

'I see you believe in adjusting to their requirements,' he said appreciatively.

'That's right. Ready for anything.' She chuckled. 'It makes life interesting.'

'Miss Jenson—'

'Please, I think we've passed the point where you could call me Pippa.'

She didn't add, *After the way you saw me*, but she didn't need to.

'Pippa—I'm sorry if I embarrassed you last night. I only wanted to return your property.'

'It wasn't your fault. It was just unlucky that you turned up…well…at that moment.'

'He seemed to feel very strongly about you.'

She sighed. 'He's a nice boy but he can't understand that I don't feel the same way. We went out for a while, had some fun, but there was nothing in it beyond that.'

'Not on your side, but surely his feelings were involved?'

For a moment Roscoe fancied a faint withered look came over Pippa's face.

'And if it had been the other way around, do you think he'd have cared about my feelings?' she asked quietly.

'Perhaps. He seemed to have really strong emotions about you.'

The look vanished so fast he couldn't be sure he'd seen it. 'Life's a merry-go-round.' She shrugged. 'You have to look forward to the ups but always be ready for more downs.'

'So there's nobody special in your life at the moment? Or are there a dozen like him ready to spring out like last night?'

'Possibly. I don't keep count. Look, I just wanted to

apologise for the way I flew at you. After what you did for me, you deserved better. Today was a triumph. I had two job offers as I was leaving the court, and without those papers I'd have got nowhere. So I owe you, big time. I meant what I said. I'd have hunted you down through all London to tell you that.'

'And if I hadn't known exactly where to find you, I'd have hunted you down too. I have a job that only you can do.'

'Are you the client David mentioned?'

'That's right.'

'Ah, I begin to see. You want someone good with figures, right?'

'Among other things,' he said carefully. 'The case I want you to take concerns my younger brother, Charlie. He's not a bad lad, but he's a bit irresponsible and he's got into bad company.'

'How old is he?'

'Twenty-four, and not very mature. If he was anyone else I'd say he needed to be taught a lesson, but that—' he hesitated before finishing stiffly '—that would cause me a certain amount of difficulty.'

'You couldn't afford to be connected with a convict?' she hazarded.

'Something like that.'

'Mr Havering—'

'Call me Roscoe. After all, what you said about me calling you Pippa—well, it works both ways, doesn't it?'

For a moment the naked nymph danced between them and was gone, firmly banished on both sides.

'Roscoe, if I'm to help you I need full information. I can't work in the dark.'

'I'm a stockbroker. I have clients who depend on me, who need to be able to trust me. I can't afford to let anything damage my reputation.'

His voice was harsh, as though he'd retreated behind steel bars. But the next moment the bars collapsed and he said roughly, 'Hell, no! You'd better know the real reason. If anything happens to Charlie, it would break my mother's heart. He's all she lives for, and her health is frail. She's been in a bad way ever since my father died, fifteen years ago. At all costs I want to save her from more suffering.'

He spoke as though the words were tortured from him, and she could only guess what it cost this stockbroker to allow a chink in his confident facade and reveal his emotions. Now she began to like him.

'Why is he in trouble?' she asked gently.

'He went out with his friends, had too much to drink. Some of them broke into a shop at night and got caught. The shopkeeper thinks he was one of them.'

'What does Charlie say?'

'Sometimes he says he wasn't, sometimes he hints he might have been. It's almost as though he didn't know. I don't think he was entirely sober that night.'

Pippa frowned. This sounded more like a teenager than a young man of twenty-four.

'Do you have any other brothers or sisters?' she asked.

'None.'

'Aunts, uncles?'

'None.'

'Wife? Children? Didn't you mention having a daughter?'

'No, I said *if* you were my daughter I'd give you a piece of my mind.'

'Ah, yes.' She smiled. 'I remember.'

'That'll teach me not to judge people on short acquaintance, won't it? Anyway, I have neither wife nor children.'

'So, apart from your mother, you're Charlie's only relative. You must virtually have been his father.'

He grimaced. 'Not a very successful one. I've always been so afraid of making a mess of it that I…made a mess of it.'

Pippa nodded. 'The worst mistakes are sometimes made by people who are desperately trying to avoid mistakes,' she said sympathetically.

Relief settled over him at her understanding.

'Exactly. Long ago, I promised my mother I'd take care of Charlie, make sure he grew up strong and successful, but I seem to have let her down. I can't bear to let her down again.'

It felt strange to hear this powerful man blaming himself for failure. Evidently, there was more to him than had first appeared.

'Does he have a job?'

'He works in my office. He's bright. He's got a terrific memory, and if we can get him safely through this he has a great future.'

'Has he been in trouble with the police before?'

'He's skirted trouble but never actually been charged with anything. This will be his first time in court.'

She wondered what strings he'd had to pull to achieve that, but was too tactful to ask. That could come later.

'Was anyone injured?' she asked.

'Nobody. The shop owner arrived while there were several of them there. They escaped, he gave chase and got close enough to see them just as they reached Charlie. He began yelling at them, which attracted the attention of two policemen coming out of the local station, and they all got arrested.

'The owner insists Charlie was actually in the shop with the others, although I don't see how he can be sure. He must have just seen a few figures in the gloom.'

'What about the others? Haven't they confirmed that he wasn't in the shop?'

'No, but neither do they say he was. They hum and haw

and say they can't remember. They were really drunk, so that might even be true. But the owner insists that he was there and is pressing charges.'

She considered. 'Any damage?'

'None. They managed to trick their way in electronically.'

'So the worst he might face is a fine. But he'd have a criminal record that would make his life difficult in the future.'

'It's the future I'm worried about. They're a bad crowd, and they're not going to stop. It will get worse and worse and he'll end up in jail. I've got to get him away from that bunch.'

'Doesn't he begin to see that they're bad for him if this is the result?'

'Charlie?' Roscoe's voice was scathing. 'He doesn't see the danger. So what if he's convicted for something he didn't do? He'll just pay the fine and laugh his way home. There's a girl in this crowd who's gained a lot of influence over him. Her name's Ginevra. He's dazzled by her, and I think she gets her fun by seeing what she can provoke him into doing.'

Pippa frowned. 'You mean he's infatuated by her. There's not a lot I can do about that.'

'But there is. You can break her hold over him. Instead of being dazzled by her, he could be dazzled by you. He's easily led, and if Ginevra can lead him into danger you could lead him into safety.'

'And suppose I can't get that kind of influence over him?'

'Of course you can. You're beautiful, you've got charm, you can tease him until he doesn't know whether he's coming or going. If you really set your mind to it you can get him under your thumb and make him safe. I know you can do it. I've known you were the perfect person ever since we met and I learned who you worked for.'

So carried away did he become, explaining his plan, that he missed the look of mounting outrage in Pippa's eyes.

'I hope I've misunderstood you,' she said at last. 'You seem to be saying that you want me to be a…well…'

'A mentor.'

'A mentor? That's what you call it?'

'You point the way to the straight and narrow and he follows you because he's under your spell.'

'Ros— Mr Havering, just what kind of a fool do you take me for? I know what you want me to be and it isn't a mentor.'

'A nanny?'

The discovery of what he really expected from her was making her temper boil again. 'Be careful,' she warned him. 'Be very, *very* careful.'

'I may have explained it badly—'

'On the contrary; you've explained it so perfectly that I can follow your exact thought processes. For instance, when did you decide that you wanted me for this job? I'll bet it was last night when you arrived at my home. One look at me and you said to yourself, "She's ideal. Good shape. Handy with her fists and no morals". Admit it. You don't want a lawyer, you want a floozie.'

'No, I want a lawyer, but I can't deny that your looks play a part.'

'So you admit I look like a floozie?'

'I didn't say that,' he said sharply. 'Will you stop interrogating me as if I were a prisoner in the dock?'

'Just demonstrating my legal skills which, according to you, are what you're interested in. Tell the court, Mr Havering, exactly when did Miss Jenson first attract your attention? Was it when she was naked, or several hours earlier when you saw her in the graveyard? You saw her swapping jokes with a headstone and decided she was mad. Naked *and* mad! That's a really impressive legal qualification.'

He took a long breath and replied in a slightly forced manner. 'No, I too sometimes talk to the headstone when I visit my fa— Never mind that. I didn't know we were going to meet. It was pure chance that your—that Miss Jenson's car broke down, we got talking and she told me where she worked. That firm has handled legal work for me before and I was planning to approach them about Charlie. I saw that she would be the ideal person to take his case.'

'You decided at that moment, knowing nothing about her legal skills? But of course those weren't the skills that counted, were they? What mattered was the fact that she was a vulgar little piece—'

'I never—'

'A ditzy blonde with curves in the right places, who could be counted on to seduce your brother—'

'I'm not asking you to—'

'Oh, please, Mr Havering, credit the court with a little common sense. If you'd managed to set them on the road together, that is where it would have led eventually. At the very least, the question would have come up. You don't deny that, do you?'

'No, but—' He stopped, seeing the pit that had opened at his feet.

'But perhaps you were counting on this vulgar, unprincipled young woman to deal with him as effectively as you saw her deal with another man. A good right hook, a well-aimed knee—who needs legal training?'

She stopped, slightly breathless as though she'd been fighting. She couldn't have explained the rising tide of anger that had made her turn on him so fiercely. He wasn't the first client whose attitude had annoyed her, but with the others she'd always managed to control herself. Not this time. There was something in him that sent her temper into a spin.

'I think we've said all we have to say,' she informed him, beginning to gather her things. 'I'm sorry I won't be able to meet your requirements, but I'm a lawyer, not an escort girl.'

'Please—'

'Naturally, I shan't be charging you for this consultation. Kindly let me pass.'

He had her trapped against the wall and could have barred her exit. Instead, he rose and stood aside. His face was unreadable but for the bleakness in his eyes. Despite her fury, she had a guilty feeling of having kicked someone who was down, but she suppressed it and stormed out.

Just around the corner was a small square with fountains, pigeons and wooden seats. She sat down, breathing out heavily and wondering at herself.

Fool! she told herself. *You should just have laughed at him, taken the job, knocked some sense into the lad, then screwed every penny out of Havering. What came over you?*

That was the question she couldn't answer, and it troubled her.

Taking out her cellphone, she called David.

'Hi, I've been hoping to hear from you,' he said cheerfully. 'Wait until you've heard my news. The phone's been ringing off the hook with people wanting you and nobody but you. You made a big impression in court today, producing those figures like a magician taking a rabbit from the hat. Working for Roscoe Havering will do you even more good. Everyone knows he employs only the best.'

'Tell me some more about him,' Pippa said cautiously.

'Hasn't he told you about himself?'

'Only that he's a stockbroker. I—want to get him in perspective.'

'He doesn't boast about what a major player he is, that's true. But in the financial world Roscoe Havering is a name that pulls people up short. They jump to do what he wants—well, I expect you've found that out already. What he doesn't readily talk about is how he built that business up from collapse. It was his father's firm, and when William Havering committed suicide it smashed Roscoe.'

'Suicide?'

'He didn't tell you that?'

'No, he just said his father had died and his mother never really recovered.'

'There was a car crash. Officially, it was an accident, but in fact William killed himself because his life's work was going bust. Roscoe worked for his father. He'd seen the financial mess they were in and tried to help, but there was little he could do. Secretly, I think he blames himself. He thinks if he'd done more he might have prevented the disaster—used his influence to pull William back from the brink. It's nonsense, of course. He was only twenty-four, little more than a beginner. There was nothing he could have done.

'After William's death he managed to save the business and build it into a massive success, but it changed him, not really for the better. His ruthless side took over, but I suppose it had to. You won't find him easy. What he wants, he wants, and he doesn't take no for an answer.'

'But do you realise what it is that he wants?' Pippa demanded. 'Am I supposed to seduce this boy, because you know what you can do with that idea.'

'No, of course not,' David said hurriedly, 'but let's be honest, you've had every man here yearning for you. You'll know how to get this lad's attention.'

'I'm not sure—'

'You haven't turned him down?' David sounded alarmed.

'I'm thinking about it,' Pippa said cautiously.

What are you talking about? raged her inner voice. *Just tell him you've already said no.*

'Pippa, please do this, for the firm's sake. Roscoe brings us a lot of work and, between you and me, he owns our office building. He's not a man I want to offend.'

David was a good boss and a kind man. He'd taught her well, while keeping his yearning admiration for her beauty behind respectable barriers.

'I'll get back to you,' she said.

She was thoughtful as she walked back to Cavelli's, trying to reconcile the contradictions that danced in her mind. She'd perceived Roscoe Havering as an older man, certainly in his forties, but if David's facts were correct he was only thirty-nine.

It was his demeanour that had misled her, she realised. Physically, he was still youngish, with dark brown hair that showed no hint of grey or thinning. His face was lean, not precisely handsome but intelligent and interesting. It might even have been charming but for a mysterious look of heaviness.

Heaviness. That was it. He seemed worn down by dead weights that he'd carried so long they were part of him. They aged him cruelly, but not permanently. Sometimes she'd surprised a gleam of humour in his eyes that hinted at another man, one it might be intriguing to know.

She quickened her steps, suddenly eager to talk to him again, wondering if he would still be there. He might have walked out. Or perhaps he was calling David to complain about her.

But as soon as she went in she saw him sitting where she'd left him, staring into space, seemingly full of silent sadness. Her heart was touched, despite her efforts to prevent it.

Control, warned her inner voice. Stay impartial. His outrageous request must be considered objectively.

How?

She approached quietly and pulled out a chair facing him. He looked up in surprise.

'I'm sorry I stormed out like that,' she said. 'Sometimes I get into a temper. Shocking loss of objectivity, especially in a lawyer. A wise man wouldn't want to employ me.'

'There's such a thing as being too wise,' Roscoe said gently. 'I'm sorry, too. I never meant to offend you. I expressed myself badly, and you were naturally upset.'

'You didn't express yourself badly. You laid out your requirements for your employee, making yourself plain on all counts, so that I'd understand everything before committing myself. That was very proper.'

He winced. 'I wish you wouldn't talk like that.'

'I'm merely trying to be professional.' She gave a wry smile. 'It's just not very nice to have people thinking I'm a tart. It's even worse when that's my chief qualification for a job.'

'I never said that,' he disclaimed hurriedly. 'Nor did I mean it. But you do seem to have the ability to love 'em and leave 'em.'

'Oh, I believe in leaving 'em. I just manage without the love 'em bit.'

'That's what I want. You can cope with Charlie better than a more naive girl would. You could handle him, keep him in order, make him see things your way. What's funny?' Her sudden chuckle had disconcerted him.

'You are,' she said. 'You're making such a mess of this. What you really want is a heartless woman who can take care of herself, and you're tying yourself in knots trying to say so without actually saying the words. No, no—' she held up a hand to silence his denial '—we've covered that ground. Let it go.'

'Will you help me?' he asked slowly.

'If I can, but things may not work out as you plan. You've

assumed that he'll take one look at me and collapse with adoration. Suppose he doesn't?'

'I think that would be a really new experience for you,' he said, trying to sound casual.

'Not at all. The world is full of men who are indifferent to my charms.'

'You just haven't met them yet.'

'I've met plenty.'

'Splendid! Then you'll know what to do. Just use whatever methods you normally use to overcome their resistance.'

Her lips twitched. 'I could take that as another insult.'

'Yes, you could—if you were determined to.'

'What does that mean?'

'I means that I've realised that you can twist everything I say into an insult, and you do it whenever it suits you. So now I'm fighting back.'

'How?'

'By refusing to let you bully me,' he said firmly. 'I am *not* going to cower and watch every word in case you misunderstand. You don't actually misunderstand anything. You know I don't really mean to insult you, so don't try to score points off me. I don't want you to seduce Charlie. I want you to beguile him, make his head spin until he'll follow your lead. You'll do a good job and I'll respect you for it. And if we fight, we fight openly. Agreed?'

There was a definite no-nonsense tone to his voice, making it clear that he meant every word. He was putting his foot down, asserting himself, warning her not to mess with him— all the powerful, dominant things that she had instinctively associated with him.

And yet—and yet—

Far back in his eyes, that look was there again—a gleam that might have been conspiratorial humour.

Or perhaps not.

After a moment Pippa held out her hand to him. 'Agreed.'

They shook. She took out a notebook and spoke formally. 'I need to know as much about the gang he's running around with as you can tell me.'

'They're all young people who seem to live on the edge of the law. They don't even have proper addresses. They squat, which means they move on a lot as they get caught. I don't know for a fact that they steal, but they don't have any regular source of income. Charlie definitely gives Ginevra money. They live from hand to mouth, which he finds exciting. Here. That's the two of them together.'

From an inner pocket he took out a photograph that seemed to have been taken in a crowded room, probably a squat. In the centre, a young couple lay back in each other's arms.

'He keeps that as a treasured souvenir,' Roscoe observed curtly. 'I wanted you to see it, so I stole it from him.'

'Good for you,' Pippa murmured. Studying the picture, she felt a rising tide of excitement. 'Yes, now I begin to understand. She's up to her old tricks.'

'You know her?' Roscoe demanded, startled.

'Yes, and her name's not Ginevra, it's Biddy Felsom. I suppose she thought the new name sounded more glamorous. Her hobby is teasing the lads to do daft things to win her favour. She's done a lot of damage in her time. What's the matter?'

The question was surprised from her by the sight of Roscoe's face, filled with shock and dismay as he stared over her shoulder. The next moment she heard, above her head, the petulant voice of a young man.

'So there you are, Roscoe. Hiding from me, I suppose. You must have known I'd be over here as soon as I found out what you were up to.'

'Charlie—'

'Well, you can forget it, do you hear? I know exactly the

kind of creep you'll want to hire for me, all settled and respectable. Let's be respectable, whatever else happens. No
way. I'll find my own lawyer—someone who understands
the world and lives in the present. *Ow!*'

He hopped back, wincing as Pippa's chair was pushed out
hard against his leg.

'I'm so sorry. I didn't mean that to happen,' she said
untruthfully.

Gazing up at him, she knew he had a grandstand view of
her face and the generous curves of her breasts, with just one
button of the sedate blouse undone. Now the smile, soft and
warm, dawning slowly, suggesting that she'd been pleasantly
amazed at the attractions of the young man looking down at
her.

'Hello,' she said.

CHAPTER FOUR

CHARLIE drew a long, slow breath, visibly stunned. This was useful, Pippa thought, bringing a professional mind to bear on the situation, because it gave her the chance to study him.

He was certainly handsome. His face was slightly fuller than his brother's, just enough to give it a vivacious quality that was alluring. His mouth was attractively curved, and she guessed that many a girl had sighed hopelessly for him. He was too boyish to attract her, but he seemed pleasant.

'Hello,' he murmured, distracted. Then he recovered his poise and seated himself next to Pippa. 'Look, I'm sorry. I'm only mad at him.' He indicated Roscoe.

'He must be an absolutely terrible person,' she said sympathetically.

'He is. Definitely.'

'And now he wants to force his choice of lawyer on you—someone middle-aged and ignorant of the modern world, who won't understand you. Oh, yes, and *respectable*. Shocking!'

She couldn't meet Roscoe's eye. He was leaning back, regarding her performance with wry appreciation.

'By the way, I'm Charlie Havering,' the young man said, holding out a hand.

'I'm Pippa Jenson,' she said, taking it. 'And I'm your lawyer.'

Charlie grinned. 'Yeah, right!'

'Seriously. I'm a solicitor. I work for Farley & Son.'

'But you can't be,' Charlie protested. 'You don't look at all respectable.'

'Watch your manners, Charlie,' Roscoe said. 'This is a highly qualified lady you're talking to.'

'I can see that,' Charlie said, taking her hand. '*Very* highly qualified.'

Roscoe caught his breath as he found himself surrounded by double entendres. 'I only meant,' he said carefully, 'that she's a professional—no, not like that—'

He swore inwardly as he realised what Pippa could make of this, but she surprised him, bursting out laughing. Laughter possessed her utterly, making her rock back and forth while peals of merriment danced up from her and Charlie regarded her with delight. In fact Roscoe realised that everyone in the place was smiling at her, as though just by being there she brightened the day.

She reached across the table and took Roscoe's hand. 'Oh, shut up,' she told him, still laughing, 'You make it worse with every word.'

'I don't mean to. I was considering your feelings,' he said stiffly, withdrawing his hand.

'Heavens, we're way past that. Enough. It's finished.'

'As you wish. But Charlie, behave yourself.'

'Why, when I'm talking to the most gorgeous girl I've ever met? *Hey!*'

One moment he was leaning close in a seductive conspiracy. The next, he was bouncing with agitation at something he'd seen.

'It's him,' he yelped, leaping to his feet. 'Just let me get to him.'

Across the restaurant, a long-haired young man turned in alarm, then vanished between some curtains, closely followed by Charlie.

'What was that?' Pippa said, looking around.

'A man who owes him money,' Roscoe observed. 'One of many.'

'So that's your brother. He'll be an interesting client. Yes, I think I'll accept his case.'

It was on the tip of Roscoe's tongue to tell her to forget it because he'd changed his mind. But he controlled the impulse, as he controlled so many impulses in his life, and sat in tense silence, a prey to opposing feelings. On the surface, things were working out exactly as he'd wanted. The smile she'd given Charlie was perfect for the purpose, and it had had the desired effect. His brother had been transfixed, just as Roscoe had meant him to be. So, what more did he want?

He didn't know. All he knew for certain was that he hated it.

'Pippa,' he said edgily, 'I must be honest, I think you're going about this the wrong way.'

'What?' She stared at him. 'I'm doing what you said you wanted.'

'Yes, but I had in mind something a little more—' He hesitated, made cautious by the look in her eyes.

'A little more what?' she asked in a voice that was softly dangerous.

'More subtle,' he said desperately.

'Mr Havering, are you telling me how to do my job?'

'I wouldn't dare.'

'Really? I'm not sure of that. Perhaps we should have discussed this before now, so that you could tell me exactly how a woman goes about beguiling a man? After all, I know so little about the subject, don't I? How stupid of me not to have taken lessons from you! Why don't you instruct me now so that I'll know which boxes to tick?'

'All right,' he said quickly. 'Of course you know more than I do about this.'

'Which I thought was why you hired me. Anyway, I'm not doing well, since his attention was so easily distracted. One hint of an unpaid debt and he's off. Hmm! Perhaps I should review my strategy.'

'I feel sure your strategy is quite up to the challenge.'

'It's the first time a man has walked away from me when I was trying to mesmerise him. I could feel quite insulted by that.'

'You're having a bad day for insults, aren't you?'

'Between you and him, yes.'

'Then I may as well add to my crimes by pointing out that he didn't walk away from you, he ran away at full speed. Perhaps I've hired the wrong person.'

'You could be right. Desperate measures are called for. I must lure my prey into a net from which he cannot escape.'

'Always assuming that he returns at all,' Roscoe pointed out. 'You may have to go after him.'

'Please!' She appeared horrified. 'I never "go after" a man. They come after me.'

'Always?' he asked, eyes narrowed.

'If I want them to. Sometimes I don't bother.' Thoroughly enjoying his discomfiture, she smiled. 'And never mind condemning me as a hussy, because that's exactly what you hired me for.'

'Is there any point in my defending myself?' he growled.

'None whatever,' she assured him.

She was curious to know what he would say next, but Charlie spoiled things by reappearing, cursing because his prey had escaped.

'Did he owe you very much?' Pippa asked, turning from Roscoe with reluctance.

'A few thousand.'

'Perhaps we can recover it by legal action,' she suggested.

'Ah…no,' he said awkwardly. 'It's a bit…well…'

'All right, let's leave it,' she said quickly. 'The sooner we get down to business, the better.'

'Yes, we must have a long talk over dinner,' Charlie said. 'The Diamond is the best place in town. Come on, let's go.'

'First you ask Miss Jenson if she is free,' Roscoe said firmly. 'If she is, then you ask if she can endure an evening with us.'

'*Us?* Ah, well—I didn't actually mean that you should come with—'

'I know exactly what you meant, and you can forget that idea. Miss Jenson, could you put up with the two of us for a few more hours?'

'I'll do my best,' she said solemnly. 'We have serious matters to discuss.'

'I agree, so we can forget The Diamond,' Roscoe said, taking out his cellphone and dialling. 'Hello, Mother? Yes, it's me. We're on our way home and we have a guest. I've found a first-rate lawyer for Charlie, so roll out the red carpet for her. Fine. See you soon.' He ended the call.

Charlie, who had been spluttering fruitlessly, now found his voice. 'What about how I feel?' he demanded.

'The Diamond is no place for a serious discussion.'

'And doesn't Pippa get a say?'

'Miss Jenson has already done us the honour of agreeing to dine with us. Since this is a business meeting, I'm sure she feels that the venue is irrelevant.'

'Certainly,' Pippa said in her briskest tone. 'I have no opinion either way.'

'You're going to just let him walk over you?' Charlie demanded.

Pippa couldn't resist. Giving Roscoe a cheeky sideways

look, she leaned towards Charlie and said, 'It can't be helped. In my job you get used to clients who want to rule the roost.' She added conspiratorially, 'There are ways of dealing with them.'

The young man choked with laughter, jerking his head towards Roscoe. 'Think you can get him on the ropes?'

'Think I can't?'

She was watching Roscoe for his reaction. There was none. His eyes were on her but his face revealed nothing. Clearly, the notion of tussling with her, whether physically or emotionally, caused him no excitement.

'Just promise that I can be there to see you crush him beneath your heel,' Charlie implored.

'When you two have finished,' Roscoe said in a bored voice.

'Just a little innocent fun,' Charlie protested.

'Sorry, I don't do fun.' Roscoe's voice was so withering that Pippa threw him another quick glance. For a moment his face was tight, hard, older.

'That's right, he doesn't,' Charlie said.

'OK, I'm here,' said a voice overhead.

Charlie groaned, then bounced up as he recognised the man who owed him money, now holding out an envelope.

'I only ran to get this,' he said. 'I always meant to repay you.' He dropped the envelope and fled. The reason became obvious a moment later.

'There's only half here,' Charlie yelped. 'Hey, come back!' He resumed the pursuit.

Alone again, Roscoe and Pippa eyed each other, suspicion on one side, defiance on the other.

'How am I doing?' she asked.

'You've certainly got his attention. I'd give a lot to know what he's thinking.'

'He believes what he wants to believe,' she said with a

small flash of anger. '*Men always do*. Didn't you know that? I know it. And so does any woman who's ever had a man in her life.'

'And when a woman knows it she makes use of it?'

'She does if she has any sense of self-preservation. And may I remind you again, Mr Havering, that I'm doing what you hired me to do? You're paying for my skills, but you don't get to dictate what skills I use or how I use them.'

'Don't I?'

'No, because if you try I'll simply step aside and let Charlie see you pulling my strings.'

He drew a sharp breath. 'You really know how to fight dirty.'

'Have you only just realised that?'

He regarded her. 'I think I have.'

'Good, then we understand each other. Now he's coming back. Smile at me so that he'll know that all is well between us.'

'I wonder if that day will ever come,' he said softly.

But the next moment he was smiling as she'd suggested, even talking pleasantly, loud enough for Charlie to hear. 'My mother's housekeeper is an expert cook. I promise that you'll enjoy tonight's meal, Miss Havering.'

'Pippa,' she said. 'After all, we're fighting on the same side.'

His eyes warned her not to push her luck, but he only inclined his head before rising and saying, 'I'll get the car. Be waiting for me outside and don't take too long.'

She longed to salute him ironically and say, *Yes sir, no sir. I obey, sir.* But he was gone before she had the chance.

'That's his way,' Charlie said, correctly interpreting her seething. 'People give up arguing. You will too.'

'Will I? I wonder. Did you catch up with that man?'

'No, he escaped again. But at least I got some of the money.

And now we're alone, can I tell you that you are the most beautiful creature I've ever met?'

'No, you can't tell me that,' she said. 'For one thing, I already know and, for another, your brother wouldn't approve.'

'Oh, forget him. What does he have to do with us?'

Pippa frowned. 'He's protecting you. Don't you owe him some kind of consideration?'

'Why? He's only thinking of himself. The good name of Havering must be defended at all costs. The truth is, he cares for nobody.'

'And nobody cares for him?' she murmured slowly.

Charlie shrugged. 'Who knows? He doesn't let anyone inside.'

It sounded so convincing, but suddenly there was the whispered memory of Roscoe saying, 'If anything happens to Charlie, it would break my mother's heart... At all costs I want to save her from more suffering.'

This wasn't a man who cared nothing for anyone. He might care so much that he only admitted it under stress.

Or perhaps Charlie was right. Which of the two was the real man? Impossible to say. Unless...

Suddenly the waiter hurried up to them, almost stuttering in his agitation. 'He's in the car...says he told you to be out there waiting for him. He's good 'n mad.'

They ran outside to where Roscoe's car was by the kerb, engine running. When they had tumbled into the back seat, Pippa said politely, 'I'm really sorry,' but Roscoe only grunted, his eyes on the traffic as he edged his way into the flow. She supposed she couldn't blame him.

Their destination was an expensive London suburb, full of large detached houses standing in luxurious gardens. A woman was waiting by the gate, smiling and waving at the sight of them. She was thin and frail-looking, and Pippa recalled Roscoe saying that she'd been in a bad way ever since his father's death, fifteen years earlier.

But her face was brilliant with joy as Charlie got out of the car and she could hug him. He handed Pippa out and she found herself being scrutinised by two bright eyes before Angela Havering thrust out a hand declaring that she was *so* glad to meet her.

Roscoe drove the car away.

'He has to park at the back,' Charlie explained. 'He'll join us in a minute.'

'Come inside,' Angela said, taking her hand. 'I want to know all about you, and how you're going to save my dear boy.'

She drew Pippa into the house, a lavishly elegant establishment, clearly furnished and tended by someone who'd brought housekeeping to a fine art, with the cash to do it.

In the kitchen they found Nora, a cheerful, middle-aged woman in a large apron, presiding over a variety of dishes.

'I hope I didn't make your life difficult, coming unexpectedly,' Pippa said as they were introduced.

'There's plenty to eat,' Angela said. 'It's always been one of my husband's maxims that a successful house has food ready all the time.'

Pippa smiled, but she had a strange, edgy feeling. Angela spoke almost as if her husband were still alive.

Nora poured wine and Angela handed them each a glass and raised hers in salute.

'Welcome to our home,' she said to Pippa. 'I'm sure you're going to make everything all right.'

It was a charming scene, but it would have been more charming, Pippa thought, if she'd waited for Roscoe to join them. It was a tiny point, but it troubled her.

From the kitchen window, she had a view of the back garden, with a large garage at the far end. As she watched,

Roscoe came out of a side door of the garage and began walking to the house.

'Here he is,' she said, pointing.

'Oh, good. I was afraid he'd keep us waiting. Honestly, he can be so inconsiderate.'

Over supper, Angela was on edge, constantly turning an anxious expression on Charlie, then a frowning gaze at Roscoe, as though silently criticising him for something. To Pippa, it seemed as though she'd given all her love to one son and barely registered the existence of the other.

Of course, she argued with herself, Charlie was a vulnerable boy threatened with disaster, while Roscoe was a powerful man, well able to take care of himself. But still…

Charlie's cellphone rang. He went out into the hall to speak to the caller and, as soon as he'd gone, Angela clasped Pippa's hand.

'You see how he is, how he needs to be cared for.'

'And he's lucky to have a brother who cares for him,' Pippa couldn't resist saying.

'Oh, yes, of course there's Roscoe. He does his best, but when I think of what might happen to my darling…maybe prison…'

'He won't go to prison,' Pippa said at once. 'It's a first offence, nothing was stolen and nobody was hurt. A fine, and perhaps some community service is the worst that will happen.'

'But he'll have a criminal record.'

'Yes, and that's why we're working so hard to defend him.'

'Oh, if only my husband were here,' Angela wailed. 'William would know what to do. He always does.'

Roscoe's eyes met Pippa's and a little shake of his head warned her to say nothing. She nodded, feeling all at sea, glad to keep quiet.

'But you've got me to help, Mother,' Roscoe reminded her.

'Oh, yes, and you do your best, but it's not the same, is it?'

'No, it's not the same,' Roscoe said quietly.

'If only he hadn't gone away. He should be here now that we need him so much.'

Again, she might have been speaking of a living man, and Pippa wondered uneasily just how much she lived in the real world.

As she spoke, Angela fiddled constantly was a ring on her left hand. It was an engagement ring, with an awesome central diamond, surrounded by smaller diamonds.

'That's my engagement ring,' Angela said, seeing her glance. 'It was much too expensive and William couldn't really afford it in those days, but he said that nothing was too much for me. All these years later, I still have it to remind me that his love never died.' Her voice shook.

Pippa was uncertain where to look. Angela's determination to thrust her emotion on everyone was difficult to cope with, even without knowing that it was misplaced.

Charlie returned after a moment, bearing a cup of tea which he set before his mother.

'Why, darling, how kind of you to think of me!' She turned to Roscoe. 'Isn't Charlie a wonderful son?'

'The best,' Roscoe agreed kindly. 'Now, drink up, and have plenty of sugar because that always does you good.'

'Here,' Charlie said, spooning sugar madly into the cup. His mother beamed at him.

So the spoilt child got all the credit, Pippa thought, while Roscoe, who was genuinely working hard to ease her troubles, was barely noticed.

Then she reproved herself for being over-emotional. Roscoe was only doing what was sensible, supporting his mother and Charlie so that the family should not disintegrate. The idea that he might be saddened by being relegated to the shadows of Angela's affection was too sentimental for words. And if there was one thing Roscoe was not, it was sentimental.

And neither was she, she reminded herself.

Nonetheless, she couldn't help warming to him for his generosity and patience.

A little later Angela went away into the kitchen, and she seized the chance to tell Charlie about Ginevra. He was reluctant to believe the worst, but Pippa was firm, saying, 'I don't want you to contact her unless I say so. Give me your word.'

'All right, maybe I was a bit mad but she made my head spin.'

'Well, it's time to stop spinning. Mr Havering, do you have a computer here that I could use?'

'It's upstairs,' Roscoe said. 'I'll show you.'

'Beware,' Charlie warned. 'He's taking you up to his bedroom, a place where no sensible woman goes.'

'Cut it out,' Roscoe advised him wearily. 'Miss Jenson, I hope you know you have absolutely nothing to fear from me.'

'That's not very flattering,' Charlie protested illogically.

'Unflattering but sensible and businesslike,' Pippa said. 'Mr Havering, let me return the compliment by declaring that I too am entirely free from temptation. Now, shall we go?'

'I'll come too,' Charlie declared. 'To protect you.'

'I need no protection,' she declared firmly. 'Ask your brother how I deal with troublesome men.'

Charlie's eyes widened. 'Hey, he didn't—?'

'No, I didn't,' Roscoe said, exasperated. 'But I witnessed the fate of someone who did. Take it from me, you wouldn't like it. Stay here and look after Mother.'

Roscoe's room was much as she would have expected—full of straight lines, plain, unadorned, unrevealing. The bed was narrow and looked hard, the wallpaper was pale grey, without pattern. There was a television, modest, neat, efficient; a set where a man would watch the news. A monk could have lived in this room.

But his real home was an apartment elsewhere, she reminded herself. She wondered if that was any different, and doubted it.

But then she saw something that made her stare and gasp with delight.

'Wow!' she breathed. 'How about that? Let me look at it. Can you just—? Yes, that's right. Oh, it's the most beautiful thing I've ever—yes—yes—yes—' Her hands were clasped in sheer ecstasy, her voice full of joy, her eyes glowing with blissful satisfaction.

Roscoe regarded her, fascinated. It wasn't his first sight of a beautiful woman in transports—in his arms, sometimes in his bed.

But this one was looking at his computer.

A touch of the switch had caused the machine to flower into glorious life, making her watch, riveted, as one state-of-the-art accessory after another leapt into the spotlight.

'Oh, goodness,' she breathed. 'Why haven't I ever—? I've never even heard of some of these.'

'One of my clients owns a firm that makes software and computer peripherals,' Roscoe said. 'He's at the cutting edge and I get everything ahead of the game. I'll tell him you're interested and I'm sure he'll fix you up.'

'Oh, yes, *please*! And look at the size of that screen, the biggest I've ever seen.'

'You should try one,' Roscoe said. 'It's useful for having multiple documents open at once.'

'Ah, yes,' she murmured. 'Useful. How do I go online?'

He touched a switch and in a moment she'd connected with her work computer, entered the password and brought up a list of documents. A few more clicks brought Ginevra's face to the screen just as Charlie entered the room.

'Hey, that's her!' he exclaimed. Then he stared at the caption. 'But who's Biddy Felsom?'

'She is,' Pippa said. 'Known to the police as a small-time offender and pain in the neck. She enjoys getting stupid boys to do things they shouldn't, pulling their strings, like she pulled yours.'

'Well, she's history,' Charlie said. 'I know that you'll save me from her.'

'Good. Now it's time I was going home,' Pippa observed.

'I'll drive you,' Roscoe said.

'No you won't, I will,' Charlie was quick to say.

'Neither of you will,' Pippa said. 'Mr Havering, will you call me a taxi?'

'I'll drive you,' Charlie insisted.

'Shut up!' his brother said impatiently. 'Can't you see she's had enough of the pair of us tonight? Miss Jenson, I suggest that the next meeting should be at my office. My secretary will call you to fix a time.'

'Certainly,' she said in her most efficient tone.

'I know you can rescue me,' Charlie said. 'We'll do it together because I'm going to take your advice in *everything*.'

He said the last word with a breathless sincerity that made her regard him wryly. His eyes twinkled back at her and they laughed together.

Angela came in and demanded to know what was happening. Charlie proclaimed his faith in Pippa, which made his mother embrace her.

Roscoe took no part in this. He was calling the taxi.

Just before it arrived, Charlie came to stand before her. 'There's something I've just got to know,' he breathed.

'I'll tell you if I can,' she promised. 'What is it?'

'This,' he said, putting a hand behind her head and whipping out the clip in her hair, letting her glorious locks flow free.

'I've wanted to do that ever since we met,' he said.

'Then you should be ashamed of yourself,' Roscoe growled. 'That's no way to treat a lady.'

'Pippa's not offended,' Charlie pleaded. 'Are you?'

'No, I'm not offended, but right this minute I feel like your nursemaid. I think you should call me Nanny.'

'Not in a million years,' he said fervently.

She gave a crow of laughter. 'Well, my taxi seems to be here, so I'm leaving now. I'll see you soon.'

Charlie and Angela came with her to the gate, but Roscoe stayed back, declaring curtly that he had work to do. At the last minute he pushed a scrap of paper into Pippa's hand and turned away to climb the stairs.

As the taxi drew away she strained to read what was on the paper, mystified by Roscoe. When her hair flowed free she'd caught a glimpse of his face, full of shock as though he'd been stunned. But that made no sense. He'd seen her hair the night before. There was nothing to surprise him. Yet a man who'd been punched in the stomach might have looked like that.

Now he was giving her secret notes, and she wondered if his stern facade had melted long enough for him to send her a personal message. Could he be reacting to her as a man to a woman? She found herself hoping so. There was something about him that made her want to know more. In another moment she would find out...

Then she passed under a street lamp long enough to see what he'd written to her.

It was the address of his client's computer firm.

CHAPTER FIVE

NEXT morning Roscoe's secretary called and they set up the appointment at his office for the following day. An hour later Charlie came on the line, wanting to see her that night. Since there was still much she needed to discover she reluctantly agreed to let him take her to The Diamond, although a nightclub wasn't the place she would have chosen.

She supposed she should notify Roscoe, but she stopped her hand on the way to the phone. He was just a tad too controlling for her taste, and yielding to it would only make him worse. She would make a report afterwards.

That evening she dressed carefully, choosing a fairly sedate black satin gown with a long hem and modest neck. She'd beguiled Charlie enough to secure his attention, but she had no wish to entice him further.

Downstairs, he had a car waiting, complete with chauffeur.

'I hired it for the evening,' he said, getting in beside her. 'I don't want to drive, I want to concentrate on you, now I have you all to myself.'

'That's lovely,' she said. 'Just you, me and my notebook.'

'Notebook?'

'Well, this is a professional consultation, isn't it? You're going to fill me in on any aspects of the case that were overlooked before.'

He grimaced.

At The Diamond she had to admit that he was a skilled host, recommending dishes from the elaborate menu, knowing which wine to order. He seemed in a chirpy mood, but at last she looked up to find his face pervaded by a wry, almost hangdog look.

'I guess you were right about Ginevra,' he said. 'I tried to call her. I know you told me not to, but I had to try.'

'What happened?'

'She hung up. I can't believe I was taken in so easily. But at least now I've got you. You're my friend, aren't you? Really my friend, not just because Roscoe has hired your legal skills?'

'Roscoe does a lot for you,' she reminded him.

'I know I should be grateful to him. He's always looked after me, but…but he does too much, so that sometimes I feel I don't know who I really am. What would I do if I was left to myself? Stupid things, probably.'

'Why don't you tell me about it?'

Once Charlie started to talk, it all came tumbling out—the years of growing up in the shadow of tragedy, the crushing awareness that he was all his mother lived for, the feeling that he could never be free.

'My dad killed himself,' he said sombrely, 'but Roscoe won't allow it to be mentioned, especially to Mum. That's his way. "Do this, Charlie, don't do that. Join the firm, Charlie—"'

'Did he make you join his firm?'

'He suggested it, and what Roscoe "suggests" tends to happen.'

'Couldn't you have held out against him?'

'I suppose. Actually, I feel a bit guilty about Roscoe. I get mad at him, but I do know the truth.'

'Which is?'

'That he's always had the rough end of the stick. I think Mum blames him for Dad's death, not openly but she says things like, "If only he hadn't been so tired that day, he might not have crashed." And she says other things—so that I just know she thinks Roscoe wasn't pulling his weight.'

'Do you believe that?'

'No, not now I'm in the firm and know a bit about how it works. Roscoe was the same age I am now, still learning the business, and there was only so much he could have done. And I've talked to people who were there at that time and they all say there was a big crash coming, and nobody could believe "that kid" could avoid it.'

'"That kid,"' she murmured. 'It's hard to see him like that.'

'I know, but that's how they thought of him back then. And they were all astounded when he got them through. I respect him—you have to—but I can see what it made him. Sometimes I feel guilty. He saved the rest of us but it damaged him terribly, and Mum just blames him because...well...'

'Maybe she needs someone to blame,' Pippa suggested gently.

'Something like that. And it's so unfair that I feel sorry for him. Hey, don't tell him I said that. He'd murder me!'

'And then he'd murder *me*,' she agreed. 'Promise.' She laid a finger over her lips.

'The reason I don't deal with Roscoe very well is that I'm always in two minds about him. I admire him to bits for what he's achieved in the firm, and the way he puts up with Mum's behaviour without complaining.'

'Does he mind about her very much?'

'Oh, yes. He doesn't say anything but I see his face some-times, and it hurts him.'

'Have you tried talking to him about it?'

'Yes, and I've been slapped down. He shuts it away inside

himself, and I resent that. He's been a good brother to me, but he won't let me be a good brother to him. That's what I was saying; one moment I admire him and sympathise with him. The next moment I want to thump him for being a tyrant. I'm afraid his tyrant side outweighs the other one by about ten to one.'

'If you weren't a stockbroker, what would you have liked to do?' she asked.

'I don't know. Something colourful where I didn't have to wear a formal suit.' He gave a comical sigh. 'I guess I'm just a lost cause.'

She smiled, feeling as sympathetic as she would have done with a younger brother. Beneath the frivolous boy, she could detect the makings of a generous, thoughtful man with, strangely, a lot in common with his brother. Charlie wasn't the weakling she'd first thought. He had much inner strength. It was just a different kind of strength from Roscoe.

'You're not a lost cause,' she said, reaching over the table and laying her hands on his shoulders. '*I* say you're not, and what I say goes.'

He grinned. 'Now you sound just like Roscoe.'

'Well, I *am* like Roscoe.' Briefly, she enclosed his face between her hands. 'He's not the only one who can give orders, and my orders to you are to cheer up because I'm going to make things all right.'

She dropped her hands but gave him a comforting sisterly smile.

'D'you know, I really believe you can,' he mused. 'I think you could take on even Roscoe and win.'

'Well, somewhere in this world there has to be someone who can crush him beneath her heels.'

'His fiancée couldn't.'

'His fiancée?' Pippa echoed, startled. Since learning that

Roscoe lived alone, she had somehow never connected him with romantic entanglements.

'It was a few years back. Her name was Verity and she was terribly "suitable". She worked in the firm, and Roscoe used to say that she knew as much about finance as he did.'

'I dare say she'd need to,' Pippa said, nodding.

'Right. It makes you wonder what they talked about when they were alone. The latest exchange rate? What the Dow-Jones index was doing?'

'What did she look like?'

'Pretty enough, but I think it was chiefly her mental qualities he admired.'

'Charlie, a man doesn't ask a woman to marry him because of her mental qualities.'

'Roscoe isn't like other men. Beauty passes him by.'

'Then why did you warn me against going up to his room yesterday?'

'I was only joking. I knew he had no interest in you that way. Don't you remember? He said so himself.'

'Yes,' she murmured. 'He did, didn't he?'

After that, she relapsed into thought.

Another bottle of wine was served and Charlie drank deeply, making Pippa glad he wasn't driving.

'Was he very much in love with her?' she asked.

'I don't know. Like I said, he doesn't talk about his feelings. He wanted her in his way. The rest of us look at a beautiful woman and think *Wow!* Roscoe thinks, *Will she do me credit?* I don't think he's ever thought *Wow!* in his life.'

Oh, yes, he has, she thought, gazing silently into her glass.

Noticing nothing, Charlie continued, 'She could be relied on to know what was important—money, propriety, making the world bow down before you. And she'd give him intel-

ligent children who would eventually go into the business.
What more could he want?'

'Surely you're being unfair?'

'Well, losing her didn't seem to break his heart. He didn't
even tell us at the time. One day I mentioned that we hadn't
seen her for a while and then he said they'd broken up weeks
ago. Any normal man would drown his sorrows in the pub
with his mates, but not him. He just fired her and she ceased
to exist.'

'He actually fired her?' Pippa was startled.

'Well, he said she'd left the firm, but I reckon he made her
understand that she'd better leave.'

She felt as though someone had struck her over the heart,
which was surely absurd? From the start, she'd sensed that
Roscoe was a harsh, controlling man, indifferent to the feelings of others as long as his rule was unchallenged. So why
should she care if her worst opinion was confirmed?

Because she'd also thought she saw another side to him—
warmer, more human. And because Charlie himself had
spoken of that softer side. But the moment had passed. Charlie
had switched back from the sympathetic brother to the rebel-
lious kid, and in doing so he'd changed the light on Roscoe
who was now, once more, the tyrant.

She knew a glimmer of sadness, but suppressed it. Much
better to be realistic.

It was time for the cabaret. Dancers skipped across the
stage, a crooner crooned, a comedian strutted his stuff. She
thought him fairly amusing but Charlie was more critical.

'His performance was a mess,' he said as the space was
cleared for dancing. 'Listen.'

To her surprise, he rattled through the last joke, word perfect and superbly timed. Then he went back and repeated an
earlier part of the act, also exactly right, as far as she could
judge.

'I'm impressed,' she said. 'I've never come across such a memory.'

He shrugged. 'It convinced Roscoe that I was bright enough to be a stockbroker, so you might say it ruined my life.'

He made a comical face. She smiled back, meaning to console rather than beguile him. But the next moment her face lit up and she cried out in pleasure, 'Lee Renton, you devious so-and-so! How lovely to see you.'

A large man in his forties was bearing down on them, hands extended. He was attractive, and would have been even more so if he could manage to lose some weight.

'"Devious so-and-so!"' he mocked. 'Is that any way to address your favourite client?'

'That's not what I say to my favourite client. To him, I say, "Sir, how generous of you to double the bill!"'

Lee roared with laughter before saying, 'Actually, I'll gladly pay twice the bill after what you did for me.' He seemed to notice Charlie for the first time. 'I'm Lee Renton. Any friend of Pippa's is a friend of mine.' He pumped Charlie's hand and sat down without waiting to be invited.

'I did a court appearance for Lee the other day,' Pippa told Charlie. 'It went fairly well.'

'Don't act modest,' Lee protested. 'You're the tops and you know it.'

'Meaning that I saved you some money?'

'What else?' he asked innocently.

'What are you doing here?'

'My firm provided the entertainment here tonight, and I'll probably buy the place. I'll call you about that.' He blew her a kiss. 'You look ravishing, queen of my heart.'

'Oh, stop your nonsense!'

'Do you say that as a woman or as the lawyer who recently handled my divorce?'

'I say it as the lawyer who'll probably draw up your next pre-nuptial agreement.'

He bellowed with laughter. A passing waiter caught Charlie's attention and he turned, giving Renton a chance to lower his voice and say, 'Quite a performer, your companion—I overheard him retelling those jokes and he was a sight better than the original comedian. Does he do it professionally?'

'No, he's a stockbroker.'

'You're having a laugh.'

'Really. He's actually a client and we were discussing his case.'

'Yeah, right. This is just the perfect place for it. All right, I'm going. I have work to do. Stockbroker, eh?' He thumped Charlie on the shoulder and departed.

Charlie frowned, turning back from the waiter. 'Lee Renton? I've heard that name somewhere.'

'He's very big in entertainment. He buys things, he promotes, he owns a television studio.'

'*That* Lee Renton? Wow! I wish I'd known.'

He looked around, managing to spot Lee in the distance, deep in conversation with a man whom he overwhelmed by flinging an arm around his shoulders and sweeping him off until they both vanished in the crowd.

The waiter brought more wine and he drank it thoughtfully. 'Do you know him well?'

'Well enough. I'll introduce you another time.'

He drained his glass. 'Come on, let's dance.'

He was a natural dancer, and together they went enjoyably mad. The other dancers backed off to watch them, and when they finished the crowd applauded.

Charlie's eyes were brilliant, his cheeks flushed, and Pippa guessed she must look much the same. In a moment of crazy delight, he put his hands on either side of her face, just as she had briefly done to him at the table. But when he tried to kiss her she fended him off.

'That's enough,' she said when she could speak. 'Bad boy!'

'Sorry, ma'am!' He assumed a clowning expression of penitence.

'We're going back to the table and you're going to behave,' she said firmly.

Then she saw Roscoe.

He was sitting at a table on the edge of the dance floor, regarding her with his head slightly tilted and an unreadable expression on his face. Beside him sat a woman of great beauty in a low-cut evening gown of gold satin, with flaming red hair. Pippa saw her lean towards him, touching his hand gently so that he turned back to her, all attention, as though everyone else had ceased to exist.

'What's up?' Charlie asked, turning. '*What?* Damn him!'

He hurried her to the table, muttering, 'Let's hope he doesn't see us. What's he doing here?'

'Who's that with him?'

'I don't know. Never seen her.'

'Did you tell him you were coming?'

'No way!'

'Then perhaps it's just bad luck.'

'Not with Roscoe. I've heard him say that the man who relies on luck is a fool.'

'Yes, in stockbroking—'

'In everything. He never does anything by chance. He's a control freak.'

Pippa had no answer. She, whose presence here was a result of Roscoe's commands, knew better than anyone that Charlie was right. She shivered.

Now she could see Roscoe leading the woman into the

dance. The band was playing a smoochy tune and they moved slowly, locked in a close embrace. Pippa shifted her seat so that she had her back to them and began to chatter brightly about nothing. Words came out of her mouth but her mind was on the dance floor, picturing the movements that she'd avoided seeing with her eyes.

At last the music ended and Charlie groaned, 'Oh, no, he's coming over.'

Roscoe and his partner were bearing down on them. Without waiting to be invited, they sat at the table.

'Fancy seeing you here!' Roscoe exclaimed in a voice of such cheerful surprise that Pippa's suspicions were confirmed. This was no accidental meeting.

He introduced everyone, giving the woman's name as Teresa Blaketon. Charlie was immediately on his best behaviour in the presence of beauty, Pippa was amused to notice.

'I think we should dance,' Roscoe said, rising.

It would have been satisfying to ignore the hand he held out so imperiously, but that was hardly an option now, so she let him draw her to her feet and lead her back to the floor, where a waltz had just begun. She decided that there was nothing for it but to endure his putting an arm about her and drawing her close.

But he didn't. Taking her right hand in his left, he laid his right hand on the side of her waist and proceeded to dance with nearly a foot of air between them. It was polite, formal and Pippa knew she should have been glad. Yet, remembering how close he'd held his lady friend, she felt that this was practically a snub.

'I'm glad to see that you're taking your duties seriously,' he said. 'For you to spend an evening with Charlie is more than I'd hoped for.'

'Don't worry, it'll appear on the bill,' she said cheerfully. 'And, as it's my own time, I'll charge extra. Triple at least.'

'Don't I get a discount for the meal he bought you, and the first class champagne?'

'Certainly not. I drank that champagne out of courtesy.'

'I see you know how to cost every minute,' he said softly.

'Of course. As a man of finance, you should appreciate that.'

'There are some things outside my experience.'

'That I simply don't believe,' she said defiantly, raising her head to meet his eyes.

He was looking down on her with a fixed gaze that made her suddenly glad her dress was high and unrevealing. Yet she had the disconcerting sense that he could see right through the material. Even Charlie hadn't looked like that, and for a moment she trembled.

'You flatter me,' he said. 'The truth is, I'm mystified by you. When I think I understand you, you do the opposite to what I was expecting.'

'Just like the financial markets,' she observed saucily. 'You manage well enough with them.'

'Sooner or later, the financial markets always revert to type. With you, I'm not so sure.'

'Perhaps that's because you don't really know what my type is. Or you think you know, and you're mistaken.'

'No—' he shook his head '—I'm not arrogant enough to think I know.'

'Then let me tell you, I'm devoted to my job and to nothing else. I promised to get to know Charlie and "beguile" him, but I couldn't have done that in an office. It was necessary to work "above and beyond the call of duty."'

'And how is your case going?'

'Fairly well. He's seen through Ginevra.'

'And if you can persuade him to grow up, he's all set for a serious career.'

'You mean in the firm with you? Suppose that isn't what he wants?'

'He'll thank me in the end, when he's a successful man and he realises I helped to guide him that way.'

'Perhaps you should stop guiding him and let him find his own path.'

'Into a police cell, you mean?'

That silenced her.

After a moment he said, 'Why are you frowning?'

'I'm just wondering about your methods.'

'I don't know what you mean.'

'You don't really expect me to believe this is coincidence, do you? You knew Charlie was going to be here.'

'I see. I'm supposed to have every room bugged, and to bribe half the staff to bring me information. Shame on you, Pippa.'

She blushed, feeling foolish for her wild fantasies.

'I suppose I might be the evil spy of your imagination, if I needed to be,' he said in a considering tone, 'but when my brother conducts every phone call at the top of his voice I simply don't need to be. I happened to be passing his office when he booked the table.'

'And you made immediate arrangements to put him under surveillance. Or me.'

'I made immediate arrangements to have an enjoyable night out.'

'Teresa must have been surprised to be summoned at the last minute.'

'Teresa is a lovely woman, and she enjoys nightclubs. It gives her a chance to display her beauty, which, you must admit, is exceptional.'

It was on the tip of her tongue to ask if he'd hired his companion as he'd hired her, but her courage failed her. Besides, the memory of how he and Teresa had practically embraced as they danced, was all the answer she needed. It seemed to underline his sedate demeanour with herself.

She wasn't used to that. Men usually seized the opportunity to make contact with her body. One who behaved like a Victorian clergyman was unusual. Interesting.

Annoying.

The floor was getting crowded. Dancers jostled each other until suddenly one of them stumbled, crashing into Pippa, driving her forward against Roscoe, cancelling the distance he'd kept so determinedly between them. Taken by surprise, she had no time to erect barriers that might have saved her from the sudden intense awareness of his body—lithe, hard, powerful.

It was too late now. Something had made her doubly aware of her own body, singing with new life as it pressed up to his, and the sensation seemed to invade her totally—endless, unforgettable. Shocking.

She tried to summon up the strength to break the embrace, but he did it for her, pushing her away with a resolution that only just avoided being discourteous.

'We'd better return to the table,' he said.

Then he was walking off without a backward look, giving her no choice but to follow. Which *was* discourteous. She might have been irritated if she hadn't had an inkling of what was troubling him. She too needed time to think about what had just happened; time to deny it.

Charlie had reached the point of talking nonsense and Teresa looked relieved to see them.

'How did you get here?' Roscoe said, placing a hand on his brother's shoulder with a gentleness that contradicted the roughness in his voice.

'I hired Harry and his car. He's waiting for us.'

'Good. He can take you home while I take Pippa.'

'Hey, Pippa's with me—'

'And the less she sees of you in this state the better. Waiter!'

In a few minutes he'd settled everything—Charlie's bill as well as his own. They escorted Charlie out to the side road where the chauffeur was waiting. Teresa helped to settle him in the back seat, which gave Pippa the chance to mutter to Roscoe, 'I'll take a taxi home.'

'You will not.'

'But I don't want to be a gooseberry,' she said frantically. 'You and she…I mean…'

'I know exactly what you mean and kindly allow me to make my own decisions.'

'Like you make everyone else's?' she snapped.

'I won't pretend not to understand that, but you can't have known my brother a whole two days without realising that he's vulnerable. I don't want people to see him like this. Do you?'

'No,' she said. 'Just let me say goodnight to him.'

But Charlie was dead to the world and she stood back while Harry drove off with him. Watching Roscoe get into the driving seat of his car, she realised that she'd seen him drink only tonic water, and after several hours in a nightclub he was stone cold sober and completely in control.

Which was typical of him, she thought crossly.

Teresa didn't seem annoyed at having Pippa foisted on her when she would no doubt have preferred to be alone with Roscoe. As they sat together in the back she chatted merrily, mostly about Charlie, whose company she had enjoyed, especially as he had entertained her by running through some routines by another more talented comedian he'd recently seen perform.

'He's really good,' she recalled.

'You shouldn't encourage him,' Roscoe said over his shoulder. 'He's a sight too fond of playing whatever part he thinks people want.'

'Which will surely be useful in a stockbroker,' Pippa observed. 'He must need various personalities, depending on whether he's buying shares or selling them, manipulating the market, or manipulating people. With any luck, he'll be almost as good at that as you.'

Teresa rocked with laughter. The back of Roscoe's head was stiff and unrevealing.

Outside her apartment block, he got out and held open the door for her, a chivalrous gesture that also gave him the chance to fix her with a cool, appraising stare. She returned it in full measure.

'I hope your evening was enjoyable, Miss Jenson.'

'I hope yours was informative, Mr Havering.'

'More than I could have imagined, thank you.'

'Then all is well. Goodnight.'

Once in her apartment with the door safely shut behind her, Pippa tossed her bag aside, threw herself into a chair and kicked off her shoes, breathing out hard and long.

'Phew! What an evening! Get him! More informative than he could have imagined. I'll bet it was! Hello, Gran! Don't mind me. I'm good 'n mad.'

She was addressing the photograph that she kept on the sideboard, showing the wedding of Grandmother Dee and Grandfather Mark. Dee had once confided to her that there had been complications about that wedding.

'I was pregnant,' she'd said, 'and that was scandalous in nineteen forty-three. You had to get married to stay respectable, and I wondered if he was only marrying me because he had to.'

'And was he?' Pippa had wanted to know.

Dee had smiled mysteriously. 'Let's say he had his own reasons, but it was a while before I discovered what they were. On our wedding day I still couldn't quite believe in his love.'

Yet the young Dee in the picture was beaming happily, and in Pippa's present mood it all looked delightfully uncomplicated.

'Fancy having to be married before you could make love,' she mused.

In her mind she saw Roscoe dancing with Teresa, holding her in an embrace that spoke of passion deferred, but not for long. Right this minute they were on their way to her home, or perhaps to his, where he would sweep her into the bedroom and remove her clothes without wasting a moment.

She knew the kind of lover he would be: no-nonsense, not lingering over preliminaries, but proceeding straight to the purpose, as he did with everything. As well as pleasuring his woman efficiently, he would instruct her as to his own needs, with everything done to the highest standards. Afterwards, Teresa would know she'd received attention from an expert.

For a while Pippa's annoyance enabled her to indulge these cynical thoughts, but another memory insisted on intruding— his care for his mother, his patience, his kindness to her. All these spoke of a different man, with a gentle heart that he showed rarely. Was that gentleness also present in the lover?

'And why am I bothering?' she asked aloud. 'Honestly, Gran, I think you had it better in your day.'

Dee's smiling face as she nestled against her new husband seemed to say that she was right.

Pippa sighed and went to bed.

The night that followed was the strangest she'd ever known. Worn out, she had expected to sleep like a log, but the world was fractured. Two men wandered through her dreams—one gentle, protective and kind, the other a harsh authoritarian who gave his orders and assumed instant obedience. Both men were Roscoe Havering.

In this other world he danced with her, holding her close, not briefly but possessively, as though claiming her for ever. Unable to resist, she yielded, resting against him with a joy that felt like coming home. But then she awoke to find her flesh singing but herself alone.

In a fury, she threw something across the room. It was time to face facts. Roscoe had appeared at The Diamond the night before in order to study her and see if she was doing her job as a hired fancy woman. Whatever gloss he tried to put on it, that was the truth. Curse him!

Unable to lie still, she rose and began to pace the room, muttering desperately. 'All right, so I felt something. Not *here*—' she laid a hand quickly over her heart '—no, not there, but—' she looked down at her marvellous body '—just about everywhere else. Only for a moment. And he needn't think I'm giving in to it. I've done with that stuff for ever. So that's settled. Now I need to get some more sleep.'

CHAPTER SIX

WHEN Pippa finally awoke it was to the memory of the appointment at Roscoe's office that morning.

'Oh, no,' she groaned. 'I'm not going!'

But she knew she was. The professional Miss Jenson didn't tamely back off. She got out of bed, showered in cold water for maximum alertness and ate a hearty breakfast, calculated to enhance energy and efficiency. The fact that she was inwardly fuming was of no interest to anyone else. Certainly not Roscoe Havering.

Now that the first hint of winter snow was in the air, she chose her attire for warmth: severe suit, long coat, flat shoes. With a face free of make-up and her hair scraped firmly back, she decided that she looked just right: a lawyer, not a fancy piece, whatever a man with no manners might think.

She put in a hard morning's work at her office, then David looked in for a quick word.

'Off to see Roscoe? Good. You've probably learned all about him by now.'

'The odd detail,' she said, assiduously hunting for something inside her desk.

'Then you'll have heard that there's nobody in the business with a higher reputation. His speciality is discretionary dealing.'

Pippa knew that some brokers simply followed their

clients' instructions, but did not give advice. Others would give advice, but not make final decisions. Most demanding of all was discretionary dealing, where the broker ascertained the clients' long-term objectives, and then had authority to make decisions without further consultation. Only the best and most trusted brokers could do this, and it came as no surprise to know that Roscoe Havering was one of them.

'A lot of brokers came out of the recession looking bad,' David told her. 'Not him. If anything, his trade has doubled because clients have flocked to him, disillusioned with the others. Plus there are rumours of a link-up with the Vanlen Corporation that would make Havering one of the richest and most powerful men in the financial world.'

Pippa mulled this over on the journey to Threadneedle Street, in the financial heart of London. Now the snow had properly started and, as she stepped out of the taxi, she pulled her coat tight, relieved that she would get her car back tomorrow.

Roscoe's office was located in a historic building, converted to modern day requirements. Dark deeds had occurred there centuries ago. Dead bodies had once been discovered in the cellar, one of which was a man known personally to the reigning monarch of the time. But only the building's outside reflected the dramatic past. Inside, all was corporate efficiency, bland colours and straight lines.

But I'll bet there are still plenty of dark deeds, Pippa reflected as she hurried into the elevator. *Just a different kind.*

She was curious to see how well Roscoe's establishment reflected the man, and it was no surprise to discover that he was on the top floor, with a view down on the world. As expected, she found the atmosphere subdued, even slightly haughty.

The receptionist showed her to a seat. 'I'm afraid there'll

be a slight delay,' she said. 'Mr Vanlen just walked in without warning. He's going to Los Angeles for some big international gathering, and he's annoyed because Mr Havering won't go too. But Mr Havering says those meetings are all talk and no substance, and he won't budge. Vanlen did a quick detour on his way to the airport, so at least he can't stay long.' She made a wry face. 'He never seems to think that other people might be busy.'

'I know the type,' Pippa said with feeling.

From behind a door she could hear a voice raised in argument. 'We can't waste time. This is a big deal for both of us. When everything's signed we're going to be the kings, and you want that as much as I do... What's that? The hell with keeping my voice down! Let them know that they've got to be afraid of you, that's what I say. It's where half the pleasure lies.'

The secretary groaned. 'You hear him. That's how Vanlen thinks. Heaven help us all when that tie-up goes through. Mr Havering's a tyrant now but when he—'

She stopped as Vanlen's voice was raised again. 'I can't believe you're really not coming to Los Angeles. Surely that's—?'

'I'd better go in,' the secretary said hastily. 'Mr Havering is fed up with that subject.'

She hurried over and knocked on Roscoe's door, opening it just in time for Pippa to hear him saying harshly, 'I'm not going and that's final. I don't have the time. Anyway, the conference starts tomorrow and I'd never change my mind at this late date.'

Too right, she thought. Anyone who tried to divert Roscoe from the course that suited him was in for a nasty surprise.

'Hey! It's you!' The delighted voice came from Charlie who'd just appeared, his eyes shining at the sight of her.

'Thanks heavens you're here!' he exclaimed, coming to sit beside her. 'This place is doing my head in!'

'I gather great things are afoot,' she said.

'You mean Vanlen? Oh, yes! We're going to be the greatest. No one will be able to touch us or compete with us, and then Roscoe will have everything he wants.'

'Nobody has everything they want,' she protested.

'That depends what they actually do want,' Charlie pointed out. 'If you keep your wants down to very few, it would be quite easy.'

'And what are his wants?' she asked curiously.

'Him up there, you down here saying, "I obey, I obey!"'

He said the last words in a mechanical voice of such fine comical effect that she couldn't help laughing.

'You ought to have gone on the stage,' she said.

'Yes, I used to think that might be nice, to stand up there in the spotlight, with the audience in the palm of my hand, knowing they were hanging on my every word.'

'Which means you've got a lot in common with Roscoe after all,' she pointed out.

'Yes, I suppose I do. But I want to make them laugh and love me. He wants to make them cower and fear him. And, like I said, when he's teamed up with Vanlen, he'll have everything he wants in the world.'

She was temped to agree, but illogically her sense of justice came to Roscoe's defence. 'Aren't you being a bit unfair? What about the "other Roscoe" you told me about at The Diamond—the nicer one, with feelings?'

'You imagined that.'

'No, I didn't. I remember every word you said.'

'All right, that Roscoe exists too, but only rarely. You'll be dealing with the strong one, so never drop your guard.'

'Careful, Charlie, I don't think you know him as well as you think you do.'

He eyed her shrewdly. 'So he's still exerting his charm over you, is he? He can do that, if he thinks it's worth it. But beware the day when you're no further use to him.'

This was probably good advice, she realised. She was about to ask Charlie to tell her more but he'd already tossed the subject aside to concentrate on something that interested him more.

'Wow! Get you!' he said, his eyes caressing her from head to toe. 'I know what you're doing with that severe look,' he went on. 'But it doesn't work. You're still gorgeous. Aren't you going to take that coat off?'

It was hot in the building and she was glad to let him ease the thick garment from her shoulders. But he took advantage of the situation to slip an arm around her waist, so that she edged away, muttering, 'Not here!'

'Here, there and everywhere,' he persisted. 'There's nobody else around.'

He managed to get both arms around her, resisting her attempts to escape. She groaned, exasperated by the silly boy who couldn't understand that this wasn't the time or the place.

'Someone's coming,' she said frantically. 'Charlie, stop that.'

He was reaching up to free her hair, sending it cascading in joyous beauty around her shoulders. He'd done this before, but that time had been in the privacy of his own home, with only his family there. Now it was in front of Roscoe's door as it opened and a man emerged.

He was thin, with a face that was so pleasant and humorous that at first she couldn't believe this was the man she'd overheard. But his grinding voice was the same, asking, 'Am I interrupting something?'

'Yes,' Charlie said defensively. 'You certainly are.'

'Sorry.' Vanlen held up his hands and backed off.

His glance at Pippa was appreciative and his look said all too plainly that he was a man of the world in these matters. She had met this attitude before and dealt with it too efficiently to be offended now, but she could cheerfully have throttled Charlie. Vanlen departed just as Roscoe appeared in the doorway, his eyes frosty as he regarded his brother.

'Is this fellow bothering you, Miss Jenson?' he demanded. 'If so, say the word and I'll defenestrate him.'

'You will not,' Charlie said, hastily getting behind a chair.

Pippa tried not to choke with laughter, and failed.

'It means throw you out of the window,' she assured Charlie.

'Oh. Are you sure that's all?'

'Quite sure. Stop worrying.'

He returned to her side, addressing Roscoe belligerently. 'I was just telling *Miss Jenson* that it's no use her trying to hide beneath dull clothes. She's still gorgeous beyond belief. Or perhaps you don't think so.'

'I think Miss Jenson looks acceptably professional,' Roscoe said in an indifferent voice. 'Which is exactly what I'd expect of her.'

Cheek! she thought.

He seemed strained and she wondered how long he had dallied in Teresa's bed, and how much had she exhausted him. But he showed her courteously into his office and enquired politely after her car.

'It took some time for my brothers to find the spare part it needed,' she said, 'but they finally managed it, and I'm getting the car back tomorrow.'

She and Charlie sat facing the desk, behind which Roscoe surveyed them from a position of authority, which was how, Pippa guessed, he felt most comfortable.

He pressed a buzzer and spoke to his secretary. 'We don't want to be disturbed.'

'Ah—no!' Charlie squealed. 'I'm waiting for a call. I've told my secretary to fetch me.'

'Then we'd better hurry,' Roscoe said ironically. 'We mustn't keep the betting shop waiting.'

'I got a hot tip,' Charlie explained. 'If it comes in, it'll get me out of trouble on a lot of fronts.'

'I don't know why I bother to teach you about stocks and shares,' Roscoe groaned. 'You're only happy making ridiculous bets.'

'But surely buying stocks and shares is a kind of betting?' Pippa observed innocently.

Charlie gave a muffled choke of laughter. Roscoe's glance told her that he didn't appreciate that remark.

'All right,' she said hastily. 'Let's get on. I've been reviewing the matter and it seems to me—'

The discussion became serious. Pippa put forward her most professional aspect, but all the time she had a strange feeling that it was a mask. There was an uneasy tension in the air, not between herself and Charlie, but between herself and the man who'd held her at a distance last night while burning her with his eyes, a man who eyed her with suppressed hostility, who challenged her every movement.

'I've told the police I wasn't in that shop,' Charlie complained. 'They just say, "Come on, now. Why not just admit it?"'

'They also keep saying things like, "We know what you lads are like,"' Roscoe said. 'As though they were all exactly the same. What's the matter?'

Charlie had suddenly started coughing, but he recovered in a moment. 'Nothing, nothing,' he said with the sudden urgent air of someone who wanted to change the subject. 'Now, where were we?'

He plunged back into serious discussion, talking so sensibly that Pippa's suspicions were aroused. Only one thing could make Charlie sensible, and that was the need to divert attention. She became sunk in thought and had to be recalled by Roscoe, who was staring at her in astonishment.

'Just let me catch up with my notes,' she said hastily. 'Ah, yes, here—'

She got no further. The door was flung open with a crash and a wild voice said, 'I've got to talk to you.'

Turning, she saw a man of about forty with a haggard face and dishevelled hair. His eyes were bloodshot and he seemed on the verge of collapse.

'Mr Franton, I gave orders that you were not to be admitted,' Roscoe said in a hard voice.

'I know. I've been trying to see you for days, but I can't get in. If I could just talk to you, make you understand—'

'But I do understand,' Roscoe interrupted him coldly. 'You deceived me and a lot of other people, and you very nearly involved this firm in a scandal from which it might never have recovered. I've always made it clear that insider trading is something I wouldn't tolerate.'

Pippa understood. Insider trading meant making a profit by the use of privileged information. If a business was on the verge of bankruptcy but only a few people knew, those people would be sorely tempted to sell their shares while they were still worth something, saving themselves financially while others were ruined. It could even happen that the sudden surge in sales precipitated a collapse that might otherwise have been avoided.

In a stockbroking firm such inside knowledge was common and often misused. A spy could earn a handsome profit by selling it on.

Yet Franton didn't look like an evil conspirator. He seemed

ordinary, slightly pathetic, and Pippa couldn't help a surge of unwilling sympathy for him.

'I never meant it to happen the way it did,' he pleaded.

'Understand me once and for all,' Roscoe replied in a hard voice. 'I care nothing for what you meant. I care only for what you did. And what you did was this. You ignored my specific instructions. You lied. You spread unsubstantiated rumours and caused a false rise in prices that cost a lot of people a lot of money—'

'Including you.' Despite his pathos, Franton couldn't resist a spiteful sneer.

'Yes, including me, but it's not the money that counts. It's my reputation that you've damaged and I don't want to see you on these premises ever again. You're out, and that's final.'

'But I need a job,' Franton screamed, collapsing again. 'I've got a family to support, debts—*look*!'

He ran to the window, pointing out to where the snow could now clearly been seen cascading down.

'Snow,' he cried. 'Christmas is coming. What do I tell my children when they don't get any presents?'

'Don't try playing the pathetic card with me,' Roscoe said coldly. 'You nearly caused a disaster throughout the financial world, and you did it by dishonesty. If you've brought a tragedy on yourself the responsibility is yours.'

'You heartless swine!'

Roscoe's face was as stony as his voice. 'Get out,' he said, softly threatening. 'Get out and stay out. You're finished.'

His last card played, Franton seemed to collapse. Slowly, he backed out, casting one last beseeching look. Roscoe didn't even see it.

'Now, perhaps we can finally get on,' he said, seating himself. 'Miss Jenson, I have some papers here—'

'Wait a minute,' Charlie said. 'You're not just going to let him go like that?'

'He can think himself lucky I'm not doing worse.'

'But this is Bill Franton—he's been here for years and he's a family friend—'

'Not any more.'

'Wait,' Charlie said, dashing out in pursuit.

'I'm afraid Charlie is too soft for his own good,' Roscoe said. 'One day I hope he'll learn a sense of reality.'

'Of course insider trading is dishonest and can't be defended,' Pippa agreed, 'but that poor man—'

'Why do you call him a "poor man"—because you saw his distress? You didn't see the distress he caused other people, and the much worse distress that was narrowly averted.'

'I suppose you're right,' she sighed.

'But you don't really think so, do you? I guess I'll just have to endure the burden of your disapproval.'

'It certainly doesn't bother you.'

'I've met it before and it's based on sentimentality.'

'Is it sentimental to say you can attach too much importance to money?' she demanded indignantly.

There was an ironic humour in his eyes, as though he was enjoying a grim joke at her expense.

'Not money, Miss Jenson,' he said. 'Honesty. That's where I attach importance. Nowhere else.'

And he was right, she thought furiously. He was beyond criticism, totally honest, upright, honourable, incorruptible.

And merciless.

'Ah, Charlie, there you are.' Roscoe sounded coolly collected at the sight of his brother. The last few minutes might never have been.

'Roscoe—'

'Come and sit down.'

'But Franton—'

'The subject is closed.' Roscoe's voice was final and Pippa shivered.

She made a mental note not to get on his wrong side, but reckoned that was probably easier said than done.

Then she pushed all other thoughts aside to concentrate on the case, but now that was hard because something was causing Charlie to become uncommunicative, as though protecting a secret. When his secretary looked in, saying, 'That call has come,' he vanished at once.

'How do you think it's going?' Roscoe asked her.

'I think there are problems. He's holding something back.'

'You amaze me. Last night he didn't seem to be holding anything back. You're doing brilliantly, as I expected.'

'That's why you came along, to keep watch, is it? To make sure I didn't lead Charlie along the wrong path?'

'Are you angry with me?'

'I suppose I might be. I can't think why.'

She spoke ironically, but there was truth as well. Beneath the polite surface, this meeting seethed with undercurrents of mistrust. The visit to Roscoe's home had left her feeling more kindly to him, but last night had reversed that. Now she remembered the awkwardness on which their relationship was based and she couldn't wait to get away from him.

'Maybe I'm not managing this very successfully,' he said, 'but it's a new situation for me too.'

'You mean you don't hire women for romantic relationships every day? You amaze me. I thought you were an old hand.'

'All right, attack me if you wish. You're angry about last night, and perhaps you have reason, but I only wanted to… to study the situation.'

'You wanted to find out if you were getting what you paid for. Or if Charlie was getting what you paid for.'

'Stop it!' Roscoe snapped, suddenly finding his nerves fraying. 'Don't talk like that.'

'I'll talk as I like. It's been "like that" ever since you hired me. Well, I don't sleep with the men I date. None of them. Sorry to disappoint you.'

'How dare you say that?' he raged.

Far from disappointing him, Pippa's words gave him a surge of joy so intense it was almost frightening. Until now, he hadn't known how much it mattered. But the discovery left him more confused, even more angry. He wanted to roar up to the heavens.

'Don't ever say anything like that,' he commanded, breathing hard. 'It wasn't our bargain, and you have no right to imply that it was.'

'Maybe not in words, but it's what you were thinking.'

'Don't *dare* tell me what I'm thinking. You know nothing. *Nothing!*'

'Perhaps I know more than you realise.'

'Pippa, I'm warning you—'

'Then don't. What right do you have to warn me? You're so arrogant, you think you can give orders left, right and centre, but not to me.'

'*I'm* arrogant?' Roscoe snapped. 'What about you? You assume all men are slavering for you and you despise them accordingly. I only hope one day you'll meet a man who's totally indifferent to your charms. It would teach you a lesson.'

'But surely,' she said with poisonous sweetness, 'I've met him already—in you. Haven't I?'

If she'd been easily scared she might have quailed at the look he threw her.

'You *are* indifferent to my charms, aren't you, Roscoe?'

'Totally!' he said in a voice of ice.

'And, since I'm equally indifferent to yours, neither of us has a problem. Just the same, I think it's time this arrangement came to an end. Another lawyer will suit you better.'

She rose and made for the door, but he was there before her.

'Don't be absurd. You can't just go like this.'

'So anyone who disagrees with you is absurd? No, I was absurd the day I let myself get embroiled in this. I should have had more sense of self-preservation. Now, please stand aside.'

'No,' he said stubbornly. 'I'm not letting you leave here.'

'Roscoe, stand aside. I won't be treated like this.'

Pippa thought he would defy her again, but then his shoulders sagged.

'All right, I'll stand aside,' he said. 'But I'm going to say something first.'

'Then get on with it.'

'Don't go. Hate me as much as you like, but don't abandon Charlie, *please*.'

'Roscoe—'

'I'm begging you, do you understand that? Begging.'

His eyes left no doubt that he meant it. They were brilliant, feverish, amazing her so that she couldn't speak.

'Well?' he asked. 'Do you want me to go down on one knee?'

'Oh, don't be ridiculous,' she said, backing away. 'Suppose someone came in.'

'Then they'd see me as never before, and they'd think it was a good laugh. Is that your price? You want me to make a fool of myself, and then you'll do as I ask? Is that it?'

'Suppose I said yes?' she asked. 'Would you pay the price?'

'Yes,' he said simply. 'Shall I? Go on, you've been wanting to take me down a peg since we met. Now's your chance.'

'No!' she exploded. 'That's the last thing I'd want. I'm not that kind of harpy.'

'Then what is your answer? Will you stay?'

'*Yes!* Now get back behind your desk and stop talking nonsense.'

He gave her a wry look, but moved away behind the desk.

Suddenly the door came flying open and Charlie stood there. 'I won!' he carolled.

'You don't mean that three-legged hack came home?' Roscoe asked ironically, and only Pippa noticed the strain in his voice.

'Ten to one!' Charlie yipped joyfully. 'I made a packet. Hey, I'll be able to pay you back the money I owe you—well, some of it, anyway.' He gave Pippa a bear hug. 'And it's all due to you. Since you came into my life, everything has gone well. The sun shines, the world is beautiful. Isn't that so, Roscoe?'

'Miss Jenson is certainly having a beneficial effect,' he replied loftily. 'In fact I was explaining how pleased we are with her efforts when you came in. Now, if you'll kindly sit down, Charlie, we can return to work.'

Pippa had to give him ten out of ten for a sense of wicked irony. She tried to meet his eyes, perhaps even encourage him to share the joke. But he wasn't looking at her. The paperwork seemed to absorb him.

The rest of the meeting was conducted with strict propriety, with as few words as possible. Pippa asked questions, made notes and finally rose briskly, declaring, 'I'll be in touch when I've investigated some more.'

'Tonight,' Charlie said eagerly.

'Tonight I've got some boring reception to go to. Don't be in a rush. I'll see myself out.'

She escaped.

CHAPTER SEVEN

PIPPA had spoken the truth about the coming evening. A client was giving a lavish reception to celebrate acquiring sole rights to a piece of valuable computer software and had offered several invitations to Farley & Son, whose work had been crucial in securing the contract in a bidding war. A little group of them were going, including David and herself.

'Dress up to the nines,' he told her. 'Knock their eyes out. It's good for business.'

She laughed but did as he wished, donning a shimmering white dress that combined beauty with elegance. The reception was held at London's most costly hotel. They arrived in a fleet of expensive cars and were shown upstairs to the Grand Salon where their hosts were waiting to greet them effusively.

One of the younger wives, friendly with Pippa and new to this kind of function, was in transports. 'Everybody who's anybody in finance is here tonight,' she said. 'You probably know most of them.'

Pippa did indeed recognise many faces and began working the room, champagne in hand, charm on display, as was expected of her. As her friend had said, the cream of London's financial establishment was gathered there, so it shouldn't have been a surprise when her eyes fell on Roscoe Havering. Yet it was.

'Good evening, Miss Jenson.'

'Good evening, Mr Havering.'

'I suppose I shouldn't be surprised to see you here,' he said, unconsciously echoing her own thought. 'It's the sort of gathering in which you shine.'

'Strictly business,' she said. 'I can help to attract new clients here, and that's what David expects me to do, so, if you'll excuse me, I must get to work.'

'Wait.' His hand on her arm detained her. 'Are you angry with me?'

'Certainly not.'

'Then why are you so determined to get away from me?'

'Because, as I've tried to explain, for me this is a business meeting.'

'Tell me the real reason. That's not just efficiency I see in your eyes. It's coldness and hostility. How have I offended you now?'

'You haven't.'

'Little liar. Tell me the truth.'

'You haven't offended me, but I can't pretend that you're my favourite person.'

'Because of Charlie?'

'No, because of…lots of things.'

'Name one.'

'Stop interrogating me. I'm not in the dock.'

'No, your victim is usually in the dock with you pressing home the questions. So, you can dish it out but you can't take it?'

'How dare you!'

'Name something I've done to offend you—a new offence, not one you've told me about before.'

She ground her teeth, wondering how she could ever have sympathised with him.

'All right,' she said at last. 'Franton.'

'Who?'

'You've forgotten him already, haven't you? That poor man who burst into your office this morning.'

'That "poor man"—'

'Yes, yes, I know. Insider trading is wrong, but he's not the only one who's sailed a bit close to the wind, is he? I know someone else whose activities threaten your firm's good name, but he doesn't get chucked out. He gets protected. You hire a lawyer to keep him on the straight and narrow.'

'He's my brother—'

'And Franton is a man with a wife and children. Maybe he doesn't deserve a position of trust any more, but you threw him onto the scrap heap without a second thought.'

Pippa waited for Roscoe to speak but he was staring as though he'd just seen her for the first time.

'All right,' she said. 'I'm a soppy, sentimental woman who doesn't understand harsh reality and sticks her nose into what doesn't concern her. There, now, I've saved you the trouble of saying it.'

'Soppy and sentimental is the last thing I'd ever call you,' Roscoe said. He seemed to be talking in a daze.

'Well, anyway…since you're employing me I suppose I had no right to fly at you like that.'

His voice was unexpectedly gentle. 'You can say anything you like to me.'

'No, really—it's none of my business.' Suddenly she was desperate to get away from him.

'I wish I could explain to you what the pressures are—I think I could make you understand, and I'd like to feel that you did.'

'As you say, I don't know what it's like for you.' She gave a brittle laugh. 'I don't suppose I could imagine it.'

'Pippa—'

'Don't let me keep you. We both need to drum up new business.'

She gave him a brilliant smile and moved firmly away. She didn't even look back, but plunged into networking—smiling, laughing, making appointments, promising phone calls. It was an efficient evening and by the end of it she'd made a number of good contacts.

At last she found herself on the edge of a little group surrounding the managing director of the firm celebrating its triumph. He was growing expansive, making jokes.

Roscoe, standing nearby, joined in the polite laughter, while his eyes drifted over the crowd until he saw the person he wanted and watched her unobtrusively.

'It's been a good celebration,' the managing director said. 'Of course, I really wanted to arrange this evening a couple of weeks later, so that we could make it a Christmas party as well, but everyone's calendar was crowded already.'

'Such a shame,' said a woman close by. 'I simply adore Christmas.'

There were polite murmurs of agreement from almost everyone.

But not from Pippa, Roscoe realised. Beneath the perfectly applied make-up, her face had grown suddenly pale, almost drawn. She closed her eyes, keeping them shut just a moment too long, as though retreating into herself.

David spoke in Roscoe's memory. *The nearer to Christmas it gets, the more of a workaholic she becomes... It's as if she's trying to avoid Christmas altogether.'*

He studied Pippa, willing her to open her eyes so that he might read something in them. At last she did so, but when she saw him she turned quickly, as though she resented his gaze.

As she moved away a strange feeling assailed him. She was young, beautiful, the most alluring, magnetic woman in the room. And she was mysteriously alone. No man claimed her, and she claimed none either. For a blinding moment the sense of her isolation was so strong that it was as though everyone else had vanished, leaving her the sole occupant of the vast, echoing room.

Or a vast, echoing world.

He told himself not to indulge fanciful thoughts. But they wouldn't be banished. He started to go after her but somebody called him, forcing him to smile and go on 'business alert'. When he managed to escape, Pippa had vanished.

Along the front of the hotel were some elaborate balconies, decorative stonework wreathed in evergreen. Pippa wandered out, thankful to escape the air inside, heavily perfumed with money, seduction and intrigue. But it was too chilly to stay out long and after a few minutes she turned back. Then she stopped at the sight of the man standing there.

'Good evening,' he said.

After a moment memory awoke. This was the 'big noise' in the financial world, with whom Roscoe would soon merge his firm, becoming, if possible, more powerful and autocratic than he already was.

'Mr Vanlen. I think we met briefly in Mr Havering's office.'

'You could say we "met". It was more you putting yourself on display. Mind you, there's plenty to display, I'll give you that. You knew you were driving me crazy, and you meant to do it. Fine, I fell for it. Let's talk.'

'No, I—'

'Oh, spare me the modest denials. You came out here knowing I'd follow you.'

'No, I didn't know you were here.'

'I've been watching you all evening. Don't pretend you didn't know. Here's the deal. You and I, together, for as long as it suits me. And you'll find me generous.'

'You're mistaken,' she said coldly. 'I am *not* interested in you in any way, shape or form. Is that clear?'

But, as his self-satisfied smirk revealed, he interpreted this in his own way.

'Evidently I didn't make *myself* clear,' he said. 'Does this say it plainly enough?'

Pulling out a flat black box, he opened it to reveal a diamond pendant of beauty and value.

'And that's just the start,' he added.

She regarded him wearily. 'I'm supposed to be impressed by this, aren't I?' she said. 'But I'm not interested. Can't you understand that?'

'Come, come. You're a woman of the world. You know the score. You're used to rich, powerful men and you like them that way, don't you?'

'Only if they're interesting. Not all rich men *are* interesting. Some of them are plain bores.'

'Money is never boring,' he riposted. 'Nor is power. You see them?' He flung a hand in the direction of the room behind them. 'The richest, most powerful men in London, and there isn't one of them I couldn't crush. Ask Havering. His investigations about me have shown him a few things that surprised him.'

'He's had you investigated? You sound very cool about it.'

Vanlen shrugged. 'It's no more that I expect, ahead of our tie-up. I've done the same to him, and I found things that surprised me too. It's par for the course.'

He was right, she realised. This level of sharp-eyed suspicion was normal in the world of high finance where Roscoe inhabited a peak. But it made her shiver.

'I know a few things about you too,' Vanlen went on. 'You like to play the field. No permanent lover to make things awkward. Fine, then we understand each other.'

His hand slid around her shoulder, making her move away quickly.

'The one thing you don't seem to understand is the word no,' she snapped. 'I'll say it as often as I have to.'

'But you don't mean it,' he protested. 'Come on, just one little kiss to seal our bargain.'

Before she could stop him, he'd pulled her close and brushed her lips with his own. Exerting all her strength, she wrenched free.

'Try that again and I'll slap you so hard you'll bounce into next week,' she said breathlessly.

What he might have done then she never found out, for a cough from the shadows made them both turn. Roscoe was standing there.

'I came to fetch you, Vanlen,' he said. 'There's a big deal going on and they want you to be part of it.'

'On my way,' the man replied and vanished without a backward glance at Pippa. The scene between them might never have happened.

'Thank you,' she said coolly. 'He was becoming a bore.'

He made a wryly humorous face. 'Don't tell me I arrived in time to save a damsel in distress?'

'Certainly not. Another moment and I'd have tossed him off the balcony, so you might say you spoilt my fun.'

'My apologies.'

The feel of Vanlen's mouth was still on hers, filling her with disgust and making her rub her mouth hard with tissues.

'Yuck!' she said.

'It's a pity he affects you like that. You could have been queen of London.'

'Don't you start. Did you hear what he said about you?'

'Investigation? Sure. We each know enough to confront the other. Pippa, are you all right?'

She was still rubbing her mouth, and he caught himself up at once.

'No, of course you're not all right. Stupid of me. Don't go at it so hard, you'll hurt yourself.'

'I can't help it. He's disgusting.'

'Here, let me.' Taking a clean handkerchief from his pocket, he began to rub gently.

'It's no use,' she sighed. 'I can still feel him. Perhaps another glass of champagne would wipe him away.'

'I know something better,' he said softly and laid his mouth against hers.

It was over in a second. His lips touched hers for a brief moment, just long enough to obliterate Vanlen, then they were gone.

Through the dim light, he saw the wild astonishment in her eyes and could just make out her lips shaping his name.

'I'm sorry,' he said stiffly. 'I thought it might help.'

'I—'

'Come on.' Taking her hand firmly, he led her back to where the crowd was beginning to disperse.

David was there, looking around, brightening when he saw her. 'Ready to go?' he asked cheerfully.

'Yes…yes…'

'I think she's tired,' Roscoe said. 'The sooner she goes home, the better. Excuse me.'

He was gone.

In the car home Pippa pretended to be asleep so that she could avoid talking. But later, when she got into bed, she lay awake all night, staring into the darkness, trying to see what could not be seen and understand what could not be understood.

The following evening she went to have a family dinner at her beloved grandparents' house on Crimea Street, and where she herself had lived for the last two years of their lives. These days Frank, his wife and children, lived there, with her other brother, Brian, just down the street. Now they returned her car with an air of triumph at having made it usable again.

Pippa hadn't been back to the old home much recently, and for a while she could enjoy the company of her parents, nephews and nieces, most of whom lived no more than two streets away.

With so many children, it was inevitable that the Christmas decorations should go up early.

'I keep telling them that it's still too soon,' Brian's wife, Ruth, said in laughing despair. 'But you might as well talk to the moon. As far as they're concerned, it's Christmas already. Hold that paper chain, would you?'

Pippa smiled mechanically. It was true, as David had suggested, that she had her own reasons for shying away from Christmas—for her, it had been a time of heartbreak. But this was no time to inflict her feelings on her family, so she spent a conventional evening climbing a stepladder and hanging up tinsel.

There was a moment of excitement when a box was brought down from the attic. Dust rose as it was unpacked, but the contents were disappointing.

'A couple of tatty scarves,' Ruth said disparagingly. 'Gloves. Some old books. Let's throw them out.'

'No, give them to me,' Pippa said quickly. She'd recognised the gloves as a pair Dee had worn, and it would be nice to keep them as a memento.

She wandered through the house, glancing into the bedroom where they had slept together until the end. Pippa's mother Lilian crept in behind her and surveyed the double bed, which was still the same one where the old people had embraced each other as they'd drifted contentedly to the end of the road.

'They were very happy together,' she sighed. 'And yet I can never see this room without feeling sad.'

'I came in one morning to find that Gran had died in the night,' Pippa remembered, 'and Grandma was holding him. It wasn't very long after they took that trip to Brighton, the honeymoon they never had.'

'And they wouldn't have had even that if you hadn't taken them,' Lilian recalled. 'They told me it was the last thing that made everything perfect. Afterwards, they just slipped away.'

'And that was what they both wanted,' Pippa said. 'Even missing them terribly, I couldn't be unhappy for them. All they cared about was being together, and now they always will be.'

'And one day that's what you'll have,' Lilian said, regarding her tenderly. 'Just be patient.'

'Honestly, Mum, I don't think like that any more. You start off telling yourself, "Never mind, there's always next time". But there isn't really. There won't be a next time for me, and it's better if I face that now.'

'Oh, darling, don't say that,' Lilian protested, almost tearful. 'You can't live your life without love.'

'Why not? I have a great time, a successful job, a good social life—'

'Oh, yes, every man falls at your feet in the first ten minutes,' Lilian said with motherly disapproval.

'Not quite every man,' Pippa murmured.

'Good. I'm glad some of them make you think.'

'Mum, please stop. I did my thinking years ago when a certain person did his vanishing act. That's it. The man who can change my mind hasn't been born.'

'You're only talking like this because you're always depressed at Christmas, but I just know that one day someone will make your heart beat faster.'

'You mean like Dad does with you?' Pippa asked mischievously.

'I admit your father's no romantic hero, but he's a decent man with a sweet temper. If he'd only stop breeding ferrets I'd have no complaints.'

'Is someone talking about me?' came a voice from the stairs as Pippa's plump, balding father appeared.

In the laughter that followed, the subject was allowed to die and she was able to escape.

They all think it's so easy, she mused. *Find a man who makes your heart beat faster and that's it. But suppose you don't like him because he's hard and cynical, and he looks down on you even while he's looking you over. Suppose he infuriates you because you can't stop thinking about him when you don't want to, so that you just get angrier and angrier. Suppose he's the wrong man in every possible way but that doesn't seem to help because when he looks at you it makes you think of things you'd rather not think of. And then he does something—the last thing you expected—and it makes you want…it makes you want…oh, to hell with it! And him!*

Charlie called her the next day and they arranged to meet for dinner the following evening.

'And don't worry about Roscoe turning up because he's gone to Los Angeles,' Charlie added.

'Los Angeles?' she murmured, recalling the words she'd overheard in his office. 'But he was so definite about not going, said it was a waste of time.'

'I know, and then suddenly he changed his mind, which is something he never does.'

'Everybody does sometimes,' she said mechanically, trying to ignore certain thoughts that clamoured for entrance to her mind.

They were astounding thoughts. They said he'd gone away to escape her after their two encounters, so confusingly different. He seemed to fight with her and kiss her, just as easily.

No, she corrected herself quickly. It hadn't been a kiss, just a kindly gesture; almost medical in intent. But it had misfired. Meaning only to obliterate the memory of Vanlen's lips, he'd replaced it with his own. Which surely hadn't been his intention.

She remembered how quickly he'd backed off, clearly shocked. By himself, or by her? What had he read in her eyes that had sent him flying to the far side of the world?

The memories and questions raged inside her, warning her that the time was coming when she would have to face the truth. And the truth scared her.

At her insistence, Charlie took her to a sedate, conventional restaurant, where he was on his best behaviour. And, without Roscoe there, Pippa could raise the suspicion that had been nagging at her since the office meeting.

'Now tell me the truth,' she said. 'You never did go into that shop, but Ginevra did, probably dressed in jeans with her hair covered. In the near darkness she looked like a man, so when she escaped and the owner caught up with you—well, it was her, wasn't it?'

Charlie set his chin stubbornly. 'You're just imagining things.'

'You gave the game away when Roscoe said people thought all lads were the same and you had that coughing fit. I suddenly saw what had happened. You were mistaken for her, and she just ran off and left you to suffer.'

'Look—we were good together once and I can't just drop her in it.'

Nothing would budge him from this position. Pippa seethed with frustration and ended the evening early.

Before going to bed, she sent an email to Roscoe. For some

reason it wouldn't come right and she had to reword it three times, eventually settling on:

Mr Havering,
I've just had a worrying talk with your brother. He didn't break into the shop. It was Ginevra and three others. Mr Fletcher caught them but they ran off and by the time he caught up she'd vanished, and he assumed Charlie was the fourth.

Charlie's having an attack of daft chivalry. I've tried to make him see sense, but he's deaf to reason.

I'm afraid the 'charms' for which you hired me are drawing a blank, and it seemed only right to inform you of my failure.

I await your further instructions.
Yours sincerely,
Philippa Jenson

She read it through repeatedly, finally losing patience with herself for shilly-shallying and hitting the 'send' button violently. Then she threw herself into bed and pulled the covers over her head.

Next morning, she checked for a reply. But there was nothing.

Too soon. Think of the time difference. He must be asleep.

At work she accessed her home computer every hour, sure that this time there would be a response. Nothing.

Her email would have gone to his London office, she reasoned, and perhaps he wouldn't see it until he returned. No way! An efficient man like Roscoe would link up from Los Angeles. He was ignoring her.

Her disappointment was severe—and irrational, she knew. This didn't fit with her mental picture of him as a better man inside than he was on the outside. She felt personally let down.

She worked late that night, finally reaching home with relief.

Then she stopped, astounded, at the incredible sight that met her eyes. Roscoe was in the hall, seated on an ornate wooden bench. His head leaned back against the wall, his eyes were closed and his breathing suggested that he was asleep. He looked almost at the point of collapse.

CHAPTER EIGHT

PIPPA touched him gently on the shoulder and his eyes opened slowly.

'Hello,' he said.

'Roscoe, what on earth—? Come upstairs.'

He retrieved the two suitcases near his feet and followed her into the elevator, where he closed his eyes again until they arrived and she led him out, along the corridor and into her apartment.

'Sit down,' she said, pointing to a comfortable sofa.

'You must be thinking—'

'Tea first, explanations later,' she said.

'Thank you.'

She was smiling to herself as she filled the kettle. Her email had brought him home. The world was good again.

He drank the tea thankfully, but didn't seem much more awake.

'When did you last sleep?' she asked.

'I can't remember. I was unlucky in catching a flight. I reached the airport just in time to miss one plane and I had to grab the next one. Only it went to Paris, so I had to get a connecting flight to London.'

'You walked out on your conference?' she breathed.

He shrugged. 'After your email, what did you expect me to do?'

'Email me. Text me. Call me.'

'No, I had to talk to you properly.'

And for that he'd walked out on business.

Of course he'd done it for Charlie and his mother, Pippa reminded herself.

But common sense spoke with a feeble voice, defeated by the surge of awareness of Roscoe as a man. A man who'd tried to escape her and been defeated.

What was happening between them alarmed him because it threatened the life he'd achieved with such a struggle. But he'd seized an excuse to come back to her and now he was here, laying his gesture at her feet, waiting to know what she would do with it.

She was silenced for a moment. She'd misjudged him so badly.

'The flight to Los Angeles is eleven hours,' she said at last, 'and then you came straight back—'

'And I don't even like flying,' he ground out. 'In fact, I hate it.'

'I hate it too,' she admitted. 'It's boring, you're trapped, and I'm always sure we're going to crash at any moment.'

He gave her a faint grin of understanding.

'No wonder you're exhausted,' she said. 'But why did you wait downstairs? There's a sofa in the hall outside my front door where you could have been more comfortable.'

'Yes, but I wasn't sure if you'd be coming home alone, and if your companion had seen me lolling by your door… well…'

'Am I understanding you properly?' she asked, regarding him with her head on one side.

'I just didn't want to embarrass you.'

'You've got a nerve,' she breathed, feeling a return of the annoyance he could inflame so easily in her.

'I'm only suggesting that you might have company tonight. What's wrong with that?'

Pippa drew a deep breath, but instantly checked herself.

'No—no!' She held up her hands with the air of someone backing off. 'Let's leave it for now. I'll say it later, when you're back in the land of the living.'

'Thank you for that mercy,' he said. 'So when "later" comes I can expect to be knocked sideways, beaten to a pulp—'

'Walked over with hobnailed boots,' she agreed. 'But first I'll make you some supper.'

'Just a little, thank you. I'll probably fall asleep over it.'

'Then I shall wake you and make you eat something anyway.'

Roscoe gave her a look of appreciation. Then he followed her into the kitchen and tried to help, but finished up sitting on a stool, watching her out of bleary eyes.

'It's not just tiredness,' he said. 'It's jet lag, which always hits me like a rock. I don't know why I get it worse than most people. Everyone else seems to brush it off, but not me. And it's not just the flight home. I'm still lagged from the flight out there, so I'm—' he made a helpless gesture '—not at my best.'

'That's what comes of dashing off to conferences at the last minute,' she suggested gently.

'Yes, well…things happen. You can't always plan for…' again the gesture '…well, anyway…'

'Did you hear anything useful while you were there?' she asked in a neutral voice.

'I couldn't tell you,' he said with a humorous sigh. 'I can't remember a thing.'

'Is this Roscoe Havering talking?' she asked lightly. 'The man who makes the financial world tremble, whose tough decisions can shake the market—?'

'Oh, shut up!' he begged.

She laughed. 'Sorry.'

'You're not.'

'Hey, you're right. I'm not.'

She made a light meal of scrambled eggs on toast, and he pleased her by eating every last crumb.

'That was delicious. Do you want some help with the washing up?'

'No, thank you,' she said with more haste than politeness. 'But you've made your offer so you can go and sit on the sofa with a clear conscience.'

'That's what I like. A woman who understands.'

He wandered away with the air of a man who had arrived in heaven.

When she joined him a few minutes later he said, 'Do you really think Charlie's protecting Ginevra?'

'Oh, yes. But I can't prove it without his help. I guess I'm just not doing my job properly. I haven't beguiled him very well if he's defending her against me.'

'Charlie's loyal. If he had feelings for her once, he wouldn't drop her in it now.'

'That's nice of him but don't you see what it means?'

'It means my brother's an idiot, but we knew that.'

'It means I've failed. He was supposed to be so much under my spell that he'd do anything I said. Hah! Some spell! I'm useless.'

'That's enough. You're not useless. It's only been a few days.'

'But you thought he'd take one look at me and become my willing slave,' she said wryly. 'Or something like that. This isn't what you expected when you hired me. Perhaps you should get someone else.'

'Someone else?' he echoed. 'Someone else with your eyes, your laughter, your charm? *Is* there anyone else? Pippa, you knocked Charlie sideways in the first moment.'

'You're just being kind.'

'I'm not known for my kindness,' he said drily. 'And once you'd have been the first to say so. I knew from the start that you were exactly what I wanted—for Charlie, I mean. And you're doing well. Look how you found out about this. I had no idea.'

'But I'm failing.'

'Why are you so hard on yourself? It's not like you.'

Now she was all at sea, taken by surprise by his understanding.

'You don't know what's like me,' she muttered.

'Don't I? Well, perhaps I'm learning, and perhaps the things I'm learning are surprising me.'

She tried to be sensible, but it was hard with Roscoe's gentle eyes on her.

'Obviously I don't have the hold on him that you wanted,' she murmured.

'I think you do. The other night, when you were dancing together and he tried to kiss you at the end—'

'That didn't mean anything,' she said quickly. 'He just saw it as part of the dance.'

'But earlier that evening, when you were at the table and you—'

'I didn't kiss him.'

'No, but you did this.' Roscoe leaned forward, putting his hands on either side of her face and looking into her eyes. 'You did this,' he repeated. 'Don't you remember?'

'Yes,' she said breathlessly. 'I remember now.'

She waited for him to release her, but for some reason he didn't. She had the strangest impression that he was imprisoned in himself, wanting to move but unable to. Then she knew that the feeling was there inside her also. His hands were warm and firm against her cheeks, his eyes uncertain and questioning as she'd never seen them before. How dark and mysterious they were, inviting her to explore depths that enticed her. His lips, so often set in a firm line, were slightly parted, the sound of his breathing reaching her softly.

He'd been watching her all the time in the nightclub, she realised; not just dancing but when she was sitting at the table with Charlie, laughing with him, smiling at him. He'd noted every gesture, every moment of warmth.

She felt a tremor go through her and realised that it came from him. He was shaking. She drew in a sharp breath and in the same moment he dropped his hands, as though the touch of her burned him.

And she saw fear in his eyes.

His alarm had an instant effect on her, reminding her of her own caution about getting too close.

'You misunderstood what you saw,' she said quickly. 'It was just friendly. That's all I can ever manage. Just friendly. That's why you didn't have to worry about me bringing anyone home tonight. I know what I look like, but it's not real. People would be amazed to know how virtuously I live.'

'I wouldn't,' he murmured, but she didn't hear him.

'It's all front, all presentation,' she hurried on, gabbling slightly. 'So I suppose that makes me a tease. I meet a man, we go out, have a good time, exchange a few kisses—oh, yes, I don't deny that—and he thinks that sooner or later he's going to have a night of pleasure. I don't intentionally deceive them, but pretty soon I realise that I can't go through with it. He isn't "the one" and the kindest thing to do is tell him.'

'Yes, I saw that the first night,' he reminded her. 'But why, Pippa? You could have any man you wanted.'

'No, I couldn't,' she said. Pippa turned sharply away and walked to the window, filled with shrieking alarm at the way the distance between them was closing by the minute. It was safer to pull apart now.

But perhaps Roscoe's courage was greater than hers

because he followed and stood just behind her, not touching but barely an inch apart.

'What happened?' he asked softly.

'It doesn't matter.'

'Yes, it does. It matters because you've made it your whole life. If it didn't matter, it wouldn't scare you as much as it does.'

'I'm not scared,' she said brightly. 'What is there to be scared of?'

'You tell me—if you can put it into words.'

'You're making something out of nothing. I had a bad experience, but so does everyone.'

'Yes, but yours went deep enough to damn near destroy you,' he said in a voice that was mysteriously fierce and gentle at the same time.

That almost shattered her control. Out of sight, she clenched her hands and forced herself to shrug.

'Look, I lost the man I wanted and it cured me of silly fantasies.'

Hands on her shoulders, he turned her to face him. He was frowning slightly. 'And what do you define as "silly fantasies"?'

'Love lasting for ever. Moon rhyming with June. It's all a con trick. Have fun, but don't start believing in it, that's my motto.'

'Do you really not believe in people truly loving each other, wanting to give to each other, make sacrifices for each other?'

She gave a little laugh. 'I believed in it once. Not any more. Let's leave it.'

'What happened?'

She shrugged. 'It turned out that he didn't believe in it, that's all. Unfortunately, he discovered that rather late in the day. The wedding was planned, everything booked—the church, the honeymoon. So we had to cancel the arrangements. Very boring, but a useful lesson in reality.'

She finished with a tinkling laugh that made him look at her shrewdly.

'I see,' he said, nodding.

'Do you? I wonder. I don't suppose you know much about being jilted.'

He didn't reply for a moment. Then he said simply, 'Don't jump to conclusions.'

Suddenly, as though he too had heard the sounding of an alarm, he stepped back, asking, 'Is there any more tea?' in a voice whose brittleness matched her own.

'Yes, I'll make a fresh cup. Sit down and wait for me.'

He'd revealed more than he'd meant to and was hastily blocking a door he'd half opened. Pippa understood the feeling, having done the same. Now she was glad to escape to the kitchen and have a few moments alone to calm her riotous feelings.

When she felt she'd returned to some sort of normality, she took in the tea and found him studying Dee and Mark's wedding picture.

'They were my grandparents,' she said. 'They married during the war.'

'You're very like her,' he said.

'Really? Nobody's ever said that to me before.'

'Not in features, but she's got a cheeky look in her eyes that I've seen in yours. It says, "Go on, I dare you!"'

'Hey, that was her exactly.'

'Did you know her well?'

'I lived with the two of them near the end of their lives. When she died, she left me some money on condition I used it to train for a career. It's funny, I love both my parents, and my brothers, but I was closer to Gran than anyone else. She didn't stand for any nonsense.'

'You see; I said you were like her.'

'Well, she taught me a lot, especially how to get the better of a man.' She gave a merry chuckle. Now that the dangerous moment had passed, she was slipping back into the persona of Pippa the cheeky urchin. '"Let him think he's winning", that was her motto. "Make sure he doesn't find out the truth until it's too late".' She glanced at the picture on the sideboard. 'And I was a good pupil, wasn't I, Gran? Top of the class.'

'You want to be careful having that kind of conversation with your grandmother,' Roscoe said, grinning. 'Your grandfather might eavesdrop and discover your secrets.'

'If he doesn't know them by now—' She stopped suddenly, aghast as she heard herself talking as though they were living people. She must sound really mad. 'That is…' she resumed hastily '…what I mean is…'

'Pippa—' he interrupted her gently '—you don't have to tell me what you mean. You really don't.'

And she didn't, she realised with a surge of thankfulness. Roscoe understood perfectly.

'How long were they married?' he asked.

'Sixty years. We had a big celebration of their anniversary, and neither of them lived very long after that. He died first, and then Gran was just waiting to join him. She used to say he appeared in her dreams and told her to hurry up because he could never find anything without her. In the end, she only kept him waiting three weeks.

'I remember her saying that she wanted to outlive him, but only by a little. She wanted to be there to look after him as long as he needed her, but then she wanted to follow quickly. And she got her wish.'

Roscoe gave her a strange look. 'So love does sometimes last for ever?'

'For their generation, yes. In those days it was expected.'

'And that's why they stayed together for sixty years? Because of convention?'

'No,' she sighed. 'That's not why. They loved each other totally, but just because they could manage it doesn't mean that everyone… Drink your tea before it gets cold.'

'Then I must call a taxi and go home. Perhaps you'd have lunch with me tomorrow, when I'm more awake. We'll discuss the most sensible way to proceed.'

He took out his cellphone but, instead of making the call, he stared at it, then put it down suddenly as though reeling from a blow.

'If I can just rest for a moment,' he murmured.

'Not just for a moment,' she said. 'All night.'

'What was that?'

'You're not leaving while you're in this state. You'd forget where you were going and end up heaven knows where. Come on.'

She reached for him to help him to his feet. Dazed, he let her support him into the bedroom, where a gentle push sent him tumbling onto the bed. She went to recover his suitcases and when she returned he was sprawled out, dead to the world. Quietly, she drew the curtains and turned out the light.

'Goodnight,' she whispered, closing the door.

She washed up quietly so that no noise should intrude on him even through the door. As she worked, she tried to believe that this was really happening. Her email had brought Roscoe flying home, despite his problems with jet lag, despite his work, despite his intense need to stay ahead of the game. Despite everything, he'd come speeding back to her.

Before retiring for the night, she opened the door of the bedroom just a crack. Roscoe was lying as she'd left him, his breath coming evenly. She backed out and went to curl up on the sofa.

Who would have imagined that he had an unsuspected

frailty? she thought. More—who would have imagined that he would allow her to see it?

Just before she fell asleep, she wondered if Teresa had ever been allowed to know.

She awoke in darkness, feeling slightly chilly. The weather was growing cold as autumn advanced, so she turned the heating up, then recalled that the bedroom radiator was sometimes temperamental.

Quietly, she slipped into the room, realising that she'd been right. The temperature was low and it took some fiddling before the radiator performed properly. In the darkness she could just make out Roscoe, lying still, then turning and muttering.

He must be cold, she thought, taking a blanket from the cupboard and creeping to the bed, hoping to lay it down without waking him. But his eyes opened as she leaned over.

'Hello,' he whispered.

'I just brought you this so that you don't catch cold,' she said.

She wasn't sure if he heard her. His eyes had closed again while his hands found her, drawing her down against him. There was nothing lover-like in the embrace. She wasn't even sure he knew what he was doing. But his arms were about her and her head was on his chest, and he seemed to have fallen asleep again.

It would have been easy to slide free, but she found she had no desire to do so. The feeling of Roscoe's chest rising and falling beneath her head and the soft rhythm of his heart against her ear were pleasant and peaceful. That was missing in her life, she realised. Peace. Tranquillity. This was the last man with whom she would have expected to find those elusive treasures, yet somehow it seemed natural to be held against him, drifting on a pleasant sea in a world where there was nothing to fear.

Which just went to show.

Show what?

Something or other.

She slept.

She was awoken by a sudden movement from Roscoe. His hands tightened on her and he looked into her face, his own eyes filled with shock.

'What…how did you…?'

'You pulled me down while I was putting a blanket over you,' she said sleepily. 'It was like being held in an iron cage, and I was too tired to argue so I just drifted.'

He groaned. 'Sorry if I made you a prisoner. You should have socked me on the jaw.'

'Didn't have the energy.' She yawned, letting him draw her back against his chest. 'Besides, you weren't doing anything to deserve getting socked.'

And what would I have done if you had? The words ran through her mind before she could stop them.

'Are you sure? Pippa, tell me at once—did I…I didn't…?'

'No, you didn't. I promise. You were right out of it. You wouldn't have had the energy to do anything, any more than I'd have had the energy to sock you.'

She was laughing contentedly as she spoke and he relaxed, also laughing.

Suddenly he said, 'What on earth is that?'

He'd noticed the shabby toy on her bedside table. Now he reached out and took it.

'That belonged to my Gran—the one in that photo,' she said. 'She called him her Mad Bruin, and I think he represented Grandpa to her. After he died she cuddled Bruin and talked to him all the time.'

Roscoe surveyed Bruin, not with the scorn she would once have expected from him, but with fascination.

'I'll bet you could tell a secret or two,' he said.

Pippa choked with laughter and he drew her close, laying the little bear aside as carefully as though he had feelings.

'Will you believe me if I say I never meant this to happen?' he murmured against her hair.

'Of course. If you'd had anything else in mind you would have gone to Teresa.'

'Teresa isn't you,' he said, as though that explained everything.

'Ah, yes, you couldn't have talked stern practicalities with her.'

'As a matter of fact, I could. She's my oldest friend.'

'She's a great beauty,' Pippa mused. 'Useful kind of "friend".'

'The best. She's helped me out of several awkward situations. Her husband was also my friend. In fact I introduced them. He died a few years ago but she's never looked at anyone else, and I don't think she ever will. She's still in love with his memory.'

Roscoe wondered why he was telling her all this. Why should he care what she thought? Then he remembered her with Charlie the other night, holding his face tenderly between her hands. And he knew why.

He waited for her to say something, and was disappointed when she didn't. He couldn't see that she was smiling to herself.

CHAPTER NINE

AFTER a moment Pippa summoned up her courage and said, as casually as she could manage, 'So you went on being friends with her husband? He didn't steal her from you?'

'Goodness, no! Teresa and I had just about reached the end of the line by then. She was a lovely person—still is—but that connection wasn't there. I don't know how else to put it. I enjoyed our outings, but I wasn't agog with eagerness for them.'

'Now that's something I can't imagine; you, agog with eagerness—not over a woman. A new client, yes. A leap in the exchange rates, yes. But a mere female? Don't make me laugh.'

He was silent and she feared she'd offended him, but then he said quietly, 'It might really make you laugh if you knew how wrong you were.'

The proper response to this was, *You don't have to tell me. I didn't mean to pry.*

But she couldn't say it. She wanted him to go on. If this lonely, isolated man was about to invite her into his secret world then, with all her heart, she wanted to follow him inside. If he would stretch out his hand and trust her with his privacy it would be like a light dawning in her life.

'Well, I've been wrong in the past,' she mused, going carefully, not to alarm him. 'If you knew the things I was thinking about you that first day, and even worse on the second day.'

'But I do know,' he said, and even from over her head she could hear the grin in his voice. 'You didn't bother to hide your terrible opinion of me—grim, gruff, objectionable. And that was when you were thanking me for helping you over those lost papers. When I landed you the job from hell with Charlie your face had to be seen to be believed.'

'But I soon realised that you were right,' she said. 'I'm the ideal person to do it because I can enjoy the game. A woman with a heart would be in danger.'

'And you don't have a heart?'

'I told you, my fiancé finished all that.'

'I've begun to understand you,' Roscoe said slowly. 'You come on like a seductive siren but it's all a mask. Behind it—'

'Behind it there's nothing,' she said lightly. 'No feeling, no hopes, no regrets. Nothing. Just a heartless piece, me.'

'No!' he said fiercely. 'Don't say that about yourself. It's not true. Once I thought it was but now I know you better.'

'You don't know me at all,' she said, fighting the alarm caused by his insight. 'You know nothing about me.'

'You're wrong; I do know. I know you're kind and sweet, gentle and generous, loving and vulnerable—all the things you've tried to prevent me discovering, prevent *any* man discovering.'

'Nonsense!' she said desperately. 'You're creating a sentimental fantasy but the truth is what's on the surface. I have no heart because I've no use for one. Who needs it?'

'That's your defence, is it?' he asked slowly. 'Who needs a heart? I think you do, Pippa.'

'Mr Havering, I am a lawyer; you are my client. My private life does not concern you.'

Her voice was soft but he heard something in it that was

almost a threat, and he backed off, worried more for her than for himself. There seemed no end to the things he was discovering about her, but he feared to put a foot wrong, lest he harm her.

'All right, I'm sorry,' he said in a soothing voice. 'It's none of my business, after all. Don't cry.' He could feel her shaking against him.

'I'm not crying,' she said. 'I'm laughing. Me, saying I'm a lawyer and you're a client, when we're lying here—'

'Yes, we've got a bit beyond that point, haven't we?' he said. 'We've both experienced things to make us bitter. Like the way when someone has promised to marry you, they become the person above all others you have to beware of.'

'That's true,' she said in a voice of discovery. 'Once you start twining your life with theirs, they have a whole sheaf of weapons in their hands—the house you chose together, the secrets you tell each other—all the things they know about you that you desperately wish they didn't. Ouch!'

She gasped for Roscoe's hands had suddenly tightened.

'Sorry,' he said.

'Did that last one—?'

'Struck right home,' he agreed, drawing her head down against his chest once more. 'You brood about it, which is nonsense because she and her new love have other things to talk about apart from you. But you picture them laughing, and wonder how you could ever have trusted her so much.'

'And then you don't want to trust anyone again,' she whispered. 'So you promise yourself that you won't.'

'But it isn't so easy. If you go through life drawing away from people, at last you turn into a monster. I don't want to turn into a monster, although several people would probably tell you that's what I am.'

'Sometimes it feels safer,' she agreed.

'I won't believe anyone's ever said it of you.'

'Why? Because I've got a pretty face? Haven't you ever heard of a pretty monster? It's all part of the performance, you see. The lad who was here the first night, the one I half crippled, don't you think he sees me as a monster?'

'That doesn't mean you are one,' he said with a touch of anger in his voice. 'Stop this.'

'I led him on, didn't I? You'd think I'd know better by now, but a girl must have some fun in her life. You knew that, even then. That's why you hired me.'

He groaned and raised his hands to cover his eyes. 'And this is what he did to you? Your fiancé?'

'Or maybe I was always like that. It's hard-wired into me and it took him to bring it out.'

'You don't really believe any of that stuff.'

'Don't tell me what I believe.'

'I will because someone's got to show you how to see yourself straight. You're as beautiful inside as you are out.'

She pulled herself up on the bed so that she could see him better in the dim light and pull his hands down.

'We've known each other only a few days,' she reminded him.

'I've known you a lot longer than that. I knew it when I saw you in the graveyard, swapping jokes with a headstone. It was the kind of mad, daft—'

'Mutton-headed,' she supplied.

'Glorious, wonderful—I knew then that you had some secret that was hidden from me, that you could teach it to me and then I'd know something that would make life possible.'

He lay looking up at her, defenceless, all armour gone, nothing left but the painful honesty with which he reached out to her.

Pippa felt dizzy, knowing that she'd come to one of those moments when everything in her life might depend on what she did now. Roscoe's eyes told her that this was her decision, and she was stunned by how quickly it had come to pass. Just a few days.

He was reasonably attractive without being handsome. Yet the experience he'd given her tonight—of peace, joy and safety—had astounded her by outshining all other experiences in her life, and now the desire to kiss him was the strongest she had ever known. The tantalising half kiss he'd once given her had lived with her ever since, taunting and teasing her onwards to discover everything about him.

His eyes asked a silent question. Would she kiss him? The decision was hers.

And yes! Yes! The answer was yes!

As she adjusted her position he saw her intention and opened his arms. A little smile curved her lips, one she hoped he would understand. He did understand. The same smile was there on his own lips as she leaned forward, closer—closer—

The doorbell shrieked.

In an instant the spell died. They froze in dismay.

'At this hour of night?' Pippa whispered, aghast.

Stiffly, she moved off the bed and made her way to the front door, calling, 'Who is it?'

The voice that answered appalled her.

'Pippa? It's Charlie. Let me in.'

She turned to see Roscoe standing in the bedroom doorway. Horrified, they stared at each other. Nothing more terrible could have happened.

'Let me in,' Charlie cried.

'No, I can't,' Pippa called back. 'Charlie, go home; it's late. We'll talk tomorrow.'

'Oh, please, Pippa. I've got something to say that you'll be glad to hear. Open up!' He rapped on the door.

'Stop making so much noise,' she cried. 'You'll wake my neighbours. Just give me a minute.'

She was talking for the sake of it while her gaze frantically went around the apartment, seeking evidence of Roscoe's presence. He was doing the same, seizing his baggage, hurrying with it into the bedroom. When he was safely out of sight, Pippa opened her front door.

Charlie immediately came flying through and seized her in his arms.

'What…what do you think you're doing?' she spluttered.

'Telling you that I've given in. I'll do it your way. I'll tell the police about Ginevra. I've been thinking for hours, and I know I have to do what you think is right.' He searched her face. 'Aren't you pleased?'

'Pleased?' she snapped. 'Of all the selfish schoolboy pranks—waking me at this hour to tell me something you could have sent in a text message. How old are you? Ten?'

She was consumed by rage. At this moment she could almost have hated the silly self-centred boy.

'Oh, sorry!' he said. 'Yes, I suppose it is a bit late.'

'Get out, *now*!'

Reading dire retribution in her eyes, he backed out hastily, gabbling, 'All right, all right. We'll talk tomorrow.'

He was gone.

She listened as the footsteps faded, followed by the sound of the elevator going down. Roscoe emerged from the bedroom, walking slowly, not coming too close to her.

The memory of what had so nearly happened was burning within her. Another moment and she would have been in his arms, kissing him and receiving his kiss in return. She had wanted that so much and come so close—so close—and it had been cruelly snatched away.

What she saw when she looked at him made a cold hand

clutch her heart. His face was calm and untroubled. Whatever had happened to her, no earthquake had shaken him.

'I'd better leave now,' he said.

'No!' she said urgently. 'That's what you can't do. He might linger downstairs, and then he'd see you.'

Going to the window, she drew the curtain an inch and looked into the street below.

'There's his new car,' she murmured. 'But there's no sign of him. I reckon he's still in the hall, planning to come back up here.'

'You're right,' Roscoe groaned. 'I'll have to stay for a while. Sorry.'

A few minutes earlier she'd felt him tremble in her arms and known that he would gladly remain all night. Now he spoke as though staying with her was a duty that he dreaded.

'I'll stay out here,' he said, settling on the sofa. 'You take the bedroom.'

The spell was broken. And that was good, she tried to tell herself. She'd had enough of spells.

She lay awake for the rest of the night, and finally went out to find Roscoe on the phone to Angela.

'Charlie's arrived home,' he said as he hung up.

'Don't mention Charlie to me,' she said crossly. 'Turning up like that in the middle of the night! Does he think nobody has a life apart from him? I feel really sorry for your mother, pinning so many of her hopes on that overgrown infant.'

She was still full of nerves or she would have been careful not to say the next words.

'She's had so much to bear in her life already. Losing your father, knowing he killed himself—'

Too late, she saw the strange look on Roscoe's face.

'How did you know that?' he asked. 'Charlie, I suppose?'

'I already knew. David said something.'

'So you've known from the start. You never mentioned it to me.'

'I knew you wouldn't like it, and it was none of my business.'

'That's right,' he said lightly. 'Well, I'd better be going.'

She could have kicked herself. Roscoe's cool tension told her more than any words that he resented her for what she'd just revealed. In time, he might have told her, but he disliked her knowing without his being aware.

'I'll make you some breakfast,' she offered.

'No, I'd better be off. I'll be in touch.'

She doubted it. He couldn't get away from her fast enough.

There was nothing to do but stand back while he collected his things. Suddenly a chill wind was blowing. He gave her a polite smile, thanked her for everything, just as he should, but something was mysteriously over. Worst of all was the fact that she couldn't be sure what had ended, because she didn't know what had begun. She only knew that the sense of aching loss was unbearable.

Then a strange thing happened. Charlie became elusive. He didn't call, wasn't in his office and his cellphone was switched off. Without him, the trip to the police had to be postponed.

After two days, Roscoe texted: *Is Charlie with you?*

She texted back: *I was about to ask you the same thing.*

The next time Pippa's work phone rang it was the last person in the world she'd expected to hear from.

'*Biddy—or should I call you Ginevra?* Where are you?'

'Abroad; that's all you need to know. Charlie's a real gent, I'll say that for him. I'm not coming back but I've written to the police and told them it was me in the shop, not him. I wasn't going to, but then I got to thinking I owed him something, so I sent the letter from…the country I was in. I'm in a different place now, so the postmark won't help them. But I wanted you to know about something else, so listen.'

Pippa did so, growing wide-eyed as Ginevra's information grew clear.

'Thank you,' she said at last. 'That'll be very useful. Where can I get hold of you?'

'I'm moving around, but you can call this mobile number. I've sent you a copy of the letter so that you'll know exactly what I told the police. 'Bye.'

She hung up.

Pippa sat, deep in thought. Then she made a call.

'Gus Donelly? Good, I need your help, fast. Listen carefully.' After a terse conversation she swept out, announcing, 'I won't be back today.'

David, who'd been shamelessly eavesdropping, exclaimed, 'Donelly? I seem to recall that he's a private detective, and a very shady one. I hope you're careful.'

Pippa was not only careful but successful. Returning, triumphant, she knew she had all she needed to achieve a victory—thanks, ironically, to Ginevra.

Charlie presented himself at her office with a shamefaced smile that was clearly meant to win her over. She dealt with him briskly.

'So much for telling everything to the police! You offered a grand gesture that meant nothing. Now there's no need. I'll see you at the trial tomorrow. Now, go before I lose my temper.'

He fled.

The next day, they were all present in the courtroom— Angela clinging to Charlie's arm, Charlie trying to read Pippa's expression without success, Roscoe, aloof and isolated.

The court assembled, the magistrates seated themselves,

the accused were produced. Mr Fletcher entered the witness box and Pippa confronted him. There was nothing in her manner to suggest tension. On the contrary, she seemed at ease, cheerful and smiling. So that the sarcastic words that poured from her came as a greater shock.

'Tell the truth, Mr Fletcher. You haven't the faintest idea what actually happened that night, have you?'

'I certainly have,' he declared indignantly. 'I gave a full statement to the police.'

'Your statement is an invention. You should take up fiction writing, you do it so well.'

'Here—'

'You don't know what really happened because you'd spent the evening in the pub. I gather you put away quite an impressive amount, far too much for you to be a reliable witness. Isn't that so?'

'No, it ain't so. Nobody said I was drunk. The police never said so.'

'True, but then you're a past master at seeming more sober than you are, aren't you? As the police have found out to their cost before.'

'I dunno what you mean.'

'Then let me refresh your memory. About five years ago, there was a case that had to be dropped because you turned up in court the worse for wear.'

'That's not true,' Fletcher squeaked.

'Perjury is a crime, Mr Fletcher, and you've just committed that crime. I have the papers here.' She waved them. 'The case had seemed to be watertight, but then you ruined everything, as the constable in question will tell us.'

After that, it was over quickly. The policeman from the previous case, still furious at having his hard work undone by an unreliable witness, gave evidence that totally undermined Fletcher. The magistrate declared Charlie not guilty, then asserted that the case against the other three was also unsafe and should be dropped.

The court erupted.

Angela bounced around, throwing her arms about Charlie, then Roscoe, then Charlie again, squeaking and weeping with joy.

Pippa was surrounded by people congratulating her. She smiled but concentrated on gathering up her papers, the very picture of an efficient lawyer who cared only about her case. She resisted the temptation to look around for Roscoe. Secretly, she was afraid he wouldn't be there.

The lawyers for the other three defendants regarded her in astonished admiration.

'How did you *do* that?' one of them demanded.

Another one merely touched her arm, saying, 'I'll call you tomorrow.'

'You can call all you like,' David said, appearing behind her. He'd taken the precaution of coming to watch. 'Just remember she's signed up to my firm for the foreseeable future.'

'I can offer a very good fee,' said yet another.

'Forget it, she belongs to Farley & Son,' David declared firmly.

Angela embraced her wildly, declaring, 'You're a magician. You just waved a magic wand.'

'No, it was really Ginevra who waved the wand,' Pippa said. 'She's still got a soft spot for you, Charlie, especially after you helped her escape. Fancy telling me you were going to shop her to the police! You didn't mean a word of it.'

He had the grace to blush. 'I sort of meant it,' he said awkwardly. 'But then it seemed such a terrible thing to do that I got her away fast.'

'So I gathered. She wrote to the police telling them what had really happened, but that wouldn't have been enough on its own. Anyone can take the blame for anything from a safe distance. That's probably why she gave me all the other information about Fletcher's past.'

'But how did she know all that stuff?' Charlie asked.

'She has friends in the police,' Pippa said cautiously.

'Ah, yes, I see.' He grimaced.

'She told me what I needed, I hired a very good private detective and he did the rest.'

She was talking mechanically. Something was missing. Where was Roscoe? What would he say?

Then he seemed to appear from nowhere, standing before her.

'You were wonderful,' he said. 'Past my wildest hopes. When you wouldn't look at me just now I was afraid you were going to snub me. I guess I deserve it.'

'No, of course not. I'm just glad things worked out for you.'

'For me?' he queried. He added quietly, 'Or for us?'

'I don't know,' she said huskily.

'No, that's what we still have to find out, isn't it?'

He took her hand, holding it between both of his. She met his eyes and saw in them—what? Everything she wanted? No, because she didn't know what that was. But something that pointed the way.

'Yes,' she whispered. 'We still have to find out.'

'Will you come to my home tonight? I don't want to come to your place in case Charlie turns up.'

'I'll be there,' she promised.

Neither of them noticed Charlie standing a few feet away, his head on one side, a little smile of cheeky understanding on his lips.

Back at the office that afternoon, she had a long talk with David, who made it clear that her value had dramatically increased. The word 'partnership' was mentioned.

'Not right now, because it's a bit soon,' he said, 'but we've got our eyes on you and will take drastic steps to stop you being poached by any other firm. In the meantime, you'll have to make do with a raise.'

Her career was heading for the heights. She wondered when Roscoe would call her.

The phone rang. She snatched it up. But it wasn't Roscoe. It was Lee Renton, the impresario she'd last seen in The Diamond.

'You were right,' he boomed. 'I do need a pre-nuptial agreement.'

'I'll get to work—' Suddenly Pippa sat up straight in her chair as inspiration came to her. 'Lee, could you do me a big favour?'

'Name it.'

She explained what she wanted.

He listened with the occasional grunt, ending with, 'Consider it done. I'll be in touch.' He hung up.

The next call was the one she longed for.

'I'm going home now,' came Roscoe's voice.

'I'm on my way.'

CHAPTER TEN

ROSCOE'S apartment was high up in a tall, plain block, which once she would have said was typical of the man. But that was before she'd discovered the hidden, complex depths that meant there was no such thing as 'typical' of him.

Who would ever have thought that this man would be waiting at his open door, would pull her inside and crush her in his arms as though he'd waited all his life for this moment? Or hear him say in a shaking voice, 'I was so afraid you wouldn't come.'

'Never fear that. I'll always come if you want me.'

'And I'll always want you.'

He had even started to cook a meal for her. He wasn't a great cook, but he could manage a microwave and between the two of them they managed to get something onto the table. There was much more to deal with this evening, but, as if by a silent signal, they were each taking it slowly.

'So where do we go from here?' he asked, filling her wine glass. 'I leave the decision to you because it's clear you're several steps ahead of me. All those rabbits you produced out of the hat at the trial. You don't need me or anyone. You're queen of all you survey.'

'Hey, stop buttering me up.'

'Just trying to find the way forward, or hoping you can find it for us. There are so many things yet to be decided.'

'Like what?'

'Charlie. His feelings for you. I contrived the situation and, now that he's fallen for you, how can I just tell him everything has changed and he must forget you?'

She stroked his face, taking care that he should feel her warmth and tenderness towards him because her words would be a shock.

'You know something?' she said. 'Anyone hearing you say that would think you came straight out of the nineteenth century. You're a real male chauvinist pig.'

'Am I?' he asked, startled. 'How?'

'You talk about what *you* can do, but what about me? Don't I get a say? *You* fixed it so that Charlie should come under my influence, like I didn't have anything to do with it. But maybe *I* fixed it, oh, powerful one!'

'I guess I deserved that,' he said gruffly.

'Don't get me started on what you deserve. And there's one thing you have to understand. Charlie isn't in love with me. When we met, he took one look at me and thought *Wow!*, just as we both meant him to. But it was purely physical. He's up for new experiences and he pursued me when he thought he might get one. But there was no emotion in it. He's closer to Ginevra than he is to me. About an hour after the trial she texted me saying, *We did it!*'

'How did she know?'

'Exactly. Charlie must have called her.'

'Oh, no,' Roscoe said at once. 'I won't have this.'

'But it's not up to you. You've got to let Charlie be himself, not some creature you've created.'

'I only want to keep him out of danger. Is that wrong?'

She thought it might be impossible if, as she was beginning to suspect, danger was Charlie's natural medium. But this wasn't the time to say so. They had more urgent matters to attend to.

'The point is that Charlie's not in love with me,' she repeated, 'and his heart can't be broken by us. So we're free.'

'Free,' he echoed slowly. 'Free to—?'

'Free to do anything we want. Be anything we want.'

'Do you have any ideas about that?'

'Plenty. Don't ask me to list them because that would take all night.'

He became hesitant, almost as though nervous of saying the words.

'About…all night. Does it seem to you…?'

'Yes,' she whispered. 'It does.'

Like everything else in this new relationship, their love-making was tentative, cautious, watching and learning from each other. He was a patient lover, fervent, but with the control to take everything slowly. How softly his fingers caressed her breasts, and how mysterious was his smile as he did so.

She smiled back, feeling more and deeper mysteries unfold within her. The sweetness at being one with him was greater than anything she had ever known. She wanted to be with him. She wanted to *be* him. And she wanted it for ever.

Afterwards, he murmured, 'Are you really mine?'

'Can you doubt it?' she whispered.

'Yes. Nobody has ever been mine before.'

Before she could reply, he enfolded her in his arms again and in the passion that followed she forgot all else. But after passion came safety and contentment, both as precious as desire.

'Nobody was ever yours before?' she murmured. 'Surely that can't be true?'

'You'd think not, wouldn't you?' he agreed. 'I don't usually go around telling people that I need them. It's too dangerous, for one thing.'

'Oh, yes, I know. They have to discover it for themselves.'

'Yes. And they don't. Except you. But before you...' His voice died away into silence.

'What about your fiancée?' she asked. 'You must have been in love with her.'

'Yes, desperately. I thought I'd found the answer—a woman I could love and who'd love me—but it wasn't right between us. I couldn't be the man she wanted, giving her all my attention. She resented my other responsibilities.'

'Did she force you to choose between her and them?'

'In a way, yes. I can't blame her. I put them first, but how could I not? Charlie was still basically a kid and Mother was still stuck in a state of bewilderment. They needed me. In the end, Verity and I agreed to call it a day.'

But to outsiders it had looked like a cold-hearted parting, she thought. Perhaps Roscoe bore some of the blame for that, hiding his feelings and turning a blank face to the world, but it had left him in terrifying isolation. He'd said that nobody had ever been his before, and it was true. Pippa clasped him more closely, seeking to offer him a warmth and love that would make up for the aching loneliness in which he'd lived, a loneliness that left him always prepared for betrayal, ready to expect it as natural and inevitable.

Now she recalled the words with which he'd greeted her, a few hours and a lifetime ago.

'Why did you think I wouldn't come? Surely we'd agreed?'

'Yes, but I thought you'd remember that you were angry with me, and with reason. I behaved badly.'

'When? I don't remember.'

'When I discovered that you knew something I hadn't told you, about my father. You'll despise me, but I couldn't bear that. It made me feel spied on.'

'You like to control how much people know about you,' she mused. 'It's safer, isn't it?'

'Much safer. No—' he checked himself instantly '—it *feels* safer but, if you give into it, it's actually the way to go mad. Once I knew what you'd discovered, I had to head in the other direction, even though leaving you was the last thing I really wanted. But it was like being driven by demons.'

'Mmm, I know about those demons,' she murmured. 'They scream, *This way lies safety.* So you take that path, but you find that it leads to a howling wilderness, then to a cage. And you know you must escape it soon or there'll never be a way out.'

'You have to decide whether you want to live in that cage for ever, or venture out and take the risks of being human,' he agreed. 'But if you don't take those risks—' his arms tightened about her '—then you stop being human. And perhaps you need to find the one person who can make you want to take them.'

'Then maybe it's time I took a risk,' she said.

'How do you mean?'

'Asking you about your father. You've already told me to back off—'

'I didn't mean—'

'But I'm not going to do that. I'm going ahead, even if it makes you angry. Perhaps you *need* to be angry, so tell me what happened when he died. Were you very close to him?'

'Close?' He seemed to consider the word. 'I hero-worshipped him. I thought he was a great man, starting from nothing and building up a huge business. He had power and that was wonderful. Which just goes to show how naive I was. I was as immature in those days as Charlie is now.

'I was so proud when he took me into the business, told me I had the brains for it. We were a team, working together to conquer the world, so I thought. It was only after he died that I discovered the mountain of debt, the rip-offs, the deceit.

He'd lied to everyone; my mother, who never knew he had a succession of mistresses bleeding him dry; virtually everyone he ever worked with, and me, who trusted him totally, was so proud at being close to him, and then discovered that we weren't close at all.

'I'd been so smug, so self-satisfied, sure of my place inside the loop, and all the time I'd been kept on the outside, like the fool I was.'

Pippa pulled herself up, turning so that she could look down at his head on the pillow. 'Don't put yourself down,' she said.

'Why not? A fool is the kindest thing I can call myself. If you knew how ashamed and humiliated I felt at how easily he took me for a ride. He knew he could deceive me more than anyone else.'

'Because you were his son and you loved him,' she urged. 'He made use of that. Shame on him, not you.'

In the dim light she could just make out his wry smile.

'That's the sensible point of view. Back in those days it didn't help a distraught boy who'd been conned by a father he damn near worshipped and only found out when it was too late to ask any questions. He was dead. I went to see him lying on a slab—cold, indifferent, safely gone beyond the world, beyond me. I wanted to scream at him—why hadn't he trusted me? We could have fought for the business together. But he'd chosen to walk away, leaving me behind.'

'He rejected you,' she said softly, 'left you stranded without warning. No wonder you're sensitive about what other people know about you.'

'Stranded without warning,' he murmured. 'Yes, that was it. Suddenly I was standing on the edge of a cliff that I hadn't even known was there. No way forward, no way back, nobody I could talk to.'

Nobody I could talk to. The words were like an epitaph

for his entire life. His bond with his father had been an illusion, his mother took everything and gave little, Charlie took everything and gave nothing. He was like a castaway stranded on a desert island.

'Was anyone with you when you went to see him on the slab? Your mother?'

'No, she couldn't bear very much. There were so many things she mustn't be allowed to know.'

'The other women?'

'Yes. She'd heard rumours, I denied them, swore that I'd never heard of his being untrue to her. I was afraid she'd kill herself as well if she knew. It's ironic. I blame Charlie for telling stupid lies, but I've lost count of the really black lies I've told, the deceptions I've arranged, the people I've bribed to stay out of my mother's way in case they let something slip.'

'That's different. Sometimes you have to lie to protect people you love. That's not the same as self-serving lies. I don't suppose you told her the state the firm was in either.'

'Not completely. I hinted that we weren't as prosperous as we might be, but I spared her the worst. Sometimes I think stocks and shares are the only part of my life where I'm actually honest.'

'Deception doesn't make you dishonest,' she said seriously. 'It's the kind of deception that counts. You're the most honest man I've ever met. I *know* that Roscoe, because I know you.'

After what he'd told her about how he resisted anyone's eyes, it was a daring thing to say. Perhaps it was too soon for him to relax under a knowing gaze, even hers. But then she saw his face transfigured by joy and relief.

'You know me,' he echoed softly. 'That's the most beautiful thing I've ever heard. Now I'll never let you go.'

Heaven must be like this, she thought, nestling against him. If only they could be undisturbed for ever.

Pippa was to remember that feeling because, looking back, she could see that it was the moment everything began to fall apart. She wondered if it was the Christmas carol that triggered the catastrophe or if it would have happened anyway, for she awoke next morning to find herself in a dark wilderness.

She tried to shake it off, wondering how she could feel this way after the wonderful events of the night before. But the darkness seemed to be rooted in those very events and her confusion grew.

Roscoe was still clasping her with loving possessiveness, which should have touched her heart but suddenly seemed like a threat. She began to ease away.

'Don't go,' he said. 'Stay here a little longer.'

'I can't,' she said. 'I've got work to go to. So have you.'

He grinned. 'To hell with work. To hell with the markets.'

Another time she would have teased him fondly for such an attitude, but now she needed to get away from his warmth and gentleness, far, far away from everything that made him lovable. She must think, calm her howling demons, refuse to let them ruin her life.

She slipped out of bed and went to the window, pushing it open a little way. It was a bright, fresh morning with a little snow in the air and she stood taking deep breaths, trying to make the darkness lift.

She could do it—just a few minutes more.

But then Roscoe did the thing that made her efforts collapse. He turned on the radio and the sound of a Christmas carol floated out. As Pippa heard the words she stiffened.

'On this happy morning,
All is well with all the world.'

All is well. Once before she'd heard those words, just before the betrayal that had devastated her.

'Don't catch cold,' he said, coming up behind her and putting his arms about her. 'Hey, what's the matter?'

'Nothing,' she said hastily. 'Nothing.'

'You're shaking.' He shut the window and drew her back. 'Come back into the warm.'

But she tensed against his embrace, resisting him silently, unable to meet his eyes.

'Now the sun will always shine,
Joy is here for ever.'

But joy hadn't been there for ever. Joy had ended in the next few moments, leaving her unable to hear that carol again without reliving terrible memories.

Roscoe tightened his embrace, tried to draw her closer, felt her fight against it.

'Pippa, for pity's sake, what's the matter? It's not the cold, is it? There's something else.'

'No, I…I just have to be getting to work. And so do you.' She gave a brittle laugh. 'We still have to be sensible.'

'Sensible? You dare say that to me after the way we were together last night? Was the woman who lay in my arms and cried out to me to love her being sensible? Was I being sensible when I gave her everything I was and received back everything she had in her soul?'

Pippa didn't reply. She couldn't. There were no words for the terror she was feeling. Roscoe's face darkened.

'Or didn't I?' he said. 'Was I fooling myself about that, because the woman in my bed would never have wanted to be sensible?'

'Well,' she said brightly, 'perhaps that wasn't me, just someone who looked like me.'

'What's got into you? If this is a joke, it isn't funny.'

The music swelled. Now the carol was being played louder, sung by joyful voices, and her nerves were being torn. She had to get out of this or go mad.

'It's not a joke,' she said breathlessly. 'It's just that things look different in the morning.'

'Yes, they can look different,' he said slowly. 'Better or worse, depending on what you want to believe.'

'But that's the problem,' she said quickly. 'Wanting to believe is dangerous—talking yourself into things because it would be so nice if…if…'

Roscoe was still holding her, trying to understand the violent shaking he could feel throughout her body.

'What is it?' he asked urgently. 'Tell me. Don't bear it alone.'

She slumped against him in despair. How could she make him understand what she didn't understand herself? She only knew that she'd been brought to the edge of a deep pit, a place that many people found joyous but where she'd vowed not to venture. Now she stared down into the depths, appalled at herself for backing away but unable to do anything else.

Last night they'd talked happily about the risks they would take for their love. Now she knew she hadn't the courage and nothing mattered but to get away.

The words of the carol were still pouring from the radio.

'New day, new hope, new life.'

That was how it should have been and how it never would be again. It was all folly, all illusion, and she must put right the damage now.

'Pippa, my darling—'

'Don't—it's better not to call me that. We had a wonderful time last night, didn't we?'

'I thought so,' he said quietly.

'But now it's time to wake up and return to reality.'

'And what do you call reality?'

'We both know what we mean by it.' She gave another brittle laugh. 'I'm sure we'll see each other again, but nobody can live too long in that fantasy world.'

At last Roscoe released her. It was what she'd wanted but the feeling of his hands leaving her was achingly wretched because, deep inside, she knew he would never hold her again.

'I see,' he said. And now his voice was ominous. 'So that's how it is. We had a good time, now it's over and it had nothing to do with the real world. Is that what you're trying to tell me?'

Pippa summoned a carefree smile. 'Why, that's just it. A good time. And it was great fun, wasn't it? But now…well, you knew from the start that I was a good time girl. I think you even called me a few worse things in your head.'

'Before I *thought* I knew you,' he corrected harshly.

'Well, maybe first impressions are the most reliable. Floozie, tart, heartless piece—'

'Stop it!' he shouted, seizing her again. 'I won't listen to this. I never thought that of you—or if I ever wondered for a moment you showed me how wrong I was—'

'Did I? Or did I show you what you wanted to see? You were a real challenge, you know. Anyone can lure a man into her bed, but luring his heart—that's another matter.'

Pippa felt dizzy as she said these terrible words. In her desperation to escape she had gone much further than she'd meant to and for a moment she hesitated on the edge of recalling them, hurling herself into Roscoe's arms and swearing she meant none of it.

'Do you mean that?' he whispered.

She had one last chance to deny her words, reclaim all the joy life could offer her.

'Do you mean it?' he repeated. 'Is that all there's been between us? You trying to bring me down, to punish me for my attitude in the first few days? *Is that the truth?*'

One last chance.

'Now the sun will always shine,
Joy is here for ever.'

Frantically, she switched the radio off.

'You know the saying,' she said with a shrug. 'You win some, you lose some. I like to win them all.'

Now it was too late. The last trace of feeling had gone from him. His eyes were those of a dead man.

'I suppose I should be glad you came clean so soon,' he said. 'You might have taken it much further before you…but it's always wise to face the truth.'

A sneering look came into his eyes.

'So all the worst I thought of you was right after all. I should have more faith in my own judgement. Are you pleased? Does it give you a nasty little thrill to have brought me down?'

She managed a cynical laugh. 'I came to your bed and gave you a good time. That's hardly bringing you down.'

His eyes as they raked her were brutal.

'Oh, but you did much more than that,' he breathed. 'You put on the sweet, generous mask and it fooled me so thoroughly that I told you things that never before…' He drew a shuddering breath. 'Well, I hope it gave you a good laugh.'

She was about to protest wildly that he was terribly wrong, but she controlled the impulse in time and offered him a smile precisely calculated to infuriate him. It would break his heart, but if it drove him away from her it would be better for him in the long run. And for his sake she would hide her own broken heart and endure.

'I see that it did,' he grated. 'Well, don't let me keep you.'

'You're right,' she said brightly. 'We've said all we have to say, haven't we?'

He made no attempt to follow her into the bedroom as she gathered her things and when she came out he was waiting by the front door, as though determined to make sure that she left.

'Good day to you,' he said politely.

'Goodbye,' she told him, and fled.

A robot might have functioned as Pippa did for the rest of the day. Her efficiency was beyond reproach, her smile fixed, her work done to the highest standard.

'What the devil is the matter with her?' muttered David, her employer and friend.

'Why not ask her?' his secretary suggested.

'I daren't. She terrifies the life out of me.'

At last it was time to escape back to the apartment that would now be her cage. As if by a signal, Pippa began to tidy the place, although it was already tidy. From now on order and good management would be her watch words. She would concentrate on her career, be the best lawyer in the business and never again try to break out of the prison created by her nightmares. Life would be safe.

At last, when she'd put everything else away, she came to the box rescued from the attic in Crimea Street. Taking out the gloves and scarves, she discovered some handwritten books at the bottom.

'That's Gran's handwriting,' she breathed. 'But surely she didn't keep a diary? She wouldn't have had time.'

Yet the diaries went back to Dee's early life, when she had

been a nurse, and had still sometimes found the time to jot down her thoughts about the life around her. Sometimes amusing, sometimes caustic, sometimes full of emotion, always revealing an ebullient personality that Pippa recognised.

There were the long, anguished months when she'd loved Mark Sellon hopelessly, becoming engaged to him, then breaking it off because she couldn't believe he loved her. But he'd been returned to her in the hospital, shot down by enemy planes, and she'd sat by his unconscious form, speaking more freely than she could have done if he'd been awake. Dee had written:

> I told him that I must believe that somewhere, deep in his heart, he could hear me. Wherever he was, he must surely feel my love reaching out to him, and know that it was always his.

Pippa read far into the night, until she came to the passage that, in her heart, she had always known she'd find, written just after her grandfather's death.

> I saw you laid in the ground today and had to come away, leaving you there. And yet I haven't really left you behind because you're still with me, and you always will be; just as I'll always be with you in your heart, until we really are together again. It doesn't matter how long that is. Time doesn't really exist. It's just an illusion.

Pippa dropped her head into her hands. That was how love should be, how it never would be for her. She knew that now.

She laid everything away tidily, turned out all the lights and went to bed. A faint gleam from the window showed her the toy bear on her dressing table. In this poor light his shabbiness was concealed and his glass eyes seemed to glimmer softly.

'No,' she told him. 'I'm not listening to you. You want me to believe one thing, and I know it's different. I believed you once. I believed Gran. She used to talk to me about her and Grandpa, saying that one day it would happen to me. And I thought it had when I met Jack. He made me feel so safe and loved, and sure of the future. And now I don't *want* to feel safe and loved. *Ever.* Do you understand?'

But he had no reply for her.

CHAPTER ELEVEN

CHARLIE called the next day, his voice full of excitement over the line.

'Bless you for what you've done for me,' he said. 'And I'm not talking about the trial.'

'You've seen Lee?'

'Yes, I've just had a long talk and it's looking good for a couple of weeks' time. Oh, boy, wait until Roscoe hears about this!'

'Don't be in a rush to tell him, Charlie, and don't do anything rash. Wait until you're a little more certain.'

'All right, Miss Wise and Wonderful. I'll do it your way. And thank you again.'

She wondered if she would hear from Roscoe but days passed in silence. Just as well, she told herself. If she saw him she might weaken, and that must not happen. Much better this way.

But the ache persisted.

Days passed, nights passed. She told herself that it was getting easier, except that every knock at the door was him. Until it wasn't.

But then, one evening, it was.

One look was enough to tell her that if anything had changed it wasn't for the better. Now his face wasn't just cold but furious.

'We need to talk,' he said.

She stood back and he walked in, turning on her as soon as the door closed.

'My God, I never thought you'd stoop to this,' he raged.

'I don't know what you mean.'

'Oh, please, you wreck his life and then you don't know what I mean?'

'If you're talking about what I think you are—'

'I'm talking about Charlie walking out of the firm, blowing his life chances to chase a chimera. I'm talking about you persuading him to do it. How could you sink so low? Were you really that desperate for revenge?'

'Revenge?' she echoed, astounded. 'I didn't want revenge. Why should I? You did me no harm. If anything, it was me who... What did you mean about Charlie leaving the firm? That wasn't in the plan.'

'But there was a plan? You admit that?'

'Yes,' she said, her temper flaring, 'there was a plan—an innocent plan to help Charlie follow his own path in life. He's a natural entertainer and I have a friend, Lee Renton, who's in the business. He sets up those television programmes where amateurs perform and viewers vote. I recommended Charlie to him after that evening we spent at The Diamond. He did an impromptu performance for me at the table and he was so good that I thought he should take it further.

'Lee has auditioned him and because he's the big boss he's been able to pull strings and include Charlie in a show in two weeks' time. If he's no good, OK, but the top two performers go through to the next round, and I'd back Charlie to be one of them.'

'And then what?' Roscoe demanded scathingly. 'An existence spent on the grubby fringes of show business?'

'Or as a star, however it turns out.'

'However—? That's how you see life, is it? Leave it to chance?'

'What do you suggest instead? Opt for safety every time? Choosing safety doesn't always *lead* to safety. We know that, don't we? But it can, if it's your own free choice. But being a stockbroker isn't Charlie's choice. It was your choice for him, and it won't work.'

He turned away from her, walking about the room like a man who no longer knew where he was going.

'You said Charlie walked out,' Pippa reminded him. 'Did he? Or did you force him out because you were so determined to make him do it your way?'

He turned a haggard gaze on her. 'I wanted him to go on a course to learn some more about the business,' he said. 'He'd have acquired an extra qualification, boosted his prospects. He refused to go because it would have meant missing the television show. I told him he had to make a choice.'

Pippa groaned and clutched her forehead. 'Tell me I'm not hearing this,' she muttered. 'You forced him to choose and you're surprised that he chose his freedom?'

'Freedom? You call that kind of life freedom?'

'To him, yes. Freedom isn't just not being in prison. You could keep Charlie out of trouble with the law but you'd do it by trapping him behind the bolts and bars of finance. For him, that would be a life sentence. He's made his choice.'

'Or you made it for him.'

'No, I helped him do what he wants to do.'

'Behind my back. You did encourage him to deceive me, didn't you?'

'I advised him not to tell you too much too soon, in case you tried to interfere.'

'Interfere? I'm his brother.'

'Yes, his brother, not his keeper. And you did interfere with that damn fool choice you forced on him. "Do it my way or get out." The clever thing to do would be to leave the door open for him to come back if his new career failed. But you slammed that door shut so you're not really a clever man at all, are you?'

The next moment she was sorry she'd said it because his face changed. The anger died out of it, replaced by a weary sadness that broke her heart.

'No,' he said slowly. 'I guess the truth is that I'm a fool. I've always been a fool. I've trusted people who couldn't be trusted, and I never learned from my mistakes.' He gave a soft, mirthless laugh. 'How big a fool is that? The biggest in the world.'

They weren't talking about Charlie any more. He was saying that he'd trusted her, and he felt betrayed by her. Nor could she blame him when she remembered how he'd confided in her that night, talking about his father, his fiancée, his desolation at the way he'd been abandoned. He'd confided in her as to nobody else in his life, and just a few hours later she'd rejected him, her rejection coming out of the blue, with no real explanation.

And it had to stay that way. She didn't dare tell him the whole story of her inner destruction in case he opened his arms to her in sympathy and understanding. Then she would weaken, seeking his love where once she'd found the strength to reject it. And she would destroy him.

Whatever happened, she would protect him from that. Protect him from herself.

'I see you don't deny that you made a fool of me,' he said. 'And that's all I was—just one more fool among many. I fell for you totally, nothing held back. Boy, that must really have given you a laugh.'

'No, I'm not laughing,' she said quietly. 'But I do know that I'm no good for you. I'm poison, and you're better off without me.'

'Oh, please!' He warded her off again, this time actually backing away. 'Spare me the pathos. You've done so well up to now. I was a scalp you had to add to your collection. You as good as admitted it.'

'I didn't—'

'As close as, damn it. You had your victory and then I was no more use. I congratulate you. Cutting out the dead wood is good business practice, although even a heartless robot like myself hesitates before using it on people.'

'Don't call yourself a heartless robot,' she cried. 'I've never said that—'

'Can you swear you've never thought it?'

'No…never…' she said jerkily.

'You're lying. The truth is there in your face. You've thought that and worse. Charlie told you I'm a control freak, didn't he? And perhaps I am. But I'm not the only one, Pippa. Maybe I have pulled the strings of Charlie's life, but so have you. The difference is that I pull strings in the open, not behind anyone's back.'

Seeing that she was too stunned to speak, he turned with an air of finality and went to the door.

'Be sure to send me your bill,' he said, and walked out.

She could hear his retreating footsteps, followed by the sound of the elevator going down. She felt cold—deeply cold, too cold to move—with a coldness that would last for the rest of her life, freezing her heart, turning her to something inhuman.

But Roscoe already saw her as inhuman. His contempt left no doubt about that.

And that was good, she told herself resolutely. He was safer that way. As long as he was safe, she could bear anything.

Charlie called her, full of excitement about his approaching big night.

'Mum's giving a big party that night,' he bubbled, 'and

she wants you as the guest of honour because you made it all happen. She's thrilled about my new career. Roscoe can't understand it.'

'Obviously he isn't thrilled.'

'He wouldn't be, would he? I don't see him any more now I'm out of the firm, and he won't be at home on the night. OK, so I'll tell Mum you're coming.'

'Charlie—'

But he'd hung up, leaving her reflecting that Roscoe wasn't the only member of his family who liked to call the shots.

The day of Charlie's show started badly, with another car breakdown. This time Pippa faced the inevitable and dumped the vehicle. She took a taxi to the Havering house, arriving to find all the lights on and Angela waiting for her on the front step, flanked by neighbours who clapped and cheered as her taxi drew up.

'Roscoe's not here,' Angela confided. 'He's so annoyed about the programme that he's not coming.'

'How do you feel about it?' Pippa asked.

'It's what Charlie wants. And besides,' Angela added in a low, confiding voice, 'he can be a bit of a naughty boy, and if he gets into a little trouble now and then, well—it won't matter so much, will it?'

So, despite appearances, there was a realistic brain beneath that fluffy head of hair, Pippa thought. More realistic than Roscoe about some things.

Dinner was a banquet, and then everyone crowded around the huge television screen on the wall. There was the opening music and the announcer came on.

'Hello, folks! It's time for *Pick a Star*, the programme where you, the viewer, vote the star in and the dunces off. And tonight's contestants are—'

As soon as Charlie began his comedy act, everyone knew

this was the winner. None of the other seven contestants could hold a candle to him. Even Pippa, who knew how rigorously Lee had had him trained as a favour to her, was impressed by his quality.

'Now it's voting time, folks—the moment when you choose the winner. Here are the phone numbers.'

When he got to Charlie's number everyone scribbled frantically and hauled out their cellphones to ring and cast their votes. Angela dived for the house phone and put her call through.

'How long do we wait?' Angela asked.

'Half an hour,' Pippa told her, 'but Lee said there wouldn't be any question. He's sure Charlie will win and go on into the next round but, even if he doesn't, Lee's got an agent already interested in him.'

The minutes crawled past and at last it was time to gather around the set to learn the winner. When Charlie's name was announced, the room erupted.

There he was on screen, triumphantly repeating his act, his face full of delight, and more than delight: fulfilment. The applause grew, the credits rolled. It was over.

One by one, the guests departed. A beseeching look from Angela made Pippa stay behind the others and she understood that Angela didn't want to be alone. Her house was going to be very empty now.

She led the way into the conservatory and poured Pippa a glass of champagne.

'It's so kind of you to stay a while, my dear. I know everything's going to change now, and I'm ready for it as long as Charlie is doing what will make him happy.' She added in a confiding tone, 'I must admit that I hoped you and Charlie… but there, he says you're like a friendly big sister.'

'I hope I am.'

'Oh, dear, how sad.'

'Sad?'

'I would have loved to welcome you into the family as Charlie's wife.' An idea seemed to strike her. 'You don't think you could make do with Roscoe, do you?'

'*What?*'

'I know it's a lot to ask, but you never know, you might make him human.'

'Angela, please don't go thinking like that. There's no way Roscoe and I could ever…please don't.'

'No, I suppose you're right. I'm being selfish, I suppose. I've always wanted a daughter because you can't talk to a man as you can to a woman, and I've had nobody to talk to since my husband died. Charlie was just a child and Roscoe…well, he's only interested in making money. To be fair, he gives it too, but he seems to think that's all that's needed.'

'Gives it?' Pippa echoed cautiously.

'He's got charities he gives to, hospitals in the Third World, that sort of thing, but signing cheques is easy. It's affection he finds difficult.'

'But maybe it's just a different way of showing affection,' Pippa said urgently. 'Putting your arms around a sick child is fine and beautiful, but if that child is dying for lack of the right medicine, then surely it's the man who signs the cheque that buys the medicine who's shown the real feeling? At any rate, I'll bet that's what the child's mother would say.'

Angela stared at her. 'You sound like Roscoe.'

'And he's right,' Pippa said robustly. There was a curious kind of satisfaction in defending Roscoe when he wasn't there. It was when he was there that the trouble started.

'Have you ever tried to talk to him?' she asked gently. 'You might find more sympathy in Roscoe than you thought.'

'Do you think so? Have those wonderful all-seeing eyes of yours bored into him and found something the rest of the world missed?'

This was so close to the truth that Pippa was momentarily lost for words. She recovered enough to say, 'Who knows? He works so hard at not letting people see what he's really like, almost as though part of him was afraid.'

'Afraid? Him?'

'Sometimes the man with the strongest armour is the one who needs it most for…whatever reason.'

'You may be right,' Angela sighed. 'It's just that I've always found it hard to forgive Roscoe for William's death. If he'd taken on a bigger share of the work—'

'But he was just a boy,' Pippa protested. 'About the same age Charlie is now. Would you blame Charlie in the same way?'

'No, of course not, but—' Angela checked herself as though the realisation had startled her. 'Roscoe has always seemed different.'

'*Seemed* is the word,' Pippa said. 'He was young, learning the business and probably completely confused. Then his father died. Maybe he blamed himself, then he discovered that you blamed him—'

'I never said so,' Angela hurried to say. 'Oh, but I wouldn't need to say so, would I?'

'No. But he wouldn't say anything either, and so you lost each other all these years ago.'

Angela was silent, looking sad, and after a moment Pippa ventured to ask, 'Was your husband at all like that?'

'Oh, no. William was talkative and open-hearted. He told me everything—absolutely everything. Our marriage was blissfully happy.'

She held up the hand with the glittering diamond ring. 'At least I've always had this as a symbol of his love. I kiss it goodnight every evening when I go to bed, and for a moment I can imagine he's still there. We loved each other so much until he…until he…' She was suddenly shivering. 'He died in a car crash. Taken from me suddenly, with no goodbye. Oh, if he'd had the chance to say goodbye he would have been so kind—'

With a feeling of sick dread, Pippa realised that Angela knew the truth, despite her frantic denials. Beneath her smiling facade, she was hiding another self, permanently tormented. It was a self that the outside world must never be allowed to see, and in that she was just like her elder son.

Now Pippa knew what she must do. Going to sit beside Angela, she put her arms gently about her and held her close.

'You remember him as a kind man who loved you,' she said. 'And that's what really matters—all the good years you shared—loving each other—'

'Yes, yes—*no*!' Angela's voice suddenly rose to a shriek and sobs shook her. 'No, he left me,' she wept. 'He took his own life, although he knew I loved him. He went away from me because he wanted to, and it destroyed me and he didn't care. *He didn't care.*'

'That's not true,' Pippa said, tightening her arms. 'He didn't stop loving you. He was just full of despair. His mind was so dark that he wasn't his real self. It was another man who took his own life, not the one you knew. He didn't reject you. That was someone else who only looked like him.'

She wondered if she had any right to say this when she didn't really believe it. William Havering's suicide had indeed been a betrayal of those who loved and needed him, and she'd said as much to Roscoe. But this desperate woman could not have endured it.

She knew she'd made the right decision when Angela raised her head, her eyes frantically searching Pippa's face.

'Do you mean that?' she whispered.

'Yes, I do. He must have been terribly ill, and it was the illness that made him act, not his own heart. He never rejected you, and I know that wherever he is now he wants you to understand that. He can't have peace until you have it first. You still love him, don't you?'

'Oh, yes—yes—'

'Then do this for him. Speak to him in your heart and tell him you forgive him because you know he didn't mean it. Tell him—'

She stopped for the air was singing. Suddenly, Dee was there with her, pointing to the words in her diary—words she'd spoken to the man she loved, not knowing if he could hear them, if he would ever hear them.

'Tell him…tell him…'

'What is it?' Angela asked in wonder. 'You look as if you'd seen a ghost.'

'No,' Pippa whispered. 'You don't need to see a ghost to feel it.'

'What should I tell him?'

'That he's still with you,' Pippa said slowly, 'and he always will be, just as you'll always be with him in your heart, until one day you really will be together again.'

'And he won't reject me?' Angela whispered longingly. 'After so long?'

'It isn't long. Time doesn't really exist. It's just an illusion.'

'Yes, yes,' Angela said eagerly. 'I didn't understand before, but I do now. You're so kind and understanding.'

She buried her face against Pippa, still trembling, but no longer in agony.

A sound from the door made Pippa look up, and what she saw made her stiffen with shock.

Roscoe stood there. He was staring, seemingly dazed by the sight that met his eyes—his mother, in transports of joy and relief, in Pippa's arms.

This was what he was trying to do for her, but never managed it, she thought. Perhaps he'll hate me.

She recalled his chilly hostility when he'd discovered she knew about his father's suicide. To him, this would seem even more of an intrusion.

She patted Angela's shoulder. 'Roscoe's here.'

Angela raised her head. To Pippa's pleasure, she smiled at the sight of Roscoe and reached out a hand.

'Mother, what is it?'

'It's all right. Dear, dear Pippa has made me understand so much—she said such wonderful things—'

'I heard what she said,' Roscoe told her quietly. He took out a handkerchief and dabbed Angela's face. 'Don't cry, Mother. There's nothing to be sad about.'

'I know. It was wonderful. Charlie won and he'll be in the next round and, before we know it, he'll be rich and famous.'

The phone rang and she snatched it up. 'Charlie, darling, we were just talking about you—'

Pippa took a step away from Roscoe. Everything—her mind, her heart, her flesh—all were in turmoil at his appearance and the uncertainty over what he'd heard. Only one thing was sure. She must get away from him.

But she felt her hand taken between his in a grip she couldn't resist, and he drew her away, out of Angela's sight.

'How can I ever thank you?' he asked in a low, passionate voice. 'I never dreamed I could see her so at peace again, and you did it.'

He raised her hands to his lips, kissing them, while she felt a happiness she'd feared never to know again. She tried to fight it, but it wouldn't be fought.

'You don't mind that it was me?' she asked.

'If you mean would I rather have been the one who brought my mother peace again, then yes, I would. But as long as somebody can make her such a priceless gift, that's the only thing that matters.'

'Thank you,' she said softly. 'It hurt so much when we quarrelled, but at least we can part friends.'

'Part? Are we going to part?'

'We've already parted, Roscoe. You know that.'

'But I don't. Just because we said some terrible things—you pretended to be a floozie and I pretended to believe you. We can get past that if we want to.'

The turmoil of feeling that went through her was part joy at his love, part misery at the parting that she knew was inevitable, although he could not see it, and part terror that her own nerve might fail. She must leave him, but the knowledge filled her with anguish.

'Surely you're ready to try again,' he said in a pleading voice. 'The fact that you're here—'

'Charlie told me you wouldn't be here tonight.'

'He said that? Surely not? He knew I was coming.'

'Maybe I misunderstood,' she said huskily. 'But it's too late for us.'

'It'll never be too late while we love each other.'

She didn't answer that. She didn't dare.

Hearing Angela hanging up, Pippa said quickly, 'I've got to go.'

'I didn't see your car outside.'

'It's finally had it.'

'Then I'll drive you. Don't argue.'

Angela kissed her goodbye and watched them depart with a smile that said she was crossing her fingers for her hopes to come true.

'Wrap up warmly; it's snowing again,' Roscoe said as he helped her on with her coat, drawing the edges together. 'Your trouble is that you haven't got anyone to look after you. Never mind, you'll have me in future.'

She didn't protest. It wasn't true but she didn't have the strength to dispel the beautiful dream right now. There would be time enough for heartbreak later.

CHAPTER TWELVE

As THEY headed for Roscoe's car they realised that there was a ghostly figure standing beside it, half obscured by the driving snow. Pippa gasped with horror when she realised who it was.

'That's Franton,' she said urgently. 'The man you fired for insider trading. He's probably damaged your car.'

But there was nothing threatening about Franton's appearance as he stood waiting for them by the road.

'What are you doing out here in this weather?' Roscoe asked him, sounding irritated. 'Do you want to catch your death?'

Franton loomed at them through the flakes.

'I'm not staying long. I only came to thank you. I found out who got me the job.'

'I told them you'd do it well and I know you will,' Roscoe said gruffly.

'And the paper you signed…about my debts…'

'It's only a guarantee. You still have to pay them.'

'But, thanks to you, I have time now. I had to come and thank you.'

'Fine, but clear off now before you get pneumonia,' Roscoe snapped, sounding annoyed. 'Where's your car?'

'I sold it.'

'Get in; I'll drive you home.'

Franton tumbled thankfully into the back seat. Pippa, sitting in the front, tried to sort out her tangled thoughts but without success.

Why, she thought fretfully, couldn't Roscoe stay the same person for five minutes at a time?

Franton's wife and three children were waiting at the window, looking anxious. They streamed out to embrace him and Roscoe sat watching the family scene, before firing the engine and driving off.

'I don't believe what I'm seeing,' she breathed. 'You got him another job? After what happened?'

'What else could I do?' he demanded. 'You saw his family. It's not much of a job, handling the finances of a little group of shops.'

'But didn't you have to tell the owners why you fired him?'

'I'm a partner in the business.'

'So you pulled strings for him?'

He grunted.

'And you've guaranteed his debts?'

'Guaranteed them. Not paid them. Now, can we drop this?'

'I just can't get my head around it. Nobody would guess the truth about you.'

'But you think you know the truth?' he asked savagely. 'After the way you attacked me about him, what did you expect me to do?'

'I didn't expect you to take any notice of anything I said. And I'm not even sure you did. I have a suspicion that you'd have done it anyway. Scrooge outside and Santa inside.'

'How dare you?'

'I don't know,' she mused. 'But I dare.'

After a while she said, 'This isn't the way to my home.'

'I'm taking a detour. The traffic's heavy because we're close to Trafalgar Square.'

'Ah, yes. That's where they set up the huge tree that the Norwegians give us every year.'

'Let's go and see it,' he said, turning into a side road and stopping.

Taking her hand, he drew her forward to where the crowds were gathered. There was the great tree rearing up into the night, covered in lights. More lights set the fountains aglow and the huge buildings around the edge of the square. All around, carol singers gathered, their voices rising into the chilly air.

'Beautiful,' Roscoe murmured.

Receiving no reply, he turned to see Pippa standing with her eyes closed, her face wet from snow, or maybe tears. Her head was uncovered and now her glorious hair was drenched and hanging drably.

'Pippa,' he said urgently. 'Pippa, what is it? Tell me, for pity's sake.'

He shook her shoulders gently and, when she didn't react, he drew her close, kissing her with the fierceness of a man trying to reawaken life.

'Pippa,' he whispered. 'Where are you?'

'I don't know,' she said helplessly. 'But I can't escape. I'm trapped there and I always will be.'

'You can. Let me help you.'

He kissed her again and again and she gave herself up to the feeling, trying to find in it a way out of the fears that tormented her. But she knew there was no way out and she must try to make him understand.

'Let me go,' she said desperately. 'I have to get out of here.'

She wrenched herself free and darted away, vanishing into the crowd so that for a moment Roscoe lost her and looked around desperately. She had vanished into thin air, gone for ever, and for a moment the demons that pursued him seemed to be mocking him.

Then he saw her at the end of the street, fleeing him without looking back. He gave chase and managed to catch up before she vanished again.

'No,' he said fiercely. 'We can't leave it like this. It's too important. Let's go back.'

'Not to that place,' she said, pointing to Trafalgar Square, whose lights could just be seen in the distance. 'I couldn't bear it.'

'But why?'

'Christmas,' she said simply. 'I just can't cope.'

'Let's go home.'

He led her back to the car, saw her tucked in and headed back to her home. She sat in silence, her arms crossed over her chest for the whole of the journey, then let him shepherd her upstairs. She knew this moment had to come. They must have a long talk, and she must make him understand why this path was closed off to her. Then, and only then, would she be ready to face the bleakness of life without him.

When they reached her apartment he fetched a towel and began to dry her hair, which was sodden from the snow, pulling it down so that he could work on it properly. The movement reminded him of that first day, when he'd seen her hair and her young, voluptuous body in their full glory.

Now there was nothing young or glorious about her. With her hair bedraggled, her face pale and strained, he had a sudden blinding glimpse of how she would look as a weary old woman.

He had never loved her so much.

At last he tossed the towel away, but still kept hold of her.

'I can't believe the way things went wrong with us without warning,' he said.

'There may have been no warning to you,' she said. 'For me, there was.'

'But everything was beautiful between us. We made love and found that our hearts and minds were open. We could talk and trust each other. I thought it was wonderful. Was I wrong?'

'No,' she cried passionately. 'It was wonderful. But that was what scared me. It was wonderful once before. All that trust and hope for the future. I know how little it means because I had those feelings with Jack, and they ended in a smash-up. I loved him so much. I was ready to give him everything I had, everything I was, everything I might be, and I thought it was the same with him.'

She began to pace the room.

'After that night you and I spent together, I woke up full of fear. It made no sense when things were so good between us, but I had this terrible sense of darkness. I tried to force it away, and I might have managed it, but then that Christmas carol came on the radio. And suddenly I was back there with Jack.

'Christmas was coming and our wedding was set for the New Year. The church was booked, the reception, the presents had started to arrive. I went to see him at his flat, and I was so stupid that I never realised anything was wrong. I could see he had something on his mind but I thought he was planning a special surprise for me.

'There were carol singers in the street below. They were singing *that* carol; how joy was here for ever and there would be "*New day, new hope, new life*". And it seemed to fit us so exactly that I began to sing the words. Jack looked a bit embarrassed. I'll never forget that look on his face, but of course it was because he was about to tell me that it was all over.

'I had some mistletoe that I'd been keeping hidden, waiting

for the right moment to produce it. I thought it was the perfect moment. I brought out the mistletoe and held it up, saying "This is where you're supposed to kiss me."

'But he just looked more embarrassed, and suddenly blurted out that he would never kiss me again. It was over. He was marrying someone else. I just stood there, trying to take it in, and all the time those words were floating up from the street. Since then, I've never been able to hear them without a shudder, but until that day I didn't know how deep it went.'

'But one song—'

'That's what I've tried to tell myself, but it's more. That one carol seems to sum it all up. The very fact that we were so happy seems like a threat. I'm afraid of happiness. I daren't let myself feel it because I can't face what happens when it ends.'

'And you think it will end with us? You don't trust me to be true to you? How can I prove it?'

'You can't. It's my fault, not yours. After Jack, I shut out love, hid myself away from it. That's why I live as I do, because it keeps love away. Let people think of me as a floozie who doesn't need real feeling! It makes me angry sometimes, but it also keeps me safe, and safe is what I want to be more than anything in the world.'

'More than anything in the world?' Roscoe echoed slowly. 'More than everything we could have together? More than the love we would share over the years, more than our children, our grandchildren?'

'Stop it,' Pippa whispered. 'Please, please stop it.'

He moved closer, not holding her, but letting her feel the warmth of his breath on her face.

'No, I won't stop it,' he whispered. 'I won't stop because I'm going to make sure that you remember me. I won't let you just shut me out as though our love didn't count. Do you think I'm going to let you off so easily? I'm not. I'm going to make sure you remember me every moment.'

Now he touched her, laying his mouth against hers, caressing her with his lips, then whispering, 'Feel me, and remember me. I'll always be here. You'll never be rid of me, do you understand?'

'Yes,' she murmured. 'I don't want to be rid of you, but I can't be with you. I'd make you wretched and destroy you, and I won't do that.'

'Tell me that you love me.'

'I love you—I love you—'

'And you belong to me.'

'Yes, I belong to you, and I always will. But please go away, Roscoe—please forget me—'

'Never in life. When I leave this room I'll be with you. When you wake up tomorrow morning I'll be with you. When you go to bed I'll be with you. When you dream of love and feel hands touching and caressing you, they'll be my hands, although I may be far away. As the years pass I'll be with you. I won't set you free—ever.'

His kiss intensified. She felt his mouth crushing hers for one fierce moment, before it softened again, leaving only tenderness behind. Then she was alone and he was backing away to the door, not taking his eyes from her.

'Forgive me,' she cried. *'Forgive me!'*

'Perhaps,' he said quietly. 'One day.'

He walked out.

An unexpected knock on her door turned out to be Charlie, dressed in a heavy overcoat, swathed in a scarf.

'It's freezing out there,' he said, coming in. 'I came because I wanted to tell you myself. Even if I don't win the show, my agent has fixed me up with a load of dates and *I'm on my way.'*

He finished with a yell of triumph and they embraced eagerly.

'Is Ginevra pleased for you?' she asked.

'Probably. We're not in touch. Last I heard from her was a text wishing me luck and saying not to contact her any more.'

'Do you mind?'

'Nope. There's a girl…well, anyway…'

'Have fun,' Pippa chuckled. 'You've been taking things too seriously for too long.'

'Well, that's over and I'm glad. I swear I'll never take anything seriously again.'

'How's Roscoe coping with the change in you?'

'Resigned, I think. I hardly see him now. Since the tie-up with Vanlen came to nothing, he's in the office all the time.'

'There's not going to be a merger?'

'No. I'm not sure what happened but I've heard there was a big row. Vanlen wanted to go ahead and merge; Roscoe didn't. Vanlen made threats; Roscoe told him to do his worst. Vanlen stormed off.' Charlie suddenly became awkward. 'Actually, I thought you might have seen Roscoe more recently.'

'The last time I saw him was at your mother's house on the night of the show, and I only went because you assured me he wouldn't be there.'

He was wide-eyed. 'Did I say that? I don't remember.'

'Stop telling porkies. You promised I wouldn't bump into him. But he said you knew he'd be there. How did you get that so wrong, Charlie?'

'Ah—well—'

She surveyed him suspiciously. 'You set us up to meet, didn't you?'

'Who, me?' His air of innocence was perfectly contrived,

and she would have believed it if she hadn't known him so well by now.

'Yes, you.'

'How can you think that I—? Oh hell, yes of course I did. I was hoping the two of you would see sense if I helped things along.'

'You've got an almighty nerve, playing Cupid.'

'Why shouldn't I? I need a big sister, and I've chosen you. Besides which, it's always handy having a lawyer in the family. There are bound to be times in the future when—well, you know.'

Her lips twitched. 'Yes, I do know.'

Charlie became briefly serious. 'But that's not really the reason, Pippa. Both Mother and I want you in the family because you make Roscoe human. Without you he'll go to the dogs.' He resumed his clowning manner. 'So get on with it, OK? Right, now I've got to go. I just wanted to see you again and say thanks for everything.'

He gave her a brotherly kiss and was gone, taking with him her last connection with Roscoe.

At their parting she'd said a final goodbye, but still she clung to the hope that he would refuse to accept her rejection. But he neither called her nor turned up on her doorstep. In the next few days their only contact was a letter:

I had a long talk with Mother last night. I think we were both equally surprised that it was possible, but once we started it grew easier. She told me how she'd felt, things that I hadn't known, and actually asked my forgiveness if she'd failed me. I told her there was nothing to forgive. Without you, it would never have happened. For the rest of my life you can ask anything of me that you wish and it will be yours. As I am yours.

It was signed simply, *Roscoe*.

He had said that she would never be alone and she found that, mysteriously, it was true. The apartment echoed with emptiness, yet he was always present, along with her other silent companions. There was Dee, accusing her of cowardice, and Mad Bruin, echoing Dee's thoughts, as he always had.

Cowardice? Am I really a coward?

If you had any real nerve, Dee told her, *you'd go back to Trafalgar Square and face that Christmas tree and those carols.*

That's what you'd have done, isn't it? But I'm not brave enough. I'd always be watching Roscoe, wondering if his love was failing, and I won't do that to him.

It's nearly Christmas. Soon the lights will go out and it'll be too late for another year. It's now or never.

Then let it be never. Better for him. I'd only break his heart.

Yet she began wandering past Trafalgar Square every night on her way home, standing there, apart from the crowd, trying to listen to the carols without hearing them. But it was no use. The darkness did not lift and after standing in the cold for an hour she would turn and make her way drearily to the nearest underground station, trying to find relief in the thought that this self-inflicted punishment would soon be over, and she could be strong for another year.

'I won't go back in the future,' she murmured. 'I can't.' Just one last visit, she thought. Then never again.

'And you'll come with me,' she said, taking up Mad Bruin from his place by her bed. 'We'll say goodbye together, then maybe you'll understand and stop nagging me. And tell *her* to stop nagging me. Not that she ever does stop. Look at that.'

The exclamation was drawn from her by one of Dee's diaries, on which Bruin had been sitting, and which fell to the floor when he was moved. Picking it up, Pippa found it falling open at a page in the centre. Dee had written:

I suppose I'm a bit mad. I swore I'd never marry him. I even ended our engagement. That broke my heart. I thought I was doing the best thing, but who gave me the right to decide for both of us? When he came back to me, injured, vulnerable, I knew that my place was by his side, no matter what.

We're marrying now because I'm pregnant, so I don't know if he really loves me. But IT DOESN'T MATTER. I love him, and that's what matters. Nobody knows the future. You can only love and do your best. Perhaps it won't work. Perhaps he'll leave me.

Here some words were scribbled in the margin. Pippa just managed to make out her grandfather's writing: *Daft woman! As though I could.*

Dee went on:

I'll take that risk and, at the end, whenever and what-ever the end will be, I'll be able to say that I was true to my love.

'You were so strong,' Pippa murmured. 'If only I could be like you. But I can't.'

She put the diary carefully into a drawer, then tucked Bruin into her bag and hurried out.

She could hear the carol singers from a distance and ran the last few yards, suddenly eager to see the beautiful tree, its lights streaming up into the darkness, promising hope. That hope would never be hers, but she would carry the memory of this night all her life.

A vendor was wandering through the Square, holding

up sprigs of mistletoe and doing a roaring trade as couples converged on him, paying exorbitantly for tiny sprigs, then immediately putting them to good use. Tears sprang into Pippa's eyes as she watched them.

All around her people were singing. Someone was yelling, 'Come on, everyone. Join in.'

But she couldn't join in. That was the one final step that was still beyond her courage. Sadly, she pressed Bruin against her cheek before turning away.

But then someone crashed into her from behind and made her fall to the ground, sending him flying.

'No,' she cried. 'Where are you—where—?'

'It's all right; I've got him,' said a familiar voice, and she found herself looking into Roscoe's eyes.

He helped her to her feet and pressed Bruin back into her hands. 'Take care of him.'

'How long have you been there?' she stammered.

'Since you arrived. And last night, and the time before. I know why you've come here and I've followed, hoping that what you found here would make you believe in me again.'

'But I do believe in you. It's myself I don't believe in. I'm afraid.'

'You? Never. You're not afraid of anything.' He made a wry, gentle face. 'Many people are afraid of me. Not you. That was the first thing I liked about you.' He went on, almost casually, 'I could do with you around just now. Vanlen's turning nasty and your moral support would mean a lot to me.' He gave a small grin. 'Plus, of course, your legal expertise.'

'I heard the merger was abandoned and he didn't like it.'

'Since a certain night, I want nothing further to do with him. He blames me for you knocking him back.' He gave a grunt of laughter. 'If only I could believe that. I could hardly tell him that you have no more use for me than for him.'

'That's not true; you know it's not,' she whispered. 'It's because you matter so much that I—'

'If I could have spoken freely I'd have told him that you're a woman so special that I'd take every threat he could throw at me, make any sacrifice asked and call it cheap at the price. Except that there is no price. There never was and there never could be. What isn't given freely has no value.'

Pippa clutched her head, almost weeping. 'You make it sound so wonderful, but I have nothing to give.'

'That's not true. You've already given me things that matter a million times more than anything else in my life. If you choose to be more generous it will be the most precious gift of all. If not, I'll always live in the knowledge that I knew the most glorious woman in the world, and my life was better for knowing her.

'If you won't marry me, Pippa, I'll never marry anyone else. I'll live alone, dreaming of you. It'll be a sad life when I think of what could have been mine instead. Will you abandon me to that loneliness? Do you love me so little that you'll do that to me?'

'No,' she cried. 'I love you with all my heart; it's just that… the fearful part of me is still fighting it. If only I could…if only…'

Everything in her yearned towards him. If only she could find the inspiration that would take her that last step into the unknown.

But it wasn't unknown. It was filled with problems, fears, difficulties, but also with love. That much she knew. As for whether the love would be enough, that was up to her, wasn't it?

Nobody knows the future. You can only love and do your best.

Dee's words seemed to echo so resoundingly that she

gasped and looked up, almost expecting to see the mysterious presence.

'Where are you?' she whispered.

Here, the presence replied. *Here, there and everywhere. In your heart.*

'What is it?' Roscoe asked.

'Nobody knows the future,' Pippa repeated slowly. 'You can only love and do your best. She knew that. She tried to tell me.'

Roscoe had laid all that he was, all he had and all he ever could be at her feet. He could do no more. Now the future lay in her hands.

'Roscoe,' she said, reaching out to him, 'if only I could—'

'But you can,' he said. 'You can if you believe. We can do it together because now I know the way.'

The choirmaster was just waiting to start the next carol. Roscoe tugged at his arm, spoke a few words and the man nodded. The next moment the first notes of '*A New Day Dawns*' floated out on the air.

'Not that one,' she said quickly.

'Yes, that one,' he said. 'That's the one that haunts you, and once we've defeated it together, the way is clear for us. Don't you see?'

'Yes, I do, but—' Still the fear lurked.

He took her face between his hands.

'No buts. From now on we face everything together, including this. Especially this. So now you're going to sing this with me. Understand?'

'Yes,' she whispered.

'Then do it. Do it now, I order you. Yes, I'm a control freak and a manipulator, *but so are you*. When we're married I'll give my orders and expect you to do as I say. But be honest, my darling. *You'll* give *your* orders and expect me to do as you say. And I will. In the end we'll know each other so well that nobody will have to give orders. We'll each know how to please the other.

'And, since you're a bigger control freak than I am, it'll be me doing most of the obeying. But this time it's me giving the orders. Sing with me, for this hope is ours and it's time to claim it.'

Around them the voices rose, seeming to shimmer with the lights that glowed up high, to the star at the top of the tree, blazing against the darkness.

'A new day dawns, a child is born.
Behold the shining star,'

'Sing,' he said. 'Sing with me. *Sing*.'

And suddenly she could do so, clinging to him for the strength only he could give her. Now and only now the words would come.

'It leads us on to hope revived,
New day, new hope, new life'

It was there, the miracle she'd thought could never happen, rolling back the fear, setting her free, but only free as long as he was there.

She saw the question in his eyes and nodded as their voices rang out together.

'For darkness flees the coming light,
And we are all reborn.'

'Reborn,' she whispered.
'Does that mean you'll marry me?'
'Yes, I'll marry you.'

From his pocket he took a small box containing a diamond ring, which he slipped onto her finger. She gasped. 'That's your mother's.'

'She gave it to me. She said her time for wearing it was over, but yours had just begun. It's her way of welcoming you into the family, but also—I don't know how to put it—'

'She gave it to you, not Charlie. That's her way of opening her heart to you again, saying you're her son?'

'Yes. It's taken so long. I thought I was resigned, but I wasn't. After all these years it has brought me more joy than I can say, and that's another thing I owe to you. You brought us together and helped us understand each other. I could never give this ring to anyone but you, and you must promise me to wear it all your life.'

'I'll wear it as long as you want me to wear it.'

'All your life,' he repeated.

A vendor glided past them, waving a sprig of mistletoe. 'Go on, buy it,' he begged. 'Then I can go home.'

Roscoe grabbed the first note he came to and proffered it without looking to see how large it was. The vendor's eyes opened wide and he vanished quickly.

Slowly, Roscoe raised the mistletoe over her head.

'Do you remember what you said to that fool who let you slip through his fingers?' he asked.

'"This is where you're supposed to kiss me",' she recalled.

'Very willingly,' he said, lowering his mouth to hers for the first kiss of their engagement.

She kissed him back fervently, trying to tell him that she was entirely his, despite her fears. With his help she would conquer them and be everything he wanted. Nothing else mattered in her life.

Afterwards they hugged each other. Later there would be passion, but just now what mattered was the warmth and comfort they could bring each other. As her spirit soared she even managed a tiny laugh.

'What is it?' he asked, lifting her chin and gazing searchingly into her face.

'That was a twenty pound note you gave him.'

'If it had been a million pounds it wouldn't have begun to be enough for what I've won tonight.'

As they finally walked away, arms entwined, she murmured, *'New day, new hope, new life.* All the best things to wish for.'

'I don't have to wish for them,' Roscoe said. 'You have given them to me already, and they will last for ever.'

They set the wedding date for soon after Christmas. It would take place in the church belonging to the graveyard where they had first met, where Pippa's family lay in the grounds. The day before, they paid a visit together and went to look at the graves of Mark and Dee. Roscoe brushed the snow away, revealing the faces beneath, not just happy, but with a contentment that spoke of many years of successful marriage.

'I'm glad they'll be at our wedding,' she said.

'They'll always be part of our lives,' he agreed. 'Because without them we'd never have met. Do you think your grandmother likes me?'

'Oh, yes, I can tell from the way she's looking at you.'

'So can I.'

When she went to visit the other family graves he stayed behind to talk to Dee.

'You've been such an influence in her life—and mine— that I want to know you better. Without you, she wouldn't be who she is, and I wouldn't be the happy man that I am. Thank you with all my heart.'

He stepped back.

'I'll see you both at the wedding tomorrow. I hope you enjoy it.'

He walked away to find the woman he adored more than life, and even now he had the sense that two pairs of eyes were following him. He smiled, happy in the knowledge, and resolved to tell Pippa all about it.

MIDNIGHT UNDER
THE MISTLETOE
SARA ORWIG

Sara Orwig lives in Oklahoma. She has a patient husband who will take her on research trips anywhere, from big cities to old forts. She is an avid collector of Western history books. With a master's degree in English, Sara has written historical romance, mainstream fiction and contemporary romance. Books are beloved treasures that take Sara to magical worlds, and she loves both reading and writing them.

With special thanks to Stacy Boyd, Shana Smith
and Maureen Walters.
May you have a blessed and joyous holiday.

One

Another secretary to interview.

Zach Delaney stood at the window of his west Texas ranch and watched the approaching car. This candidate was prompt. He had heard this one lived in Dallas, was single, only twenty-four, a homebody who insisted on weekends free to go home. She wanted a week off before Christmas and two days after Christmas. If she could do the work, it was all right with him. He didn't know her, but she had worked more than two years at his Dallas office, which held the corporate offices of his demolition company, his trucking company and the architectural firm he owned. She'd risen fast and was highly recommended.

As Zach watched the car approach the house, he thought about the other secretaries he'd interviewed and the conversation he'd had with his brother Will, who had stopped by an hour ago.

He remembered Will laughing. "I know you—you're probably about to go up in smoke from boredom."

"You've got that right. I feel as if I'm a prisoner and time seems to have stopped," Zach replied, raking his fingers through his thick, brown curls.

Will nodded. "Don't forget—you're supposed to stay off your feet and keep your foot elevated."

"I'm doing that most of the time. Believe me, I want my foot to get well."

Will smiled. "You should have just stayed in Dallas after Garrett's wedding earlier this month. You haven't been cooped up like this since you were five and had the mumps."

"Don't remind me."

"That was twenty-seven years ago. I don't know how you've made it this long in demolition without getting hurt."

"I've been lucky and careful, I guess."

"If you don't end up hiring today's interviewee, I'll send someone out to work for you. If I had known the difficulty you're having finding a competent secretary, I would have sent one before now."

"Thanks. One secretary lasted a few days before deciding the ranch was too isolated. Another talked incessantly," Zach grumbled, causing Will to laugh. His brother's brown eyes sparkled with amusement.

"One of those women hovered over me and told me what to do to take care of myself. Actually, Will, instead of hiring a secretary to help go through Dad's stuff, maybe we should just trash it all. Dad's been gone almost a year now and this stuff hasn't been touched. It's not important. The only value that stuff can have is sentimental. That makes it worthless as time passes."

"We don't know for sure there isn't something of value in those boxes," Will argued.

Zach nodded. "Knowing our father, he could have put some vital papers, money or something priceless in these boxes, just so someone *would* have to wade through them."

"You volunteered to go through his papers while you re-cuperate from your fall. You don't have to."

"I'll do it. The secretary will help go through all the letters and memorabilia while I also keep up with work. You became guardian for Caroline and you handled a lot of the dealings to bring our half sister into the family. Ryan's knee-deep in getting his new barn built while commuting back and forth to his business in Houston. Besides, I'm the one incapacitated with time on my hands. I'm it, for now. I don't know what got into Dad, keeping all this memorabilia. He would never have actually written a family history."

"Our father was not one you could figure. His actions were unfathomable except for making money. He probably intended to write a family history. In his old age I think he became nostalgic." Will headed toward the door and then paused. "You sure you don't want to join us for Thanksgiving? I'll send someone to get you," he added, and Zach was touched by Will's concern.

"Thanks, but no thanks. You enjoy Ava's family. Ryan leaves soon to spend Thanksgiving with the latest woman in his life—I can't keep up with which one this is. I'll be fine and enjoy myself all by myself."

"If you change your mind, let me know. Also, it's less than six weeks until Christmas. We're going to Colorado for the holiday. Do you want to come along? We'll be happy to have you join us."

"Thank you." Zach grinned. "I think I'll go to the house in Italy. It'll be beautiful there and you know I don't do Christmas."

"So who is the beautiful Italian lady? I'm sure there is one."

"Might be more than one." Zach smiled. "You hadn't been into Christmas much yourself until you got Caroline. Now you have to celebrate."

"Truthfully, with Caroline, it's been fun. Come with us and you'll see."

"I love little Caroline, but you go ahead. Doc told me to stay put and this is a better place than snowy mountains in Colorado."

"That's true, but we'd take care of you."

Zach shook his head. "Thanks, Will, for coming out."

"Let me know about the secretary. I'll get you one who's excellent."

"With Margo on maternity leave, I may have to find a new one permanently. I don't want to think about that."

Now, Zach shifted his foot and glared at it, recalling the moment the pile of rubble had given way and he had fallen, breaking an ankle, plus small bones, causing a sprain and getting one deep gash. Staying off his foot most of the time was hell. He didn't like working daily in an office, and the doctor told him he couldn't go back to working on site or travel much, but he could do some work at the ranch and stay off his foot as best he could.

Zach sighed as the car slowed in front of the house. Emma Hillman. She climbed out of her car and came up the walk.

Startled, he momentarily forgot her mission. A tall, windblown, leggy redhead, who would turn heads everywhere, was striding toward his front door. With looks like hers, she belonged on a model's catwalk or doing a commercial or in a bar, not striding purposefully toward his house in the hopes of doing secretarial chores. Even though she wore a tailored, dark green suit with an open black coat over it, she had a wild, attention-getting appearance.

The west Texas wind swept over her, catching more tendrils of long red hair and blowing them around her face. Immobilized, Zach stared. She didn't look like any secretary on his staff in any office he had. Nor did she resemble the homebody type to his way of thinking. All those recommendations she had—they must have been based on her looks. His spirits sank. He would have to ask Will to find him somebody else. He needed someone who would stay on the ranch during the week. This one was a declared homebody. Add that to her looks and he couldn't imagine it working out. He also couldn't imagine her being an efficient secretary, either. He would give Emma Hillman a lot of work and in less than two days, she would probably fold and run as her predecessor had.

When the bell rang, he could hear Nigel get the door. Zach hobbled back to the middle of the room to wait to meet her. Before he sent her packing, he might get her home phone number. Actually, even if she did work out here, when the temporary job ended she'd go back to the corporate office, so getting her phone number was only wishful thinking. She'd still be an employee. Even so, eagerness to meet her took the boredom out of the morning. This promised to be his most enjoyable moment since he arrived at the ranch.

Emma Hillman pushed a button and heard chimes. Her gaze swept over the large porch. The ranch was not at all what she had pictured in her mind. She had expected a rustic, sprawling house, not a mansion that bordered on palatial. When the door swung open, she faced a slender gray-haired man.

"Welcome, Miss Hillman?"

"Yes," she said, entering as he stepped back.

"I'm Nigel Smith. If you'll come with me, Mr. Delaney is waiting."

Following him, she glanced around the enormous entrance. Wood floors had a dark appearance with a treatment that gave them an antiqued quality and probably would not show boot marks or much of anything else.

She tried to finger-comb her hair and tuck tendrils back into the clips that held her hair on either side of her head. She had been warned about Zach Delaney—that he was difficult to please, curt, all business. Actually, he had conflicting descriptions—a charismatic hunk by some; others pronounced him a demanding ogre. She had been told too many times about her three predecessors who hadn't lasted more than a day or two.

She didn't care—it was a fabulous opportunity for another promotion in the company and the pay was terrific right at Christmastime. Even though she was going to miss being in Dallas with her family, she was determined to cooperate with Zach Delaney and be the secretary who got to stay.

Nigel led her through an open door into a large room with shelves of books on two walls, a huge fireplace on another and all glass on the fourth. In a hasty glance she barely saw any of her surroundings because her attention was ensnared by the tall man standing in the center of the room.

His prominent cheekbones and a firm jaw were transformed by a mass of dark brown curls and riveting blue eyes. A black knit shirt and tight jeans revealed muscles and a fit physique. Even standing quietly, he appeared commanding.

Dimly, she heard Nigel present her and she thanked him as he left, but her gaze was locked with the head of her company, Zach Delaney. Her breathing altered, her heart raced and her palms became damp. She felt flustered, drawn to him, unable to look away. For heartbeats, they gazed at each other while silence stretched.

With an effort she offered her hand. "I'm glad to meet you, Mr. Delaney," she said. Her voice was soft in her ears.

He stepped forward, his hand closing around hers, his warm fingers breaking the spell she had been temporarily enveloped in. "Welcome to the Delaney ranch. I'm happy to meet you, and it's Zach. We're going to work closely together. No 'Mr. Delaney.' And please have a seat." His voice was deep, warm and sexy, an entertainer's voice.

Feeling foolish, yet unable to control the physical reaction she was having to him, she sat in a leather chair. Another chair was close and he turned it to face her, sitting near her. "I've read your recommendations, which are excellent. If you want this job, you're to move here for the duration of the time you work for me—five, possibly six weeks total. Your weekends are free from one on Friday afternoon until Monday morning at nine o'clock."

"That's fine with me," she replied, thinking someone should have warned her about his appeal. He rarely was in the Dallas office and executive offices were on the top floor. She had never seen him or crossed paths with him before. She had no idea she would have such an intense reaction to meeting him.

"I expect this job to end around Christmas, when my foot heals. You can return to the Dallas office and I will be on my way back to the field."

"Fine," she replied, barely able to concentrate on what he was saying for getting lost in vivid blue eyes. His conversation might have been practical, all business, but the look in his eyes was not. Blue depths probed, examined and conveyed a sensual appraisal that shimmied warmly over her nerves. "As I mentioned in our phone call, I'd like to take that week before Christmas and two days afterward if the job hasn't ended."

"That's fine. As far as your duties, you're here to help with any correspondence or business matters I have and to help me sort through some family papers. My father intended to write a family history. He had old letters and family memorabilia that have been passed through generations, that sort of thing. I volunteered to go through all of it while I'm supposed to stay off my feet," Zach said, waving his hand toward the boxes of papers nearby.

"The memorabilia should be fascinating," she remarked.

"If your ancestors wrote these letters and sent them, how did they get possession of them again?"

"Good question. They wrote other relatives, sisters, brothers, and as far as I can see, everybody saved every word that was put on paper. There are letters in those boxes that aren't from Delaneys, but are written to a Delaney who saved it. You'd think one person would have tossed them. If the letter isn't from a Delaney, there is no reason to keep it."

"I imagine some were tossed. There were probably more since you had such prolific writers in your family."

"If I were the only Delaney of my generation, I would simply shred the papers this week because I think they're junk. Some of the letters date back to the 1800s."

Horrified at the thought of shredding old letters, she stared at him. "The 1800s? It should be spellbinding to read about your relatives," she blurted before she thought about how it might sound critical of her boss's attitude.

He smiled. "I suppose it's a good thing you feel that way because you'll be reading some of this stuff for me. Anyway, that in general is what I hired you to do. Does this sound acceptable?"

"Certainly. I'm looking forward to it."

"Great. Feel free to ask questions at any time. I'll have Nigel see about getting you moved in. You were asked to come prepared to move in. Is this what you did?"

"Yes. I was told to pack for the job because you might hire me and want me to stay."

"I'm getting desperate for a secretary. The salary should make up for some of the demands," he said and she merely nodded.

"Nigel is sort of jack-of-all-trades around the house. He acts as butler, assistant and a financial manager. You'll meet more of our staff, who have homes on the ranch."

"I wonder if I'll ever find my way around," she said as she glanced beyond him toward the hall.

"Nigel will give you a map of the house. We have an indoor pool and one outside. Feel free to swim after or before work hours. We have a gym, too."

"This is a modernized ranch home."

"This house has been remodeled many times. The family room was the actual original house, built in the 1800s. Anyway, my grandfather had an elevator installed, so I'm taking it temporarily. You're welcome to if you want."

"Thank you, I won't need the elevator," she replied with a smile. "I exercise each day, so stairs are good."

"Great. Do you think we can start work this morning in about an hour?"

"Certainly."

As he stood, she came to her feet and followed him to the door. He offered his hand. "Welcome to the Delaney ranch, Emma," he drawled in a mesmerizing voice that wrapped around her like a warm blanket. She shook hands again with him, an electric current flashing from the contact while she looked into the bluest eyes she had ever seen. Dark brown curly lashes framed his mesmerizing eyes.

"I hope you find your stay here worthwhile," he said, a dry, professional statement, but his tone of voice, with those blue eyes focused on her and her hand enveloped in his, made her think of sizzling kisses. Realizing how she was staring, she withdrew her hand and stepped back. He turned to walk into the hall to talk to Nigel, nodded at her, and in seconds she left with Nigel to see where she would stay.

The next hour was a whirlwind of getting unpacked enough to function through the day. To her surprise she had more than a room—it was a suite with a sitting area, a dream bedroom with a four-poster and fruitwood furniture. Dazzled by the lavish quarters, she looked at a bathroom as large as her apartment. The bath held a sunken tub, potted plants, mirrors, an adjoining dressing room plus a huge walk-in closet. She took pictures on her cell phone to send to her sisters. She could imagine how they would ooh and aah over where she was staying. Her paramount concern was how would she work constantly around Zach Delaney. She had heard rumors at the office about how appealing he was, but not from anyone who had actually worked for him. She had talked to one secretary who had spent two days with him and thought he was a monster, piling on work until it was impossible to get done what he demanded. Another secretary had complained about him being silent and abrupt during the day.

When she saw it was time to go back to meet with him, she smoothed her hair into a loose bun and left her room. Trying to familiarize herself with the mansion, she walked to the study where she had met Zach.

He sat behind a desk and stood the minute she appeared in the doorway. Once again, she tried to avoid staring. He looked muscled and fit except for his foot that was wrapped in a bandage and in an oversize health shoe. The unruly curls were a tangle around his face, softening his rugged features.

"Let's go to the office," he said, and she walked beside him down a wide hall filled with paintings, plants, side tables and chairs.

As they entered a large room, she drew a deep breath. It was a dream office with two large desks at opposite ends of the room. Shelves lined three walls and the remaining wall was glass with a view of a small pond and well tended grounds up to a white fence. Beyond the fence were stables, a corral and pasture. Through spacious windows, daylight spilled into the room. Fax machines, shredders, computers and electronic equipment filled each end of the office.

"That's my desk," he said, pointing to the larger one that was polished, ornately carved dark wood. Forming an Lshape with the desk, a table stood at one end. The table held two computers, one of which had dual oversize monitors. Another computer was centered on his desk. Two laptops and an iPad lay on the table.

The other desk was glass, looking far newer. File cabinets were built into one wall and not noticeable at first glance.

He sat behind his desk, motioning toward a leather chair facing him. She sat, crossing her legs, catching him looking at her legs when she glanced up. She inhaled sharply. She experienced an undercurrent of intense awareness and suspected he did as well. It was unexpected, definitely unwanted. Any hot attraction between them could put her job in jeopardy and this job was important to her. She was saving to go back to college and, ultimately, become qualified to teach. This was a temporary increase in pay she could use to achieve her dream.

"Since you and I and my staff are the only people here, you can dress casually. Jeans are fine."

She nodded. "Great."

"The glass desk will be yours. You'll find a stack of papers I've signed that need to be copied and put into the mail." He leaned back and stretched out his long legs.

She realized she was going to have a difficult time for a few days, focusing on what he was saying because she got lost looking at him.

"Hopefully you'll be able to read my handwriting. I have a document there for you to type for me to sign. Another stack holds filing. There's an in-box on the corner of my desk. When you finish anything, if it doesn't go in the mail or the file, place it in my in-box. If you have any questions, always feel free to ask. Take a break when you want and feel free to get what you want in the kitchen. Did Nigel show you where the kitchen is?"

"Yes, he showed me around briefly."

"Did you meet my very good cook?"

"Yes, I met Rosie."

"Good. You can start work each day at 8:00, quit at 4:00 or start at 9:00 and quit at 5:00. You're stuck here for lunch so we'll not add that to the time."

"I prefer 8:00," she said and he nodded.

"Any questions now?" he asked, giving her a direct look that made her pulse jump another notch.

"One—where do I take the mail?"

"There's a box on a shelf near your desk that is marked Mail and you put everything in there. One of the hands who works on the ranch will get the mail to take it down to the road to be picked up."

She nodded and headed over to her desk, feeling her back prickle because she suspected Zach's gaze was on her. She sat down and looked at the piles of work in front of her, remembering the angry statements from Brenna about Zach Delaney heaping mountains of work on her. It looked like a lot now—hopefully, by the end of the day, she would have made a big enough dent in the stacks to get to keep this job.

Still conscious of him across the room, Emma reached for a stack. As she began to read the first letter, she tried to keep from glancing his way. She pushed the stack aside and picked up a tablet with a bold handwriting. The writing to be typed looked the most time-consuming, so she started with it. In minutes she managed to put Zach out of her thoughts.

When she finished each task, she placed it in the proper pile. Standing, she gathered the work she had completed and put papers for Zach into his in-box. His back was turned as he worked at his computer and she looked at the thick hair curling on the back of his head.

She had not expected to be working in the same room with him. Also, she hadn't expected to work for someone

who took her breath and set her pulse racing just by a glance
from his sky-blue eyes.

With a deep sigh, she placed letters in the box for mail and
then she started to file.

She looked across the room to see him setting papers in
a pile. He picked up the letters in his in-box, glanced at her
to catch her watching him again. She turned away to work
on her computer, in seconds concentrating on what she was
doing for the next half hour. She finished another stack and
picked them up to take to his in-box and this time when she
glanced his way, she met his gaze.

He seemed to be sitting and watching her. She picked up
the papers and carried them to his desk, all the time aware
of his steady observation.

As she started to put the letters into the box, he took them
and riffled through them before looking at her. "You're a fast
worker. And an accurate one."

"Thank you. I try to be."

"I figured with all the work I've piled on you this morning, you'd be out of here as fast as the others."

"I intend to stay," she said, amused, and realizing he might
have been testing to see how she worked. She went back to
her desk, again having that tingly feeling across her shoulders, certain he was watching her.

When she glanced at him, he had settled back to read. In
seconds, he placed the letter in the stack beside him on his
desk.

What kind of man did she work for? When she had gone
to work at Z.A.D. Enterprises, she hadn't given much thought
to the head of the business because she'd heard he was rarely
in the Dallas office. The business comprised primarily of demolition, but also had a trucking company, an architectural
firm and a concrete company. The international company had
offices scattered worldwide and she heard Zachary Delaney

traveled constantly from site to site, something she would detest. Other than that and the recent grumbling by Brenna, she knew little about him. Not one of the secretaries who had preceded her had said anything about his appeal, about his looks, about anything except he had proven difficult to work for. Maya, as well as Brenna, had thought he was unreceptive and uncommunicative. All had complained the workload was too heavy and she had to agree it was a lot, but it made time fly. On the other hand, around the office the word had always been that he was friendly. Perhaps part of his surly reputation with some secretaries was caused by his being injured and isolated on a ranch.

She returned to the stack, until she heard the scrape of a chair.

He stood and stretched, flexing muscles in his arms. When he glanced her way, she was embarrassed to be caught staring at him again.

"Want some lunch?" Without waiting for her answer, he motioned. "C'mon, we'll get something to eat. Rosie will have something fixed."

"Thank you," she said. "I still have letters, though."

"C'mon. You'll like Rosie's cooking and she'll be disappointed if you don't come eat. Those letters aren't urgent."

"Very well. You're the boss and I don't want to hurt her feelings." Glancing at her watch, Emma was surprised it was half past twelve. "I didn't realize the time."

"Time flies when you're having fun," he said, grinning at her. Creases appeared on either side of his mouth in an enticing smile that caused her to smile in return.

"So, Emma, tell me about yourself since we'll be working together for the next month or so."

Satisfaction flared because he must mean she would get to stay. "There's not much to tell. I've been at Z.A.D. for two years now. I have an apartment in Dallas and have two sisters and two brothers. My sisters, Sierra and Mary Kate, and Connor, my older brother, are married. Bobby and I are single. What about you?"

"I have two brothers, it was three, one is deceased. My older brother became guardian of our little niece, Caroline."

"That's sad. Is your niece's mother deceased, too?"

"No, her mother walked out when Caroline was a baby. She didn't want to be tied down with responsibilities, although she had a nanny and someone to cook and clean."

"I can't imagine," Emma said, staring at him.

He shrugged. "One more thing to sour me on marriage. My older brother felt the same way until this year. He just married in September."

"You don't want to get married and have a family?"

His mouth quirked in a crooked smile. "Not even remotely. The weeks I'm spending here recuperating are probably the longest I've stayed home in Texas in I don't know when. I'm a traveler."

"I've heard you work all over the world and I know Z.A.D. has offices worldwide. I have a vastly different life. I don't want to miss a weekend with my family."

"We're poles apart there," he remarked with a smile, directing her into a large kitchen with an adjoining dining room that held a table and chairs, a sofa, a fireplace, two wingback chairs and a bar.

"What's for lunch, Rosie? Something smells tempting," he said, raising a lid on a pot on the stove. A stocky woman in a uniform bustled around the kitchen. Her graying hair was in a bun and glasses perched on her turned-up nose.

"Chicken soup there and I have quesadillas or turkey melt sandwiches—your preference."

"How about soup, plus—" He paused and looked questioningly at Emma. "Either of the choices have any appeal?"

"Of course. Quesadillas, please."

"Good choice. Rosie's are special. Soup and quesadillas it is. We can help ourselves, Rosie."

Bowls and plates were on the counter. With that steady awareness of him at her side, Emma helped herself to a small bowl of soup, surprised when Zach set down his dishes and held her chair as she sat down. The gesture made their lunch together seem far less like boss and secretary eating together than a man and a woman on a date. Rosie appeared with a coffeepot, which Emma declined and Zach accepted.

When he sat, she said, "I'm sure everyone asks, what drew you to demolition?"

"A child's love of tearing something down, probably. I have an engineering degree and I almost went to architecture school. I have architects working for me so we build where we tear down. We build sometimes where nothing has stood. I find it fascinating work."

"I hear you go all over the world." She didn't add that she knew he was wealthy enough he would never have to work a day if he didn't want to.

The Delaney wealth was well publicized. She had never known anyone like him before. His love of travel was foreign to her. His disregard for family and marriage dismayed her even more than his apparent disregard for his family history. He had a lifestyle she could not imagine, but the head of the company was light-years from her clerical job, which provided an excellent way to save money to finish her college education.

"So, Zach, your favorite locale is where?" she asked as Rosie brought a platter with steaming quesadillas to set between them.

"There's too many to have a favorite. I love Paris, I love Torres del Paine, Iguazu Falls, the city of New York. They're all interesting. Where's your favorite?"

"Home with my family," she said, smiling at him, and he shook his head.

"Okay, I'll rephrase my question," he said. "Where's your favorite place outside of Texas?"

She lowered her fork. "I've never been outside of Texas."

One dark eyebrow arched as surprise flashed briefly in his blue eyes. "Never been outside of Texas," he repeated, studying her as if she had announced she had another set of ears beneath her red hair.

"No, I'm happy here."

"You might be missing something," he said, still scrutinizing her with open curiosity.

"I don't think so, therefore, that's really all that matters, right?" she asked, certain after today he would have satisfied his curiosity about her and lunch with the boss would cease.

"You're missing some wonderful places and you don't even know it."

She smiled at him again, thinking he might be missing some wonderful family companionship and didn't even know it. "As long as I'm content, it doesn't matter."

"So tell me about this family of yours and what they all do."

"My family lives near me in Dallas. Dad is an accountant and my mom is a secretary. My younger brother works part-time and is in school at the University of North Texas. I've taken classes to become a teacher. This semester I didn't enroll, but I hope to start back soon."

"How far along are you?"

"I have a little more than half the credits I need. Back to my family—in addition to my siblings, I have five small nieces and three nephews. We have assorted other relatives, grandparents, aunts and uncles, who live in the same general area."

"Big family."

"My siblings and I visit my parents on weekends," she said.

"So do my aunts and uncles. There are anywhere from twenty to thirty or forty of us when we all get together."

He paused as he started to drink his water, giving her a polite smile as if she said they spent every weekend at the park so they could play on the slides and swings.

"My family is definitely not that together," he said. "We go our separate ways. Dad's deceased and Mom disappeared from our lives when we were young."

"We have different lifestyles," she said, thinking this was a man she couldn't possibly ever be close to even if circumstances had been different. His world and hers were poles apart. Their families were so different—hers a huge part of her life, his nearly nonexistent, what with his father being deceased and his mother walking out years earlier. Those events had to influence him and make him the man he was today. This job would be brief and then she probably would never see him again. "The quesadilla is delicious," she said.

"I told you Rosie is a good cook. So, is there any special person in your life right now? I assume no one objected to you taking this job."

"Not at all and there's no special person at the moment. As long as I can go home for the weekends and holidays, I'm fine."

"I'm not sure I've been involved—friends or otherwise— with someone as tied into home and family."

"I'm your secretary—that's different from your women friends."

"We can be friends," he said, looking amused, and a tingle ran across her nerves. In tiny subtle ways he was changing their relationship from professional to personal, something she did not want. With every discovery about him, she saw what opposites they were. This was not a man who would ever fit into her world or her life other than on a physical level. She definitely did not fit into his.

Surprised that he was even interested, she had to wonder. She had never heard a word of gossip about him even remotely trying to have an outside relationship with an employee. Far from it—occasional remarks were made to new single women to forget about impressing the boss—if they even got to know him—except through efficient work.

"We can be friends to a degree in a professional manner," she said, wondering if she sounded prim.

"Emma, we're going to be under the same roof, working together for weeks. Relax. This isn't the office and it's not that formal. If I have something critical, a letter I just have to get out, an appointment that has to be made by a certain time, I'll tell you."

"Fair enough," she said, feeling as if their relationship just made another subtle shift. Or was it her imagination because she found him so physically attractive? "So you don't gather often with the family, you travel a lot—what else do you do?"

"Most of the time for the past few years my life has been tied up in my work. I have a yacht, but I'm seldom on it. I ski. I have a villa in Italy. I have a condo in New York, one in Chicago and I spend the most time between Paris and Chicago where we have offices. I like cities."

She placed her fork across her plate and stood. "That was a delicious lunch. If you'll excuse me, I should get back to the letters."

"Sit and relax, Emma. Those letters aren't urgent and they'll be there after lunch. I'm enjoying talking to you. There's no rush. And I suspect some tidbit will appear for dessert."

Surprised, she sat again. "I'm not in the habit of arguing with my supervisor. I don't think I can possibly eat dessert. This was more lunch than I usually have."

"Indulge yourself while you can," he said. Pushing his plate forward, he placed his arms on the table and leaned closer. "Emma, this is lunch. We're not at work. Forget the supervisor-secretary relationship, which doesn't have to exist 24/7. This is just two people having lunch together," he drawled in that husky voice that was soft as fur. Vivid blue eyes held her attention while his words poured over her and the moment shifted, holding a cozy intimacy. "Beautiful green eyes, great red hair—they sort of lend themselves to forgetting all about business," he said softly.

"We're about to cross a line we shouldn't cross," she whispered while her heart hammered.

"We crossed that line when you came in the door," he replied.

Two

Her heart thudded because his words changed their relationship. She realized her reply would set the standard. For a fleeting second, how tempted she was to flirt back, to give him a seductive reply that was on the tip of her tongue. For the moment, she wished he were someone else and not her boss.

Following the path of wisdom, practicality and caution, she smiled and chuckled, shaking her head and trying to diffuse the electrifying tension that had sprung between them. "I don't think so," she replied lightly. "We can't. I'm here for a secretarial job, which sets definite limits. I'm not crossing that line. If that's part of my work—then tell me now."

"Definitely not part of the job," he said, leaning back and studying her with a faint smile and amusement dancing in his blue eyes. "As rare for me as for you in an employer-employee situation. But we're not going to be able to shut it off that easily. As a matter of fact, I think the chemistry is in spite of both of us, not because of either of us wanting it to happen. That's a big difference and rather fascinating."

"We'll not pursue it," she persisted. Rosie appeared with a tray that held four choices of desserts. "What would you like, Miss Hillman?" she asked.

"Please just call me Emma," she said, looking at luscious desserts. She was no longer hungry, yet Rosie stood with a broad smile and Emma knew how her own mother liked for everyone to take some of her desserts, so she selected a small slice of chocolate cheesecake.

Zach took a monstrous concoction of vanilla ice cream and brownies topped with fudge sauce with a sprinkling of fresh raspberries.

"You must work out big-time to turn that into muscle," she observed and the moment the words were spoken, she wished she could take them back because she had just tossed the conversation back to the personal. "This is so much food. What does Rosie do with leftovers? Save them for dinner?" Emma interjected, trying to get the conversation on a different note as rapidly as possible.

He flashed a slight smile as he shook his head. "I work out and my injured foot has thrown me off schedule. As for the leftovers—there are a lot of people on this ranch. She'll pass them on after lunch and they'll be gone by midafternoon. You think all those hungry cowboys won't light into her cooking? They'll devour it."

She smiled, glad the moment had been diffused and they were back on a harmless topic. "This is delicious," she said as she ate a bite. She looked up to meet his steady gaze that fluttered her insides.

"She'll be glad to know you liked it. Rosie's been cooking for us since I was a little kid."

She smiled and they enjoyed their desserts, then she said, "Do you mind if I put a few family pictures on my desk?"

"Emma, within reason, put whatever you want on your desk or around your desk or in your room upstairs. I don't care what you do unless you want to paint something or make a permanent change."

"Of course not. Thanks. Now, if you'll excuse me, I think this time I will get back to work," she said, folding her napkin and standing. When she picked up her plate, he touched her wrist lightly.

"Leave the dishes or you'll get a Rosie lecture. She's in charge here and she wants to do things herself and her way," he said, releasing her wrist as he stood and walked around the table.

Smiling, she set her plate down. "I know how my mother and one of my sisters are. Sometimes they just want all of us out of the kitchen."

"You're so tied into your family. Are you going to be able to stay away from Dallas for the length of this job?"

"I gave that some serious thought, but this isn't permanent and as far as I can see, this assignment is a great opportunity because it's a hike in pay, even temporarily, and I'm saving money to finish my education. And I did ask for the weekends off to go home."

"We both hope it works out. So far, so good. I'll admit, I didn't expect you to last the morning, because several before you didn't. I've been pleasantly surprised."

"Glad to hear I'm up to snuff. So far so good in working for you," she replied with a smile.

One dark eyebrow arched quizzically as he looked down at her. "You expected an ogre. Aah—let me guess—rumors from your predecessors."

Still smiling, she nodded. They entered the office and she left to return to the correspondence and filing. Within the hour she noticed he had stopped heaping work for her and she could see where she would catch up with all he had given her.

No matter how lost she got in the assignments, she couldn't shake her awareness of him. Carrying papers to his desk, she often met his gaze while he talked on the phone. Each time it was the same as a physical contact with a sizzle.

Common sense warned this job would not be as simple and straightforward as she had envisioned. When he talked on the phone, his voice was usually low enough that she couldn't hear much of what he was saying and she made no effort to try to hear. She caught snatches of words, enough to know he was discussing problems involving his work.

As she placed a letter in the box for mail, Zach got off his phone. "Emma, take a break. The afternoon is more than half gone."

"I'm fine."

"Take a break—walk around the place, go outside, go to the kitchen and get a snack—whatever you want to do. Don't argue or I'll come get you and we'll go for a stroll. As much as I can stroll right now."

She laughed. "What a threat," she said, placing mail in the box and hurrying out of the room as she received a grin from him. She hoped he didn't guess moments like that played havoc with her insides. How tempting to head back to work just to get him to spend the next few minutes with her.

She stood in the wide, empty hall and wondered what to do, finally going toward the kitchen to get a cup of tea. She suspected there was a very well-stocked pantry.

"Afternoon, Emma," Rosie greeted her.

"It smells wonderful in here."

"Roast for dinner. Can I get you something?"

"Yes, thank you. If possible, I'd like a cup of hot tea."

"Of course," Rosie replied. "Looks as if you might be the one who stays."

"I hope so."

Rosie chuckled. "Those others looked frazzled and un-happy from the first morning. I would have sent one packing faster than Zach did. Have a seat and I'll brew your tea—or if you want a breath of fresh air, go outside and I'll bring it to you."

"Thanks, Rosie."

"You can take it back to your desk if you want. Zach isn't particular about food in the office if you don't leave crumbs or make a big mess."

"I won't," Emma replied, smiling. "I'll wait outside," she added, stepping out onto the patio and strolling to the pool to look at the crystal water that was almost the same blue as Zach's eyes.

When she finished her tea, she went to her room to retrieve a small box of family pictures. She had already distributed some pictures in the bedroom. When instructed to arrive with her things packed she had brought what she really wanted with her. She stopped to look around again, still amazed at the size and beauty of where she would stay.

When she returned to her desk, Zach was on the phone and she had more work waiting. After placing her pictures on her desk and table, she focused on correspondence, so lost in concentration she was startled when Zach spoke to her.

"It's half past five. Just because the work is here in the house, you don't need to stay all hours. We'll close the office now. I eat a late dinner, but you can eat whenever you want— Rosie will be in the kitchen until eight. After that she'll have cold or easily heated choices on a chalkboard menu."

"Thanks," she said, wondering if she had eaten her last meal with the boss. If she had, it would be the wisest thing to happen. At the same time, she couldn't prevent her slight disappointment.

"You've done good work today, Emma. I hope you like the job."

She wanted to laugh and say that he sounded surprised. Instead, she merely nodded. "Thank you. I think this will be good."

He gave her a long look that killed the impersonal moments that had just passed. Once again her nerves tingled, invisible sparks danced in the air and she could feel heat rising. In spite of logic, she didn't want him to go.

Turning away, he walked out of the room without saying anything further. She stared at the empty doorway. The chemistry had not changed. He seemed to fight it as much as she, which was a relief and made the situation easier.

Zach continued to pile on a lot of work. While there wasn't as much as that first morning, letters to write, papers to proof, appointments to set, phone calls and various tasks streamed to her desk. Time passed swiftly as she worked diligently and kept up with what he sent to her. There were no more lunches together. Sometimes he worked straight through and then stopped about four. Sometimes he ate at his desk. He continued to make an effort to keep their relationship impersonal, which suited her completely. No matter how cool he was, there still was no way to stop that acute consciousness she had of him as an appealing male.

Thursday the work he gave her in the morning was done by noon. When she returned after lunch he sat by a large cardboard box filled with papers.

"Want to tackle some of the old letters and memorabilia?"

"Sure," she replied, watching him pull another chair near his. "That's a lot of letters."

"Many were written by my great-great-grandfather to his sister, his brother, later his wife. They were all saved and somehow ended up back with our family. Probably some relative didn't want them and another one took them."

"Zach, that's wonderful. I'd think you'd want to read each of these yourself."

"Hardly. They are letters from an old codger who settled out here and struggled to carve out a life on the plains. He was probably a tough old bird and about as lovable as a prickly porcupine. I think you are romanticizing him. Sit here beside me so whenever you have a question you can ask me. Want anything to drink before we start?"

"No, thank you, I'm fine." As she crossed the room, his gaze raked briefly over her, making every inch tingle. She became aware of the navy sweater and matching slacks she had pulled on this morning, her hair in a ponytail.

Catching a whiff of his enticing aftershave, she sat beside him.

"The big basket is for letters and papers that go to the shredder," he instructed. Sitting only inches from him, she was lost in his blue eyes and could barely focus on what he told her. She was even closer than she had been that first morning and it was distracting beyond measure.

"As far as I'm concerned, I think it would do the family a favor to shred all papers that don't contain pertinent information that would affect our lives today," he said. His voice deepened a notch and he slowed his speech. Was their proximity having an effect on him, too?

Lost in depths of blue, she was mesmerized. Her breath caught and held. He leaned a fraction closer. Her heart raced. With an effort she looked away, trying to get back to their normal relationship. Leaning away from him, she touched the yellowed envelopes in the large box as she tried to get back to his instructions.

"If there is anything about money, boundary rights, water rights, that sort of thing, then place the paper in the box marked Consider and I will read it. If you find maps, drawings, etc., then place them in Miscellaneous."

As what he had told her to do sank in, she frowned. She picked up a tattered, yellow envelope with flowing writing across the front. "This was in the 1800s. Look at the address on it. It's just a name and the county. You want to shred it?"

"If it doesn't have anything pertinent to the matters I listed—rights, boundaries, money. Something significant."

"The letter is significant if it has nothing like that in it. Isn't it written by one of your ancestors?"

"Probably my great-great-grandfather. Maybe further back than that by one generation."

"You can't shred it. It's wonderful to have all these letters from your ancestors and know what they were like," she said, staring at him and wondering how he could care so little about his own family history. "How can you feel that way about them?"

With a smile he shook his head. "It's past and over."

"You have an architectural firm, so you must like old buildings."

"Old buildings are more reliable than people. People change constantly and you can't always count on them. An old building—if it's built right—might last through centuries and you can definitely rely on it."

She stared at him, wondering who had let him down so badly that he would view people as unreliable. Had it started when his mother had walked out on the family? Three young boys. Emma shivered, unable to imagine a mother leaving her young sons. Maybe that was why Zach kept his feelings bottled up. "This is your tie to your past. And your ancestors were reliable or you wouldn't even be here now."

"Okay, so read through the letters. If they're not significant in the manner I've told you, toss them in this basket. Give me two or three of the most interesting and I'll read them and see if I can discover why I should keep them. I think when you get into it, you'll change your mind. I don't want to save letters that tell how the sod roof leaks or the butter churn broke or a wagon needs a new axle."

"I think all those things would be interesting." She tilted

her head to study him. "Family really isn't important to you, is it?"

Shaking his head again, he continued to smile. "Sure it is. I'm close with my brothers. That doesn't mean I want a bunch of old letters none of us will look at twice. They're musty, rotting and of no value." He leaned closer, so close she blinked and forgot the letters. He was only inches away and his mouth was inviting, conjuring up her curiosity about how he kissed.

"You're looking at me as if I just sprouted fangs."

She couldn't get her breath to answer him. His eyes narrowed a tiny fraction and his smile vanished. The look in his eyes changed, intensifying. Her pulse drummed, a steady rhythm that was loud in her ears. "I can't understand your attitude."

"Well, we're alike to a degree there—I can't understand yours," he said lightly. Again a thick silence fell and she couldn't think about letters or the subject of their conversation or even what he had just said. All she thought about was his mouth only a few inches from hers. Realizing the lust-charged moments were happening too often, she shifted and looked away, trying to catch her breath and get back on track.

She stood and stepped away, turning to glance back. "I'll get a pen and paper in case I need to take notes."

"I'll help sort some of these," he said, studying her with a smoldering look.

She wanted to thank him and tell him his help wasn't necessary. It definitely wasn't wanted. She needed to keep space between them. Big spaces. This wasn't a way to start a new assignment. She had no such attraction to men she worked with in Dallas, or anywhere else for that matter. Why was Zach Delaney so compelling?

It was certainly not because he was great fun or because they had so much in common. The only similarities they had were living in Texas at the same time in history and being connected in business to the same company. She had to get a grip on her reactions to him.

In every way he was not the man to be attracted to. Her boss, a world traveler, cared almost nothing for all the things that were important to her, family most of all.

Picking up a tablet, a pen and an empty wooden tray, she returned to her chair, pulling it slightly farther from his, but she couldn't move away because the basket and box to put the old documents in stood between them. She placed the wooden tray on the floor beside her chair.

When she opened the first envelope, a faint, musty odor emanated as she withdrew thin, yellowed pages covered in script. She read the letter from a man who wrote about frontier life, the "beeves" he had rounded up, and his plans to take them north to sell.

"Zach, if this is your great-great-grandfather, you should read this letter and see what kind of life he had," she said impulsively. "It's fascinating. He writes about a wagon train that came through and camped on his land. Is that this same ranch?"

"Same identical one," he remarked dryly, amusement in his expression.

"Listen—'their leader was Samuel Worthington,'" she read. "'Samuel asked if they could stay. He said they had traveled from Virginia and were going west. They had lost four people in their group. The four unfortunates drowned when they crossed a treacherous river after a rain. I gave them flour and beef so they had fresh supplies. Worry ran high about finding water in days to come so I drew Samuel a map of the land I know and showed him where to find water when they left my home. They have great expectations regarding their journey.'"

She lowered the letter to look at Zach. "I think that's wonderful. Don't you feel you know a little now about your great-

great-grandfather? He was kind and generous with those travelers. I would be so excited if these were letters written by my great-great-grandfather."

Zach smiled at her as if facing a bubbling child. "Okay. My great-great-grandfather was a nice guy who was good to people passing through. That knowledge really doesn't bring me closer because he lived years ago. It doesn't change the course of life. He was a rancher in the old days of the longhorns and he had a tough life. He worked hard and was successful and built on the land to pass that on to the next Delaney son. I don't need to wade through all his old letters about life on the plains in the early days."

She tilted her head to study Zach. She was both annoyed by his attitude and at the same time, mesmerized again by his enticing smile. "Do your brothers feel the way you do?"

"We haven't talked about it. I'll ask before I shred these. I would guess that Will might want them and Ryan will feel the same as I do."

She shook her head. "I can't understand your family. You must not have been close growing up."

He shrugged and shook his head. "When our mom walked out and divorced Dad, he sent us away to different boarding schools. I suppose he had some reason that seemed logical to him. We're close in some ways, but we were separated most of the time for a lot of years. It made a difference."

"That's truly dreadful."

He smiled again and her pulse fluttered. "Don't feel too sorry for us. Our father spent a lot of money on us."

"Money doesn't make up for some things."

"We could argue that one all night," he said, leaning back and placing his hands behind his head. The T-shirt stretched tautly across his broad shoulders and his muscles flexed. As he stretched out, she could not keep from taking one swift glance down the length of him. Feathers were holding a dance inside her. Everything quivered and lustful thoughts flashed in her mind. She realized silence was growing again and he watched her with a look of interest. Her mind raced for something, trying to think where the conversation had ended.

"Your great-great-grandfather—I wonder if any of you resemble him."

"You can see for yourself. In the last years of his life, someone painted his portrait. It hangs in the library." He put down his arms and leaned forward. "C'mon. I'll show you."

"You don't need to walk there now. I assume you're supposed to be staying off your foot."

"I can walk around," he said, getting the crutch. "I go to the doc next week and hope to get off this crutch. I'll still be in some kind of crazy medical shoe, but at least I may lose the crutch. C'mon. We'll go look at my old ancestor. I suspect he was a tough old bird. My dad was in his own way. I'm amazed he kept the letters. He didn't have a sentimental bone in his body until the last couple of years of his life. Or maybe since Caroline's birth. That little granddaughter changed him."

"That's family—little children wrap around your heart."

He gave her another big smile. "You're sentimental, Emma."

"I certainly am," she replied cheerfully.

He led the way into the library that held shelves of books from floor to ceiling. A huge portrait in a gilt frame hung above the fireplace and she looked at a stern-faced man with prominent cheekbones, straight gray hair, mustache and beard.

"I can't see that you look like him in any manner at all."

"No, I don't think so either." He gestured across the room. "Over there are portraits of my paternal grandfather and my dad."

She crossed the room. "You don't look like them either."

"If I have a resemblance to any forebears, it's my maternal grandfather. People say I look like him. I don't see it much myself except for the hair. No pictures of him here."

She returned to the fireplace to study the picture, thinking about the letter she had just read. "I'd think you'd want to read every letter in that box."

"I'm leaving that to you."

She turned to find him looking at her intently, a look that was hot and filled with desire, giving her heart palpitations. In spite of his injured foot, he looked strong and fit. Muscled arms, broad shoulders, flat belly. She stepped toward the door.

"We better go back and let me start reading them," she said, heading out of the room, aware that he fell into step beside her. "You said you have brothers. Do they have ranches around here or do all of you gather here?"

"Both. I'm not a rancher, so I've probably spent the least time here, but we were here plenty growing up. Plenty to suit me. I'm not a cowboy and not a rancher and my brothers can ride the horses. No, thanks. Will's ranch adjoins this one. Caroline loves it there, so they go quite often. Ryan's ranch is farther away. He's a cowboy through and through. Maybe it's because he spent too much time out here with Granddad."

"So will your brothers come here this week for Thanksgiving?" she asked, lost in thoughts about her own family's plans. She was taking a corn casserole and a dessert for everyone.

"No. Ryan's with a friend and Will and family are going to his home in Colorado."

"I can't imagine not being with family, but if you're with close friends or a close friend and family, that works," she said, glancing at him to see a grin. "You're staying out here alone, aren't you?" she blurted, aghast to think his brothers were going their own way and Zach had no plans. She started to invite him to her house, but she remembered that her predecessors had not lasted more than a few days at best on this job. If she invited him and then he dismissed her, it would be awkward.

"You're staring, Emma, and you have pity written all over your face," he said. "A new experience in my adult life. I can't remember anyone feeling sorry for me for any reason before."

Heat flushed her cheeks, and she forced a faint smile, hoping the pitying expression would vanish. They had stopped walking and were gazing at each other. He placed a hand on her shoulder lightly. The feathery touch with anyone else would have been impersonal, but with Zach, it was startling.

"It's my choice," he said. "Stop worrying."

"Zach, you can come to our house," she said, changing her mind about inviting him because it was sad to think of him being alone. "My family would be happy to have you. We've always invited friends who would have been alone on Thanksgiving, so I know my family will welcome you."

His grin widened. "Thank you for the very nice invitation, but I rarely notice holidays and don't celebrate them."

"Is this a religious thing?" she asked.

"No. It's a 'my thing.' As I mentioned, my brothers and I grew up in boarding schools, and sometimes we were left there on holidays because our folks were in Europe or heaven knows where," he explained. While he talked, she was acutely conscious of his hand still lightly on her shoulder. His gaze lowered to her lips and she could barely get her breath. It took an effort to pay attention to what he was saying. "None of us care much about holidays. Will is changing because of Caroline and his wife, Ava. I'm usually not in the country on Thanksgiving, but this year spending it alone here on the ranch is what I choose to do. Thank you anyway for your invitation," he said, turning to walk again.

Still physically too aware of him at her side, she strolled beside him. The hot attraction that obviously affected both of them tainted this job. If she got to stay, could she keep their relationship impersonal? She didn't think it would be much of a problem.

This loner, besides being her boss, was not the man to be attracted to. How could he possibly want to spend Thanksgiving alone? Even though he came from enormous wealth, he must have had a cold, lonely childhood. He seemed a solitary person who stayed out of the limelight and worked in distant places where he was unknown. She had seen pictures of his brother in the newspapers and in Texas magazines, but never Zach. He clearly kept a low profile.

As they entered the office, she parted with him and went to her desk to try to concentrate on work.

Over an hour later Zach received a phone call. She continued with her work, but by the time half an hour had passed and he had had three calls, she realized there must be a problem somewhere. He sat with his back to her, his feet propped up on a nearby computer table. The room was large enough that she couldn't hear exactly what he said. When she caught snatches of a few words, she guessed the language was German.

She worked until five to get everything done he had given her. He was still engrossed in phone calls when she shut off her computers and left the room. In her room, she spent over an hour reading and replying to emails from family and close friends before going to the kitchen for dinner.

Thinking of the loner in the office the entire time.

Lowering his feet Zach had swiveled in his chair and watched Emma leave the room, but his many phone calls had demanded his focus. Now, he glanced down at a letter on his desk she had typed. "I'll make the call at 8:00 in the morning your time and see if we can't get this worked out quickly," he said into the phone. "Right, Todd. I'll let you know. It's too late there to call anyone now." He replaced the receiver, glanced at his watch and sighed.

His cell phone indicated a call and he answered because it was Will.

"Can you talk now?" Will asked.

"Yes. We've had problems on a job and I've been on and off the phone for the past two hours."

"I've gotten a busy signal once. How's it going with the new secretary or is it too early to tell?"

Zach glanced again at the letter on the desk. "She's a good secretary. I don't think she'll last though. She's totally wound into her family in Dallas, which is several hours away from here, probably too far. They live, breathe, eat and stay together most of the time."

"Just say the word and I'll get someone else sent out."

"Not yet," Zach said, thinking about Emma's green eyes. "She's efficient. She's sentimental—you'd think these old letters were worth a million the way she views them. She can't keep from telling me I shouldn't shred them."

Will laughed. "Another one telling you what to do?"

"No, not like the first one. Emma's just so into families, she can't understand that I'm not treasuring every word from our ancestor. He was probably a tough old guy, even tougher than Dad. Why would I treasure every word he uttered?"

"You're a little more irreverent than most descendants would be. I'm a little curious about them, so I want to read a few and see what's in those boxes."

"You can have them, Will."

"No. You volunteered. You just need the right secretary to help you. Sounds to me as if you don't have a good fit yet and I should send someone."

"No. She's an excellent secretary. I've piled on the work and she's done it accurately and quickly. I don't want to dump her because she likes the box of old letters."

"True. At least she may really read them."

"Oh, she'll read them all right," Zach said, smiling as he remembered Emma poring over the one, her head bent. Her red hair held gold strands and a healthy shine. She had it pinned up, but strands spilled free and indicated long hair. Long hair and long legs.

"We'll leave in a few weeks for Colorado. If you change your mind and want to come along, or to spend Thanksgiving with us, let me know."

"Thanks, but I'm fine. My new secretary was a little shocked when she learned I'm spending the holiday alone. She invited me to join her family."

There was a moment's pause. "You two are getting to know each other."

"How can we avoid it? Remember, we work all day together and there are just the two of us here except when we see Rosie or Nigel."

"If you were Ryan, I'd ask if she's good-looking, but I've heard you talk too often about avoiding dating employees."

"You and I have agreed that's a complication no one needs in his life. I don't want any part of that kind of trouble," he said, thinking about her full lips and hearing a hollow sound to his words. "There's no need to bring emotions into the workplace—at least the kind of emotions that a relationship would create. Common sense says no way," he added, more to himself than Will.

"It worked with Ava."

"Yeah, but you hired her to work with Caroline—that was different from an office situation and you know it. It's not going to happen here. I get looks from her like I'm from another planet with my feelings about holidays, families and memorabilia."

Will laughed. "I can imagine that one. There are times

you get those looks from me. Ryan is the baby brother and he accepts whatever we do."

"Yeah. I do get those looks from you, but I don't know why because you're like me about sentiment. Or at least you were until Ava and Caroline. Especially Caroline. They've mellowed you until I hardly know you."

"You ought to try it sometime," Will answered lightly. "I'll talk to you before we leave for Colorado."

"Sure, Will. Thanks for the invitation. Tell Ava I said thanks." Zach ended the call and swung his chair around to look out the window without really seeing anything outside. Envisioning Emma, he wanted to be with her again. He had just blown the sensible course. He should have let Will send out another secretary, yet how could he get rid of Emma when her secretarial skills were excellent and she wanted the job? He couldn't send her back because of the steamy chemistry between them.

"Keep it strictly business," he whispered, lecturing himself. Stay away from her except when working. Don't share lunches or dinners or anything else outside of the office and work. Willpower. Resoluteness.

Thinking of the problems on the project in Maine, the buildings the company had bought and intended to replace with one large building, a parking garage and a landscaped area, he tossed down a pen and returned to thinking about Emma. He wanted to have dinner with her, but hadn't he just resolved to avoid her? He didn't want to get involved with an employee, especially a sentimental homebody who could barely leave her family and especially an employee living under the same roof with him. It could complicate his life beyond measure to have her expect some kind of commitment from him and to have rumors flying at the office. He didn't want tears and a scene when he told her goodbye. Thoughts of any of those things gave him chills.

She didn't look like a sentimental homebody, at least his idea of one. Her full red lips, the mass of red hair that was caught up on her head hinted at a wild, party-loving woman. The reactions she had to just a look from him implied a sensuous, responsive lover.

"Damn," he said aloud. Taking a deep breath, he yanked papers in front of him.

Wiping his brow, he leaned over his desk and tried to concentrate on tasks at hand. After two minutes he shoved aside papers and stood. He should send her away, get her out of his life, but the chemistry he wanted to avoid made it impossible to think about giving her up. No matter what he'd just told himself, he wanted to be with Emma—what could a dinner hurt?

With a glance at his watch, he saw he had probably already missed her and a hot dinner from Rosie. Annoyed he would have to eat alone, he headed to the kitchen, hoping Emma was still there.

His disappointment when she wasn't bothered him even more than her absence. Since when had he started to look forward to being with her so much?

Three

The evening was quiet and after dinner Emma stayed in her room. She had eaten alone, experiencing a mix of relief and disappointment that Zach hadn't appeared. It was wiser that he had not eaten with her. The less they socialized, the better, even though there was a part of her that wanted to see him.

On Friday, he appeared wrapped in business and he kept his distance. That afternoon, he told her to leave at one so she could get to Dallas ahead of the traffic.

"Thanks," she replied, smiling broadly. "I'll accept that offer." Shutting down her computer, she was on the road away from the ranch twenty minutes later. They had gotten through the first week, so she must have the job. They also had kept a distance between them. He had been professional, quiet, but there was no way she could feel she had imagined the chemistry simmering just below the surface. Any time they locked gazes, it flared to life, scalding, filled with temptation, an unmistakable attraction.

Now she could believe rumors she had always heard that

he never dated employees, never getting emotionally entangled with anyone on his staff, never even in the most casual way. She intended to keep that professional, remote relationship with him and this job would be a plus on her resume.

If she could just keep from dreaming about him at night—with a sigh, she concentrated on her driving and tried to stop thinking about Zach Delaney. Instead, she reflected on the fun she always had at home with the family and with her nieces and nephews.

Monday when she returned to work, she dressed in jeans, a T-shirt sprinkled with bling, and sneakers. Zach had said jeans were fine and that's what he had worn every workday. Even so, she felt slightly self-conscious when she entered the office.

He was already there and looked up, giving her a thorough glance.

"You said jeans are acceptable," she stated.

"Jeans are great," he said in a tone that conveyed a more personal response. "Yours look terrific," he added, confirming what she thought.

"Thank you," she answered, sitting behind her desk and starting to work.

"This afternoon I'm going to Dallas to see my doctor. Hopefully, I can toss this crutch when I come home."

"You can return to your traveling?"

"How I wish. No. He's already told me that I'll have to wear this and continue to stay off my foot except to get around the house. Still, it'll be an improvement."

"Sure," she replied.

He returned to whatever he had been doing and they worked quietly the rest of the morning. When she left for lunch, he stayed in the office. In the afternoon, she read more Delaney letters, occasionally glancing at the great-great-grandson, continuing to wonder how he could care so little about his history.

The next morning the crutch had disappeared. Zach remained professional and slightly remote. She noticed he hobbled around and kept his foot elevated when he was seated.

On Thursday afternoon she dug inside one of the open boxes of memorabilia and picked up a small box and opened it. Yellowed paper was inside and when she pushed the paper away, she gasped when she discovered a beautiful pocket watch.

"Zach, look at this," she said, turning to take the box to him. He stood by a file cabinet. Today his T-shirt was navy, tight and short-sleeved, revealing firm muscles and a lean, fit body. Dark curls fell on his forehead. As he came around his desk, she handed him the box. Their fingers brushed, sending ripples radiating from the contact.

"This is beautiful," she said. She looked up from the watch, meeting his gaze, ensnared, while tension increased between them. She could barely get her breath. It was obvious he felt something as he focused on her. His attention lowered to her mouth. Her lips parted, tingled while her imagination ran riot. How long before he kissed her?

"Zach," she whispered, intending to break the spell, but she forgot what she had been about to say. He shifted, a slight closing of the space between them. His hand barely touched her waist as he leaned closer. She couldn't keep from glancing at his mouth and then back into crystal blue that held flames of desire.

The air heated, enveloped her, and the moment his mouth touched hers, she closed her eyes. His lips were warm, firm, a dangerous temptation. Her insides knotted, dropping into free fall. Protests vanished before being spoken. Her breath was gone. His lips settled, opened her mouth.

His arm went around her waist tightly, holding her close against his hard body.

She spun away, carried on his kiss. A dream kiss, only it was real, intensifying longing, burning with the impression of a brand that would last. Her hands went to his arms, resting lightly on hard, sculpted muscles.

As his tongue probed and teased, her heart pounded. Passion swamped her caution. She wrapped her arm around his neck and kissed him in return. Standing on tiptoe, she poured herself into her kiss. His arm tightened and he leaned over her, kissing her hard and possessively, making her light-headed. She wound her fingers in his hair as she kissed him, barely aware he was tangling his hand in her own hair.

It was Zach Delaney she kissed wildly. The reminder was dim, but gradually stirred prudence. "Zach," she whispered, looking up at him. Her heart thudded because the look in his eyes scalded, sending its heat to burn her. His mouth was red from kisses, his eyes half closed. His expression held stormy hunger.

"Emma, you like this," he whispered, winding his hand in her hair behind her head, pulling her head closer again.

She wrapped both arms around his neck, holding him and kissing him back. Her heart raced as she gave vent again to desires that had smoldered since she met him.

Their breathing grew harsh while he slipped his hand down her back to her waist.

Again, she grasped at control and raised her head. "I wasn't going to do this."

"I've wanted to since the first minute I saw you," he declared in a rasp. His blue eyes darkened, a sensual, hot look that melted her and made her want to reach for him again.

Instead, she stepped away. "I came over here for a reason," she whispered, unable to get her voice. Her gaze was still locked with his and he looked as surprised as she felt.

His kisses had shaken her. Desire was a white-hot flame. She wanted him in a manner she had never experienced before and the attraction shook her even more than that first day she had met him.

"Zach, I should quit this job right now," she whispered. He gave her a startled look and she could feel her face flush.

"Over a few meaningless kisses?" he asked.

She didn't want to answer him. He stood there looking at her in that sharp manner he had while she struggled to get the right words.

"The kisses—" She paused. She didn't want to admit more to him, but he wanted an answer. "Kisses weren't like others. This was different. We have something—" She waved her hands helplessly.

He inhaled, drawing deeply, his chest expanding as longing flared again in his eyes.

"Common sense tells me to walk away now," she whispered. "You have a reputation for never going out with an employee."

"I never have," he answered. "That doesn't mean I can't."

"That wasn't what I wanted to hear. I want this job."

"We'll do something," he replied, his voice raspy and quiet. "Don't quit. We'll try to stick to work."

She shook her head, looking at his mouth and feeling her pulse speed as they talked. "I can't. I'm quitting. I don't think you need more notice than that. You can find a wonderful, efficient secretary soon enough."

"No," he replied, jamming his hands into his pockets while a muscle worked in his jaw. "I'll double your salary and you stay."

"Double my salary?" she repeated, shaking her head.

"You don't need to pack and go because we kissed. We're adults. If we kiss, it's not that big a deal. There's nothing between us—no history, no ties. If you don't want to get involved, we can both exercise control. With my offer, you'll earn twice as much. Don't walk out on that over a few casual kisses."

Exasperated and stung over his dismissal of kisses that had shaken her, she stared at him. "There's no relationship between us. There's not even any emotional bond. We're practically strangers. But those kisses weren't casual to my way of thinking," she whispered.

She stepped close, put her arm around his neck and placed her mouth on his, kissing him with all the heat and fury she felt over his dismissive attitude. After one second that probably was his surprise holding him immobile, his arm banded her waist and he returned her kiss. Fully. He pressed against her, his tongue going deep while she kissed him, trying to set him on fire. In seconds she broke off the kiss and looked up with satisfaction.

"I'd say your body's reaction isn't casual."

With his eyes darkened, his breathing was ragged. She had felt the hard throb of manhood against her and his heart pounding.

"Okay. Kisses damn well aren't casual, but I'm trying to get us back there," he said. A muscle worked in his jaw. When his attention focused on her mouth, she stepped back.

"Do you still want to double my salary—or do you want me to go?"

"I'll double your salary," he replied, grinding out the words.

"You'll double my salary to get me to continue as your secretary. You know I can't turn that down."

"I hope not. You're a good secretary," he answered in a more normal tone of voice.

Inhaling deeply, she promised herself she would exercise better control.

"Against good judgment, I'll stay. I can't say no. I need the money for my college plans."

"That's settled." They stared at each other until she realized what she was doing.

"I came over here for something," she said, feeling foolish, struggling against stepping into his arms again, yet determined to regain her composure. She looked around and spotted the small box on the corner of Zach's desk. She retrieved the box, clinging to it as if it were a lifeline.

"Look at this."

He was still gazing at her and his blue eyes had darkened again. His expression no longer appeared as impersonal. Her heart drummed while her lips tingled. The urge to reach for him tormented her. With a deep breath he looked down, picked up the watch and turned it in his hand.

"This is a find," he said, his voice deep, becoming hoarse, and she was certain the husky tone was not caused by the watch he held. "This watch is worth going through the box of stuff." Turning it in his hand, he studied the gold back. "These are my great-great-grandfather's initials," Zach said, extending it to her and she looked down, stepping closer to gaze at the watch, which she had already studied. "Warner Irwin Delaney," Zach read. "This we'll keep, thank you, Emma."

"It's a beautiful pocket watch. I'm glad you're keeping it. I'll research to find one like it to pinpoint how old it is. For the moment, I'll see what else I can find."

"I'll help for a while," he said. "The watch makes poking around in all the old stuff more interesting."

She returned to her chair, mindful of him pulling one up nearby. The awareness of him was sharp, intense and disturbed her concentration. She wanted to take a long look at him, but she didn't want to get caught studying him.

She tried to focus on a letter and realized her concentration was on Zach only. His kisses had been fantastic, setting her on fire in a blaze that still burned. She wanted more kisses, wanted to dance and flirt and make love—reactions that shocked her. Ones she had never experienced before in this manner. The men in her life had always been friends, family-oriented guys she had been comfortable with. Never anyone she had been very serious about either. Why did he hold such appeal for her?

She could barely think about the jump in salary for thinking about the man. Any other time in her life she would have been overjoyed at the increase in pay, but now it kept slipping her mind, replaced by thoughts about Zach.

The wise thing to do would be to pack and go no matter what salary he offered. She couldn't do it. The salary was important. College—and her classes on the internet—was expensive. This boost in salary filled a great need. Without thinking, she glanced at him. He was studying her openly and she felt her face flush as they looked into each other's eyes.

The glance had the same effect as a touch.

They worked in silence. As he methodically shoved aside letters, she realized he was looking for more things like the watch. She became absorbed in her reading.

"I feel as if I know part of your family," she said, folding a letter. "After the Civil War, Warner Delaney started building this ranch house. He brought his family out here. Earlier, he met a woman in Kansas City and is going to ask her to marry him."

"My great-great-grandmother? Her name was Tabitha, I think."

They heard a commotion in the hall and a tall man in Western boots, jeans, a navy sweater and a Stetson entered the room. He held the hand of a little black-haired girl who smiled broadly at Zach and then glanced shyly at Emma.

"Will. Caroline. How's my prettiest and favorite niece?" Zach asked, lifting her up and holding her to kiss her cheek.

She laughed and giggled as he set her on her feet. "Hey, Will. Where's Ava?"

"Stopped to talk to Rosie and leave Muffy with her. Muffy is a dog," he explained, glancing at Emma.

"Emma, this is my niece, Caroline, and my brother Will Delaney. Ah, here is Ava. Emma, meet Ava Delaney. This is Emma Hillman, my secretary."

As she shook hands with the adults, Emma gazed into warm welcoming green eyes of a sandy-haired blonde. Caroline, holding a small brown bear, could not stop smiling.

"C'mon, let's go into the family room where it's more comfortable and Caroline has things to play with while we talk," Zach suggested.

Will smiled. "We were on our way back from Dallas and stopped for a few minutes to see about you."

"Zach, all of you go ahead," Emma said. "I can stay in here. I don't want to intrude—"

"C'mon, Emma, or we'll all have to sit in here on these hard chairs," Zach said with a shake of his head.

"Please join us," Ava said. "Don't leave Caroline and me alone with these two."

Emma smiled and nodded, knowing Ava was teasing and it was nice that they would include her. Will was strikingly handsome without the ruggedness of Zach. She would not have picked them out of a crowd as brothers because Will's dark eyes were nothing like Zach's vivid blue ones. Their facial structure was as different as their hair.

"Well, the offer is still open for you to have Thanksgiving with us," Will said.

"Thanks. I'll still stay here. You know Rosie will cook a big turkey."

"You should join us, Zach," Ava said. "The snow will be beautiful and we'll have a great time."

"Thanks, Ava. I'll do fine here," he replied without glancing at Emma.

When they entered the family room, Emma mulled over his turning down the offer for Thanksgiving. How could he turn down Will and stay alone on the isolated ranch? She would never understand how Zach could possibly avoid being lonely and miserable. Was this all a carryover from childhood hurts, seeking isolation because it was a shield against times he had been left alone and deeply disappointed?

"So how are you doing with the memorabilia?" Will asked.

"I want to show you what Emma found in that box of old letters. I'll put it with anything else of value we find."

"I'll get it," Emma said. "You talk to your family." Before Zach could protest she hurried from the room. In minutes she returned to hand the box to Zach.

As she sat down, he took the watch and held it up. "Look at this."

"That looks like a fine watch and something nice to keep since it belonged to a Delaney ancestor," Will said. Zach carried it to show it to Ava and Caroline who crowded around them. Will got up to join them.

"If this isn't just like Dad," Zach said. "I'll bet he found the watch and stuck it back in with the letters to let us find it."

"I don't know. I had the feeling he had never gone through that stuff before," Will remarked.

"Maybe not. No telling what else I'll find. Or Emma will find."

"I hear you're the one reading the letters," Will said, smiling at her.

"Yes, most of them."

"She's far more interested and views them as sacred chunks of our family history and Texas history, but I don't have quite the same respect for them."

The men returned to their seats and Zach placed the watch in the box on a table.

Emma's mystification about Zach's solitary way of life grew as she listened to the brothers and realized they were close and enjoyed each other's company. And Zach was good with Caroline. When Caroline walked over to him, he lifted her to his lap and focused his attention on her.

Shortly she climbed down and went to get into Will's lap and turn his face so he looked at her. She whispered in his ear.

"Yes, we will right now," Will said, looking at Zach. "Caroline has some family news to tell you."

Caroline couldn't sit still and had a big smile. She climbed down and ran to Zach to stand at his knee. She gave another shy glance at Emma and Emma suddenly suspected she was interrupting a family moment. She wanted to leave them to themselves, but she was afraid that would be even more disruptive, so she sat quietly.

Caroline's big smile broadened. "Uncle Zach, I'm going to become a big sister."

"You are!" Zach looked over her head at his brother. "Congratulations!"

"It's early, but we told Caroline because we want to do some remodeling and build a nursery, not only in Dallas, but at my ranch here and in Colorado."

"That is great news, Caroline," Zach said. "Wow! You'll be a big sister and I'll be an uncle again."

She laughed and turned in a circle.

Zach crossed the room to hug Ava lightly. "Congratulations. That's wonderful."

"We think so," she said, her eyes sparkling. She looked radiant as she glanced at her husband and exchanged a look with him. They were obviously so much in love Emma felt slightly envious. Ava reached out to hug Caroline and Will picked her up, holding her while she wrapped her arm around his neck. "We're thrilled," Ava added.

"Congratulations to all of you," Emma said. "You have wonderful news." She looked at Caroline. "Caroline, you'll have lots of fun with your little brother or sister."

Caroline nodded and smiled.

"We're excited," Will said. "And we'll let you both go back to work. We need to get to the ranch. Caroline has been promised to get to ride her horse."

"It's been nice to meet you," Ava said to Emma. "We're glad you're working here. Zach needs help with all the old papers."

"Just keep him from shredding them," Will remarked dryly.

"I find them fascinating," Emma said. "I'm beginning to feel as if I knew Warner Delaney. It was so nice to meet all three of you and it was good of you to include me in your family moment."

"Do you think my unsentimental brother would care who he shares family news with?" Will remarked dryly, grinning at Zach.

As they left the room, Emma stayed back and returned to her desk. She didn't go back to work, but sat staring into space, thinking about Zach. What a waste of someone's life to take away the fabulous moments shared with family and friends. How could he turn down Ava's invitation to spend Thanksgiving with Will and his family? Instead, he would sit in isolation at home on the ranch—a sad choice.

She sat by the box to read a letter, finally concentrating on her work.

When Zach returned, her pulse jumped. He was off-limits, a danger to her peace of mind because her volatile reactions to him had not dwindled even a degree.

"I enjoyed meeting your family. They're great and that's fantastic news they shared."

"My brother amazes me. He'd been as opposed to marriage as any of us, yet he is so in love with Ava, it's ridiculous. And he's great with Caroline. None of us have ever been around children and to become her guardian was really tough for him."

"Well, from what little I saw, Caroline is a very happy little girl."

"Ava and Will have been terrific for her. Ava was the one who suggested Muffy, a little puff of a dog that brought Caroline out of her grief from losing her father more than anything or anybody else."

"Did I hear her call him 'Daddy Two'?"

He nodded. "We've gotten used to that. Will is her second dad since her blood father died and I think she wanted a mom and dad. You noticed she calls Ava Mom?"

"Yes, I did. They seem incredibly happy. How could you not want to be with them for Thanksgiving?"

"I'm my own company. I get along fine."

She shook her head. "Amazing," she said, reaching for another letter. "Do all of you get together for Christmas?"

He gave her a lazy smile and she guessed his answer. As shocked as she was over Thanksgiving, her surprise was greater this time. "You're spending Christmas here alone? You can't do that."

"Of course I can," he replied with laughter in his voice.

"I'd think all of you would gather here since this is the family ranch. Isn't this where you had Christmas celebrations when you were growing up?"

"Maybe twice when Granddad lived here. Never, after he was gone. My mother hated the ranch. Any ranch. If we celebrated together, it was in Dallas. After Mom walked, we didn't even come home for Christmas."

"Zach—"

His jaw firmed and an eyebrow arched. She realized she should stop talking about his personal life. She shrugged and turned away, going back to work without saying anything else. He did the same and she fought the urge to stare at him. How could he spend Christmas all alone? She couldn't imagine anyone doing that through choice.

They worked for the next hour and Zach stood, stretching again.

"Enough of this," he said. "Let's break. I'll go lift weights and do what I can do without involving my foot. We have treadmills or the track. Or an exercise bicycle. Nigel will be there because if any of us lift weights, he appears. He doesn't want us alone if we're working out with weights. That's a long-standing rule and he walks around the track, which is probably good for him. If you prefer, you can sit in the family room and have a lemonade or a cup of hot tea or anything else you want."

"Enough choices," she said, putting down a letter. "I'll change quickly and get on a treadmill. I'd rather sit on the terrace after work."

"Good enough. See you in the gym."

She left him, hurrying upstairs to change.

If only Zach felt about holidays the way Nigel felt about working out. That one shouldn't go it alone.

With Nigel walking on the indoor track, Zach hoisted a bar, lifting it high and lowering it slowly when he saw Emma enter the gym. He set the bar in place and wiped his forehead with a towel while watching her. She wore blue shorts and a blue T-shirt that revealed lush curves, a tiny waist and heart-stopping long legs.

She smiled and waved, going to a treadmill to start it.

He should have let her go back to Dallas. She was a great

secretary, as well as pure trouble. Their kisses were dynamite and the last kiss—when she wanted to prove their kisses couldn't be called casual—had ignited fires that still blazed. Her sudden kiss had shocked and electrified him. It had been a spunky, devil-may-care, I'll-show-you challenge that he would never have expected from her. If he could have burned to cinders from a kiss, he would have with that one. His reaction had definitely not been casual and she knew it. She had more than proven her point. She had driven it home with a wrecking ball.

She had a backbone and he suspected she was as strong-willed as he. Not his kind of woman in any manner except physically. She had been aghast over his plans for a solitary Christmas. He would bet the ranch he hadn't heard the last on that one. She would want to take him home with her for Christmas. The whole thing would be humorous and he could ignore it easily, except she was getting to him in a manner he hadn't thought possible. The hot kisses he had labeled "casual" blasted his peaceful life with constant fantasies about holding her and making love to her.

He wasn't concentrating well on his work. It took real effort to avoid eating lunch or dinner with her. He had offered this exercise time when he should have left the office, worked out with only Nigel and let her continue with her secretarial duties. Common sense said to either practice more self-control or get rid of her.

His lusty body just wanted to seduce her.

Frustrated, he returned to working out.

At one point he paused, glancing over to see Emma running on the treadmill. She was going at good clip, had an easy stride and looked as if she had done this before. She looked fit and tempting. The T-shirt clung, the blue darker where it was damp with perspiration. She had a sexy bounce as she ran and her long legs were as shapely as he had imagined.

With a groan, he returned to his weights. When he stopped, she had finished and had a towel around her neck as she stood talking to Nigel. He smiled, glancing at Zach who waved Nigel away as a signal he was leaving the gym. Since Zach was finished, Nigel headed for the door and, without a glance, Emma followed close behind.

Zach hung behind. He hobbled out of the gym, wanting his foot to heal so he could get back to normal. He went to shower, wrapping his foot in a plastic boot and keeping it out of the shower to avoid getting it wet.

He constantly thought about taking her out when his foot healed and taking her to bed even sooner. If he didn't want to complicate his life, that would not happen. She definitely would have her heart in an affair, something he had always avoided. In spite of what he knew he should refrain from doing, he could not keep from wanting to be with her and fantasizing about it.

Heat climbed, erotic images of Emma in his arms tormenting him. She was getting to him in ways no other woman ever had. So far, her resistance had been almost nil until he offered to double her salary. He suspected they both had acted impulsively. He couldn't bear the thought of losing his excellent secretary and to be truthful to himself, he just didn't want her to go out of his life yet. She hadn't been able to resist because she was trying to save money to finish her college courses. Had part of her wanted to stay because of the attraction?

Out of the shower, he decided not to go back to the office. He could work somewhere else in the house the rest of the day and keep space between them.

He ate dinner alone as he had most nights of his adult life. He had had affairs, but they had usually been brief, casual, on-and-off relationships. His job added to his solitary life. Tonight, he was restless, still drowning in thoughts of Emma. Finally, he had enough of his own company and went to look for her, hoping she had not shut herself in her room for the night.

But she had. He had to remember it was for the best.

Four

Monday, they returned to their regular work routine. Late that day local meteorologists began to warn of a large, early storm from the west predicted to reach Texas on Thursday or Friday. Each day they checked the weather, Emma surprised that Zach ate lunch and dinner with her, flirting, friendly and heightening desire with every encounter.

By Thursday, pictures were coming in from the west of all the snow. "We're ready for the storm, here at the ranch," Zach told Emma. "We have supplies of every sort and enough food for weeks. I think you're stuck, Emma, unless you want to take off work and head to Dallas this afternoon." They both listened as the TV weatherman showed a massive storm dumping twelve inches of snow in the mountains in New Mexico and blanketing Interstate 40, closing it down.

"Now they're predicting it'll come in here Friday," Zach repeated. "If you beat the storm home, you'll be stuck there, which is fine if you want to do that."

"I can miss one weekend at home," she said. "Actually, I

can go ahead and work and get more of the letters read and go through things."

"If you're sure. I've told Nigel and Rosie the same thing. Rosie's cooking up a storm herself, but if we get what they're predicting, neither of them will come in. I've told them to stay home."

"I'll stay here, Zach. I don't want to get caught in bad weather. From what they're predicting, it will come and go and be clear for me to go home for Thanksgiving next week."

"If you decide to stay, I'll pay you overtime."

"That isn't necessary. I'm happy to be out of the storm. Mom's already called worrying about me."

"Call her so she can stop worrying."

"Thanks, Zach."

"I wish I could take you out dancing Saturday night, but that's out because of the storm and my foot. We can have a steak dinner—I'll cook. We can have our own party here."

She laughed. "Sounds great, but you don't have to do that."

His blue eyes held a lusty darkness and his voice lowered. "I want to. Even though it might not be the wisest thing for either one of us, a cozy evening in front of a fire while it snows outside sounds fun. Now I can't wait for the first flakes to fall."

Shaking her head, she smiled at him while her insides fluttered. Saturday night with Zach would not be the same as working together in a spacious office. "In the meantime, let's go back to work," she said, pulling her chair close to the open box of letters.

She read more letters—some were by his great-grandfather, most by his great-great-grandfather, all of them mixed together. She had trays she would place them in according to generation. She had made trays labeled by dates, water rights, and "boundary disputes." She tried to sort them all the ways that would be helpful. If she had time before the job ended, she would put them in chronological order.

She had read five letters when she shoved her hand into the box to get more and felt a hard lump beneath the letters. She moved them carefully, placing them to one side in the box, and found two objects wrapped in cloth. "Zach, there are some things in this box. They're wrapped in rags." She carefully continued to remove letters as he crossed the room. He bent over to plunge his hand in.

"Zach, be careful with the letters."

"Ah, Emma, these letters are not priceless heirlooms."

"They may be to some of your family."

"I'll be damned," he said, grasping something wrapped in cloth and pulling it out of the box. He tossed away the rags. "This is a Colt. It's a beauty." He checked to see if it was loaded—it wasn't. "This is fantastic. You said there were two things."

He placed the Colt on an empty chair and turned to reach into the box to withdraw the other object wrapped in cloth.

"It's a rifle," he said, unwrapping strips of rags that had yellowed with age. Zach tossed them into a trash basket and held the rifle in his hands, checking to be certain it was not loaded. "It's a Henry. I'll say my ancestors knew their weapons. A Colt revolver and a Henry rifle." He raised it to aim toward the patio. "This is a find. Why would anyone stick these in with a bunch of letters? If I had been the only descendant, I would have pitched the boxes and never given them another thought."

"Well, aren't we all glad keeping the heirlooms was not left to you alone," she said sweetly and he grinned.

"The Henry was a repeating rifle that came out about the time the Civil War began. This is fabulous," he said, running his hand over it. "Now I can feel a tie with my ancestors with these two weapons. Ryan is going to love both of these. So will Will."

"You make it sound as if all of you are gun-toting cowboys, which I know is not the case. Far from it. You're a man of cities."

"I still love this. It's a beaut and Will and Ryan are going to love it. Garrett—he's a family friend—won't be so wound up over it, I don't think. He's the city person, which makes it funny that Dad willed this ranch to Garrett and not to any of his sons. It's also why Garrett is in no rush to claim it. This Henry is something."

She picked up an envelope. "If you'll excuse me, you can go drool over your guns while I read." She withdrew a letter. "Want me to read aloud?"

"I don't think so, thank you," he said, smiling. He picked up the revolver and carried a weapon in each hand back to place them on his desk. As soon as he sat, he called Will to tell him about the latest find.

They talked at length before he told Will goodbye and then called Ryan to tell him about the revolver and the rifle. She shook her head and bent over the latest letter, still thinking the letters were the real treasure.

It was an hour before he finished talking to both brothers. With his hands on his hips, he looked at the boxes. "Some of the boxes have objects of value. There's one more box. I wonder if each one will hold its own treasure. I'll start looking through this box," he said, sitting down and pulling a box close. He took out a bunch of letters and put them on the floor.

"These letters are not packed away in any apparent order," she said. "Put the letters in this box because it's almost empty now. You'll tear them up, dumping them out like that. I'll help you."

"The precious letters. I'll take more care," he said, and began to shift them to the box she had beside her. When his box was three-fourths empty, hers had been filled. He bent over his box and felt around. "I don't feel anything, except letters."

"Try reading a few," she suggested.

He frowned slightly and picked up a letter to skim over it. "Nothing," he said, tossing it into the discard box and taking another. After an hour, Zach was clearly tired of his fruitless search. "I can't find anything worth keeping."

"Maybe I *should* get in the car and go home now. It's sort of tempting fate to stay."

"You made a decision to stay. If you were going you should have left hours ago. You made your decision, so stick with it. If you leave now, you could get caught if the storm comes in early. You'd be in the snow in the dark. Not a good combination. Just stay."

Stay, she'd have to.

On Friday the storm arrived as predicted, the first big flakes falling late morning. Emma went to the window. "Zach, this is beautiful. I have to go outside to look." She left the office and went out the back to the patio to stand and watch huge flakes swirling and tumbling to earth. She stuck out her tongue, letting an icy flake melt in her mouth. She also held up her palm, watching for the briefest second as a beautiful flake hit her and then transformed into a drop of icy water.

In seconds she heard the door and glanced around to see Zach hurrying outside with a blanket tossed around his shoulders.

"I thought you might be cold," he said, shaking it so it was around her and over her head as well as covering him. With his arm around her shoulders, he held the blanket in place. Shivering, she pressed closer, relishing the cozy warmth of Zach beside her.

"Isn't this beautiful! I love the snow. It would be fun to have a white Christmas if it didn't keep people from their families."

"Your family will probably build snow forts and snow-men this weekend."

She smiled. "Our yard will be filled with snow sculptures, bunnies, snow dogs, forts, tons of snowballs, snowmen. Our local paper came out one year and took pictures. We have sleds and everyone will go sledding if they can."

"I guess in their own way, your family really enjoys life."

"In the best way possible, they enjoy life," she said, look-ing up at him. "Okay, I'm ready to go back in." She tossed the blanket over his shoulder and dashed for the back door, feeling her cascade of hair swing as she ran.

Inside she stomped her feet to get the snow off and wiped her shoes on the mat. Zach appeared and did the same, best he could with his still-injured foot. "Want coffee, tea or hot chocolate to take back to the office?"

"Sure, hot chocolate."

In minutes she had a mug and was at her desk, concen-trating on work and trying to forget about Zach and how he had looked with big snowflakes in his thick brown hair and on his eyelashes.

"Emma," Zach interrupted her during the afternoon. "Look outside now."

She had been concentrating on work and forgotten the snow. The wind had picked up and when she glanced out, she gasped.

Snow was "falling" horizontally and the entire world was white. Everything in sight was buried in snow except the tall trees that were dark shadows as a blizzard raged.

"I didn't notice. Oh, my word. I'm glad I didn't get caught out in that." She walked to the window and heard him coming to join her. Once again he draped his arm lightly across her shoulders.

"Tomorrow night, we'll have our fancy steak dinners. Tonight it will be informal and cozy with Rosie's Texas chili and homemade tamales. We can curl up by the fire and watch a movie or play chess or whatever you want to do. I can think of a few other possibilities," he added in a huskier tone.

"Chess and a movie sound perfect. Forget the other possibilities. Stop flirting."

"We'll see what the evening brings," he said, caressing her arm lightly. "And at the moment, I can't resist flirting."

"Try," she said, taking a deep breath. She looked outside again, shivering just because the storm looked icy and hazardous. Once again she was thankful she wasn't traveling. "I'm glad Rosie and Nigel are off. No one should be out in this. What about your livestock?"

"That's who is out there fighting the elements and working—the cowboys who take care of that livestock at times like this. Just hope there's nothing unusual happening with any of the stock."

She nodded. "I'll go back to work. I've received a text from Mom and all my family is home now except those who work close and they'll be home soon. Some businesses have closed early."

"Our Dallas office closed two hours ago. I have a policy with my CEO and with the vice presidents—whoever is in charge when I'm away—I don't want anyone caught in this getting home. They've all had time to go home."

"That's nice, Zach," she said as she returned to her desk.

They worked until five when Zach stood and stretched. "Time to quit, Emma. Actually past time to stop."

"We're out of the storm and I don't mind continuing."

"I mind. Come on—knock off and we'll meet back down here for a drink and then dinner. Want to meet here at six?"

"Sure," she said, shutting down her computer while he turned and left the room. She closed up and went to her room to shower and change. Dressing in a bright red sweater and matching slacks, she brushed her hair and tied it behind her head with a scarf.

Eagerly, she went downstairs to search for him. She followed enticing smells to the kitchen and found Zach stirring a steaming pot. He put the lid back in place. The minute she saw him, she forgot dinner. He wore a bulky navy sweater that made his shoulders appear broader than ever, and faded jeans that emphasized his narrow hips and long legs. He was in the health shoe and his loafer. Tangled curls were in their usual disarray. Zach's eyes drifted slowly over her, an intense study that had the same results as a caress. Then his gaze locked with hers and her mouth went dry. She was held mesmerized while her heart became a drumbeat that she was certain he could hear. Captured by his look, she remained still while he stopped stirring and set aside the spoon to saunter toward her.

Her heart thudded as she tingled in a growing temptation. "Zach," she whispered, uncertain if she protested or invited because she wanted to do both.

He reached for her, drawing her to him to kiss her.

Her stomach lurched while longing blazed. His passionate kiss demanded her response. Trembling, she returned his kisses, her tongue stroking his and going deep, exploring and tasting. He smelled of mint and deep woods. His lean body was hard planes against her softness, building her excitement.

Zach reached beneath her sweater, sliding his hand up to flick free her bra and then cup her breast as his thumb stroked her. Pleasure fluttered over her nerves and tickled her insides while she clung tightly to him. Finally, she looked up at him.

"Zach, this is exactly what I intended to avoid."

"So did I," he whispered. "It's impossible. Just plain, downright impossible," he added before kissing her.

Moaning with pleasure again, she twisted against him. He was aroused, ready to love. He unfastened her slacks, pushing them off, and they tumbled around her ankles. Kicking off her shoes, she stepped out of them.

Tearing herself away from his kiss, she gasped. "Zach, we're crossing a line."

"I told you, we crossed that line the day you walked into my office for this job. This was inevitable."

"So ill matched and not what I want," she said, looking into eyes that had darkened to a cobalt blue. "A total disaster."

"You want this with all your being. You can't stop," he whispered. His mouth ended her argument. Knowing he was right, she wanted him and she wasn't inclined to stop. She kissed him even though she'd declared their lovemaking a disaster and meant every word.

With deliberation he held her away to look at her and she stepped out of her pooled slacks. He pulled free her red sweater and her unfastened lacy bra went with it. His seductive gaze inched slowly over her, made her pulse race.

"You're beautiful," he whispered, caressing her breasts. Pausing, he tossed away his sweater and she inhaled deeply at the sight of his chest that tapered to a flat washboard belly ridged with muscles.

His hands rested on her hips as his gaze dallied over her, taking in the sight with measured thoroughness. "You're gorgeous," he whispered hoarsely. "You take my breath."

She tingled beneath his sensual perusal. Wherever his gaze drifted, she reacted as if it were his fingers instead of eyes that trailed over her.

He untied her hair, pulling loose the delicate silk scarf, letting the free end slip down in a feathery whisper over her breast before he let go and the scarf fluttered away.

"Your hair is meant for a man's fingers. I've thought that since I saw you get out of your car the first day."

"Zach," she whispered, shaking with need as she reached to pull him close. He resisted, catching her hands, finishing his study. Caresses followed with his fingers touching where he had looked.

"Zach," she gasped, closing her eyes, trembling when she reached for him. He held her away, continuing his sweet torment. His feather strokes started at her throat, moving to her nape and down her back, up her side and then over her breasts, lingering, circling a taut point with his palm. She inhaled and moaned. "Zach," she protested, tugging on his waist because she wanted to press against him and kiss him, to caress him. "We shouldn't kiss."

"Neither of us wants to stop. You want this and I want you. We've been headed for this moment from the first. Ah, Emma," he whispered. His fingers slid over her belly, drawing light circles that tormented and heightened desire.

She throbbed with need. Hunger to love him built swiftly. His fingers slipped up the inside of her thigh and she gasped, spreading her legs. Then he caressed her intimately. Her heart pounded and her eyes flew open as she pulled him roughly to her and kissed him, pouring out her need.

With shaking fingers, she unfastened his belt and then his jeans, shoving them off.

"Your foot?"

"It's protected by the shoe. Ignore it." He yanked off his loafer and then his briefs followed.

She drew a deep breath at the sight of him.

His arms held her tightly. His rock-hard muscles pressed against her while his manhood thrust insistently. He picked her up to carry her in front of the fire, lowering her to an area rug. Flames warmed her side, but she barely noticed for looking into hungry blue eyes.

"You're beautiful." Kneeling, he showered kisses on her. She couldn't stop. Couldn't tell him no. A disaster was blowing in with the storm that raged outside. His hands strummed over her, building need. Her pulse thundered in her ears as she wrapped her arms around his neck, wanting to devour him.

As his hands stroked her, her hips arched to meet him. She wanted more, had to have his hands on her. He stretched out beside her, turning her into his arms while he kissed her and his hand stroked her thighs, moving between them to heighten her pleasure.

"Zach," she breathed, sitting up and leaning over him. She trailed her fingers over the hard muscles, tangling her hand in his chest hair, showering kisses on his shoulder and down over his chest to his belly, moving lower.

As she kissed and caressed him, Zach combed his fingers through her hair. In minutes he sat up to roll her over while he kissed her.

"Zach, I'm not protected," she whispered.

"I'll be right back," he whispered, his tongue trailing over the curve of her ear, stirring waves of sensation while his hand drifted down over her. He rolled away and stood, crossing to get something from the pocket of his jeans and return. He came down to hold her and kiss her, loving her until once again she thrashed beneath him.

Kneeling between her legs, he picked up a packet he had laid aside earlier. She drank in the sight of him while her heart thudded with longing. She had gone beyond the point of saying no, caught up in passion, wanting him.

Stroking his thighs, rough brown curls were an erotic sensation against her palms. He lowered himself, kissing her. His tongue went deep into her mouth, stroking her while she returned his kiss and clung to him. He eased into her, pausing, driving her to a desperate need as he thrust slowly.

Her pounding heart deafened her. Consumed by passion, she wanted him, longed to give herself to him. She had shut off thought earlier and was steeped in sensation, knowing only Zach's body and his loving.

She arched, moaning, crying out until his mouth covered hers again and his kiss muffled sounds she made.

Zach maintained control. Sweat beaded his brow as he continued to thrust slowly. Dimly, she was aware he held back to heighten her pleasure, a sensual torment that made her want more. Urgency tore at her. As she clung tightly to him, beneath her desire ran a current of awareness that she bonded with Zach during this snowy night. This would be a forever event, always in her memory, burning deeply into her life no matter what he felt.

She tossed wildly beneath him until his control vanished. Zach pumped frantically, thrusting deep, his hips moving swiftly.

She arched, stiffened and cried out, her hips moving while ecstasy burst over her, showering her with release.

He shuddered while she clung to him, moving with him, for once both of them, in this moment, well matched. Maybe the only such time. Rapture spread in every vein, running in streams of satisfaction. Sex was breathtaking, incredible, earthshaking in her world.

She could no longer turn back time or erase the occasion. Zach had just become a facet of her life. He could disappear tomorrow, but this night had happened.

"How did we get here?" she whispered, stroking damp curls off his forehead.

"We walked in here with our eyes open. We're where we both wanted to be. You can't deny that."

She kissed his shoulder lightly. "No, I can't," she said, smiling at him and winding her arms around his neck. Tonight she had made him significant in her life, something she shouldn't have done.

"I think it's the perfect place to be," he said, combing long strands of her hair away from her face. "Snow outside, cozy and warm in here, you in my arms, wild lusty love. Totally gorgeous. Best sex ever. I couldn't ask for anything more."

"At the moment, I have to agree."

"For the first time, I'm glad I hurt my foot. Otherwise, our paths would have never crossed. If I had passed you in the Dallas office, I would have noticed you, but I wouldn't have gotten to know you. Not unless you had become my secretary there."

"Not likely. This Friday night hasn't gone according to plan."

"It definitely changed for the better," he whispered, showering kisses on her face and caressing her. "How about a hot tub together?"

"I think that's a great suggestion, but I thought you had to keep your foot out of water."

"I do. I've gotten very adept at hanging my foot out of the shower. I'm sure I can prop it on the edge of the tub."

"You can't hop into a tub," she said, laughing.

He laughed and stood, scooping her into his arms. "I'll carry you to a hot shower instead."

"No," she said, alarmed. "Zach, put me down. You'll hurt your foot."

"Nonsense. I carried you earlier and I didn't hear a protest. We'll do it this time the same way," he said, kissing her and ending her argument.

Carrying her to a bedroom with an adjoining shower, he set her down. He had to give up showering together. As soon as they returned to bed, he pulled her into his embrace to kiss her.

Past midnight Zach held her close. "Ready now for some of Rosie's chili?"

Emma stretched lazily, kissed his cheek and smiled at him. "I think I've lost my appetite."

"I've found mine. Let's go and when you smell it, you'll probably want some. Want a glass of wine or one of my margaritas first?"

"Seems like this is the way we started the evening," she said, wrapped in contentment. She suspected she had already complicated her life and she refused to worry about it on a wonderful night that had turned special. Tomorrow's worries would come soon enough.

"I think you're right."

He stepped out of bed, went to a closet and returned wearing a navy robe. He handed her a dark brown robe. "For you, although I definitely prefer you without it."

"No way, for dinner."

Zach placed his arm around her shoulders as they walked to the kitchen.

"The chili has cooked on low all evening, so it's ready," he said, getting out a covered dish. "I'll get our margaritas, build a fire and we'll eat when we're ready."

In minutes he had drinks mixed and logs stacked to get a fire blazing. He turned out the lights, leaving just firelight and the snowy view outside.

She walked to the window. "Zach, it looks even more beautiful than earlier today. Tomorrow morning we have to build a snowman if it's wet snow."

"Don't count on it. This is a cold night outside. It couldn't be hotter in here," he added in a husky voice.

She smiled at him. "When did you last build a snowman?"

"Probably when I was five. I don't remember exactly, but we did when we were little. A bunch of little boys—of course, we did."

She smiled and he walked to her, carrying their drinks.

"Here's to the very best night ever."

Surprised, she touched his glass with hers. "I'll drink to that and I agree," she said. She sipped the margarita and looked at the snow. "It's beautiful out there, but I'm ready to sit by the fire."

"In front of the fire is much cozier than here by cold windows."

Tossing a bunch of pillows from the sofa to the floor in front of the fire, he held out his arm. "Come here and enjoy the warmth."

She sat on the floor and he drew her back against him. "This is great, Zach."

He curled a lock of her hair in his fingers. "When do you plan to go back to college?"

"I'm saving money and this job helps. I hope to start again next September. I'll take night or Saturday classes or on the computer."

"You can't just take a year off to go back to college?"

"I like my job at your office. I hate to leave it."

"I can promise you it'll be there if you want to come back."

She smiled at him. "Thanks, but I probably need the income, too. I don't think I can save that much."

"Do you have to get presents for that enormous family of yours?"

"The adults draw names. We all give to Mom and Dad. Right now we don't draw names for the kids because there aren't that many and they're little, so they're easy, but I expect the year to come when they do draw kids' names. Our family is growing and two of us are still single."

He took her drink and placed it on the table. One look in his eyes and her pulse jumped while he drew her to him.

"Zach," she said with longing. Sliding her hands over his muscled shoulders, she wrapped her arms around him to kiss him as he pulled her down on the pillows.

Hours later Zach emerged from his bathroom and went to the kitchen. Emma wasn't there and the fire was dying embers. The longer he had been with her, the more he had wanted her. Now he felt insatiable. Lovemaking should have cooled him. He had broken his own rules to avoid emotional and physical entanglements with employees. With Emma, he couldn't turn back time and now he didn't want to. Last night had been fantastic, red-hot and unforgettable, making him want her more than ever. He grew hot just thinking about her. She excited him beyond measure and was unbearably sexy. He hoped she didn't expect more than he could give because she was sentimental, someone he never expected to become involved with.

She was totally the type of woman he had always avoided going out with. Always, until now. They were captives of circumstances that placed them in the same room, close proximity day and night. There were too many sparks between them to avoid fire. When had he been unable to use more control or maintain his cool resistance and good judgment?

"Here I am," she said, coming through the door.

"You changed," he said, looking at her jeans and thick blue sweater. "You look great."

"I was just going to tell you that. And you also changed. I like your black sweater. And your tight jeans," she said, wriggling her hips.

"You'll never get dinner if you keep that up," he said, a husky note creeping into his voice as his temperature jumped just watching her twist her hips.

She held up a hand. "No, no. I get to eat."

"I know what I want."

"Let's try chili right now. If it isn't cooked beyond the point of being edible."

"Not at all. Cooker on low, remember? Rosie left us salads in the fridge. I'll get them before I serve the chili. Want a glass of wine or margarita first?"

She laughed. "I think we've done that before. We can't seem to get past it to dinner."

"It wasn't the drinks that interrupted. We'll try again. Do you want wine?"

"I'll take the margarita. Maybe this time, I'll actually drink one."

He left to mix her drink and she followed him to the bar.

"Before I forget," he said, "let me go get something that came in the mail earlier." He set down his bottle of beer and left to return with a large envelope. "Since you like family so much, here are pictures of our half sister's wedding to Garrett, our CFO and a longtime family friend. Bring your drink and we'll look at the pictures together."

She sat down on the sofa, and Zach sat beside her, removing a book of bound pictures from the envelope.

"Garrett has married Sophia, our half sister. We didn't know we had a half sister until the reading of Dad's will. You can imagine the shock, particularly to my mother. I thought we might have to call an ambulance and I'm not joking about it. She had no clue. No one could understand my dad. Not any of us, definitely not my mother. I don't think she even tried. Maybe Sophia's mother. He never married her, but he kept her in his life until the end."

"Sounds sad, Zach."

"Don't start feeling sorry for me over my dad. All of us wanted Sophia in the family. First, we really wanted her— that should please you. Second—Sophia, as well as all of us, stood to inherit a fortune from Dad if she became involved with the Delaney company. It was his way of forcing us to get her into the family. And forcing her to join us. Sophia was incredibly bitter over Dad and wanted no part of this family."

"Even though you were her half brothers?"

"That's where Garrett came in and you can see the results. We all like her and Garrett loves her."

Emma looked over the photographs. "She's beautiful and they both look radiantly happy."

"You're enough of a romantic to think that no matter what the picture shows."

Emma stuck her tongue out at him, making him grin.

He looked at her profile while she studied the pictures. Her skin was flawless, her lashes thick and had a slight curl. Locks of red hair spilled onto her shoulders. He set down his beer, took her drink from her hand and then placed it and the book of pictures on the table. He pulled her into his arms to kiss her.

Her mouth was soft, opening like the petals of a rose. Heat spilled in him, centering in his manhood. He couldn't get enough of her, relishing every luscious curve, her softness sending his temperature soaring. She wrapped her arms around him, kissing him in return, and he forgot dinner again.

Five

By Monday morning a bright sun made snow sparkle and icicles had a steady drip as ice and snow melted. When Emma went to the office she glanced out to see the snowman they had built Sunday afternoon. She had pictures of Zach clowning by the snowman.

Zach had run inside and returned with one of Rosie's aprons to put on the snowman. He removed the snowman's hat and placed sprigs of cedar for hair so he had a snow-woman. He posed for a picture with his arms around the snow-woman's waist and with Zach puckered to give the snow-woman a kiss.

Remembering, she smiled. They had turned the snow-woman back into a snowman because Zach said he needed to return Rosie's apron. She'd reminded him that *he* wore that very apron to cook their steaks Saturday nights, a point he'd conceded.

Monday was uneventful except she couldn't lose the constant awareness she had of Zach. She was getting too close to him, enjoying his company too much. The weekend had brought intimacy and an emotional bonding that she may have been the only one to experience. She thought about the job ending soon and not seeing Zach again, so the problem would resolve itself. In spite of the weekend, it seemed wiser to put the brakes on a relationship. How deeply did she want to get involved with him? They were totally different with different priorities and vastly different lifestyles. The weekend had been magical, but they were shut away into almost a dream world, isolated in the storm on the ranch. She should develop some resistance and keep from sinking deeper into growing close to him. At least she should try. The intimate weekend was over and she should avoid another if she could dredge up the willpower.

That evening she learned that he was having his dinner in the office. Disappointment was coupled with knowledge that she was better off not seeing him. As she filled her plate in the kitchen, she quizzed Rosie about how Zach spent his holidays and received the same version she'd heard from Zach.

"Christmas decorations are in the attic and haven't been touched in years because it's been so long since any of the family has been at the ranch at Christmas," Rosie said. "Nigel used to put them up in case the family came, but he stopped years ago because the Delaneys were rarely at the ranch in December. Actually, this house has been closed most of the time for the past ten years and the foreman runs the ranch."

Emma picked at her dinner, her focus on Rosie.

Peeling and cutting carrots, Rosie stood at the counter. "When Adam, Zach's eldest brother, was born, Mrs. Delaney was delighted and gave him her attention. He had a nanny and Nigel and I worked for them in the Dallas home. Back then, they had lots of help. By the time Will was born, Mrs. Delaney was losing interest. When Zach came along she wasn't happy and she told me herself—no more babies. They had their family."

"Rosie, that's awful," Emma said, thinking how every baby was so welcome in her family. Each birth was a huge celebration.

"That's the way she was. In those days she and Mr. Delaney were going their separate ways. When she got pregnant with Ryan, Mrs. Delaney had a screaming fit. She didn't want another child and she made that clear. She had lost interest in her boys."

"I can't imagine," Emma said, deep in thought about Zach.

"No. They were good boys. Adam was eight, Will was seven, Zach, five. She couldn't wait to get them out of the house and into boarding school. She sent Adam that year. Next year, Will went. Two years later, Zach went."

"That seems too young to send them away."

"Zach was never the same. He closed up and shut himself off. As a little fellow, he would hug me and climb into my lap. That all stopped. He was getting too big to get on my lap, but the hugs vanished. He was quieter, more remote."

"You and Nigel both seem to have a close relationship with him."

"Zach is nice to work for and I love him like another son, but he keeps his thoughts to himself. Any woman who thinks she'll come into his life and change him is in for a big disappointment."

"I can't imagine his solitary life," Emma said. "My family is like yours and we all gather together on holidays."

"Their mother just turned off the love, if she had ever really loved them. It hurt those boys. Maybe not Adam and Will so much because they were the oldest and had had more of her attention."

"I don't understand how she could do that."

"She's hardly ever laid eyes on Caroline who is her only

oldest grandchild, the daughter of Adam, who sadly passed away. She has no interest in the little girl. Caroline is showered with love by all those around her, so I don't think she's noticed or realized yet, but when she gets older, she will. Mrs. Delaney's interest is in herself. She doesn't come see them. Anyway, this is the first Christmas for a Delaney to be here on the ranch in years. I don't think Zach pays much attention to Christmas. He hasn't been home in years for a holiday celebration."

"I can't imagine that either. At Christmas, home is the only place I want to be."

"I agree," Rosie said, smiling broadly. "Open the pantry door."

Emma did and saw snapshots of children, babies, adults, teens.

"That's my family," Rosie said. "Zach has given me time off and I will be with my family for Christmas." She wiped her hands and came close to tell Emma the name and relationship of each person.

"That's wonderful, Rosie. I know you can't wait to see them."

"Most are in Fort Worth, but others are scattered across Texas. Dallas, San Antonio, Fredericksburg. I'll be off for three weeks."

"This will be a fun Christmas for you," Emma said, wondering if Zach would enjoy being alone as much as he said he did.

Later, while as she ran on the treadmill, Emma thought about all Rosie had said. Emma suspected Zach would not put up any Christmas decorations. She glanced at the ceiling, thinking about the room upstairs that led into the attic. Emma's jaw firmed. She would decorate for Zach. She wanted Christmas reminders in her room and on her desk, but while she was at it, she would decorate the house a little if she found the Christmas decorations.

Nigel was gone by six each evening. By now Rosie might have left. As soon as she finished on the treadmill and showered, Emma pulled on fresh jeans and a red T-shirt. In the attic it took only minutes to find containers, systematically marked Christmas and each box had an attached list of contents.

She carried a box to the office and placed decorations around her area. She glanced toward Zach's desk and debated, leaving it alone except for one small Christmas tree she placed to one side.

Wondering whether she would encounter Zach, she carried another box to the family room. In the attic she had spotted a beautiful white Christmas tree covered in transparent plastic and tomorrow she intended to ask Nigel to help her get it into the family room.

Maybe the decorations would get Zach into the holiday spirit.

In the family room she placed artificial greenery on the mantel and then placed sparkling balls, artificial frosted fruit. She set long red candles in a silver candelabra in the dining room, arranging them on the mantel. The scrape of a shoe made her turn toward the door as Zach entered.

He stopped to glance around. His black T-shirt and faded, tight jeans set her insides fluttering.

"What are you doing?" he asked.

"Decorating a bit for Christmas since the holiday approaches."

Zach's gaze met hers as he crossed the room. "I don't care about your room or your desk. Otherwise, don't put this stuff up in the house. Your intentions are nice, but this isn't what I hired you to do," he said, stopping only a few feet away.

"I'm not using work hours to do this," she said. "I thought you'd like it."

"No. I don't want the clutter. It's old stuff and doesn't conjure up warm memories. I'll get Nigel to see that it's cleared away."

"I can take it out," she said. "I didn't know it would be hurtful."

"It isn't hurtful," he said, with a slight harshness to his tone. "I just don't want it around and it's time-consuming to put up and take down. Besides, you shouldn't be lugging those heavy boxes out of the attic. The decorations are meaningless. These are old decorations that should be tossed."

"You don't think your family, Caroline in particular, might enjoy them?"

His eyes narrowed. "I'm having an argument over Christmas decorations. Caroline's house in Dallas and the house in Colorado will probably be decorated from top to bottom. She doesn't need more here."

"You don't think she'll see you as Scrooge?"

"No, she won't. I'll have presents for her and she's so excited over the baby, she won't care what's happening here. Caroline has reverted back to a very happy child, which is what she was before she lost her dad. These decorations won't matter to her. When she's older, she'll accept me the way I am. Maybe view me as her eccentric uncle."

"Very well," Emma said quietly.

"I'm fine about Christmas and the holiday isn't about decorations. Stop looking at me as if I've lost my fortune or some other disaster has befallen me."

"I don't think losing your fortune would be as disastrous as what you are losing. And I know Christmas isn't about decorations. You childhood doesn't have to carry over in the same way now."

"Stop worrying about me being alone," he said, smiling,

his voice growing lighter as he stepped closer and placed his hands on her shoulders. His blue eyes were as riveting as ever. Her heart thudded and longing for his kisses taunted her.

He glanced around and walked to the big box of decorations to rummage in it.

"What are you doing?"

"What you wanted. I'll observe one old Christmas custom. There are some decorations I want."

Smiling, wondering what he searched for, she stepped closer.

"Here's one," he said, pulling out a decorative hanging cage filled with sprigs of artificial mistletoe. "I'll put mistletoe up all over this part of the house. Let's see if we can follow one Christmas tradition," he added, his tone lowering another notch, strumming over her nerves. "You can help with this."

"I don't think that's such a great idea," she whispered.

"I think it's fantastic." He attached the ornament to the hook on the top of the door, then stood beneath it. "You want some Christmas traditions in my life. Well, here's one," he said, winding his arm around her waist to draw her closer as he leaned forward.

His mouth was warm, his lips firm on hers. She opened to him, melting against him while her unspoken protests crashed and burned.

Wrapping her arm around his narrow waist, she held him tightly. Her heart thudded and she could feel his heart pounding. Desire fanned heat as an inner storm built.

Her moan sounded distant. Longing strummed over every nerve. She had intended to avoid moments like this, stay coolly removed from anything personal with him. Instead, she was tumbling into fires that consumed her. Need became a throbbing ache, more demanding than before.

Their passionate kiss lengthened, became urgent. She wound her fingers in the tight curls at the back of his neck.

Time vanished and the world around them disappeared. Zach's kisses were all she wanted.

How could it seem so right to be in his arms? To kiss him? They were far too different in every way that counted for it to seem like the best place to be when he held her. His kisses had become essential to her, yet their lifestyles clashed. She held him tightly as if his kisses were as necessary to her as the air in the room.

One hand wound in her hair while he kissed her, his other hand caressing her nape.

Finally, she leaned away. "Zach, this isn't what I planned."

He raised his head, his blue eyes filled with hunger. He glanced overhead. "I'm surprised the mistletoe hasn't burst into flames. Now I'm glad you got out the Christmas box. Let me see if there's more mistletoe in there." His husky voice conveyed lust as much as the flames in his crystal eyes. He turned to rummage in the box again. "Here are three more bunches. I have just the places. Come help me hang these."

"I still don't think I should. Zach, we're sinking deeper into something we were going to avoid."

"You started this. You can't back out now. C'mon." He left the family room and headed for the office, stopping in the doorway to hand her two of the bunches. "This is perfect," he said, giving her a long look that shivered through her. "You wait while I get a hammer."

He disappeared into the hall. Common sense urged restraint. Now she wished she had left Christmas decorations alone. In minutes he was back. She watched him reach up to push a tack into the wood to hold a sprig of mistletoe tied with a red ribbon. He tapped it lightly with the hammer. She passed him, crossing the office to her desk. She wanted space between them.

She could hear him hanging the mistletoe, but she didn't want to watch. She straightened her desk and wondered if she could tell him to take the last sprig and go. She would put the box of decorations away when Zach wasn't around. She had never thought about mistletoe, never expected to even see him tonight.

She thought about the sharp tone in his voice when he had first spotted the Christmas decorations. Was he all bottled up over old hurts? When it came to interacting with other people, from what she had seen, Zach was warm and friendly. Were old hurts still keeping part of him locked away from sharing life with those closest to him?

After he hung the mistletoe, he turned to her as he stood beneath it. "Emma, come here a minute."

"Don't be ridiculous," she said, wanting to laugh, yet feeling her insides clinch over his invitation.

"Emma, come here," he coaxed in a velvet tone.

"Zach," she said, sauntering toward him while thinking about his past, "I'll come there if you'll go somewhere with me either this week or next."

"Deal," he said, clearly not giving that much thought.

With her pulse racing, she stopped inches away from him.

He took her wrist to draw her to him. "Now we'll test this one," he said, framing her face with his hands as he placed his mouth on hers to kiss her again.

He tasted of mint while his aftershave held that hint of woods. She slipped her arms around his waist and kissed him. His arm banded her, pulling her close against him while he leaned over her and his kiss deepened.

When they paused, she took deep breaths, trying to get back to normal.

"We have a deal," she said. "Come home with me for the weekend and see what it's like to be with a family who wants to be together." She wanted him to see what a joy a loving family could be. Billionaire or not, she felt incredibly sorry for Zach, certain he was missing the best part of life and maybe with her family, he would see it. "When you see what you're missing, you'll want to start accepting your brothers' invitations to join them." Her last words tumbled out and she expected that curt tone and coolness he'd had earlier.

"You took advantage of me."

"Oh, please," she said in exasperation.

"Besides, I'm supposed to stay home to stay off my foot," he said. "I shouldn't be going anywhere for the weekend. That's the whole point of being stuck on the ranch." His voice held the husky rasp. His breathing was still ragged and his lips were red. His expression conveyed a blatant need that he made no effort to hide. Even though he argued, she suspected he was giving little thought to their deal.

"I'll drive and you can put your foot up in the car. At my folks' house, you can keep your foot elevated all the time you're there. We'll all wait on you. You'll have a good time."

"Emma, I don't want to go to my brothers' homes for holidays. Why would I go to your parents' when I don't know anyone except you?" he asked.

"Because you just agreed to do so."

He stared at her and she could feel a clash of wills and imagine the debate raging in his mind. "If I go home with you, won't your whole family think there's something serious between you and me?"

She smiled at him. "No. We all bring friends home a lot. Growing up, I'd say we often had at least one person eating with us who wasn't a family member."

"So how many men have you brought home?"

"None until now," she admitted. "It still doesn't mean anything other than you're my boss and I would like you to meet my family."

"Who takes her boss home to meet the family?" he asked and she was sure she blushed with embarrassment, but she wasn't giving up. Zach needed to see some real family life.

"As long as you're coming this weekend, you might as well come for Thanksgiving."

"Oh, hell, Emma, that's an extra two days."

"You said you would and you'll enjoy yourself and you can sit off in a room alone whenever you want and prop your foot up all you want."

"Dammit." He stared at her again with his jaw clamped shut and she was certain he would refuse. She felt silly for trying to get him to come. Her world-traveler billionaire boss was light-years away from her ordinary family.

"All right. If I'm going home with you for Thanksgiving, I get more than that one kiss," he said, pulling her back into his embrace and kissing her hard while he pulled her up against him. "A lot more," he added.

Startled, she was frozen with surprise for a few seconds and then her arms wrapped around his neck and she kissed him in return. His hand slipped down her back over her bottom, a long, slow caress, scalding even through the thick denim of her jeans.

His fingers traveled up again, slipping beneath her shirt, cupping her breast lightly, a faint touch causing streaks of pleasure. He pushed away the lacy bra, his warm fingers on her bare skin.

She moaned in delight, spreading her fingers wide and slipping her hand beneath his T-shirt to stroke his smooth, muscled back. Pleasure and need escalated swiftly.

Taking his wrist to hold his hand, she looked up. "Zach, we have to stop this for now. I can't—"

"Yes, you can" he said, showering kisses on her temple, her cheek, her throat. Protests faded into oblivion. She kissed and caressed him until he carried her to a bedroom where they made love for the next hour.

During the night she eased off the bed and slipped away from him, gathering her clothes as she went. She returned to her room, thankful for the space and the haven where she could be alone to think. In her own room, she fell into bed, her mind on Zach. Their lovemaking was binding her heart to him with chains that would hurt to break. Zach was becoming more important, more appealing and exciting. Was she tumbling headfirst, falling in love with him? A love that would never be returned. This past weekend, Zach had just become a bigger danger to her well-being and her heart. A weekend of love, three nights of passion, now another night. How long would it take her to get over what she already felt for him?

She fell asleep to dream about Zach and awoke early the next morning. Longing to go find him, kiss him awake and love again was strong. She slipped out of bed and looked at the clock, knowing she would follow a sensible course and get ready for a workday.

They both needed to step back and get things under control again. Just thinking about Zach, she wanted to be in his arms. Surprise lingered that she had asked him to go home with her and that he had accepted.

What had seemed a good idea at first, began to look like complication after complication. She had to let her family know. She thought about the family letters she had read and how little Zach cared and decided to hold him to his acceptance. She wanted him to see a family who relished being together and made the most of their moments. Maybe he would join his brothers more on holidays and participate with his own family.

Touching her lips lightly with her fingertips, she remembered his kisses. After Christmas she would return to her job in Dallas, and Zach would disappear from her life. She would be with him less than a month more. Despite her earlier worry, she *could* keep from falling in love with him because they had nothing between them except physical attraction. She didn't like his lifestyle, his attitude toward family, his disregard for all the things she loved so much. Maybe her heart was safe in spite of the attraction that was pure lust. She pulled out her phone to text her mother that company was coming. Company with an injured foot.

By Thanksgiving afternoon Zach wondered how he had gotten himself into this. Since he was twelve years old, he had been able to say no or get out of most things he didn't want to do unless it involved his father. Even with his father, by age twenty-one, he had become adept at escaping his father's plans for him.

He was in the center of a whirlwind. He had met four generations of Hillmans. They encompassed ages two to ninety-something. Brody, Emma's father, had made him feel welcome, as well as her mother, Camilla.

Zach tried to keep the names straight, learning her parents and siblings quickly. Connor, the married older brother, his wife, Lynne, Sierra, Emma's oldest sister, and Mary Kate, the youngest, both sisters married, Bobby, the younger brother. Zach mentally ran over the names of people seated around him while they ate the Thanksgiving turkey. He received curious glances from Connor and could feel Connor being the protective big brother even though they were far across the long table from each other.

The dining room table seated eighteen and other tables held more of the family with grandparents, aunts, uncles, nieces and nephews gathering together today.

Until the subject came up during the Thanksgiving feast, Emma had neglected to warn him that it was family tradition to decorate for Christmas after Thanksgiving dinner, which was eaten early in the afternoon. After dinner everybody under eighty years of age changed to jeans and T-shirts or sweatshirts. Also, the decorations didn't come out until the men had set up the Christmas trees in various rooms in the house, which they did while others cleared the tables.

Once trees and lights were up with an angel or a star at the top of each tree, the women and children took over with the decorations while the men decorated the porch.

As soon as Zach started to join the men, Emma took his arm to lightly tug him toward the living room. "You sit and elevate your foot. You can help the kids with the decorations. The little kids can't put the hooks on the balls and that sort of thing."

"Emma, I can do a few things outside."

"We need you in here and you know you should stay off your foot. The more you don't walk on it, the sooner you'll heal," she lectured, looking up at him with wide green eyes. His gaze lowered to her mouth and he longed to be alone with her and saw absolutely no hope until they left Dallas.

In minutes he began to help the little kids with ornaments while he sat with his foot resting on a footstool. Boxes of shiny trimmings were spread around him and on the table in front of him. Emma and her mother had a table over his propped-up foot to keep the kids from bumping his injury. The living room held what Emma had called the real Christmas tree. It was a huge live balsam pine that touched the ceiling. Spread around him were boxes of a family history of decorations with shiny ornaments mixed with clay and paper trimmings made by kids. Once Emma stopped beside him. "How are you doing?"

"You owe me," he said. "I intend to collect."

Her cheeks turned pink and he wondered what she was thinking. He remembered their lovemaking and wished with all his being he could be back at his ranch and alone with her. Instead, what seemed like a hundred people and kids were buzzing around him like busy bees. He had to admit she had a fun family and he'd had a good time through dinner. What he knew he would remember most, was when she had come down for Thanksgiving dinner. The whole family dressed for the occasion, which she had warned him about just before they had left the ranch.

He had been standing in the front hall and looked up as she came down the stairs. She wore an emerald green dress that came only to her knees and her red hair was caught up in a clip with locks falling free in the back. She looked stunning. The sight of her had taken his breath and he longed to be able to hold her and kiss her.

After a time Emma took away the table that sheltered his injured foot. "You're excused now to go watch football. They've finished decorating the porch and the guys turned on a game. We'll help the kids decorate and then clean up the Christmas tree mess. I'll take over your job."

"I don't mind doing this."

"Go watch football with the guys in the family room."

"You won't have to tell me again," he said, smiling at her and still wanting to kiss her. He stood and she slipped into his chair while he limped away.

During the second half of the game, his cell rang and he excused himself to answer Will's call.

"Happy Thanksgiving, Zach."

"Happy Thanksgiving to you and Ava and Caroline. Let me talk to Caroline," Zach said as he stepped farther into the hall so his conversation wouldn't interfere with everyone listening and watching football. He talked briefly to his niece and then Will came back on the line.

A touchdown was scored and the family members watching the game cheered and applauded.

"Where are you?" Will asked. "You sound as if you're at a game."

"I'm at Emma's house in Dallas," Zach admitted, certain there was too much background noise for him to convince

Will he was home alone at the ranch. He braced for what he knew was coming.

"You're where?" Will asked.

"You heard me. I sort of got finagled into this," he tried to say quietly.

"I can't hear you. You're at your secretary's house with her family?"

"That's right, Will. And I need to go. Happy Thanksgiving to you." As he ended the call, he was certain he had not heard the last from Will. Returning to his seat, he looked at the room filled with Hillman men and the older boys. This room held a huge white Christmas tree. Their attic had been filled to the brim with all the decorations that now covered the various trees in the house. With a deep sigh he settled to watch the game. The evening promised to be incredibly long, but he had to admit, the Hillmans had fun and obviously loved being together. To his surprise, he'd had a good time with them. They were nice people and her brothers were great to be around, actually making him miss seeing his own, which gave him a shock when he realized he was thinking about calling both of them, even though he'd just spoken to Will. He had to admit, Emma had been right about the weekend with her family versus his staying at the ranch by himself. He looked at her laughing at something her sister said to her. His insides knotted and he wanted badly to be alone with her and to hold her in his arms.

It took several hours to get the decorations up and the empty boxes put away. A sweeper was run. Finally the entire bunch of people settled in the family room, sitting on the floor, chairs, sofas. When the football game ended, Emma's sister, Mary Kate, sat at the piano to play Christmas carols and they all joined in singing. Emma came to sit beside him and to his amazement, the kids found him interesting, so they had squeezed onto the sofa beside Emma and him. Being crowded together suited him because he could put his arm around Emma's shoulders without it seeming a personal gesture. He had an arm around two of the little kids on the other side of him, but he enjoyed having Emma pressed against him.

To his surprise, he remembered the old songs he hadn't sung in years. Finally when they stopped singing, they began to pull coats out of closets.

"We're going outside because Dad turns on the Christmas lights, a tradition that means the Christmas season is officially kicking off at the Hillman house."

Zach laughed. "I don't know how I let you get me into this."

"I know exactly how," she said, giving him a sultry look, and his smile disappeared.

"Emma—" Smiling, she walked away and he watched her hips covered in tight jeans as she walked away from him to get her jacket.

The entire family and dogs gathered on the front lawn and waited for the light ceremony. In minutes the lights came on and it was bright as noontime. Zach stood next to Emma and applauded with the others when the lights sparked to life. "Emma, I've fallen into *Christmas Vacation*. This is the Griswold house," he said softly.

She laughed. "Except the lights all came on at the first try. Dad loves Christmas. Actually, we all do. It's wonderful."

The family stayed up talking until one when they began to say good-night. By the time Emma and her younger brother, Bobby, turned in, they had to lock up and switch off lights.

She had an apartment nearby, but she had told him she would stay at her parents' house. He hadn't known they wouldn't sleep at her place until they were almost to Dallas. A huge disappointment to him.

At her door, Zach placed his hand on the jamb to block

her way. He tugged on a lock of her hair to draw her closer and leaned forward to brush her lips with a light kiss. The instant his mouth touched her soft lips, his body reacted. He ached with wanting her. His arm tightened around her waist while he kissed her long and fervently. "I want you, Emma," he whispered.

The look in her eyes made his pulse pound. He inhaled deeply, fighting the urge to reach for her again. This wasn't the time or the place, so he told her good-night before going to the room given to him for his weekend visit.

He wanted to be alone with Emma now and couldn't wait to get back to the ranch, but the holiday had been a pleasant surprise.

By Saturday, the weather had warmed. The family sat at a long picnic table, made from five tables pushed together with Zach at one end, his foot propped on a wooden box. Emma's mother was to his right and Emma sat on his left. Her father was at the far end while various relatives lined both sides of the table. They sat in a sunny spot in a wooded park not far from Emma's parents' home.

It was easy to see where Emma got her looks. Her auburn-haired mother, Camilla, was a good-looking woman and appeared far younger than she had to be since she was the mother of Emma's older brother and older sisters. Brody Hillman, Emma's dad, had welcomed him, but Zach could feel the unspoken questions and saw the speculation in Brody's expression. Even more open about his curiosity was Emma's older brother, Connor. Connor studied Zach and Zach could feel disapproval simmering just beneath the surface. Connor had been friendly, but only in a perfunctory manner and Zach thought it was just a matter of time before Connor quizzed him about his relationship with Emma.

There had been enough curious looks from all of them to

remind him that Emma did not bring men home with her for the weekend. He had wished a hundred times over that he had not accepted her invitation, He would have to last until tomorrow afternoon when they would leave for his ranch.

"Zach," Emma said, "my nieces are so impressed with you. I told them you are a world traveler. They want to know the scariest trip you've had or scariest place you've been."

He smiled at a row of little girls staring at him expectantly and told about waking up with a huge snake in his tent, but that was not as scary as swimming and discovering a shark approaching him. By the time he got to that part, the boys had gathered around to listen. The girls sat quietly, their eyes opening wider, and he didn't want to scare them. "Those were scary moments. Then there was a time I was camped far from a town. My things kept disappearing. I thought someone who worked for me was taking them until I discovered it was a very sly monkey. We found the stash and I got back my things, except my golf cap. I left that for him and hoped I'd see him wearing it, but I never did."

As the girls laughed, he glanced at Emma to see her smiling while she watched her nieces.

He got out his phone. "I have pictures," he said, opening it and quickly finding his electronic scrapbook. He held out the phone and Emma had to join the kids to look. She gasped, maybe only slightly less than the little girls. She bent closer, looking at a massive snake that was held by four men.

"Zach, is it alive?" she asked.

"Yes, but it had been fed, so it wasn't moving much and everyone was safe."

She glanced at Zach, and he suspected he had just dropped a notch in her estimation of his lifestyle. He suspected she liked homebody types who spent their weekends playing with the kids versus someone who traveled and encountered wild snakes and ran some big risks.

After lunch, they cleaned up and when everything was put away, a tag football game was planned with everyone participating.

"You can be scorekeeper, Zach. We always have two or three scorekeepers, so no one person has to keep up with all of us," Brody said. "There's a lot of give and take to score-keeping for one of our family games. Usually we end up with about as many different scores as scorekeepers, so don't take any of this too seriously. You'll see."

Zach agreed to the task, sitting on the sidelines with his foot resting on a cooler. Brody's sister, Beth, joined him as scorekeeper along with Brody's mom, Grandma Kate. Emma's maternal grandmother, Grandma Nan, was on the field to play; she looked too young to be a grandmother. The oldest of the nieces and nephews was only six, so everyone played around the kids. As three-year-old Willie grabbed the ball and tried to run with it while the family cheered, Zach joined in, laughing at the child clutching the football as if it were a lifeline.

Zach glanced at Emma on the playing field. She had leaves in her hair. She had shed the bulky sweatshirt and wore a bright pink T-shirt with her jeans. She was watching him, laughing with him over the kids, and desire stabbed him. That electrifying tension flared to life, as unwanted and un-expected as it had been the first time she had walked into his home. He wished they were alone. Someone stepped between them and the tension eased, but it did not vanish.

The kids provided constant laughs with their antics and he saw why she liked to come home for the weekend. They were all happy with each other, having great fun. He had known fun with his brothers, but life had been tense if both his parents were present unless they were entertaining a house filled with their friends. Even then, it had never held this re-laxed closeness. He realized he was enjoying a whole family of people who loved each other and exhibited a joy in being together. He had this now with his brothers, but they seldom were all together and until Caroline, there had been no small children around.

He could see why Emma thought he was missing something and why she had hated to leave him alone. He looked at her parents, thinking how different they were from his own. The love they shared showed constantly even though they were across the field from each other, or at opposite ends of the long table earlier. He realized he had never seen that kind of warmth between his parents. He looked at Emma, laughing with a small niece. Maybe Emma was the wealthy one after all.

Breaking into his thoughts, he looked down into big brown eyes as a little boy walked up to him. "Did you give my team a point?"

He wasn't certain which child stood before him, guessing it was Jake. "Yes, I did give your team a very big point," he answered, amused that the little kid was checking on him.

The child nodded. "Thank you." He turned to his great-grandmother. "Did you give my team a point, Gran-Gran?"

"Yes, I did," she said, leaning forward to hug him. "You're playing a good game," she said.

"Thank you." Smiling broadly, he ran off, half skipped to his dad, who asked him a question, glancing over his head at Zach. The child told his dad something and his dad smiled at Zach and turned back to play.

Zach was unaccustomed to sitting out anything active. During the time-out, he motioned Emma over.

"I hate sitting on the sidelines. If three-year-old Willie can play, so can I."

"Zach, you have to stay off your foot."

"This shoe protects my foot. I am not accustomed to being a spectator. I'll stop if my foot hurts. It's only tag football."

"You'll be on my team then, so I can keep up with you."

"Don't hover. Your family will really think we have something going."

Zach got into the game, enjoying himself even though he knew he was being foolish and risking more injury, but he hated doing nothing except keeping score. He had never been one to sit on the sidelines and he didn't want to miss out now. He hobbled around and it was easy to keep up when they had geared down to a three-year-old level.

Before dinner they gathered wood to build a fire in a stone fireplace. When Zach started to help, Emma stopped him.

"This isn't a chore you have to do. Go sit and we'll get the wood."

"I'm not doing much," he said, brushing past her. Minutes later as he picked up a dead branch and turned, Connor blocked his way.

"Thought you were supposed to stay off your foot."

"A few branches and I'll quit. I still can't get accustomed to sitting around."

"Which is why Emma works on your ranch?"

"Right," Zach said. He could feel anger from Connor and see curiosity in his expression.

"You've been all over the world, so you're pretty sophisticated and experienced. Emma's not. Did she tell you she's never brought anyone home before?"

"We work together. I don't know what she's told the family, but I think I'm here because she feels sorry for me."

"Yeah. We heard you were alone. I just don't want to see my sister hurt."

"I wouldn't want her hurt either."

"Zach," Emma called, hurrying to join them. "Give those sticks to Connor and come sit. You shouldn't be on your foot. Just watch everyone."

All the time she talked, Zach looked at Connor who gazed

at him with a flat stare that held a silent warning. When Emma tugged on his arm to take the wood from him, Zach turned away.

"I think Connor was being a big brother and jumping to ridiculous ideas. Pay no attention to him," she said.

"Your older brother is a little difficult to ignore since he's five inches over six feet tall and probably weighs in at 250."

"Come on. They're getting the fire started and we'll cook dinner and then sit and sing and later, tell stories."

Amused, he went with her, hobbling along.

As they got dinner on the tables, Emma carried a hot dish and set it on the table, then turned to find Connor beside her.

"Emma." He glanced over her head and she realized they were the only two standing at the end of the long table. "Be careful. I don't want you to get hurt."

"I hope, Connor, you didn't threaten him. He's my boss."

"If that's all he is, that's fine. Guys like Zach Delaney do not marry into families like the Hillmans."

"I brought him home for the weekend because I didn't want him to spend Thanksgiving alone. We've always invited people who might be alone on holidays. I felt sorry for him. There's nothing more to it than that."

"It looks like more," Connor said, frowning.

"This is a temporary job that is on the verge of ending. When it does end, I'll never see him again. Most of the time he works abroad. There's nothing to be concerned about."

"I hope not. Take care of yourself."

She smiled. "I will. Stop worrying."

He jammed his hands into his pockets and walked away. She watched him and shook her head. Connor was forever the big brother.

As she got more dishes of food on the table, Mary Kate approached with more delicious looking food.

"Is Connor being big brother?" she asked.

"Ever so," Emma replied, rolling her eyes.

"Emma, *should* Connor be big brother?"

"No. I didn't want Zach to be alone over the holiday and he would have been. Anyone in this family would have invited him if they had been in my place."

"Are you sure?" Mary Kate asked, tilting her head to study her sister. "Here he comes." She moved away before Emma answered. She forgot her siblings. Zach approached and he was the only person she noticed.

After dinner they played a word game around a blazing campfire. When the sun went down the air cooled with a fall chill and the fire felt good. Emma sat close beside him and Zach longed to put his arm around her, but he did not give in to the impulse. It would look far too personal for a boss and secretary. The dancing red flames highlighted gold streaks in Emma's hair. She sat beside him playing a simple game where they sang and clapped and the little kids could play. Emma's dad sat with his arm around her mother while she clapped.

Zach continued to marvel at her family. Outside of old movies, he hadn't known families like this really existed. He completely understood why Emma treasured her weekends at home and her holidays. As a little kid he had hoped for this, but it had never happened with his own family or any that he visited and he finally had come to the conclusion such families did not exist, but Emma was proving him wrong.

Once as she sang, she glanced at him and smiled. More than ever, he wanted his arm around her or just to touch her, but he knew that wasn't a possibility now. If he wasn't careful, her family would have them engaged.

It was after ten when they began to break up. He helped clean until he was told to put his foot up. Finally he went with Emma back to her parents' house. Tonight, everyone was heading home except her younger brother, and Zach wanted to return to her apartment and be alone with her.

Instead, they sat up talking to Bobby until one in the morning. While Bobby and Emma talked about Bobby's school year, Zach looked at the Christmas tree. He had counted eight Christmas trees of various types and sizes that had been set up and decorated in the Hillman home.

Besides celebrating Thanksgiving, he was immersed in Christmas. The mantels in the family room and living room were covered in greenery and red bows. Decorations were everywhere he looked. No wonder she had tried to decorate the ranch a little. His attention shifted to Emma and his longing to be alone with her increased.

Finally, when Bobby went to bed half an hour later, Emma came to sit by him. He made room for her and she leaned against his chest, his arm around her and her feet beside his on the sofa.

"It's been fun, Emma. You have a great family."

"You really mean that?" she asked, twisting to look at him. She was in his arms, her face so close to his. "I love Thanksgiving," she said, turning and settling back against him. "I love Christmas. Look at the tree. It's beautiful and so many ornaments remind me of a special thing or person or time. I couldn't bear Christmas without a tree."

"I'm not as tied in to Christmas as you well know by now."

"You should get into the spirit and enjoy Christmas. If you did, you would never return to spending it the way you do now." She yawned and stretched. "I'm ready to turn in, Zach." She stood and he came to his feet. She walked to the tree and carefully lifted free a glass Santa to show to him. "This is my favorite."

He looked at the ornament and her delicate, warm hand. "I hope you have years of wonderful Christmases," he said quietly.

"I hope you do, too."

"This is turning into one so far."

"It's Thanksgiving and the start of the Christmas holiday. There's a month to go." She returned the Santa to the tree. "I love each ornament, Zach." He came to stand beside her and put his arm around her waist. "Look at our reflection," she said, touching a shiny green ball.

"I'm going to start carrying a sprig of mistletoe in my pocket," he said, turning her to him to kiss her.

His arm tightened around her waist and she slipped her arms around him, kissing him while her pulse drummed. She quivered while desire ignited. Finally, she raised her head. "We should go to bed."

"If only you would always say that at the ranch," he replied. He smiled and kept his arm around her waist to walk beside her as they headed toward the stairs.

"Night, Zach," she said and disappeared into the room where she slept. In his own room, he lay in bed with his hands behind his head, thinking about the day and the evening with her and her family. He couldn't imagine spending every weekend this way, but sometimes it would be fun. He still thought she was missing out on a wonderful world and when his foot was healed, he would try to show her some place exciting out of Texas since she had never even been beyond the boundaries of the Lone Star state. As soon as he thought of traveling with her, he knew it would never happen. When the job ended, she would go out of his life. She had been correct when she said they had vastly different lifestyles. Neither one was the right person for the other in even a casual way.

In spite of that knowledge, his common sense, caution and experience, he couldn't stop wanting her and he couldn't shake her out of his thoughts.

He finally drifted to sleep, still yearning to be alone with her.

After Sunday dinner, Zach and Emma left for the ranch. She drove again while he sat with his foot propped up across the backseat and resting on bags placed on the car floor.

"You have a nice family. I see why you value your weekends. Your family shows they enjoy being together."

"Thank you. You seemed to like being with your brother and his family."

"I do, but I don't think my brothers and I have the closeness your family does."

Emma could see Zach in the rearview mirror. "You can have that closeness. From what you've said, you're all congenial. Maybe you are alone so much because you keep up your guard, Zach. It might carry over from childhood and times you were alone. Life's different now. You don't have to keep everything all bottled up. You can enjoy your brothers and now there's a half sister. You and Will seem very close."

He sat in silence. She met his gaze when she glanced at him, but then she had to turn her attention back to the road. "You might be right," he said finally. "I've never looked at it that way. I was disappointed as a kid. So were they. We were dumped and couldn't even be home together some years. I don't know—maybe my feelings are a guard left from childhood hurts. As a little kid, I couldn't keep from resenting it."

"Well, the nice thing now is that you don't have to be alone," she said, smiling at him.

"Maybe you're right. I'll admit it's fun when my brothers are together. And now I enjoy having Caroline and Ava there, too. Your family certainly has a great time together."

"We do and in a crunch, we can count on each other too. I'm happy you came with me."

"I enjoyed the weekend. Neither of your brothers were thrilled. I got looks from them the whole time. If they intended to send me warnings, they succeeded."

"Pay no attention to them. You'll never see them again."

Zach smiled and looked at her as she glanced in the rear-view mirror at him. "I'm not invited back?"

Emma felt her cheeks flush. "Of course you are. Whenever you would like to go home with me. I just figured you wouldn't want to again. I sort of trapped you into this time."

He grinned. "I'm teasing you."

"Zach, would you like to come home with me for Christmas?" she asked sweetly. "We'll have the whole family and they would be delighted to have you."

"No, they wouldn't be delighted. Thank you for asking me. I'll stay home and give my foot a rest."

"They would be pleased to see you again, except perhaps Connor, but you can ignore him."

"Home on the ranch is where I belong."

When they stepped inside the empty ranch house, Zach dropped their bags and switched off alarms. As she picked up her bag, he turned to take it from her and set it back on the floor. He slipped his arm around her waist. "Now what I've waited all weekend to do," he said in a husky voice. "You do owe me."

Six

When his mouth covered hers, her heart lurched. Wrapping both arms around his neck, she pressed tightly against him. His mouth was warm, insistent, and she kissed him eagerly. She clung to him, returning his kiss while the air heated and her heartbeat thundered. How could he melt her in seconds? Why did he weave such a spell with her? She didn't care. All she wanted at the moment was to hold and kiss him. She felt as starved to make love as they had on the snowy weekend.

"Emma, I want you," he whispered.

Each kiss was more volatile than the last. At the moment she didn't care about caution and what was wise in dealing with him. All she wanted was to be in his arms and kissing him.

Still kissing her, he picked her up and carried her through the house to the family room. He sat on the sofa, cradling her on his lap. Her hands drifted over him while her heart raced. She was glad they were together. Running his fingers in her hair, he kissed her. Why did this seem necessary? Why did his loving seem so right and special? The questions were dim, vague speculation that was blown away by passion.

She combed her fingers through his thick curls and played her hand over his muscled chest.

His hand slipped beneath her T-shirt. His fingers were warm, his hand calloused and faintly abrasive against her skin, a sensual, rough texture that heightened feeling. In seconds he had pushed away her bra to caress her. Pleasure streaked from his slightest touch, fanning sexual hunger to a bigger flame. Emma sat up, her thick red hair falling on both sides of her face as she tugged his T-shirt free and pulled it over his head. His eyes darkened and he had her shirt whisked away in a flash.

Knowing she was pursuing a reckless course, but wanting him desperately, she sat astride him and leaned forward. They embraced each other to kiss, his sculpted, warm chest pressed against her with the mat of chest curls a tantalizing texture.

Desire raged while she struggled to dredge up control. Dimly, she thought about her fears of how hurt she would be when the job ended and she told Zach goodbye. The hard knowledge that when that time came, he would be gone permanently from her life was a cooling effect. And it hurt. Was she falling in love with him? Was she *already* in love?

She leaned away slightly to frame his face with her hands. "To my way of seeing, our continuing to make love is a road to disaster. I want to back up a little and think about what we're doing." As she talked, she shifted off Zach and stood in front of him. While he watched her, his fingers caressed her, dallying along her hip and down her thigh, causing her to pause. She inhaled sharply, closed her eyes and stood immobile while his hands created magic and made her want to go back to kisses and loving him.

After seconds or minutes, she didn't know, she grabbed his wrists and opened her eyes. "Zach, wait."

He stood, his arms wrapping around her. She ran her hands over his chest. "I want you, Emma. I want to make love to you all night."

"Part of me wants that. Part of me has enough sense to know that's a reckless course to follow. Getting involved with you isn't what I hired on to do. And that first day that's what you agreed to avoid. I don't want last weekend every night until this job is over. If we do, I'll never want to leave."

"I just know what we both want right now. Kisses don't have one thing to do with business or your job or mine. I wasn't even going to keep you that first day, but you proved to be such a damn good secretary, I did. Emma, I've spent the past four days wanting you. I've been with you, watching you, aching to hold and kiss you."

His words echoed her feelings. Constantly through the holiday, she had glanced at him, wanting to go somewhere they could be alone to kiss and love and lose themselves as they had the weekend before. At the same time, she knew the hopelessness of getting more deeply entangled with him.

"You and I are way too opposite to get closely involved. You might not care at all and that means nothing to you, but it means a lot to me. You saw my family. My lifestyle and background are totally different from yours. If we continue to make love now, it will mean certain things on an emotional level to me that lovemaking won't to you. We'll get more deeply involved with each other. I can't separate that from my deepest feelings."

Standing, he reached out to take her into his arms again. "We'll just kiss. You say when to stop."

"If we do this, Zach, you'll have my heart."

"Maybe you'll have mine," he whispered, showering kisses on her temple to her cheek and then on her mouth. He kissed her insistently, holding her close against him, ending her arguments. She wanted him and her hunger overcame the logic, her caution, her arguments. She held him, kissing him with fervor that grew. The weekend had been another chain binding her heart. She held him tightly. She couldn't stop now. Later, he picked her up, kissing her as he carried her to the closest bedroom to make love to her.

Near dawn she stirred and rolled over to look at Zach who lay sleeping beside her. She rose up, brushing a curl off his forehead. A dark stubble covered his jaw. He was muscled and fit except for his injury that would heal. With their loving and Zach going home with her, he became more appealing each day. It didn't matter. There was no way he could ever be the man for her. No matter what her heart wanted. They were far too opposite. Even if they both were wildly in love, there was no possibility she could ever accept his lifestyle. She had told him if they continued making love, it would mean more to her and it would hurt deeply when she had to break it off and leave. And should he want her to stay, or wanted to marry her, which was impossible with a man like Zach, she couldn't accept. Not with his nomadic lifestyle.

While he had been good about the weekend with her family, she suspected there was no likelihood he would ever settle. She hurt and the hurt would grow worse later, but they were mismatched and neither wanted change.

He had met her family now and knew enough about her that he should understand what she told him. She suspected this job would end soon because he had a doctor's appointment this week and she had noticed he was getting around far better each day.

She studied him, with his shadowy long lashes on his cheeks. As he slept, she took her time. Looking at his firm lips, she thought about their kisses. Unable to resist, she leaned closer to kiss him lightly. His arm banded her waist and his eyes opened lazily. He pulled her close to kiss her to make love. She stopped thinking and gave herself to feeling.

At nine o'clock, she sat up and reached across him to get his phone from a bedside table. "Zach, it's after nine. We have to—"

He kissed her and stopped her announcement. In minutes he raised his head. "We don't really have to do anything except stay here in bed."

"Oh, yes, we do," she said, stepping out of bed and tugging free the sheet to wrap around herself. "We need to get back to our business relationship. We're already deep enough in a personal one. It's time to slow this part down." He placed his hands behind his head, smiling and watching her.

"I'll see you in the office," she said, scurrying out of the room, praying she didn't encounter Nigel before she got away from Zach and got her clothes back on.

It was an hour before she had showered and dressed in fresh jeans, a blue cotton shirt and loafers. With an eagerness she couldn't curb, she went downstairs to the office to find Zach sitting behind his desk.

He smiled when she came in and stood to come around his desk. He looked sexy, more appealing than ever in fresh, tight jeans and a black sweater. The warmth in his eyes held her immobile, unable to look away, and her pulse drummed in her ear. Her breath caught as he closed the distance between them to take her into his arms and kiss her a long time.

"Good morning," he said in a deep voice that was like fur wrapping around her.

"Good morning," she whispered in return, aware she was in love with him to the extent she might not ever get over it. This was a man she absolutely had to get over. He would never be the man for her and she could never be the woman for him.

"We weren't going to do this in the office. Use some self-control," she teased, trying to make light of the moment and end it.

"Sure. For now," he replied, heading to his desk. As Zach circled his desk, she noticed that he no longer limped and she was certain he would be able to go back to his normal life very soon and would no longer need her. The thought of telling him goodbye hurt with a pain that ran deep. She had faced the truth that she was in love with him. Hurt was inevitable.

They both were busy and lunch was brief, but he ate with her and she was glad. She wanted to be with him and the clock was ticking. Their time together would end too soon. She wanted more than just dining with him, of course, but each time they made love, her heart was bound more tightly with his.

Zach sat with work in front of him, but he couldn't keep from continually watching Emma. She was filing, moving around from desk to file cabinet, paying no attention to him. The tight jeans molded her hips and long legs. Her hair was tied behind her head with a ribbon and through lunch he had wanted to reach over and untie it.

He should have told her goodbye when they got back last night and he should have eaten lunch on his own today. He thought about her brother; he had meant it when he had told Connor he didn't want to hurt Emma. He glanced at his desk calendar. He would go to the doctor tomorrow and he suspected he would be told he had recovered and could return to his usual activities, which meant her job would be over.

If someone had bet him everything he owned that he would go home with a secretary who was a homebody deluxe, he would have lost every cent he owned. All during the ride back in the car, he had longed to lean over the seat to kiss her. When they arrived home, their lovemaking was inevitable. He could not resist.

He thought of what she had said in the car about the way he was with his family. Was his solitary life because he didn't know how to open up with his brothers or risk his emotions again and get them trampled as he had when he was a child?

He was leaving the ranch and the country as soon as he could. He would probably spend Christmas in Italy. He thought about the fun she would have with her family and couldn't keep from comparing that with thoughts about him rattling around the house in Italy all alone. The Italian home didn't hold near the appeal it had a month earlier.

Thoughts of her heated him. He wanted her right now and he wanted her in his bed again tonight. What would it be like to marry Emma and have her in his bed each night? The question shocked him because it was the first time he had contemplated even a thought of marriage with any woman he was friends with. How emotionally entangled was he with Emma? She stirred responses and emotions in him no other woman ever had. But there was no way he could have a permanent relationship with her.

She made her choices and she knew the job would end soon and they would part and not see each other again. There was absolutely no future in seeing her after she returned to Dallas. This wasn't the woman for him. Except in bed. He couldn't get enough of her there. Just watching her and thinking about her, he was getting aroused.

Knowing he had to get his mind off her and cool down, he turned to pick up the weekend mail, trying to concentrate on business.

It was almost four when Zach's phone rang. Emma had closed her computer and it looked as if she were clearing her desk to get ready to go. Zach answered the phone to hear Will.

Zach turned to ice, swearing quietly, causing Emma to look at him. "I'll be there as fast as I can get there." He replaced the phone.

"Caroline's gone," he said, glancing at Emma as he punched a number on his cell phone while he came around his desk.

"Oh, no. How long ago?" Emma rushed to keep up with him. She hurried beside him. "What happened? What will you do?"

"Go look for her. You can stay or you can come with me." Zach broke off to talk to his foreman. "Carl, Zach. Caroline's dog ran off and she went after it. They don't know where she is. Organize the guys and get them to head over to Will's ranch to help look for her. I'm going now." He listened and then ended the call. He grabbed a jacket he kept in the back hallway. He tossed her one of his. "Take this if you're coming with me."

She yanked on the heavy jacket, half running to keep up with him.

"Will and Ava are in Dallas. They were going to the symphony," Zach explained as they hurried toward the eight-car garage. "They're flying back now."

"How did Caroline disappear?"

"Muffy got out and Caroline went after her. The nanny, Rosalyn, went after Caroline, but Rosalyn slipped and fell. They think she hit her head on a rock because she lost consciousness briefly. When she regained consciousness, Caroline was gone." He was tempted to tell Emma to stay at the ranch because he could go faster without her, but they probably would need everyone they could get to help search for Caroline. His insides were a knot thinking about the little girl wandering around on the ranch with night coming.

"Thank heavens the weather is warmer than last week," Emma said, half running to keep up with his long stride.

"Will already has a chopper in the air and he's calling Ryan. He'll notify the county sheriff after he talks to Ryan," Zach said. He was chilled with fear for Caroline and couldn't wait to get to Will's ranch to start searching. Hazards spun in his mind and he tried to not think about them. How long would it take Caroline to get to the highway? From what Will said, she must have been near the house when last seen. He'd think forty minutes to an hour at best before she could possibly reach the highway. He glanced at the sky. It probably would be dark in another two hours.

"Damn, there are some canyons and some woods on Will's land," he said. "She's just so little."

Climbing into a pickup, with Emma rushing into the passenger seat, Zach headed toward the highway pushing the truck as fast as he dared.

Emma called her mother, relaying the situation. "My family can at least say a few prayers," she explained to Zach. "How long has Caroline been gone?"

"Not long. The minute she regained consciousness, Rosalyn called Will on her cell, so it was just a brief time. The bad thing was Rosalyn had no idea which direction to go to look for Caroline."

"Surely she hasn't gone far from home. Maybe she'll find her way back soon."

"She'll be chasing that little dog," he said, explaining about how easily Caroline could find her way to the highway. "Little kids can go fast sometimes and they like to run."

"I think we'll find her. She hasn't had time to get far."

"We've got a creek that has a few deep spots. She swims, but it's cold and I don't know what she'd do if she panicked. We have rattlesnakes in abundance," he said, clamping his mouth closed. "At least it's winter and the snakes won't be the same problem as in summer," he said, aware he was thinking out loud. Caroline was too little, her life too sheltered, to have any idea how to take care of herself.

"Hope for the best, Zach," she said, looking every which

way out the windows. "I know she can't be this far out, but I can't keep from looking around."

He gritted his teeth. He couldn't understand Emma's hopeful tone as if finding Caroline had become a certainty. There had been only rare moments in his adult life he had felt terrified, but he did now. He never had to this extent.

The car left a cloud of dust in the graveled road as he sped along, sliding on curves, sending plumes of dust into the air. They reached the highway in record time and he was amazed his driving hadn't scared Emma. Feeling a grim foreboding, Zach pushed the truck to its limit, speeding on the flat road. He gripped the steering wheel until his knuckles hurt.

"When we get close to Will's land, especially in line with the house, should you slow to watch for her?"

"I'm going to the house to find out where Rosalyn last saw her. We have to find her before night falls. We have mountain lions, coyotes. She can't stay out alone tonight."

"She can't have gotten far," Emma said with a strong, positive tone. "We'll find her before dark. We'll split up to look," Emma said. "No point in staying together. Maybe Muffy will just go home."

"I don't think so," Zach replied, his nerves on edge and not helped by Emma's cheerful optimism. "That little dog isn't any more accustomed to being out on her own than Caroline is. Muffy won't know the way home. Damn, I've never felt so helpless."

"Have you ever been this panicked about yourself?"

He gave her a startled look. "That's entirely different."

"Have you ever been this concerned about another adult?"

"No. Adults are different. Caroline is vulnerable."

"You're going to help. There are lots of people to help in the search. I'm sure we'll find her."

"Emma, I don't know how you can be so certain we'll find her," he said, trying to avoid snapping at her. "All the odds are the other way." If he and Emma were opposites, it had never been more so than at this moment. He glanced at her and saw her watching the land spreading away from the county road.

"There are a lot of people to look for her and she hasn't been gone long," Emma replied.

She was right, but it was a huge ranch with too many hazards for a child. Caroline would be completely unpredictable because she had never been out alone before. He hurt for Will and Zach was terrified for Caroline, trying to avoid thinking about how afraid she must be.

They lapsed into another silence until Zach waved a hand. "We're less than a mile from the turn into Will's ranch."

A barb wire fence bounded the property and the land near the road was flat with mesquite scattered across it. "You can see a lot from here." Shortly, he spotted the gate ahead and beyond it a thick grove of trees. The road curved out of sight and two tall cottonwoods bordered the county road. "Let me out along here, Zach," Emma said.

"I don't think she's had time to get this far. I hope not."

"I'll start walking back toward the house. Maybe I'll meet her." She patted his arm. "Don't worry until you have to."

"How the hell can I not worry?" he snapped, knowing he was being sharp, but he was filled with worry and fear for Caroline and he couldn't understand or appreciate Emma's positive attitude.

"Let me out as soon as you turn off the highway please."

"Emma, I don't want to have to worry about you, too."

"Don't be ridiculous. I have my phone. Stop the car and I'll go on foot."

He slowed, turned and stopped.

"Be positive, Zach. We'll find her." She jumped out quickly and he drove away.

At least she had a phone and knew how to use it. He suspected Emma knew little more than Caroline about being out on her own on the ranch, but she was an adult and would be okay. She was insulated in her positive feelings while he had none. As he drove around a bend in the road, Emma disappeared from sight in his rearview mirror.

Emma stood still, her gaze searching the dark woods. It would be five soon and since it was winter, the daylight would fade quickly. Saying another prayer, she began to walk inside Will's fence, continuing on in the direction they had been headed before Zach turned onto the ranch drive. She had told him she would walk toward the house, but she wanted to look along the highway a bit first. The highway worried Zach and she could see why. She studied the darkness beneath the thick grove of trees as she went. Surely if a child and a dog were nearby, they would make noise.

"Caroline," Emma called, the cry sounding small, pointless in all the emptiness around her.

Emma walked briskly for ten minutes, following the wide curve of the road, listening for any sounds of a child and then she heard voices. The road still curved and whoever was talking was lost to sight, but it sounded like more than two people.

Emma jogged, following the road, and finally she saw a pickup ahead. It had pulled off the side of the road. Relief and joy swamped her because it was a couple standing and talking to Caroline. The child held a white dog in her arms.

"Caroline!" Emma lengthened her stride and ran, breathing deeply when she reached them.

"Caroline, everyone is looking for you," she said as she hugged the little girl lightly.

She looked expectantly at the couple standing watching. She offered her hand. "I'm Emma Hillman," she said.

"We're Pete and Hazel Tanner," a deeply tanned, white-haired man said. His wide-brimmed hat was pushed back on his head. "We saw the dog and stopped and in a few minutes the little girl came running into sight. She gave us a number to call and they are coming to get her."

"Thank you so much," Emma said. "I'll call her uncle and tell him in case he hasn't gone to the house." She turned slightly, calling Zach to tell him.

"I'm the one coming back to get her," Zach said. "When I drove up, they told me the Tanners had called. Thank goodness you're with them. I should be there in minutes."

"She's fine, Zach. And she has her dog with her. These nice people stopped to see about Muffy and then Caroline came along."

"Just wait and I'll get all of you. I won't be long."

"I'm sure you won't," she said smiling and thinking how fast he had driven. She called her mother to let her know Caroline was found safe.

Scratching Muffy's head while Caroline held her, she talked to the couple for a few minutes. She wanted a hand close to the dog in case Muffy decided to run again.

"Caroline told us her name and how her little dog ran away and she couldn't catch her. She said her nanny was probably looking for her," Mabel Tanner said.

"A lot of people are searching for Caroline," Emma stated, smiling at the girl.

Emma heard the car before she saw Zach and then she watched him pull onto the shoulder to park. He had a leash in his hand and hooked it on Muffy's collar after he had hugged Caroline. Picking up Caroline, he handed the end of the leash to Emma while he talked to the Tanners.

"Thanks beyond words for helping," he said, shaking hands with the couple and talking briefly to them. In minutes they climbed into their pickup while Zach held the door for Emma and Caroline. As Caroline buckled herself into the back, Zach buckled the leash in beside her. Caroline pulled Muffy onto her lap. Zach leaned in to brush a kiss on the top of Caroline's head. "You gave us a real scare," he said softly.

"I'm sorry." She smiled up at him, and he stepped back to close the door.

He slid behind the wheel and glanced at Emma. "After I talked to you and knew you were with Caroline, I called Will to tell him to go on to the symphony because everything is okay here. He's already landing. He said he wants to come home to hug Caroline."

"I can understand that," Emma answered. She turned in her seat to talk to Caroline.

"Caroline, did you have trouble finding Muffy?"

"No. I could see her, but she wouldn't come back to me. I had to run fast."

"I'll bet you did," Emma replied. "You ran a long, long way."

Caroline nodded her head. "She sat to wait for me and then she'd run. I think she wanted to play."

Emma had to laugh. "I'm sure she had great fun."

"Everyone was very worried about you and Muffy. I'm glad we found you and Muffy didn't cross the highway," Zach said.

"Mr. and Mrs. Tanner told me that they saw Muffy and stopped because they thought she was a lost dog. Then they saw me. When I told them I was alone, they called Daddy Two. I told them his phone number."

"That was the right thing to do," Zach said. "He'll be here soon."

Caroline's eyes narrowed. "Am I in trouble?"

"I don't think so," Zach said. "We'll just be glad to have you and Muffy home again. Rosalyn is very worried. We all were worried about where you were and if you were safe. You gave us all a big scare, Caroline," he said.

"I would have gone home, but I couldn't catch Muffy."

"Would you have known how to find home?" Zach asked her.

"I could have followed the fence. Except I got scared when I saw Muffy running toward the highway."

"I'll bet you were scared. How did Muffy get loose?"

"The back gate wasn't closed all the way. Someone had left it open and Muffy squeezed out."

"Well, we'll put a little sign on that gate to keep it closed," Zach said and Caroline smiled.

Caroline hugged Muffy who had stretched out to sleep. "Thank you for coming to get me, Uncle Zach."

"You're welcome," he said.

Soon they were home and as they approached the house, Rosalyn waited on the porch. Pulling her coat close around her, she came down the steps to greet them. With a bandage on her forehead, she looked pale and she walked slowly, carefully hanging to the rail.

"Rosalyn doesn't look so great," Zach said quietly.

They climbed out of the car, and Caroline ran to Rosalyn to hug her while Zach got Muffy out and held her until they were inside the fenced yard. He set the small dog on her feet to remove her leash.

Emma greeted Caroline's nanny and stood quietly while Zach talked to her about her fall. "You should get off your feet, Rosalyn."

"I will. I just had to come hug Caroline. She didn't know I fell. She thought I was probably coming behind her. I can't tell you how worried I've been. About as much as Mr. Will. I caught my foot on a root and I couldn't keep from falling. I hit something, and then I was just out. When I came to, Caroline was gone. I've never had such a scare," she said, looking at Caroline who was tossing a ball for Muffy.

"She's back with her dog so you mend. Take it easy and get well."

"I intend to," she said, smiling at him.

A car came up the drive and Will spilled out, hurrying around to open the door for Ava. They both rushed through the gate. The instant Caroline saw them, she threw out her arms and ran toward them.

Will picked her up to hug her and hold her out so she and Ava could hug.

"We'll go say hello and goodbye. Leave the family to themselves," Zach said.

Will turned to greet them, shaking Zack's hand. "Thanks for coming on the run and thanks, Emma, for finding her with the Tanners on the highway. They live over in the next county and we know each other to say hello. I couldn't believe Caroline made it to the highway in that time."

"We're all happy now," Zach said. "We'll leave you to talk to Caroline and Rosalyn. Night, sweetie," he added, kissing Caroline's cheek. Slipping a small, thin arm around his neck, she hugged him and Zach smiled at her.

He took Emma's arm to go to his car and in minutes they were on the road driving back to his ranch.

"I'm going home, kicking back and having a beer. Caroline looks so little and frail. That scared me. I still feel as if my insides are shivering." He glanced at her. "How did you keep so calm?"

"You were calm."

"I just had it all bottled up, but it's coming out now."

Emma was amazed, because Zach seemed so tough, and today, cool when he had taken charge to call his men and then get to Will's ranch quickly. He had traveled and worked in dangerous jobs all over the world where he'd had to keep his wits, yet now he was coming apart. She saw his hands had a tremor. "I don't know how you were calm," he repeated.

"Positive thinking and prayers, Zach. Expecting a happy outcome."

"You're the eternal optimist," he stated, shaking his head. "I've seen too much, Emma. Positive thinking and prayers can't guarantee happy endings."

"Neither can giving up hope and imagining all sorts of scary scenarios. Then if something happens, because of your imagination, you've suffered more than once. We're very different people."

"Amen to that one," he said. "There's the one thing we can agree about," he added and she smiled.

As soon as they were inside the house, Zach built a fire, got the wine she requested and a beer for himself. While he sipped, he stretched out on the floor. Firelight flickered over him and her breath caught. He looked virile, appealing. Broad shoulders, long legs, thick curls. She wanted to join him, but that was a path to deeper complications.

"How do people have kids and not have nervous breakdowns when they do something like Caroline just did?" he asked.

"You cope with it, just the way you and Will and Ava did. You do whatever you can," Emma said.

"I'll never understand how you could stay cheerful and optimistic that we would find her. I know the reason you gave me, but I still don't get it"

"We did find her," she reminded him, sitting near him to sip her drink. He removed it from her hands and drew her down into his arms to kiss her. "I just try to focus on the positive, Zach. And Caroline hadn't been gone long when everyone started looking for her."

"I keep thinking she had reached the highway and if the Tanners hadn't come along—"

"But they did come along, so don't think about the other possibilities," Emma said. He held her in his embrace as they were stretched on the floor together. She had been frightened for Caroline, but certain they would find her. Now to know

Caroline was safe and with Will, Emma felt as if they had been given the biggest Christmas gift early.

Desire, relief, joy all buoyed her and she wrapped her arms around Zach to kiss him hungrily. Instantly, his arm tightened around her waist and he pulled her closer. "I need you tonight, Emma," he said in a rasp. "This is an affirmation of life and all's right with our world," he said, his blue eyes darkening as he drew her closer.

Seven

Relief transformed into lust, and loving Zach *was* an affirmation of life.

Heat from the fire warmed her, but not as much as Zach's kisses that sent her temperature climbing.

Sex with him became paramount. To be alive, to be able to make love with Zach, to have loved ones safe—her emotions ran high and she threw herself into kissing him, tangling her fingers in his thick hair.

She thought Zach was caught in the same emotional whirlwind, relieved, celebrating life and that all was okay now because his kisses became more passionate as he concentrated totally on pleasuring her.

In seconds they loved with a desperate hunger. With ragged breathing, she kissed him while her fingers traced muscles and planes of his body. Wild abandon consumed her and when they were joined, they rocked together until she cried out his name with her thundering release.

"Zach, ah, love," she gasped, the word slipping out and

she hoped he hadn't heard her. Rapture enveloped her, a moment in time when they were in unison and meant something to each other. A moment she wanted to hold, yet would be as fleeting as the snowflake she had caught and watched disappear in her warm palm.

Afterwards, as they drifted back to reality, he held her close in his arms while he showered her face and shoulders with light kisses that made her feel adored.

She turned on her side to look at Zach, drawing her fingers along his jaw to feel the rough, dark stubble. "This isn't what I expected tonight. Yet it's a rejoicing of sorts."

"A definite celebration of life for me." He sighed and traced his fingers over her bare shoulder. "I hope next week is another occasion for cheer. I have a doctor's appointment and I have high hopes I can get back into a normal shoe."

"When you do we'll be through here. Zach, I still urge you to keep those letters. You don't know if Caroline will want them one day. If you destroy them, you can't get them back."

"I know you've scanned most of them into the computer, so now we have electronic copies."

"The original letters are far more important."

He smiled. "Emma, you're a hopeless romantic. You're talking about letters written over a hundred years ago."

"I feel as if I know that part of your family. They were brave, intelligent and your great-great-grandfather had a sense of humor. I've found touching letters by your great-great-grandmother, too. I think the letters are priceless. And the fact that the letters date from over a hundred years ago has value, Zach. The electronic copies hold *no* value except they are copies if the originals are destroyed."

"I think you're placing too high a value on old letters. Now the things we've found mixed in with the letters, the gold watch, the Colt revolver, the Henry rifle—those are valuable. I can't believe someone put a Colt or a rifle in a box of letters."

"They put together what was important to them."

"No way are those letters as valuable as that Colt."

"Maybe not in dollars, but I think the letters are more valuable. The letters are a window into your ancestors' thoughts and dreams and lives."

He rose on an elbow to look at her. "We are polar opposites in every way. How can we possibly have this attraction that turns my insides out?"

"It does other things to you," she said, caressing him.

"You know what you're doing to me now," he said in a deep voice.

"Zach," she whispered, knowing the one part of their lives where they were totally compatible. "You're an incredibly sexy man," she added.

"That, darlin', is the pot calling the kettle black, as the old saying goes." His eyes darkened and his gaze shifted to her mouth as he leaned closer to kiss her.

She held him tightly while the endearment, his first, echoed in her mind and how she wished he had meant something by it. When it came to Zach, she couldn't hang on to that optimism she had everywhere else in her life.

Through the night they made love and slept in each other's arms. It was late morning before they dressed and ate. While Zach talked on the phone to Will, she sat at the kitchen table and gazed outside at the crystal blue swimming pool, the color reminding her of Zach's eyes. She thought about all she loved and admired about him—his generosity, his care for Caroline and his family, even if he didn't spend time with them, he obviously loved them. He was intelligent, talented, capable of running the businesses he owned and she had heard he started all of them, not his father. He was caring and fun, exciting, obviously a risk-taker although that wasn't a part that held high appeal for her.

As soon as he told Will goodbye, she stood. "Zach, I'm going back to work. I can still get a lot done today."

Nodding his head, he stood as she left the room. Her back tingled and she was tempted to turn around to stay with him and postpone work, but there was no point and no future in spending a lot of time with him. After this job ended, she did not expect to see him again.

Each day the rest of the week she spent nearly all her time reading the letters. When she returned Sunday night after the weekend at home, she was certain this would be her last week to work for Zach. A new concern nagged her constantly—for the first time, her period was late. They had used protection, so she dismissed the likelihood of pregnancy, but she didn't know what was wrong. Tuesday morning she called to make an appointment to see her family doctor the following week when she would be at home in Dallas.

Later that day, forgetting time or her surroundings, she read a yellowed letter on crackling paper.

"Zach, do you have a moment? Listen to this letter," she said. "This one is from your great-grandfather when their first child, a son, was born. Was your grandfather the oldest son?"

"Yes, he was," Zach said, leaning back in his chair.

She bent over the paper spread on her knees, her hair falling forward around her face.

"My dear sister. Lenore gave me a son today. He is a fine, strong baby and I am pleased. He has my color eyes and his mother's light hair. He has a healthy cry. I am certain his cries can be heard at the creek.

"With her long hair down Lenore looks beautiful. She has given me life's most precious gift. I feel humble, because there is nothing as valuable that I can present to her in return. I have done what I hope will please her the most. To surprise her I have ordered a piano for her.

"I wish I could give her fine satin gowns and a palace, but

she would merely laugh if I told her my wish. Instead, I hope she likes her piano. It will be shipped to Saint Joseph, Missouri, on the train. I will send four of the boys with a wagon and a team to go to Missouri to pick up the piano. They must protect it from the elements, thieves and all hazards because they will have to cross more than one treacherous river. They have promised they can get the piano and bring it back here."

Pausing, she looked up as Zach crossed the room to her. "Surely, that letter means something to you."

Taking the letter from her fingers to drop it back into the box, he pulled her to her feet, putting his arm around her waist. "I still say you're a romantic."

"If you destroy these, I think you'll have regrets."

"That's impossible for me to imagine. Today I'm filled with positive moments because I expect a great prognosis when I go to the doctor this afternoon. I think he'll say I'm healed and can wear regular shoes. After Christmas I want to take you dancing."

Her heart felt squeezed. She was thrilled while at the same time, that was only postponing their final parting.

"We'll see when the time comes," she said, placing her hands on Zach's chest. She could feel his heart beneath her palms and wondered if his reaction to her was half as strong as how he affected her. His blue eyes darkened with desire, causing her heartbeat to quicken. "You may not be able to dance as soon as you think. What is more likely—you'll be half a world away by that time."

"I don't think that's why you aren't accepting, is it?"

"I don't see much future for us. I think when you fully recuperate, you'll be gone. You'll return to life as you've always lived it. You have to agree."

"I might hang around Texas for a while. There are things I can do here. Wherever I am, I can fly home when I want to."

"I don't know how you can even call one place home.

This is the family ranch, now Garrett's, not your home. You don't stay in your home in Dallas," she argued breathlessly, having to make an effort to concentrate on their conversation when all she could think about was being in his arms and wanting him.

He smiled at her. "I'll ask again." Sparks arced between them, the air crackling. Just as it had been between them that first encounter, she was caught and held in his steady gaze that made her even more breathless.

"Zach," she whispered, sliding her arms around his neck.

He kissed her. Tingles streaked across her nerves. Awareness intensified of every inch of him pressed so close. Holding him tightly, she refused to think about the future, the job ending, her saying goodbye to Zach. Each day she was more in love with him. The world, work, letters, her future, all ceased to exist in her thoughts that focused totally on him.

His kiss turned her insides to jelly, ignited fires, heat sizzling in her. She pressed against him more firmly, taking what she could while he was here in her arms because too soon he would be gone forever.

Finally, she gave a thought to their time and place.

"Zach, there are other people in the house now," she whispered, wondering if her protests fell on deaf ears.

He kissed her, silencing her conversation. When she felt him tug on her sweater, she grasped his wrists. Breathing hard, he looked at her as she shook her head.

"We're downstairs. Nigel and Rosie are here. Within the hour you should leave for your flight to Dallas to see your doctor. We have to stop loving now."

Combing long strands of hair from her face, Zach looked at her mouth. "You're beautiful. We'll come back to this moment tonight when I get home."

"We shouldn't," she whispered. "You need to get lunch now before you go."

"I know what I'd rather do."

She shook her head. "Lunch is on the schedule."

"Ok, come eat with me." She nodded, walking beside him, unable to resist. Through lunch he was charming, making her anxious for his return before he had even left the house.

While he was gone the house was quiet and she read, stopping occasionally to stretch, or pacing the room and reading as she walked.

Late afternoon shadows grew long and she added a log to the fire. It was winter and the days had grown shorter with a chill in the air. She heard his whistle before he appeared. When he came through the office door, he closed it behind him. Her heart thudded against her ribs. She took one look at him and knew her job was over.

Vitality radiated from him as if he had been energized while he was in Dallas. She didn't have to ask what the doctor had said. Zach crossed the room to pull her to her feet and kiss her heatedly

In minutes, clothes were tossed aside. The fire was glowing orange embers, giving the only light in the darkened room during early evening.

"Zach, we're downstairs and not alone in the house."

"The door is closed. No one will bother us," he whispered between kisses. "I want you, Emma." He kissed her before she could argue and she yielded, loving him back with a desperate urgency.

They moved to the rug in front of the fire. Heat warmed her side while Zach's body was hot against her own. He got a condom from a pocket and returned to kneel between her legs while he put it in place.

Orange sparks and embers highlighted the bulge of muscles and his thick manhood while the planes of his cheeks and flat stomach were shadows. Another memory to lock away in her mind and heart.

A log cracked and fell, sending a shower of sparks spiraling up the chimney. The sudden flash of red and orange dancing sparks illuminated Zach even more for a brief moment. He looked like a statue, power and desire enveloping him. She drew her fingers along his muscled thighs and heard him gasp for breath.

Lowering himself, he wrapped his arms around her to thrust slowly into her, filling her. He was hard, hot, moving with a tantalizing slowness as she arched beneath him.

"Zach," she whispered, wanting to confess her love, longing to hold him tightly and tell him she loved him with all her heart.

Their rhythm built, increasing need and tension, until release burst, spinning her into ecstasy, taking him with her seconds later.

She lost awareness of everything except Zach in their moment of perfect union. A physical bonding at the height of passion that carried with it an emotional bonding. Clinging to him with her long legs wrapped around him, she did not want to let go as if she could hold the moment and delay time itself. This man, so totally different from her, had become vital to her. Right now she couldn't face letting him go.

They slowed, calmed while she caught her breath. Her hands were light touches, caressing his shoulders and back while she drifted in paradise.

When he rolled over, taking her with him, he kissed her tenderly. There was still enough glow from embers to reflect on Zach and she touched his cheek lightly. "The doctor said your foot is healed, didn't he?"

"Yes, he did," Zach said, smiling. "I can toss this boot and wear my shoes. My own boots have to wait a while, but eventually, I can wear them."

"So my job ends this week. Christmas is coming and I wanted off anyway."

"I'll be gone for Christmas, but I'll come back afterwards and that's when I'm taking you out. I'd stay if you'd stay with me for a few weeks, but you'll want to be home for Christmas."

"Yes, I will," she said, hurting, even though she had known this time was approaching.

"I'll be in touch with you," he said. Glancing over his shoulder, he shifted away to stand and put another log on the fire. He returned to pull her close against him, warm body against warm body as he wrapped his legs with hers.

He combed her long hair away from her face with his fingers. Tingles followed each stroke and she could feel their hearts beating together.

"This is paradise, Emma."

How she longed to hear him say words of love. Common sense told her that would not happen, but wishes and dreams came with his strong arms holding her and his light kisses making her feel loved.

All were illusions that would disappear with the morning sun. For now she could pretend, wish, hope, give herself to fantasies that normally she wouldn't entertain for a minute.

She kissed him lightly in return.

The fire crackled and burned, causing dancing dark shadows and bathing Zach's body in orange.

"You're very quiet," he said.

"I'm savoring the moment."

"I'm savoring holding you close. Sometime tonight we'll get in a bed, but not yet."

Eventually, they gathered their clothing and each went to shower. They put away the dinner Rosie had cooked and made sandwiches to eat in front of the fire and sat and talked until Zach stood and took her hand.

"Let's go upstairs and I'll build a fire in my room. I can do stairs now with ease." He placed his arm across her shoulders as they climbed the stairs, leading her down the hall to his suite of rooms where he took her into his arms to kiss her.

Wednesday, she gave all her time to the letters. Zach's work had dwindled as Christmas approached, so since Thanksgiving she had devoted her time to trying to get through as many of the letters and memorabilia as she could.

She hoped someone else in the Delaney family wanted the letters because the few she had read to Zach and the ones he had read himself had not changed his feelings about them. He always sent them to the discard pile.

By Friday, the tension from being constantly around him—loving him, but not able to make him truly hers—was greater than ever. Today would change everything. Today she would return to Dallas, to her life before meeting Zach. Even though he had talked about seeing her after Christmas, she didn't expect to see Zach again.

Early that morning Rosie cooked while Emma ate breakfast. Halfway through breakfast, Emma felt sick and dashed to the bathroom. When she returned, she carried what was left of her breakfast back to the kitchen.

"Rosie, I can't eat any more. I felt sick and now food doesn't look good."

Rosie turned to study her while she dried her hands and took the dishes from Emma. "You were sick yesterday morning."

Emma looked at Rosie and met a speculative gaze. "My period is late," Emma said, confessing what had been worrying her each day. "I shouldn't be sick no matter what, but I am."

"Bless your heart," Rosie said, hugging Emma lightly. Emma stood immobile, stunned. Fear had blossomed earlier over a week ago. She had pushed away the nagging worry, telling herself it was her imagination. But it was too many days now for it to be her imagination. Two days in a row, she had been sick during breakfast and then it was gone.

"Rosie, I have two married sisters and a sister-in-law. They all have babies. I've seen both my sisters have morning sickness." Emma felt chilled and trembled. "Rosie, this wasn't in my plans."

"You don't know for certain, do you?"

"No. I'll get a pregnancy test this weekend when I go to Dallas. I already have a doctor's appointment for next week."

Rosie placed her hands on her hips while she faced Emma. "Then don't start worrying now. The stomach upset might be something you ate and your period could start tomorrow. How late are you?"

"A week now."

Emma rolled her eyes. "That's not enough to give you a worry. A few days is nothing. Wait a few weeks."

Emma nodded, but she was not reassured. "I'm extremely on time almost to the hour, so this is unique." Suddenly, to the depths, she was certain she was pregnant with Zach's baby. Her head swam and for an instant she felt light-headed. She reached out to grasp the kitchen counter to steady herself. Rosie's hand closed on her arm.

"Are you all right?"

Rosie's expression showed concern that threatened panic. "Rosie, promise me—please don't say anything yet until I know for sure."

"I would never. Don't give it another worry. That's not my business and I don't interfere in something like this. I'll not say anything." Rosie's brow furrowed and her eyes were filled with concern.

"I don't panic over things, but I feel panicky over this. I feel so out of control."

"Wait until you've seen a doctor and know absolutely," Rosie said, but her voice held only solicitude.

"This wasn't supposed to happen," Emma whispered, more to herself than Rosie.

"Some things are just out of our hands," Rosie declared. "Go back to your room and lie down if you need to." She took Emma's icy hand in her soft, warm hands, briefly and then released her. "You have a big, loving family. They'll take care of you and a little one."

A little one. Emma shook and clenched her hands. Rosie hadn't said a word about Zach being helpful. Was this going to be a huge shock—and an unpleasant one for him? Would it be a responsibility he didn't want? He had talked about how unprepared Will had been for Caroline. On the other hand, Zach seemed to truly care for Caroline and he had been a wreck when they couldn't find her. Of all men on earth— "I'm going to my room if he comes asking for me," she said, suddenly wanting to get behind closed doors and adjust to what was happening before she faced another person. "This is my last day. He doesn't need to know until I'm sure."

"I promise. You have your secret," Rosie said, nodding and going back to doing dishes.

Emma hurried out and raced out of sight, rushing to her room where she crossed the room to place her hands on her flat middle. "I can't be," she whispered.

In her dressing room she studied herself in the mirror, turning first one way and another. She had watched two sisters and a sister-in-law go through pregnancies. She looked in the mirror, running her hands over her flat stomach. There were no single mothers in her family.

Zach. How could she ever tell a man who wouldn't even spend Christmas with his family that he was about to become a father?

Eight

She was staring at her stomach in the dressing room of her suite when her stomach rolled and she ran for the bathroom. She was sick again and this time she knew it was partly with worry.

She thought of her brother, Connor. Connor was strong-willed, the take-charge oldest sibling, a total alpha male who would want to make Zach marry her. He wouldn't want to marry or he already would have talked about it. Zach would rebel and probably disappear to another country.

She shook again, chilled on the warm day. She ran a cold cloth over her face and went back to sit, knotting her fists and trying to think what to do, praying she was wrong.

She could leave, slip out without Zach even knowing and then say goodbye with a call from Dallas.

Too many things were so wrong. She had just tossed her future into uncertainty and chaos. Why had she ever stayed and worked for him? Why had she made love with him? Fallen in love with him when she had known it would be disastrous and hopeless? Why hadn't the protection worked?

The Dallas job would go, too. If she stayed there, word would get right back to him. *Just quit the company and go somewhere else,* she told herself. By the time she was ready to tell Zach, he would probably be halfway around the world, far from Texas and from her. Soon she would be only a memory to him.

Standing in front of the mirror, she inspected her figure. She could get through Christmas without anyone knowing. Common sense said to stop worrying until she was certain, but that was impossible. All her positive reactions to past upheavals were gone now. She couldn't hold the same cheerful certainty for herself and she needed to get a grip. This worry was not like her and there was a bright side. If she could just focus on the baby and try to avoid thinking about Zach. A total impossibility.

In her heart, there were no doubts. Because of their loving, she would become the mother of a Delaney. It seemed likely that Zach would help support his child, but that was all. A man whose heart was already given to traveling and his job would never be tied down by a family.

Feeling an ache of worry increasing, she rubbed her neck. Mary Kate was her closest sibling and she could tell her. The thought of Mary Kate's support lifted Emma's spirits slightly. Her sister would be a staunch ally and Emma was certain she could always count on her mother's acceptance. If she could just keep Connor from doing something wild like wanting to punch out Zach.

She remembered Will and Ava and Caroline and the love that shone between Will and Ava, plus their eagerness when they had announced a baby on the way. Emma hurt, her insides twisting into a knot while tears threatened. She wouldn't have that shared joy and love. This wasn't the way she had always dreamed about having a family. The love she had wished for was what she had witnessed between Will and Ava.

Emma wiped her eyes and got up, walking restlessly, wishing she could undo what had been done. She had no one to blame but herself. How she wished she could back up and relive her life.

Then Emma thought about the baby and put her hand protectively on her stomach. *Her* baby. Her family would be shocked, upset, angry, probably even with her, but when the baby arrived, they would all accept and love the tyke.

This baby would fit into her family and they would shower the baby and her with love. Her brothers would be dads for the baby. Her child would not come into the world unloved or unwanted.

She stretched on the bed, staring into space while her mind raced over problems and solutions.

The first hurdle was to get through today with Zach. She was already packed, ready to go home. How was she going to be able to tell Zach goodbye?

An hour later she went down to work. Zach sat stretched out, his feet on a window ledge while he talked on the phone. She sat at her desk, unable to work, looking at him and thinking about the future.

She could tell he was getting ready to end the call, so she returned to the box of letters where she had spent all of her time lately.

As she picked up a letter something rattled inside the envelope. Turning the envelope over, she shook it. A golden heart locket on a chain fell into her palm. Glittering brightly in the center of the heart was a brilliant green stone.

She withdrew the fragile letter and read, looking up to interrupt Zach. "Listen to this letter: '...this was my grandmother's locket with my great-grandmother's and my great-grandparents' pictures. I want you to have it because it should remain in the family to be passed to each generation.' This letter is signed by your great-grandfather, so this locket must be incredibly old if it belonged to his grandmother." Pausing, she put aside the letter. "Look at this beautiful locket. There are two tiny paintings inside with pictures, I suppose, of two more Delaneys, an even more distant generation." She carried the locket across the office to hand it to Zach.

Standing, he took the locket to turn it in his hand and inspect it.

Finally he looked up and held it out. "Emma, you take this. I want you to have it."

"Zach, I can't do that! You have a family and some of your relatives may want it. You should keep that jewelry. It's an heirloom and your great-grandfather wanted it to stay in the Delaney family."

"You said you feel as if you are part of the Delaneys when you read those old letters. I want you to have it as a bonus for your work and to give you a tangible memory of all this history you waded through. Here," he said, taking it from her and stepping behind her to fasten it around her neck.

"I really think you should keep this in your family," she said and then realized part of her would become part of his family. She placed her fist protectively against her stomach.

"I want you to have it," he insisted, taking her shoulders to turn her to face him as he judged how it looked on her. "It is pretty," he added, his voice deepening while it thickened with desire. He looked into her eyes. She met his blue ones, her heart beating faster. She wanted his strong arms around her. She wanted to hold him while she kissed him. As if he could read her thoughts, he drew her to him and placed his mouth on hers.

Her heart slammed against her ribs. Zach pulled her close, holding her tightly while he kissed her hard and possessively.

Her pounding heart should indicate her feelings as she

held him tightly in return. She let go all restraint, kissing him, her deepest love, the father of her baby. And she was certain she was pregnant. How she wished she didn't ever have to tell him.

"Zach," she said, on the verge of saying she would miss him. "Thank you for the necklace. Your brothers and your half sister may not be happy with you for giving away this heirloom."

"My brothers would definitely want you to have it. Sophia, I don't know. I want you to have it. Actually, I don't think I'm making you much of a gift except I suspect you think so."

She looked at the locket in her hand and got a knot in her throat as emotions choked her. "I do think so," she whispered, knowing it would go to a Delaney heir.

Zach put his finger beneath her chin to raise her face. Embarrassed because she couldn't hide her emotional reaction, she stood on tiptoe and kissed him quickly.

As their kiss became passionate, her emotions shifted. When she ended their kiss, they both were breathless and she suspected Zach had forgotten about her reaction to the locket.

"I'm going to miss you, Emma."

"You can still come spend Christmas with us," she said, certain of his answer.

He smiled. "Thanks, but I've already made arrangements. I'll be at an Italian villa I inherited. Dad always referred to it as his 'summer home.'"

His answer stung and made her leaving a reality. Yet it was for the best because now her emotions were on a rocky edge. They needed to part even though she felt as if her heart were breaking.

She placed her hand against his cheek. "I'll think about you on Christmas in your Italian villa."

"You are probably the one person in the entire world who

feels sorry for me spending Christmas that way," he said, smiling at her.

"I know what you're missing."

"We can both say that. You could come with me and let me show you that Italian villa and see how you like spending Christmas in Italy. Live a little, you have next Christmas with your family."

"Thank you, but I'll stay in Texas and you go to Italy. Zach, you get along with your family—your brothers and Caroline mean a lot to you. Realize what a treasure they are. Love and enjoy them. I think you shut yourself off in defense when you were hurt as a child. You have a wonderful family and your ancestors are fascinating. Don't sell them short. Try a Christmas with Will and family sometime, get Ryan, Sophia and Garrett there, too."

"You are a dreamer and a romantic," he said patiently. "I will enjoy my Italian villa immensely. It will be sunny, beautiful with no crowds, no schedules. You really should try it."

She shook her head. "Thank you. We'll each go where our hearts are, only I think yours is there out of an old habit more than because you really enjoy it."

"I suppose I never stopped to think about it."

She stepped away and glanced at her watch. "I need to get on the road now. The job has been wonderful." She tried to hold back tears as she stood on tiptoe to kiss him.

He held her tightly, kissing her fiercely. Finally, he paused. "You can stay this weekend if you want."

"I have plans in Dallas," she said, knowing it would be heartbreaking to spend the weekend and go through this last day again.

She stepped out of his embrace. It was time to go. She'd already said her goodbyes to Rosie and Nigel, and Nigel had already placed her things in her car.

Zach headed out with her, reaching around her to open the car door.

"You'll hear from me," he said.

"Maybe I'll see you at headquarters someday," she replied lightly, sliding behind the wheel. Closing the door, he stepped back and she started the car. As she waved and drove away, she glanced in the rearview mirror to see him standing in the drive, watching her.

She would tell her mother and sisters she had been invited to Zach's Italian villa. Connor didn't need to hear about it. An Italian villa sounded like paradise, but not at Christmas. That was definitely family time.

Family time. Worry and heartbreak stung. She couldn't keep from crying until she thought about the baby and making plans. How and when would she tell her family? She'd wait until after Christmas because she had no idea how they would receive the news.

Zach had seemed good with Caroline and interested in her. How would he be with his own child? He had told her how they had struggled to get Sophia into the family and how much they wanted to know her. Surely, if he wanted to know his half sister, he would want to know his child.

The first thing was to get a pregnancy test kit. If she wasn't pregnant, then all these worries would seem ridiculous.

Pregnant—it was a shock she couldn't absorb. It was so totally unexpected because they had always used protection. Something she had never thought would happen to her until after she was married. She had always looked forward to her own family, but in her mind, it had included a husband who was an active family man. A reassuring thought now was the knowledge she would never be alone raising this baby because her family would all participate. Clinging to that, she tried to ignore the steady hurt squeezing her heart.

Christmas with a baby on the way. Would she have to give

up college and her hope of teaching? Christmas had always been filled with magic for her, the best time of the year, and this Christmas would be so different. She would have to be responsible for someone else. It was an awesome task. She would get a present for her baby this week. And think of baby names. Her baby would not have the Delaney name. Another Hillman.

She missed Zach. As mismatched as they were, she liked being with him. He had been easy to work for. When she decided what and how she would tell him about the baby, she would get in touch with him. In the meantime, this break was as inevitable as it was necessary.

She fingered the locket around her neck. She thought it was a beautiful heirloom and she would take very good care of it. It would go into safekeeping for her baby soon.

She hoped Will prevailed on Zach to keep the letters. It would be sad to see them destroyed. Since she would be mother of a Delaney, if they decided to shred the letters, she intended to ask Zach for them.

She missed Zach badly and each mile between them increased her longing to be with him. She could have prolonged the separation, but there was no point and her emotions were on a raw edge. In a few hours she would be home and her family would keep her busy enough that the pain over parting with Zach should be alleviated.

By Monday, Zach missed Emma more than he had thought possible. He was planning to leave for Italy on Tuesday, but he had lost his enthusiasm for the trip. Should he do something else this Christmas? That was Emma's influence. He recalled times as a child that he had wanted to be with his family, but then he and his brothers had been left at their schools for the holidays. Eating at the home of an indifferent headmaster had never been fun and Zach began to count only on his own company. He would be happy in Italy once he was there.

Earlier that morning Will had called his brothers and Sophia, and the entire family was coming for lunch today to bring their Christmas presents to him, so he was having a little Christmas celebration with his family. Emma would have been relieved to hear it, but now she was wrapped up in her own family's activities. When he first was injured, Zach had given his secretary at headquarters a list of gifts to purchase for each member of his family. They'd been wrapped and delivered to the ranch.

Standing at the window, Zach looked at the dry, yellowed windswept landscape beyond the fenced yard. Why had life become empty without Emma? It had only been the weekend since she left, but it seemed eons ago. Common sense told him she was not the woman for him, not even in a casual way. He smiled at the thought. No relationship was casual to Emma. Not even the brief affair they had.

He paced the room restlessly. "Go to Italy," he advised aloud. "Pick up your life and forget her."

Memories flooded him of holding her, kissing her, making love to her. Of her laughter, her hands on him, her luminous green eyes studying him. Even the looks of pity she had given him came back to haunt him. Was he missing out on the best part of life as she had said? Was he letting that armor from childhood keep him from loving and being loved today?

Would he really want to be tied down with a family? Tied down with Emma? The last thought sounded like paradise.

Was he going to mope through Christmas? It was a time he had never given much thought to since he was grown.

He saw three limos coming up the drive so he left to open the front door.

Will, Ava and Caroline climbed out of the first limo. Ryan emerged from the second and Garrett and Sophia from the third limo. The drivers carried boxes filled with wrapped presents. Zach directed the drivers where to put the presents and then turned to greet everyone.

"Don't tell me all this stuff is for me," Zach said.

"Who else is here for us to give presents to? Although I do have one for Nigel and one for Rosie and I'll bet the rest do, too," Ryan said with a cocky grin. "You said you were giving Nigel and Rosie three weeks off."

"And I did. Come in," he said, picking up Caroline to give her a hug. He led them to the family room where the drivers had already placed boxes of presents.

A sofa beside a large wingback chair was piled high with Zach's presents for his brothers, Sophia and their families.

"You should have had Nigel bring down the Christmas tree," Will said.

"Don't you start that. Emma had decorations up and I got rid of them."

"You have turned into Scrooge," Will said.

"Hardly," Zach replied, waving his arm in the direction of the sofa with presents. "I believe I have a few presents for everyone."

"My apology," Will said, laughing. "Not entirely Scrooge. I do see mistletoe hanging over the door. That's a weird decoration to put up for a man living alone."

"Just drop it, Will," Zach said.

"Maybe I should have stopped by last week and met the secretary," Ryan said.

"Will a beer shut you two up?" Zach asked. "First, let me see about the drivers and get them settled with something to eat and drink. I'll be right back. When I do, we'll start this little family Christmas celebration that I suspect is totally for my benefit," Zach remarked dryly.

When he returned he asked them, "Eggnog, beer, wine, martini, margaritas, Scotch, an old-fashioned—none of you have to drive home and I have a full bar, so what do you prefer?" he said, going behind the bar to fill orders. In minutes he brought out snacks Rosie had left.

Ryan held up his bottle. "Merry Christmas to our newest family member, Sophia, to Ava and Caroline, to my big brothers, to Garrett who's been like a brother," he said, including Garrett as he always·had.

They all held up bottles and echoed his toast.

"Now I'll propose a toast," Will said, "and a Christmas prayer of thanks for Caroline in our lives, for Sophia becoming part of our family and for Ava. The four of us have been blessed by them."

"Here, here and amen," Ryan said and they clinked bottles together again.

In a few minutes Ryan raised his bottle high again. "Here's to the two surviving bachelors in this group. Zach, my bro, I'm going to outlast you."

All three of the others protested at the same time. "Ryan, you're next," Garrett said. "No way is anyone getting Zach down the aisle."

"They can't get him to stay in one country long enough to fall in love," Will added, making Zach grin.

"Sorry, Ryan, but I'll win this one," he said, thinking about Emma.

They soon went to the kitchen where Zach got out ribs from a Dutch oven. All night he had cooked ribs and he had baked beans that had slowcooked for hours. He got a large bowl of Rosie's cold potato salad. He replenished beers and they all gathered around the big table to feast on the rib dinner. As he passed out the beers, he thought of Emma. If she could see him now, she would know he enjoyed his family. They just weren't together as often as hers.

"When are you leaving for Italy?" Will asked.

"Tomorrow. The weather prediction is good. So when is everyone else going?"

"We're leaving tomorrow morning for Colorado," Will replied. "Caroline is hyped over going and she is almost climbing the walls now," he said, smiling at her and Caroline giggled.

"Garrett, when do you leave?"

"We'll go to my folks' house Thursday. We're going out with Sophia's friends Friday night."

"Ryan, what about you?"

"I'm leaving to go back to Houston. I need to see if I still have a drilling business, I've been gone so long. Meg and I have parties Friday night, Saturday night and Sunday night. Meg's a party girl."

"Meg?" Zach asked. "Should I know who Meg is?"

"No. I can answer for him," Will said. "Meg is just the most recent." He grinned at Ryan. "You two are kids, still doing kid stuff," Will teased.

"May be kid stuff, but it's fun. At least I'm not so decrepit I have to sit around someone's home each of those nights," he teased.

"And Zach in Italy. Who is the latest beautiful lady?"

"I'll be alone at my villa, which is fine."

"Well, all of you should come to Colorado. This is going to be the best ever Christmas," he said, smiling at Ava and then at Caroline. "We have a Santa suit for Muffy that Caroline thinks Muffy loves to wear. We'll have worlds of fun and if anyone wants to come afterwards to ski and enjoy Colorado, you're invited. Except our invalid."

"Not an invalid any longer," Zach said. "Doc's given me a big okay and I can do whatever I want. We didn't discuss skiing."

"C'mon, Zach," Ryan said. "Garrett, you, too. Let's fly

up there after Christmas and ski. I'll come, Will, right after
New Year's if you're staying that long."

"Sure. All of you come join us. You can bring anyone you
want with you."

"I'll see how it goes in Italy," Zach said. "I doubt if I'll be
back that soon."

"The bird has flown the coop again," Will teased. "You
just can't stay put. We'll see you next summer."

"I'll pass this time, but thanks," Garrett said. "I'm building furniture and Sophia is painting."

"Still the workaholic," Ryan stated. "Some things never
change."

They ate ribs until they had a platter filled with bones.
When they finished, they all cleaned up and soon they returned to the family room to open gifts.

The first gift went to Caroline and her eyes sparkled as she
unwrapped a box that held a new doll. She gave Zach a hug
and he smiled at her. "Merry Christmas, sweetie," he said,
wishing Emma was with him.

After the gifts were unwrapped and stacked neatly to go,
Zach said he had something else for them.

He left and returned with a box holding the gold pocket
watch, the Colt revolver and the Henry rifle. "My secretary
and I have been through a lot of the memorabilia. I don't
know why these things were buried under the letters. So far,
we found these three items. Why doesn't each family take
one. We can draw if you want to see who gets what, regarding this stuff."

"You ought to have something," Garrett said. "Leave me
out. These are Delaney possessions and I'm not a Delaney."

"Sophia is," Zach said immediately. "There was a locket
that I gave to my secretary. Sorry, I didn't wait to ask you,
Sophia, when I gave Emma the necklace. She has pored over

this stuff and enjoyed it. You'd think these people were re-lated to her."

"That's fine, Zach," Sophia said. "Really. I don't need it and it's nice you gave it to her."

"Sophia, you participate," Zach said. "I'm staying out of it because all of you know I don't care about the letters and the ancestors and our past. It's history."

"Our parents weren't sentimental, and you're really a chip off the old block," Will said.

"Now that remark and comparison, I can do without." Zach scribbled out words on three pieces of paper and wadded each up. "We can draw or you can each say what you want and see if anyone else wants it. Or we can go in order of age."

"Hand us the papers and that will be that," Will said.

Zach held out his hand and in seconds Will picked up the Henry rifle, Ryan the Colt revolver and Sophia the pocket watch. "Okay. Is everyone happy with what you got?" Zach asked.

"Sure," Ryan said, rubbing his hand along the Colt. "This is excellent."

"I love this watch—more than I would the rifle or the re-volver," Sophia said. "I would like one of the letters to put with it."

"Good choice. I like the watch," Garrett said, exchanging a smile with his wife.

"Go to the office and pick out whatever letters you want," Zach instructed. "We can divide them all three ways when someone finishes going through them."

"These things are treasures," Ryan said, continuing to turn the revolver in his hand.

"The Henry rifle is fantastic. I'm definitely happy," Will added.

It was late afternoon when Garrett stood. "We need to get home because we're flying back to Dallas."

Ryan stood and gathered his gifts. "I'll go, too. Soon I'll fly out for a tropical paradise, palm trees and warm breezes and a beautiful woman."

"Won't seem like Christmas," Will said. "Of course, you may not care. I'll bet you'll be ready for snow-covered mountains before New Year's."

"Probably will," Ryan replied cheerfully.

"You can bring your friend with you."

Ryan winked. "I think I'll come alone and see if I can find a new friend. See you in the summer, Zach, and thanks."

"You're welcome. I'll let your drivers know you're going."

Zach saw them out, then returned to join Will and Ava while Caroline played with her new doll. "Want one more beer? You don't have to go because they did."

"Sure, I'll have a beer. Is your foot hurting?"

"No. It's healed," Zach said, getting two beers from the bar.

"You don't look so great. Anything worrying you?"

"No. Maybe you're getting me mixed up with Ryan. He's the one who's always got a smile. Remember, I don't have his rosy outlook on life. This is my natural look all the time."

"I know that, but you aren't usually as quiet as today and you look as if something's on your mind besides Christmas and us."

"Actually, Christmas hasn't been on my mind, which I'm sure, surprises no one. "

"What do you think about the prospects for the Cowboys this next year?"

"Great," Will answered and the talk shifted to football and then moved to business while they told each other what the current projects were.

When Ava and Will finally stood to go, he paused. "Will you come back from Italy or just go to a job site?"

"Probably just go to a site. I'm through here, so I'm dumping the letters and memorabilia. It's up to you and Ryan now. Garrett, too, if you can rope him into it because of Sophia."

"I'll see. So you sent your secretary back to the Dallas office."

"Yes. We won't see each other again. She turned out to be efficient and good, Will. She's read a mountain of old letters."

"I don't want to shred them. She's right about a tie to our past."

"With time they'll disintegrate. She copied some of them carefully and put them in a scrapbook between clear acid-free sheets. She said that way we can make copies for family members who want them."

"I'm astounded they got through our parents without being destroyed. You know Mom wouldn't care at all about them. Dad didn't until the end of his life."

"Frankly, I can't work up a lot of interest."

Will chuckled. "So how did she get you to go home for Thanksgiving with her? Is there something going on here that I haven't been told?"

"Will, don't quiz your brother about his personal life," Ava said, smiling at Will. "Caroline and I will say goodbye. The ribs were delicious and thank you for the gifts. You know we'll all love everything."

"Merry Christmas, Ava," Zach said, walking her and Caroline outside. "Take care of him."

"Merry Christmas, Zach. I intend to," she answered and waited while he hugged Caroline before the two of them climbed into the limo to wait for Will.

"So how did your secretary get you to go home for Thanksgiving with her?" Will persisted.

"I think she's trying to rescue me. You can't imagine how sorry she feels for me and how much sympathy I get."

"Sympathy." The word burst from Will and he started laughing. "She feels sorry for you because you don't celebrate these holidays. Does she know how you live and how much money you spend whooping it up on holidays?"

Zach grinned as he shook his head.

"So she made you go home with her for Thanksgiving. Now what in the world incentive did she use to get you to do that?"

"Mind your own business, Will. And the best possible incentive of all."

"I never ever thought I'd see the day."

"You haven't seen it yet. Don't worry, there isn't anything serious between us and there won't be. She is one hundred percent a homebody. I'm almost one hundred percent traveler. That's not a good fit and we both know it."

"Yeah, right," Will said, smiling. "By the way, you didn't tell me that she's gorgeous. I know now why from the first you didn't want me to get someone else to work for you."

"She's an efficient secretary."

"With drop-dead looks. Well, merry Christmas," Will said, impulsively hugging his brother. Startled Zach hugged Will in return.

"I think Caroline and Ava are changing you," Zach said, stepping back. "It's a good change, Will. None of us wanted to turn out to be like Dad."

"Sure as hell not. He was as cold as ice until Caroline came along. She'll never know how she has affected this family."

"All for the better and you're good for her."

"I'm trying. Ava's the one."

"It's you, too. Don't sell yourself short," he said following Will to the limo door. The driver held it. "Merry Christmas, Will. Thanks for my presents."

Zach stepped back and watched as the driver closed the door and went around to get behind the wheel. He continued watching the limo go down the drive, but his thoughts were on Emma. Tomorrow he was scheduled to leave for a night

in New York and then to Italy. Right now, he didn't feel inclined to leave Texas. This was home more than Italy. He
was comfortable here. He had to admit, he was a lot closer
here to Emma than he would be in Italy. If he just had to see
her, he could in only a few hours' time. From Italy, it would
be a real trek.

Jamming his hands into his pockets, he went back to the
empty house. How could it seem so big and empty with Emma
gone? What was she doing at this moment? Did she miss
being with him?

Inside, he closed the front doors and heard the locks click
in place. He stood in the entryway and debated whether to
call her. It was pointless, so he went to the office, pausing
beneath the mistletoe. He reached up to take down the decoration, turning it in his hands, remembering her kisses. Sex
with Emma had been the best ever. Of all women, Emma
was the only one who had created sparks the first moment
they looked at each other. She definitely was the only one to
include him in her family gatherings, the only one to make
him rethink his past, the only one he had ever really missed.

With a sigh he tossed the mistletoe on a table. He didn't
expect her to be back at the ranch ever.

He didn't want to go to New York tomorrow. He picked
up his cell to tell his pilot they weren't going until later in the
week. He didn't have to be anywhere at any specific time so
there was no rush to leave Texas.

Tuesday afternoon he didn't feel any more inclined to leave
for New York and Italy than he had on Monday. Even without Emma, he would rather be at the ranch than in an empty
house in Italy. He didn't want to ruin his pilot's Christmas,
just because he didn't care about his own, so he told his pilot
he would stay in Texas until after the holiday. If he decided
to go, he could catch a commercial flight. Or just go to New
York and spend Christmas there.

Feeling glum, he reached for his phone to call Emma just to talk. How many times he had done that the past few days, and then decided he wouldn't call her?

He was restless and nothing interested him. Emma occupied his thoughts most of his waking hours.

Startling him, he received a call on his cell phone. Shaking his head, he was tempted to not answer when he saw it was from Will. Afraid it would be an emergency, he said hello.

"Zach, it's Will. Where are you? Italy or Texas?"

Zach swore and gritted his teeth. Will usually didn't call until Christmas day. "I'm still in Texas, but will go to Italy soon."

"I just thought you might still be in Texas. What's wrong?" Will asked.

"There's nothing wrong. Staying here is just easier."

"Right," Will said. "Could it be that you miss Emma? I imagine she invited you to spend Christmas with her family. You could, you know," Will said without giving Zach time to answer his question.

"I am not spending Christmas with Emma and sixty other Hillmans."

"So then pack and go to Italy. You'll forget her and get over her."

"Thanks. I plan to go to Italy. I'm just not in a rush," he said, thinking he wasn't going to get over Emma anytime soon.

"Well, I know it's a safe bet you haven't fallen in love, so I'll stop worrying about you. You can still fly up here if you want. Caroline will take your mind off Emma. Caroline is having a blissful time. Christmas is magical for her and she's turning it into magic for us."

"That's great, Will," Zach said with sincerity.

"Even Muffy is enjoying the snow. We have to clear paths

for her or she'll sink out of sight. Give some thought to joining us."

"Thanks. Bye, Will," Zach said and ended the call without giving Will a chance to prolong it.

Zach returned to staring at smoldering logs in his fireplace while Emma filled his thoughts. Did she miss him or was she immersed in family Christmas activities? He held up his phone, tempted to call her, finally giving in to the temptation.

At first he thought she wasn't going to answer, but then he heard her voice and his heart skipped beats.

"Zach, you're calling from Italy?"

"I haven't gone yet. I'm going to New York first," he said. "Ready for Christmas?"

"Hardly, but I will be soon. Something's always going on around here. People coming over or someone wanting me to do something or Mom needs help. I'm busier than ever. Have you heard from Will or Ryan?"

"Will today. They're having a great time," he said, longing to be with her. The phone call only made him miss her more and he felt ridiculous for calling. "I'll have to admit, the place seems empty with you gone."

There was a long silence. "I miss being there."

"No, you don't, really," he said, smiling, certain she didn't, but he hoped she missed him.

"I do miss you," she said solemnly in a quiet voice that made his heart lurch. He inhaled deeply, wanting her with him, in his arms now.

"Will you go out with me for New Year's Eve? I'll come home if you will."

There was another long pause and he held his breath. "Yes," she said. "The sensible part of me says no and I'm sure you feel the same."

"We'll have a good time," he said lightly, his heart racing with eagerness that he would see her again and go out with her. He settled back to talk, asking about her family, enjoying listening to her, glad for this tenuous connection that was still a link with her.

They talked for over an hour before Emma broke in. "Zach, my family is calling me. I promised I'd go shopping and they're waiting for me to join them."

"Sure. See you New Year's," he said.

The connection ended and he felt more alone than he had in years. He wanted Emma with him. How could she have taken such a place in his life that he couldn't get along without her now?

New Year's Eve seemed an eternity away. He stretched and walked around restlessly. He couldn't concentrate on work. He didn't want to go to Italy. He didn't want to join Will because all he would do was think about Emma.

He left to head for his gym while he stayed lost in thought about her.

Emma hurried out to join her sisters and mother to spend the afternoon shopping, but the entire time, she couldn't keep Zach out of mind. She was going out with him for New Year's Eve. Surprise had been her first reaction. She was astounded he wanted to pursue a relationship. She had debated only a moment with herself. Now that she was carrying his baby, everything had changed. Whether she or Zach liked it or not, she would be tied to him for years. Unless he totally rejected his child and she didn't think he would. Not when he seemed to care so much for his niece. She still couldn't accept having a casual relationship with him, but she would just have to see how he reacted and what he wanted.

The aching gloom that had enveloped her when she parted with him had lifted, leaving only worry over his reaction to her news. Excitement, joy over the prospect of an evening with him was tinged with concern over when and how to break the news to him about their baby. If he rejected this child, he would break her heart. Even though he had rejected her lifestyle and hadn't wanted her in his life permanently, this baby was more important now and life had changed.

By five in the afternoon, she was exhausted from shopping and wanted to go home and take a nap. She suspected her mother might be wearing down also, so she told Mary Kate she thought they should call it a day.

It was almost six before they actually unloaded the car and were settled back at home. Emma headed to her room, leaving her packages to get later. All she wanted to do was stretch out and get a quick snooze.

She hadn't been in bed five minutes when there was a knock on her door and Mary Kate appeared.

"Can I talk to you a minute?" she asked, stepping into the bedroom and closing the door. She shook her dark brown hair away from her face as she crossed the room. Her tan sweater emphasized gold flecks in her hazel eyes.

"Sure, come in. Does Mom need help with dinner?"

"No, she's lying down, too, and Sierra has gone home with her brood. So has Lynne to relieve Connor of watching their kids. They all promised to come back after a while." Mary Kate sat on the edge of the bed.

"You've got all the energy," Emma remarked.

"How are you feeling?"

"Tired. We did a lot of shopping and I guess the work I've been doing and the Christmas stuff has caught up with me. I'm sleepy."

"Sure. You were sick this morning when I came."

Emma sat up slightly. "Whatever it was, it passed."

"You know I'm here for you," Mary Kate said, her hazel eyes filled with concern and Emma took a deep breath.

"How did you know?" Emma asked, certain her sister had guessed she was pregnant.

Nine

Mary Kate shrugged. "I've been there," she said, tugging up the sleeves of her tan sweater.

Emma sat up. "You haven't been there as a single mom. Not in this family. MK," she said, reverting to the nickname, "I don't know what I'm going to do." she said. Tears threatened and she tried to get a grip on her emotions.

Mary Kate hugged her and Emma clung tightly to the sister who had stood by her through so many childhood scrapes.

As she released her sister, Emma wiped her eyes. "This was unplanned, unexpected and shouldn't have ever happened. I'm carrying Zach's baby."

"Zach Delaney. Boy, you picked one. That's what I was afraid of. Does he know?"

"No, not yet."

"Do you have any idea how he will react?"

"Not really. He seems crazy about his niece, but he's taken no responsibility for her. When her father was killed, Zach's older brother became guardian. Zach is solitary, a total loner and happy in that life. He rarely comes home. He works abroad, all over the world and loves what he does. He doesn't need the money. He travels to dangerous places and he likes it."

"I thought I heard you say he's in demolition."

"Yes. His company has other businesses, but that's the one he loves and takes an active part in. A big active part. That's how he hurt his foot. Somehow, I can't see him taking this well at all. He doesn't have serious relationships. I wonder if he goes out much because of his lifestyle. He keeps to himself and spends holidays alone, including Christmas."

"Christmas—alone? Through his own choice?"

"Yes."

Her sister's frown reflected her own feelings about Zach's view of holidays. "Wow. Well, even if he has nothing to do with you or the baby, you have a family who will be right with you."

"If Connor doesn't try to punch Zach."

Mary Kate laughed. "He won't. Connor grumbles, but he's too much like Dad to resort to fists unless someone else starts something. Do you think Zach will give you any financial support?"

"I'm guessing he will, but I don't know. If he doesn't offer, I'm not pursuing it. I'll manage and he paid me extravagantly for the job I just did, plus I have a good job with his company and money saved. I'll manage."

"I'm sure you will," Mary Kate said, shifting to a more comfortable seat on the side of the bed. "What about your education and a teaching job? That's what you've always wanted."

"I think that will have to be postponed," Emma said. "I'll use this money for the baby. Later on, I hope I can pick up where I left off, go back to college, get my degree and then teach."

"I hope Zach Delaney does what's right and gives you financial support. Marriage sounds like an unlikely event."

"It's impossible. He's totally solitary. MK, how will I tell Mom and Dad? It's Dad I'm worried about. I think this will break his heart. And I know—I should have thought of that before now."

"You're not getting a lecture from me. Dad's able to take news and he'll help you and so will Mom. I know it's hard to think about telling them, but don't worry about it. Just do it and get it over with."

"I'm waiting until after Christmas and you wait, too."

Mary Kate ran her fingers over her lips. "Absolutely. This is your deal to tell the family, not mine. I'm just here for you. And don't expect it to be long before Mom catches on. She's been through this five times."

"I know."

I better go see what the kiddos are doing. Bobby's watching them and he's as much a kid as they are. Holler if you want to talk again."

"Thanks, MK."

"Sure."

Emma settled back against pillows and watched her sister leave the room. She could count on MK. Actually, she could count on her whole family. It was just Zach who was an unknown factor.

She thought about New Year's Eve. That would be the time to break the news. As soon as Christmas had passed, she would tell the family.

She missed Zach. How long would she continue to miss him? Months, years, forever?

Christmas Eve morning, Zach sat at his desk trying to think about work and finding it impossible. Emma dominated his thoughts every waking hour. He hadn't gone to Italy and he still didn't want to go. He wouldn't do any more in Italy than he would on the ranch, so he just stayed. He felt closer to Emma here and the house reminded him of moments she had been there. How many times during the week had he pulled out his phone and started to call her?

He tossed his pen and rubbed the back of his neck. He wanted to see her and he was tired of trying to think about work and failing completely.

The phone rang and he saw the caller ID indicated Will, which was no surprise. Zach was tempted to avoid answering and the questions that would follow. Taking a deep breath, he picked up his phone to talk.

"Yes, Will, I'm here at the ranch. I decided to stay in Texas." He tried to put some cheer in his voice and realized he was failing.

"Are you sick?"

"No, I'm not."

"Is Rosie there?"

"No. You know I gave her and Nigel three weeks off. I'm okay. Merry Christmas. Let me talk to Caroline."

He talked briefly to his niece and she suddenly said goodbye and Will returned. "We're getting snow. How's the weather there?"

"I know you didn't call to get a weather report."

"No, I didn't. Just some small talk while I walked into another room and closed the door for privacy. Zach, if you're in love with Emma, do something about it. You might have to live life a little more on the ordinary side like the rest of us do."

Zach had to laugh. "And a merry Christmas to you, too, Dr. Phil. Stop giving me advice."

"Okay, but this is so unlike you. Do you want to fly up here today and spend tomorrow with us? I promise we're fun."

"I'm sure you're fun galore, but I'm happy here," he said,

giving some thought to Will's invitation. For the first time, he was slightly tempted, but he still preferred Texas where he was closer to Emma. "When have I not been happy alone?"

"Maybe since you met Emma Hillman. Well, you're a grown man and I won't give you advice, just an invitation. And a merry Christmas."

"Thanks, Will. Thanks for calling and for your invitation. I really mean it. Merry Christmas to you all."

As he hung up, Zach had to smile over his brother's ridiculous call. He paced restlessly and then stopped to look down at the largest box of memorabilia. He pulled up a chair and picked up a letter to read.

"All right, Emma. I'll try again to find something fascinating in my ancestors' lives."

He read two letters and tossed both in the discard box. He picked up another and saw it was his written by his great-great-grandfather during the second year of the Civil War.

"My dearest Tabitha:

"My love, we covered twenty miles today in the rain. It is dark and cold now and I write by firelight. I am glad we did not encounter any of our enemy because our ammunition and our supplies run low. I am fortunate to have both my rifle and my revolver, plus ammunition. Others are not so fortunate. This ghastly war between the States is tearing our country apart. My dearest, how I miss you! If I could just hold you against my heart. You and our son.

"This fighting is lonely and desperate. How I long to be with you this night and see your smile, that would be a Christmas treasure to me. Know that I send my love to you on this Christmas night. You and our little one are the most important part of my life and what I am fighting for. I dream of peace for our babe and his descendants and their offspring. How I wish I could see our son, this precious babe. My heart aches with wanting to be with you and my child on this night.

*Nothing else on this earth matters, but I fight to keep life se-
cure for the two of you."*

For the first time Zach felt a thread of kinship with this
ancestor from generations earlier. Feeling foolish for his
emotional reaction to the old letter, Zach continued to read.
*"I close my eyes and imagine you holding out your arms
and smiling at me. Someday, my love, we will be together
again. Know that I send my love to you and our son on this
Christmas night."* He could be saying those words to Emma.
Leaning back in his chair, Zach watched flames dance in the
fireplace. He missed Emma. He could imagine the ache in
his relative's life on a cold Christmas night away from his
young wife and a baby.

He picked up the letter to continue reading:

*"Know you are my life and you and our offspring have my
love always. I want this land to be safe for our son and his
sons. My family I hold dearest of everything on this earth. I
dream of when I can come home and we are together once
again. My love, how I long to hold you close to my heart. All
my love to you from your adoring husband, Warner Irwin
Delaney."*

Zach had a tightening in his chest and he placed the letter
in the discard box with the others without thinking about what
he was doing. As he finished reading, all his thoughts focused
on Emma and the letter. She would have been touched by it.

Was he missing out on life as she had said? Was he missing
the most treasured part—a woman's love and a family's love?

He had never really thought marriage could be happy and
filled with love until he had been with Emma's family, because he had never seen a loving family in his own home or
his oldest brother's or even in any of his friends. Garrett's
parents seemed the closest and Garrett had been happy growing up, but the Cantrells had not exhibited the warmth and
closeness the Hillmans had.

Will had not been married long enough for his marriage to count. Will was in euphoria and still steeped in his honeymoon. The Hillman seniors had been married for years and they were obviously in love. Zach had never thought of marrying or having a child—yet he loved Caroline and he barely saw her. How much more would he love one of his own that he saw often? Surely he would love his offspring deeply, and, if he ever had any, he intended to give them all the time and attention he possibly could.

Emma was a steadying influence, her calm faith in love, her cheer, her optimism—maybe he desperately needed that in his life. He needed her. It was still Christmas Eve morning. He reached for his phone and made arrangements to get the plane ready to fly to Dallas. He had to see Emma.

Christmas Eve at four in the afternoon Emma rushed back to her apartment. It was already getting dark outside with an overcast gray sky and a light snow predicted. Carrying an armload of packages, she hurried into her apartment building to be stopped by the doorman.

"Miss Hillman, you have a delivery."

Surprised, she waited while he disappeared into the office and returned with a red crystal vase that held several dozen red roses and stems of holly.

"That's for me?" she said, glancing at the packages filling her arms. "I'll come back to get it."

"I'll bring it up. I didn't want to leave it in the hall."

"Thank you." At her apartment she unlocked the door and stepped back to let him carry the bouquet inside and set it down.

"Merry Christmas, Miss Hillman. You have beautiful flowers."

"Thank you. Merry Christmas to you, Mr. Wilburton," she said, tipping him for carrying up her flowers.f

She dropped her packages and closed the door, hearing the lock click in place. The flowers had to be from Zach. She pulled out a card, looking at a familiar scrawling handwriting that she had seen so many times in the past few weeks.

"Merry Christmas, Emma. Zach." A pang rocked her. How she wished he were here! She missed him more each day and tried to avoid thinking about it if she could. With a glance at her watch, she realized she should get ready soon to join her family.

Hurrying to hang up her coat, she turned on her Christmas lights.

Lights sparkled on her tall green Douglas fir that held sparse ornaments, which she added to each Christmas. She had greenery and candles on her mantel, a wreath on her door and a dining room centerpiece of holly around the base of a large poinsettia that had been given to her by friends from her office.

This year she had added something new. She looked at the sprig of mistletoe she had hung above the doorway into the dining area. The mistletoe made her think of Zach and their mistletoe kisses. She wondered how he was enjoying his Italian villa. For all she knew, he might not be alone there.

Usually Christmas Eve filled her with anticipation and excitement, but this year she missed Zach and she could not keep from worrying about her baby and breaking the news to her family. In spite of her sister's reassurances, telling the family was going to be difficult, making her worry how they would take it. An even bigger concern was how Zach would accept the news.

She picked up all her packages to carry them to her bedroom and open them. She had been buying baby things because she was excited and wanted to get ready even if it was early. A bassinet stood by the window and she had a new rocking chair that had been delivered two days earlier. She began to open packages and finally had the new baby clothes laid out across her bed where she could look at them. They would all go into the wash, but she wanted to look at them first: the tiny onesies, tiny socks, little jumpers and bibs, rattles and a baby brush, plus small blankets.

She ran her fingers over the blankets. Even if Zach wanted to marry, which she knew he would not, she couldn't accept his lifestyle. He still wouldn't put family first. Travel and work would always take first place with him and fulfill the need for excitement in his life. It would never be family that would hold his interest. Sadness tinged her excitement over the baby. Sadness and worry about her baby's acceptance.

She showered to get ready to go to her parents' house for dinner and then a midnight service. Her new Christmas dress was a red crepe with a low V-neck and long sleeves. The skirt ended above her knees and she had matching high-heeled pumps. She caught her hair back on either side of her face and had clips with sprigs of holly attached. Last of all, she fastened the gold locket, stepping close to the mirror to look at it and rub the gold lightly with her finger as if she could conjure up Zach by doing so.

Startling her, her intercom buzzed. She answered to hear Mr. Wilburton.

"May I come back a moment? There's something else here."

"Sure, come up. I'll open the door," she answered, curious what he had. She gathered things to put into her purse until the bell rang. Wondering what he had forgotten, she hurried to the door to open it.

The first thing she saw was a huge stack of packages that hid the doorman.

"Come in," she said, wondering how Mr. Wilburton could have forgotten a mountain of gifts.

He turned slightly and she faced Zach. "Merry Christmas, Emma."

Stunned, she could only stare at him. "Zach? You're here? It's Christmas Eve. Where's Mr. Wilburton?"

Zach laughed. "These packages are getting heavy. Can I come in?"

Ten

"Come in," she said, her heart racing as she took presents off the top of his stack.

He rushed to her sofa to set them all down while she closed the door and trailed behind him. He was in a black topcoat over his suit. When he turned, she took one look in his eyes and she was in his arms. He had brought a rush of cold air in and his coat still was cold and smelled of the outside. As she slid her arms beneath his coat and jacket, he felt warm, holding her tightly against him while they kissed.

Her heart thudded with joy. Giddy to see him, laughter bubbled inside her. She was overwhelmed by surprise.

Desire raged, more than all else, and she pushed the topcoat away, hearing it fall to the floor. His suit jacket went with it. With shaking fingers, she unfastened the buttons to his snowy shirt. He held her away to look at her, taking in her red dress before he kissed her again.

Picking her up in his arms, Zach carried her to her bedroom while he kissed her. Emma clung to him, wrapped in his embrace and filled with longing. When he set her on her feet, she could feel his hands at the top of her zipper as he started to draw it down.

His hands grew still and he raised his head. "Is one of your sisters expecting?"

Startled, she looked up at him. "No, neither one." Zach looked beyond her at the bed and then his gaze went around the room and she realized why.

"Emma, that's a lot of baby clothes and a lot of baby things. More than you'd take to a shower."

His questioning gaze returned to her. Her heart drummed and her palms became damp. She hadn't expected Zach. All the most recent baby things were laid out. Her mouth went dry and she felt weak in the knees.

"I know only one way to tell you. I'm pregnant," she whispered.

"You're pregnant?" Sounding stunned, he stepped back to look at her. "You don't look it. You have all this ready for a baby. Are you sure? When are you due?"

"I've been to a doctor now. When I found out for certain, I couldn't wait to buy things. I know it's too early, Zach. I'm barely pregnant, but I'm excited. This isn't the way I was going to tell you, or this soon. I know you have your life and you're not the daddy type—"

"And you're not the single-mom type. I'm going to be a dad," he said and silence stretched between them. Suddenly his hands closed on her waist and he held her up while he gave a whoop.

"A dad! Emma, love," he said, setting her down and wrapping his arms around her to kiss her hard and long.

Shocked by his reaction, the last possible thing she had expected, she stood immobile for seconds until she caught her breath. Wrapping her arms around him, she held him tightly to kiss him back.

He stopped as abruptly as he started. "You're sure?"

"Absolutely. The doctor says yes. The pregnancy test was positive. My body is changing. Ask Rosie. And Mary Kate guessed."

"Rosie?" he said, looking stunned. "You knew then?"

"I suspected, but it was really early. Rosie did, too."

He laughed. "Emma, that's fabulous. We're going to be parents. My precious love, I came to ask you to marry me." He knelt on one knee and took her hand. "Emma Hillman, I love you and want you to be my wife. Will you marry me?"

"Zach, get up," she said, her smile fading because she hurt badly. He had just proposed, saying words she hadn't been able to avoid dreaming about, but there was only one answer. She looked up at him as he stood. "I love you and I'm thrilled and scared about the baby, but, Zach, we can't marry. Our lifestyles are poles apart. You wouldn't be happy. I wouldn't be happy with you gone all the time."

"Emma, we have to work this out," he said, framing her face with his hands. "I've been miserable without you. You've made me see a family can be happy and love each other. We'll work this out."

"I can't. You'll be gone and you do risky things. You won't be there to be a dad."

"Yes, I will," he said patiently. "And love isn't in one place or in a house. It's between two people. Your parents would have had the same love if your dad had traveled. You have to agree on that one."

"I guess they would have, but I don't want a dad who's gone all the time."

"I won't be. I can work more in the Dallas office and let others do the on-site requirements. For heaven's sake, I own the place. I don't have to go out and do hands-on work. I don't even have to work if I don't want to."

She didn't dare breathe as her whole being tingled and

hope flared. "You might not be happy with a desk job," she said, wondering if she dared accept his complete reversal of his lifestyle.

"I don't want to be away from you."

"You would do that?"

"Of course. Emma, you've made me open my heart and trust someone to return my love. Don't turn around and crush that now. I love you and I want to marry you. Besides that, it's been pure hell without you."

She trembled, wanting to believe him, scared to do so. "Rosie said you couldn't change."

"Well, there are some things Rosie doesn't know about me. She doesn't know I have fallen in love with the most wonderful woman in the world."

Unable to smile because of the moment for a life-changing decision, Emma stood looking into his eyes. They were both taking chances, but they loved each other and love was too precious to toss aside. As her decision came, she trembled. "Yes, I'll marry you," she answered, wrapping her arms around his neck to kiss him. Excitement and joy blossomed, enveloping her. Tears of happiness spilled down her cheeks.

"Don't cry. Not even happy tears," he said. "Darlin', this is too fabulous for even one tear. Marriage to you will be the most wonderful thing in my life. You're right, Emma. What counts in life is the people you love."

After a moment he raised his head. "How far along are you?"

"Just barely pregnant," she answered, smiling at him.

He looked beyond her at the bed covered in baby clothes. "Isn't this really premature?"

"It is, but I'm excited."

"And your family? They may not be happy with me, but when they hear we're getting married, they should be okay. Do you think?"

"They don't know. It's early, Zach. Mary Kate knows. She guessed and we're close so she asked me. No one else knows."

"Then don't tell them yet," he said. "Tonight let's announce we're getting married. Let's marry on Christmas." He smiled. "I don't want to wait any longer anyway."

"That's not possible, Zach. That's tomorrow."

"I know when Christmas is. Unless you have your heart set on a big wedding, we'll marry tomorrow with just your family. That's enough people to fill the church."

"What about your brothers and your half sister and her husband, whom you're close to?"

"Listen to me," he said. "We marry tomorrow. Then we're off on a honeymoon and I'll get you out of the state of Texas. First, the Italian villa and then Paris and back to New York, Niagra Falls and then home. How does that sound?"

"Impossible."

"No, it's not. We can get a church and just have the family and get married tomorrow afternoon. Then when we come back from a honeymoon we can have a big reception and invite everyone, including my family. We can announce the baby whenever you're ready."

Too thrilled to plan anything, she laughed. "It still sounds impossible. As a matter of fact, I have to be at my folks' home at six tonight. It's already after five."

"We have time to make some decisions. If you run late, you can call and tell them you're on your way."

"I go for the evening. We all eat there and then we go to midnight church service together. Will you go with me?"

He kissed her lightly on the forehead. "Of course, I'll go."

She smiled. "Why didn't you call me?" she asked, running her fingers over his shoulder.

"I should have, but I was going as fast as I could. I just decided to come this morning."

"You came from Italy?"

"No, I never did go to Italy," he said. "I missed you too much. Italy seemed empty and unappealing. My heart was here in Texas."

Her heart missed a beat as she gazed up at him. She combed her fingers through his thick hair. "I feel as if I haven't seen you for a long, long time."

"I know. That's the way I feel about you," he said. "I couldn't wait until New Year's Eve."

"I'm stunned," she said. "I thought you were in Italy. You said you were going."

"Italy lost its appeal and I kept putting it off until it seemed pointless to go. I've missed you," he said solemnly and another wave of happiness swamped her. She kissed him lightly on the lips.

"Zach, no one will marry us on such short notice, and not on Christmas."

"Sure they will," he replied. "Maybe you're not the optimist I thought you were. I think I can get our minister to do the ceremony. I'll call him unless you want to ask yours first."

"You get your minister. I can't imagine calling any minister on Christmas Eve and asking him to marry us on Christmas Day. That's wild, Zach," she said, dazed and unable to believe she was marrying him. "We don't have a license. We don't have what we need."

"I'll call my attorney and get him moving. He'll get it worked out. We can still marry in the church tomorrow."

"This is crazy. What'll I wear?"

"You'll look beautiful in whatever you wear and we can go from here to a dress shop and then to your parents' house. I know the perfect store and I'll see if they'll stay open until we get there."

She listened as he talked to his lawyer and her incredulity deepened. Everything seemed impossible. It was turning into a magical Christmas where the impossible became possible. Mrs. Zachary Delaney. Was she rushing headlong into disaster or into paradise? Right now, she viewed it as paradise. Zach had already made astounding changes in his life.

He called a store and talked briefly. "Grab what you need," he said to Emma. "They were just about to close, but she'll wait. You can find something you like there."

"What store?"

He told her the name of an exclusive shop that was far beyond her budget and she had never crossed the threshold even to look there.

"Zach, are you certain? We're really rushing into this and you just blithely said you'd change your whole way of living."

"I sure did. That's how much I love you. Wait a minute." He rummaged through the mound of presents he had brought with him and returned swiftly to hand her a gift in a small box wrapped in green foil paper with a red ribbon and sprigs of artificial mistletoe in the bow.

"It's too pretty to open."

"Open it. What's inside may be prettier."

She opened it with shaking fingers and he caught her hand. "You're shaking."

She looked up. "I'm thrilled and happy and so in love. And my whole life is changing before my eyes. I'm scared."

He hugged her. "I love you, Emma," he said quietly and firmly in his deep voice. "Truly love you with all my heart and want to make you happy. You think I want to be off blowing up some building when I can be home in bed with you every night?"

She laughed while tears stung her eyes. He tilted her face up. "Don't cry, love. I love you and I don't want to ever hurt you."

"Tears of joy, Zach," she whispered, wiping her eyes. She opened the box and a dazzling diamond glittered in the light. "Zach, it's magnificent," she gasped.

He removed the ring and placed it on her finger. "Emma, will you marry me?" he asked again.

"Yes, Zach," she said and kissed him.

In seconds he released her. "We better run."

"Let me think. You've got me so rattled. I'm supposed to be taking something to my parents. It's a chocolate cheesecake from the fridge. Let me get it."

She hurried to the kitchen and returned to the living room where she stopped to look at her sofa. "Zach, what are all these presents?"

"They're your Christmas presents from me. I had the ones for your family sent out to your parents' house."

"How'd you know you'd even be invited?"

He grinned. "C'mon. Someone's holding open a store for us."

She shook her head as she pulled on her coat. He carried the chocolate cheesecake that was in a plastic container.

He had a limo waiting and she climbed into the back. The limo gave her pause, a sobering moment, because it brought back how much Zach was worth. "Zach, you are part of the Delaney fortune that has been well publicized. I don't see a bodyguard."

"I have one at times. He's not with us now because our driver can cover if needed, but Will's the one in the limelight. I'm not in papers and haven't been in the country lately. Ryan could pass for any cowboy in west Texas. He's not in papers a lot either. Besides that, Ryan's a tough cowboy and he looks like the type to be packing. If I were going after a Delaney, I'd put Ryan at the bottom of the list. Ryan and I are both low-key and I don't feel threatened."

"I'm thinking about your baby."

"Don't worry about it. I'll have all the security you and I both feel we need. A baby is different. We'll have plenty of security."

She realized her life was changing drastically as she looked at her fiancé whom she loved with all her being. She pulled out her cell phone. "I want to call and let Mom and Dad know you're coming with me. Then it won't be a surprise when you walk in."

"Good idea. My presents should have arrived."

In minutes she put away her phone. "They'll be glad to see you. And they did get your presents. How in the world did you know what to buy? And how many to buy for?"

"Someone told me how many were eating Thanksgiving dinner. How many adults and how many kids. They're sort of generic presents. Electronic games for the kids, baskets of fruit for the adults."

She laughed. "Zach, our house will be buried under baskets of fruit."

He grinned and hugged her. Emma held out her hand to look at her ring. "This is the most gorgeous, giant ring I have ever seen."

"I'm glad you like it." He placed his arm around her. "Emma, I read some of the family letters. I got a touching one that you'll have to read. I saw what you were talking about. Somehow with that one letter, I actually did feel a tie to my great-great-grandfather."

"I'm glad, Zach," she said with another increase in her happiness. "I was going to ask for any of the letters you decided to shred because I'll be the mother of a Delaney. And this little Delaney is going to grow up with a love and appreciation of family."

"The mother of a Delaney, my baby's mother," he said. "That sounds wonderful to me. You've given me the best possible Christmas gift I've ever received," he whispered and pulled her close to kiss her. Pausing, he framed her face with his hands. "Emma, you've made up for all those miserable Christmases I had as kid. Will told me once to hang on, that our lives would get better."

"Zach, that makes me hurt for all three of you. But that's all in the past. You'll have so much family stirring around you on holidays, you may miss your solitude."

"No, I won't. Not as long as I have you," he said and kissed her again.

When the limo parked, Zach climbed out to help Emma. "You get whatever you want in here. I'm buying it for you, so don't even ask a price."

The second dress they brought out, a white raw silk with thin straps and a short jacket, was the one. The skirt was slim and came to mid-calf. She liked it immediately and in minutes she said that was the one she wanted. She didn't want Zach to see it until their wedding, so when she came out of the dressing room once again in her Christmas dress, his eyebrows arched.

"What's this?"

"I've picked the dress I want and you're not to see it until tomorrow."

"You've set a record for the fastest woman shopper I've ever seen. I'm falling in love all over again."

She laughed, but she wondered how many women he had taken shopping. In minutes they parked at her parents' house.

"This has to be the most decorated block in all of the state of Texas," Zach said, stepping into bright lights from her parents' decorations.

"Dad started this and then our neighbors began to get into the spirit."

"Thank heaven I'll be able to afford to have someone do ours for us," he said, eyeing her roof. As they walked to the front door, she felt butterflies in her stomach. "Zach, I feel jittery about tonight and having a wedding so fast tomorrow."

"Your family will accept what you want to do," he said.

"Would you rather take your time, marry later and have a big wedding?"

She thought a moment. "No, this is exciting and I think marrying tomorrow is a great idea. We're rushing into this—something I never thought I'd do."

"We're getting married tomorrow—something I never thought *I'd* do," he said with a broad smile and she laughed.

"Let's break the news. Get ready for a hullabaloo," she warned and opened the front door.

"You're right there."

As they walked inside, her dad came forward to greet them. Emma grasped her father's arm. "Dad, get Mom to come here. It's important."

With a glance at Zach, Brody turned to send a granddaughter on the errand and in seconds Emma's mother walked up to greet them and welcome Zach. Family members trailed after her, gathering around them.

"Mom, Dad, before someone notices and asks—Zach has asked me to marry him and I've accepted," she said, holding out her hand to show her engagement ring.

Instantly her mother hugged her while her dad shook hands with Zach and in seconds the whole family huddled around while Emma showed them her engagement ring.

From that moment on she felt as if she were in a dream. She spent an hour on phone calls, making arrangements that she couldn't believe were happening so quickly. She went through dinner in a daze and felt that way afterwards. Constantly, she was aware of Zach, even if he stood across the room. When they drove to church all the kids piled into the limo with them.

"Your life will change drastically," Emma reminded him.

"It already has," he remarked, eyeing the kids surrounding him.

Through the midnight Christmas service Zach sat close beside her. Finally they told everyone good-night and left.

"Emma, you've never even seen my home. Not any of them. Let's go back to my house tonight and I'll take you home as early in the morning as you want."

"All right. Is this where I'm going to live?"

"That's up to you. If you want a new place, I don't care. I got the Dallas place because it's comfortable and a good investment. If you want something else, fine."

"I hope you're always this agreeable."

He smiled. "I'll try. I want to call Ryan and Will. I should call Garrett, too. I want you to meet Ryan and Garrett and Sophia when we get back. I don't expect any of them to come home tomorrow. When we get back from our honeymoon, we can repeat our vows in a big church wedding if you want."

She shook her head. "I'm happy. Let's just have the reception and invite everyone. That'll be a party for all."

His limo entered an exclusive gated suburban area with a gatekeeper. As they wound through the neighborhood, through pines and oaks, she glimpsed twinkling lights indicating homes. Finally they went through another tall iron gate with a gatekeeper who waved.

"I guess I didn't need to worry so much about security."

"I have security. The family ranch is more open, but we had security around the perimeter of the yard and motion lights outside, with someone watching the grounds at night. You just didn't notice."

"You didn't tell me that," she said.

He shrugged. "I didn't expect you to leave in the dead of night without me knowing about it."

In minutes she could see lights through trees on a mansion and when it came into full view, her breath caught. "This is home?" she asked. "It's a resort hotel."

"No, it's not and we can move if you want. You'll see. It's comfortable inside."

"I can imagine," she said, unable to grasp that after tomorrow this would be her home. One of her homes.

"I feel like Cinderella," she whispered.

"And I feel like the luckiest man on earth," he said. "I called ahead and told them we were coming."

"Zach, I'm just now seeing your Dallas home. This reinforces that we barely know each other."

"I know what I want," he replied solemnly. "It's you, Emma, with all my heart. This is a house, maybe big and fancy, but it's just a house I have because of those ancestors you've been reading about and feeling so close to. You know my history, my family, my secrets, my work, me. We know each other. I know your family, your very open book growing up in a happy, loving family. Maybe you're right and you're the wealthier of the two of us," he said with a smile. "We know each other well enough. Our love will cover the rest and discovery sounds wonderful."

She hugged and kissed him briefly and then turned to look at the house. "I'm overwhelmed."

"You'll get used to the place. Nigel will work here when we return from our honeymoon. Rosie sort of goes from family to family."

They stepped out of the limo at the side of the mansion. At the door he unlocked it, picked her up and carried her inside. Setting her on her feet, he turned off the alarm.

"Now the quick tour. When we return from our honeymoon, you can have the full tour of the place."

Dazzled, she felt in a dream once again. They walked through an enormous kitchen with rich, dark wood hiding appliances, granite countertops, a smooth stone floor that held small area rugs. The adjoining informal eating area was as large as the kitchen.

Zach took her hand. "This way. You can look as we go and I'll show you around better later."

They climbed winding stairs and walked down a wide hall that held a strip of thick beige carpet down the center. Zach's bedroom was an enormous suite and the moment she stepped inside, she barely glimpsed polished oak floors, elegant fruitwood furniture and a wide-screen built into a wall.

"Come here. I called this afternoon and told my staff to put this up. Next year I'm sure we'll be as decorated as Rockefeller Center." He led her to a doorway between the sitting room and his bedroom with a massive four-poster king bed. Mistletoe hung in the doorway overhead and Zach stopped beneath it.

"I love you and I can't wait to marry you. In my heart we're already husband and wife," he said.

Her heart thudded with happiness as she hugged him while she kissed him beneath the mistletoe.

Epilogue

"Zach, I still feel like this isn't really happening to me," she said, thinking that was the way she had felt most of the time when they had been in Europe on their honeymoon. She looked at herself in the mirror, her gaze going beyond her image to Zach's. He looked incredibly handsome in his navy suit.

"My love is real, Emma," he said, brushing a kiss and his warm breath on her nape.

"All those wonderful cities and the charming small towns in France, Switzerland, Germany and Italy. They were beautiful and the people were welcoming. The places and buildings were breathtaking, so beautiful. Ah, Zach, I saw them all because of you. I will treasure the memories we have of this trip forever. It was wonderful to go and now it's grand to be home."

"The next long trip will be in this country. I want to show you special places in the U.S."

She smiled. "I'm nervous about meeting Ryan tonight."

Zach laughed. "Of all people on this earth, don't be nervous over Ryan. He's as down to earth as any man can get.
He would have flown in to meet you earlier this week when
we returned, but he had a bull-riding show in Wyoming or
Montana. I don't remember where. Don't be nervous about
any of them. Sophia is almost as new to the family as you
are. I think you two will become good friends."

"Do you still want to tell my family the news about the
baby when we go for Sunday dinner tomorrow?" she asked.

"Yes, unless you want to tell them tonight. We'll tell them
and my family and anyone else you want to let know."

"Rosie, even though she guessed, and Nigel."

"Sure. All my staff will be told. I want everyone watching out for you."

She laughed. "Don't make it sound as if I'm an invalid.
Let's tell them tomorrow."

"I love you, sweet wife," he whispered and kissed her.

She kissed him passionately, in seconds forgetting the evening until he reached for the zipper of her dress.

"Zach, we have a wedding reception to attend," she said,
wriggling away from him and smiling.

"So we do, but I'd rather make love."

"Later," she said.

"Can't wait," he replied. "I'm ready and I'll wait downstairs. You look absolutely gorgeous."

"So do you, Zach," she said, her heart beating with happiness.

An hour later she stood in a country club ballroom talking to Sophia and Ava when she saw Zach and his brother
approach. Ryan was tall, handsome, dressed in a black suit
and wearing black Western boots.

"Finally you'll meet my brother Ryan. Ryan, meet Emma,
my bride."

Ryan hugged her and kissed her cheek. "Welcome to the Delaney family," he said.

"Thank you," she answered. "All of you have made me feel welcome."

Zach clasped his brother on the shoulder. "Ladies, congratulate a champion bull rider. He just won again."

Ryan grinned as he received congratulations and Emma marveled again that the Delaneys resembled each other except for Zach. She couldn't see any similarities in his looks and theirs.

She saw Will and Garrett approaching and their circle enlarged. Will draped his arm around Ava's shoulders. "Caroline is playing with your nieces and nephews and your sister Mary Kate is with them," he said. "I told her to call my cell if I need to come get her."

"Caroline will be fine and Mary Kate loves being with the kids."

The band commenced another song and Ryan turned to Emma. "May I have this dance? If I want to get to know you, we have to get away from this crowd."

She laughed and went with him the short distance to join the dancers.

"You've worked a miracle with my brother," Ryan said. "Will and I are delighted. Sophia hasn't been in this family long enough to know how much he'd changed."

"I love Zach and I want him to be happy."

"He is. You're good for him. Will and I wouldn't have thought it was possible to get him to settle down even a little. You have a great family. I've met most of them. I told all of them to bring their kids out to my ranch and let them ride. We have gentle horses. I think Connor is going to take me up first and bring his boys."

"I'm sure they'll love it. That's nice."

He spun her around and she glanced at Zach, already wanting the reception to be over and to be alone with him again.

When the dance ended, the group had broken up and Zach waited. "You've spent enough time with her, so goodbye, Ryan," Zach said, taking her hand.

"Thanks for the dance. I don't know how he talked you into marrying him," he teased. "Try to put up with him."

She laughed. "I think I can put up with him. It was nice to meet you, Ryan."

Zach led her to the dance floor to take her into his arms. "I'm ready for this to be over now."

"So am I," she said, gazing into his blue eyes that were as fascinating as the first day she met him. "I love you so," she whispered.

He pulled her close to wrap his arms around her and she danced slowly with him while her happiness bubbled. Her wonderful husband and their baby on the way—joy overflowed and she squeezed him. "Zach, this is paradise," she whispered, and he smiled at her, his eyes filled with warmth and love.

* * * * *

WEDDING DATE
WITH MR WRONG
NICOLA MARSH

Nicola Marsh has always had a passion for writing and reading. As a youngster she devoured books when she should have been sleeping, and later kept a diary, which could be an epic in itself! These days, when she's not enjoying life with her husband and son in her home city of Melbourne, she's at her computer doing her dream job: creating the romances she loves.

Visit Nicola's website, www.nicolamarsh.com, for the latest news of her books.

For Natalie Anderson and Soraya Lane, the best
writing buds a girl could wish for.
Your support and friendship mean so much.

CHAPTER ONE

'If you mention weddings or tinsel or Secret Santa one more time I'm going to ram this wax down your throat.'

Archer Flett brandished his number-one-selling surfboard wax at his younger brother, Travis, who grinned and snatched the wax out of his hand.

'Resist all you like, bro, you know you're fighting a losing battle.' Trav smirked and rubbed a spot he'd missed on his prized board.

When it came to his family it always felt as if Archer was fighting a losing battle.

Despite making inroads with his brothers Tom and Trav, nothing had changed with his parents over the years—his dad in particular. That was why coming home for his yearly obligatory Christmas visit set him on edge. And why he rarely stuck around more than a few days.

This year would be no exception, despite Travis turning into a romantic schmuck.

'What were you thinking?' Archer stuck his board vertically in the sand and leaned on it. 'A Christmas wedding? Could you get any cheesier?'

His brother's eyes glazed over and Archer braced for some more claptrap involving his fiancée. 'Shelly wanted to be a Christmas bride and we saw no point in waiting.'

Archer placed his thumb in the middle of Trav's forehead and pushed. 'You're under this already. You know that, right?'

'We're in love.'

As if that excused his brother's sappy behaviour.

The Fletts were third-generation Torquay inhabitants, so he could just imagine the shindig his parents would throw for the wedding. The entire town would turn up.

Christmas and a wedding at home. A combination guaranteed to make him run as soon as the cake had been cut.

'You're too young to get married.' Archer glared at the sibling who'd tagged after him for years, pestering him to surf.

He'd spent the bulk of the last eight years away from home and in that time Travis had morphed from gangly kid to lean and mean. Heavy on the lean, light on the mean. Trav didn't have a nasty bone in his body, and the fact he was marrying at twenty-two didn't surprise Archer.

Trav was a marshmallow, and while Shelly seemed like a nice girl he couldn't imagine anything worse than being shackled to one person at such a young age.

Hell, at twenty-two *he'd* been travelling the world, surfing the hotspots, dating extensively and trying to put his folks' deception out of his mind.

A memory he'd long suppressed shimmered into his subconscious. South coast of Italy. Capri. Long hot nights filled with laughter and passion and heat.

Annoyingly, whenever anyone he knew was loco enough to tie the knot his mind drifted to Callie.

'So who're you bringing to the wedding?' Travis wrinkled his nose. 'Another of those high-maintenance city chicks you always bring home at Christmas?'

Archer chose those dates for a reason: women who demanded all his attention, so he didn't have time left over to spend one-on-one with his folks.

He'd honed avoidance to an art, ensuring he didn't say things he might regret. Like why the hell they hadn't trusted him to rally around all those years ago.

He wasn't the flighty, carefree surfer dude they'd assumed him to be and he'd prove it this trip. He hoped the surf school he'd developed would show them the type of guy he was—the type of guy he wanted to be.

'Leave my date to me.' He wriggled his board out of the sand and tucked it under his arm. 'Planning on standing here all day, gossiping like an old woman? Or are you going to back up some of your big talk by showing me a few moves out there?'

Trav cocked his thumb and forefinger and fired at him. 'I'm going to surf your show-pony ass into oblivion.'

'Like to see you try, pretty boy.'

Archer took off at a run, enjoying the hot sand beneath his feet, the wind buffeting his face, before he hit the water's edge. He lay prone on his board, the icy chill of Bell's Beach washing over him as the lure of the waves took hold. He'd never felt so alive. When he was in the ocean he came home.

The ocean was reliable and constant—two things he valued. Two things his parents didn't credit him as being.

He paddled harder, wishing he could leave the demons of his past behind, knowing he should confront them over the next few days.

He'd made amends with his brothers four years ago, at a time when Tom had needed his support. His relationship with his mum had thawed too, considering he didn't blame her for what happened; she'd do anything for Frank.

But things were still rough with his dad. He'd wanted to make peace many times but a healthy dose of pride, an enforced physical distance and the passing of time had put paid to that fantasy.

He'd tried making small efforts to broach the distance between them, but the residual awkwardness lingered, reinforcing his choice to stay away.

Maybe, if he was lucky, this visit home would be different.

Callie went into overdrive as an Argentinian tango blared from her surround sound.

She bounced around her lounge room, swivelling her hips and striding across the floor with arm extended and head tilted, a fake rose between her teeth.

She'd cleaned her apartment for the last two hours, increasing the volume of the music as her scrubbing, polishing and vacuuming frenzy did little to obliterate what she'd confront this afternoon.

A face-to-face meeting with her number one client.

The client her beloved CJU Designs couldn't afford to lose.

The client who might well fire her lying butt when he discovered her identity.

Archer Flett didn't do commitment. He'd made that perfectly clear in Capri eight years ago. So how would he feel when he learned he'd committed his new mega campaign to a woman he'd deliberately walked away from because they'd been getting too close.

She stubbed her toe on a wrought-iron table and swore, kicking the ornate leg again for good measure.

She was furious with herself for not confronting this issue sooner. What had she expected? Never to cross paths with Archer physically again?

Yep, that was exactly what she'd expected.

It had been three years since she'd tendered for the lucrative Torquay Tan account, completely unaware the company was owned and run by the surf world's golden boy.

It had come as a double surprise discovering the laid-back charmer she'd met eight years ago had the business nous to own a mega corporation, let alone run it. It looked as if the guy she'd once been foolish enough to fall for was full of surprises.

Now she had a chance to take on her biggest account yet: the launch of Archer's surf school in Torquay, his home town. To do it she had to meet with the man himself.

She should have bowed out gracefully, been content to be his online marketing manager for lesser accounts.

But she needed the money. Desperately.

Her mum depended on her.

The music swelled, filling her head with memories and her heart with longing. She loved the passion of Latin American music—the distinct rhythms, the sultry songs.

They reminded her of a time gone by. A time when she'd danced all night with the stars overhead and the sand under her feet. A time when she'd existed on rich pasta and cheap Chianti and whispered words of her first love.

Archer.

The music faded, along with the sentimental rubbish infiltrating her long-established common sense.

These days she didn't waste time reminiscing. She'd given up on great loves and foolish dreams.

Watching her mum go through hell had seen to that.

She was like her hot-blooded Italian father, apparently: they shared starry-eyed optimism, their impulsiveness, their passion for food and fashion and flirting. She'd considered those admirable qualities until she'd witnessed first-hand what happened when impulsive passions turned sour—her dad's selfishness knew no bounds.

And just like that she'd given up on being like her dad. She didn't give in to grand passion or fall foolhardily in love. Not any more.

Sure, she dated. She liked it. Just not enough to let anyone get too close.

As close as Archer had once been.

'Damn Archer Flett,' she muttered, kicking the table a third time for good measure.

Housework might not have worked off steam but she'd do the next best thing to prepare for this meeting.

Choose a killer business suit, blow-dry her hair and apply immaculate make-up.

Time to show Mr Hot Surfer Dude he didn't affect her after all these years.

Not much anyway.

The tiny hole-in-the-wall office of CJU Designs didn't surprise Archer. Tech geeks didn't need much space.

What did surprise him were the profuse splashes of colour adorning the walls. Slashes of magenta and crimson and turquoise against white block canvases drew his eye and brightened an otherwise nondescript space.

Small glass-topped desk, ergonomic chair, hardbacked wooden guest chair opposite. Exceedingly dull—except for that startling colour.

Almost as if the computer geek was trying to break out of a mould, trying to prove something to herself and her clients.

Well, all CJ had to prove to him was that she could handle the mega-launch he had planned for his pet project and she could hang the moon on her wall for all he cared.

He glanced around for a picture. Not for the first time he was curious about his online marketing manager.

He'd internet-searched CJU Designs extensively before hiring their services and had come up with nothing but positive PR and high praise from clients, including many sportspeople.

So he'd hired CJ, beyond impressed with her work. Crisp, clear, punctual, she always delivered on time, creating the perfect slogans, pitches and launches for any product he'd put his name to.

Trailing a finger along the dust-free desk, he wondered how she'd cope with a campaign of this size. Launching the first Flett Surf School for teens had to succeed. It was a prototype for what he planned in the surf hotspots around the world.

He'd seen too many kids in trouble—kids who hung around the beaches drinking, smoking dope, catching the occasional wave. They were aimless, trying to look cool, when in fact he'd seen the lost look in their eyes.

This was his chance to make a difference. And hopefully prove to his family just how wrong they'd been to misjudge him.

He'd never understood it—had done a lot of soul-searching to come up with one valid reason why they hadn't trusted him enough.

Had he been too blasé? Too carefree? Too narcissistic? Too wrapped up in his career to pick up the signs there'd been a major problem?

Tom and Trav hadn't helped when they'd discussed it a few years ago. He'd asked, and they'd hedged, reiterating that they'd been sworn to secrecy by Frank, embarrassed that their complicity had contributed to the ongoing gap between them.

So Archer had made a decision right then to forget his damn pride and re-bond with his brothers. They might not be the best mates they'd once been but their sometimes tense relationship now was a far improvement on the one they'd had previously—the one he still had with his dad.

It irked, not knowing the reason why they'd done it, and

their lack of trust had left a lasting legacy. One he hoped opening the surf school would go some way to rectifying.

Thinking about his family made him pace the shoebox office. He hated confined spaces. Give him the ocean expanses any day. He never felt as free as he did catching a wave, paddling out to sea, with nothing between him and the ocean but an aerodynamic sliver of fibreglass.

Nothing beat the rush.

He heard the determined click-clack of high heels striding towards the office and turned in time to see Calista Umberto enter.

His stomach went into free fall, as it had the first time he'd caught a thirty-foot wave. That rush? Seeing Callie again after all these years topped it.

While he stared like a starstruck fool, she didn't blink. In fact she didn't seem at all surprised, which could only mean one thing.

She'd been expecting him.

In that second it clicked.

CJU Designs.

Calista Jane Umberto.

The fact he remembered her middle name annoyed him as much as discovering the online marketing whiz he'd been depending on for the last three years was the woman he'd once almost lost his mind over.

His Callie.

'I'll be damned,' he muttered, crossing the small space in three strides, bundling her into his arms in an impulsive hug before he could process the fact that she'd actually taken a step back at his approach.

The frangipani fragrance hit him first—her signature bodywash that instantly resurrected memories of midnight strolls on a moonlit Capri beach, long, languorous kisses in the shade of a lemon tree, exploring every inch of the deliciously smooth skin drenched in that tempting floral scent.

Any time he'd hit an island hotspot to surf—Bali, Hawaii, Fiji—frangipanis would transport him back in time. To a time he remembered fondly, but a time fraught with danger, when he'd been captivated by a woman to the point of losing sight of the end game.

In the few seconds when her fragrance slammed his senses, he registered her rigid posture, her reluctance to be embraced.

Silently cursing himself, he released her and stepped back, searching her face for some sign that she remembered what they'd once shared.

Her lush mouth—with a ripe red gloss—flat-lined, but she couldn't hide the spark in her eyes.

Flecks of gold in a rich, deep chocolate. Eyes he'd seen glazed with passion, sparkling with enthusiasm, lighting with love.

It was the latter that had sent him running from Capri without looking back. He'd do well to remember that before indulging in a spin down memory lane and potentially ostracising his marketing manager.

'Good to see you, Archer,' she said, her tone polite and frigid and so at odds with the Callie he remembered that he almost took a step back. 'Take a seat and we'll get started.'

He shook his head, the fog of confusion increasing as he stared at this virtual stranger acting as if they barely knew each other.

He'd seen her naked, for goodness' sake. For a week straight. A long, hot, decadent week that had blown his mind in every way.

'You're not serious?'

Her stoic business persona faltered and she toyed with

the bracelet on her right wrist, turning it round and around in a gesture he'd seen often that first night in Capri.

The night they'd met. The night they'd talked for hours, strolled for ages, before ending up at his villa. The night they'd connected on so many levels he'd been terrified and yet powerless to resist her allure.

She'd been brash and brazen and beautiful, quick to laugh and parry his quips, slow to savour every twirl of linguini and rich Napolitano sauce.

She'd had a passion for everything from fresh crusty bread dipped in olive oil to hiking along pebbly beach trails to nights spent exploring each other's bodies in erotic detail.

That passionate woman he remembered was nothing like this cool, imperturbable automaton.

Except for that tell with the bracelet he would have thought she didn't remember, let alone want to acknowledge the past.

'I'm serious about getting down to business.'

The bracelet-twirling picked up pace, a giveaway that she was more rattled than she let on.

'Plenty of time for that.' He gestured towards her slim-line laptop, the only thing on her desk. 'What I want to know is why you've been hiding behind your PC all this time?'

Another hit. Her eyes widened and her tongue darted out to the corner of her mouth.

A mouth designed for culinary riches and sin.

A mouth thinned in an unimpressed line so far removed from the smiles he remembered that he almost reached out with his fingertip to tilt the corners up.

'I'm not hiding behind anything,' she said, her tone as prim as her fitted black suit.

Actually, the suit wasn't all bad. Hugging all the right

curves, flaring at the cuffs and hem, ending above her knee. Combined with an emerald silk shirt hinting at cleavage, it was better than okay.

He was just grouchy because she wasn't rapt to see him. But then again, considering the way they'd parted…

'You didn't think I might like to know that the marketing whiz I e-mail regularly is someone I…'

What? Once had memorable sex with? Once knew intimately? Once might have given up his freedom for, in another time, another place? If he hadn't still been reeling from his parents' revelations?

Her eyes narrowed. 'Someone you what?'

He should have known she wouldn't let him off lightly. She hadn't back then either, when he'd told her he was skipping out.

'Someone I know,' he finished lamely, trying his signature charming grin for good measure.

Her lips merely compressed further as she swivelled away and strode to her desk. Not so bad, considering he got the opportunity to watch expensive linen shift over that memorable butt.

Damn, he loved her curves. He'd seen his fair share of bikini babes over the years—an occupational hazard and one he appreciated—but the way Callie had filled out a swimsuit?

Unforgettable.

She sat behind her desk, glaring at him as if she could read his mind. She waved at the chair opposite and he sat, thrown by her reaction. Acting professional was one thing. The ice princess act she had going on was losing appeal fast.

'Our fling wasn't relevant to our business dealings so I didn't say anything—particularly after how things ended.'

She eyeballed him, daring him to disagree. Wisely, he kept mute, interested to see where she was going with this.

'I tendered for your account without knowing you were behind the company.'

Her next sign of anything less than cool poise was when she absentmindedly tapped the space bar on her laptop with a thumb.

'When we started corresponding and worked well together, I didn't want to complicate matters.'

'Complicate them how?'

A faint pink stained her cheeks. Oh, yeah, this was starting to get real interesting.

'What do you want me to say? Any shared past tends to complicate things.'

'Only if you let it.' He hooked his hands behind his head, enjoying the battle gleam in her eyes. At last the fiery woman he knew was coming out to fight. 'Don't know about you, but I don't let *anything* interfere with my career.'

'Like I didn't know that,' she muttered, and he had the grace to acknowledge a twinge of regret.

He'd used his burgeoning surfing career to end it in Capri. It had seemed as good as excuse as any. He might as well live down to the reputation his family had tarred him with. Anything was better than telling her the truth.

'Is this going to be a problem for you?'

He threw it out there, half expecting her to say yes, hoping she'd say no.

He wasn't disappointed to see her—far from it. And the fact they'd have to spend time together in Torquay to get the marketing campaign for the surf school off the ground was a massive bonus.

Torquay... Wedding...

It was like a wave crashing over him. He floated the solution to another problem.

They'd have to spend time in Torquay for business.

He had to spend time with his overzealous family at Trav's wedding.

He had to find a date.

A bona fide city girl who'd act as a buffer between him and his family.

Lucky for him, he was looking straight at her.

Not that he'd let her know yet. He needed her expertise for this account, and by her less than welcoming reaction he'd be hard-pressed getting her to Torquay in the first place without scaring her away completely.

Yeah, he'd keep that little gem for later.

Her brows furrowed. 'What's with the smug grin?'

He leaned forward and nudged the laptop between them out of the way. 'You want this latest account?'

She nodded, a flicker of something bordering on fear in her eyes. It might make him callous, but he could work with fear. Fear meant she was probably scared of losing his lucrative business. Fear meant she might agree to accompany him to Torquay even if she had been giving him the ice treatment ever since she'd set foot in the office.

'You know this campaign will mean spending loads of one-on-one time together on the school site down at Torquay?'

Her clenched jaw made him want to laugh out loud. 'Why? I've always worked solo before. and as you can attest the results have been great.'

If she expected him to back down, she'd better think again. He'd get her to accompany him to Torquay by any means necessary—including using the campaign as blackmail.

Feigning disappointment, he shook his head. 'Sorry, a remote marketing manager won't cut it this time. I'll need you to shadow me to get a feel for the vibe I'm trying to capture with the school. The kids won't go for it otherwise.'

Her steely glare could have sliced him in two. 'For how long?'

'One week.'

She sucked in a breath, her nose wrinkling in distaste, and he bit back a laugh.

'From your previous work I'm sure you want to do this campaign justice and that's what it's going to take. You can be home in time to celebrate Christmas Day.'

Appealing to her professional pride was a master touch. She couldn't say no.

'Fine. I'll do it,' she muttered, her teeth clenching so hard he was surprised he didn't hear a crack.

'There's just one more thing.' Unable to resist teasing her, he twisted a sleek strand of silky brown hair around his finger. 'We'll be cohabiting.'

CHAPTER TWO

CALLIE stared at Archer in disbelief.

The cocky charmer was blackmailing her.

As if she'd let him get away with that.

She folded her arms, sat back, and pinned him with a disbelieving glare. 'Never thought I'd see the day hot-shot Archer Flett resorted to blackmail to get a woman to shack up with him.'

His eyes sparked with admiration and she stiffened. She didn't want to remember how he'd looked at her in a similar way during their week in Capri, his expression indulgent, bordering on doting.

As if. He'd bolted all the same, admiration or not, and she'd do well to remember it.

For, as much as she'd like to tell him where he could stick his business contract, she needed the money.

'Blackmail sounds rather harsh.' He braced his forearms on her desk and leaned forward, immediately shrinking the space between them and making her breath catch. 'A bit of gentle persuasion sounds much more civilised.'

That voice… It could coax Virgins Anonymous into revoking their membership. Deep, masculine, with a hint of gravel undertone—enough to give Sean Connery healthy competition.

There was nothing gentle about Archer's persuasion.

If he decided to turn on the full arsenal of his charm she didn't stand a chance, even after all this time.

That irked the most. Eight long years during which she'd deliberately eradicated his memory, had moved on, had dealt with her feelings for him to the extent where she could handle his online marketing without flinching every time she saw his picture or received an e-mail.

Gone in an instant—wiped just like that. Courtesy of his bedroom voice, his loaded stare and irresistible charm.

'Besides, living together for the week is logical. My house has plenty of room and we'll be working on the campaign 24/7. It's sound business sense.'

Damn him. He was right.

She could achieve a lot more in seven days without factoring in travel time—especially when she had no clue where his house was or its vicinity to Torquay.

However, acknowledging that his stipulation made sense and liking it were worlds apart.

'You know I'm not comfortable with this, right?'

'Really? I hadn't picked up on that.'

He tried his best disarming grin and she deliberately glanced away. Living with him for the week might be logical for business, but having to deal with his natural charm around the clock was not good.

'Anything I can do to sweeten the deal?'

Great—he was laying the charm on thick. Her gaze snapped to his in time to catch his damnably sexy mouth curving at the corners. Her lips tingled in remembrance of how he'd smile against her mouth when he had her weak and whimpering from his kisses.

Furious at her imploding resistance, she eyeballed him with the glare that had intimidated the manager at her mum's special accommodation into giving her another extension on payment.

'Yeah, there is something you can do to sweeten the deal.' She stabbed at an envelope with a fingertip and slid it across the desk towards him. 'Sign off on my new rates. Your PA hasn't responded to my last two e-mails and I need to get paid.'

His smile faded as he took the envelope. 'You're having financial problems?'

If he only knew.

'No. I just like to have my accounts done monthly, and you've always been prompt in the past...'

Blessedly prompt. The Torquay Tan account had single-handedly launched her business into the stratosphere and kept it afloat. If she ever lost it...

In that moment the seriousness of the situation hit her. She shouldn't be antagonising Archer. She should be jumping through whatever hoop he presented her with—adding a somersault and a *ta-da* flourish for good measure.

She had to secure this new campaign. CJU Designs would skyrocket in popularity, and her mum would continue to be cared for.

She had no other option but to agree.

'Just so we're clear. If I accompany you to Torquay, the surf school campaign is mine?'

His mocking half salute did little to calm the nerves twisting her belly into pretzels.

'All yours, Cal.'

She didn't know what unnerved her more. The intimate way the nickname he'd given her dripped off his tongue or the way his eyes sparked with something akin to desire.

She should be ecstatic that she'd secured the biggest campaign of her career.

Instead, as her pulse ramped up to keep pace with her flipping heart, all she could think was *at what price*?

* * *

Archer didn't like gloating. He'd seen enough of it on the surf circuit—arrogant guys who couldn't wait to glory over their latest win.

But the second Callie's agreement to accompany him to Torquay fell from her lush lips he wanted to strut around the office with his fists pumping in a victory salute.

An over-the-top reaction? Maybe. But having Callie by his side throughout the Christmas Eve wedding festivities—even if she didn't know it yet—would make the event and its guaranteed emotional ra-ra bearable.

He'd suffered through enough Torquay weddings to know the drill by now. Massive marquees, countless kisses from extended rellies he didn't know, back-slapping and one-upmanship from old mates, and the inevitable match-making between him and every single female under thirty in the whole district.

His mum hated the dates he brought home each year, and tried to circumvent him with less-than-subtle fix-ups: notoriously predictable, sweet, shy local girls she hoped would tempt him to settle down in Torquay and produce a brood of rowdy rug-rats.

It was the same every wedding. The same every year, for that matter, when he returned home for his annual visit. A visit primarily made out of obligation rather than any burning desire to be constantly held up as the odd one out in the Flett family.

It wasn't intentional, for his folks and his brothers tried to carry on as if nothing had happened, but while he'd forgiven them for shutting him out in the past the resultant awkwardness still lingered.

He'd steadily withdrawn, stayed away because of it, preferring to be free. Free to go where he wanted, when he wanted. Free from emotional attachments that invariably let him down. Free to date fun-loving, no strings attached women who didn't expect much beyond dinner and drinks rather than an engagement and a bassinet.

His gaze zeroed in on Callie as she fielded an enquiry on the phone, her pen scrawling at a frenetic pace as she jotted notes, the tip of her tongue protruding between her lips.

Callie had been that girl once. The kind of girl who wanted the picket fence dream, the equivalent of his ultimate nightmare. Did she still want that?

The finger on her left hand remained ringless, he saw as he belatedly realised he should have checked if she was seeing anyone before coercing her into heading down to Torquay on the pretext of business when in fact she'd be his date for the wedding.

Then again, she'd agreed, so his assumption that she was currently single was probably safe.

Not that she'd fallen in with his plan quickly. She'd made him work for it, made him sweat. And he had a feeling her capitulation had more to do with personal reasons than any great desire to make this campaign the best ever.

That flicker of fear when she'd thought he might walk and take his business with him... Not that he would have done it. Regardless of whether she'd wanted to come or not CJU would have had the surf school campaign in the bag. She'd proved her marketing worth many times over the last few years, and while he might be laid back on the circuit he was tough in his business.

Success meant security. Ultimately success meant he was totally self-sufficient and didn't have to depend on anyone, for he'd learned the hard way that depending on people, even those closest to you, could end in disappointment and sadness and pain.

It was what drove him every day, that quest for independence, not depending on anyone, even family, for anything.

After his folks' betrayal it was what had driven him away from Callie.

He chose to ignore his insidious voice of reason. The last thing he needed was to get sentimental over memories.

She hung up the phone, her eyes narrowing as she caught sight of him lounging in the doorway. 'You still here?'

'We're not finished.'

He only just caught her muttered, 'Could've fooled me.'

As much as it pained him to revisit the past, he knew he'd have to bring it up in order to get past her obvious snit.

He did not want a date glaring daggers at him all night; his mum would take it as a sure-fire sign to set one of her gals onto him.

'Do we need to clear the air?'

She arched an eyebrow in an imperious taunt. 'I don't know. Do we?'

Disappointed, he shook his head. 'You didn't play games. One of the many things I admired about you.'

Her withering glare wavered and dipped, before pinning him with renewed accusation. 'We had a fling in the past. Yonks ago. I'm over it. You're over it. There's no air to clear. Ancient history. The next week is business, nothing more.'

'Then why are you so antagonistic?'

She opened her mouth to respond, then snapped it shut, her icy façade faltering as she ran a hand through her hair in another uncertain tell he remembered well.

She'd done it when they'd first met at a beachside vendor's, when they'd both reached for the last chilled lemonade at the same time. She'd done it during their first dinner at a tiny trattoria tucked into an alley. And she'd done it when he'd taken her back to his hotel for the first time.

In every instance he'd banished her uncertainty with

practised charm, but after the way they'd parted he doubted it would work in this instance.

'Cal—'

'Us being involved in the past complicates this campaign and I'm not a huge fan of complications.'

She blurted it without meeting his eye, her gaze fixed on her laptop screen.

He wished she'd look at him so he could see how deeply this irked, or if she was trying to weasel out of the deal.

'You said it yourself. It's in the past. So why should it complicate anything?' He didn't want to push her, but her antagonism left him no choice. 'Unless…'

'What?' Her head snapped up, her wary gaze locking on his, and in that instant he had his answer before he asked the question.

The spark they'd once shared was there, flickering in the depths of rich brown, deliberately cloaked in evasive shadows.

'Unless you still feel something?'

'I'm many things. A masochist isn't one of them.'

She stood so quickly her chair slid backward on its castors and slammed into the wall. The noise didn't deter her as she stalked towards him, defiant in high heels.

With her eyes flashing warning signals he chose to ignore, he stepped back into the office, meeting her halfway.

Before he could speak she held up her hand. 'I'm not a fool, Archer. We were attracted in Capri, we're both single, and we're going to be spending time together on this campaign. Stands to reason a few residual sparks may fly.' Her hand snagged in her hair again and she almost wrenched it out in exasperation. 'It won't mean anything. I have a job to do, and there's no way I'll jeopardise that by making another mistake.'

He reached for her before he could second-guess, gripping her upper arms, giving her no room to move. 'We weren't a mistake.'

'Yeah? Then why did you run?'

He couldn't respond—not without telling her the truth. And that wasn't an option.

So he did the next best thing.

He released her, turned his back, and walked away.

'And you're still running,' she murmured.

Her barb registered, and served to make him stride away that little bit faster.

CHAPTER THREE

CALLIE strode towards Johnston Street and her favourite Spanish bar.

Some girls headed home to a chick-flick and tub of ice-cream when they needed comfort. She headed for Rivera's.

'Hola, querida.' Arturo Rivera blew her a kiss from behind the bar and she smiled in return, some of her tension instantly easing.

Artie knew about her situation: the necessity for her business to thrive in order to buy the best care for her mum. He knew her fears, her insecurities. He'd been there from the start, this reserved gentleman in a porkpie hat who'd lost his wife to the disease that would eventually claim her mum.

She hadn't wanted to attend a support group, but her mum's doc had insisted it would help in the disease's management and ultimately help her mum.

So she'd gone along, increasingly frustrated and helpless and angry, so damn angry, that her vibrant, fun-loving mother had been diagnosed with motor neurone disease.

She'd known nothing about her mum's symptoms until it had been too late. Nora had hidden them well: the stumbling due to weakness in her leg muscles, her difficulty holding objects due to weak hands, her swallowing difficulties and the occasional speech slur.

The first Callie had learned of it was when her mum had invited her to accompany her to see a neurologist. Nora hated needles, and apparently having an electromyograph, where they stuck needles in her muscles to measure electrical activity, was worse to bear than the actual symptoms.

The diagnosis had floored them both—especially the lack of a cure and mortality rates. Though in typical determined Nora fashion her mum had continued living independently until her symptoms had made it impossible to do so.

Nora had refused to be a burden on her only daughter, so Callie had found the best care facility around—one with top neurologists, speech, occupational and physiotherapists, psychologists, nurses and palliative care, while trying not to acknowledge her mum's steady deterioration.

It was as if she could *see* the nerve cells failing, resulting in the progressive muscle weakness that would eventually kill her mum.

So she focussed on the good news: Nora's sight, smell, taste, sensation, intellect and memory wouldn't be affected. Nora would always know her, even at the end, and that thought sustained her through many a crying jag late at night, when the pain of impending loss crowded in and strangled her forced bravery.

To compound her stress she'd had to reluctantly face the fact she had a fifty-fifty chance of inheriting it too. She hadn't breathed all through the genetic testing consultation, when the doctors had explained that Nora's motor neurone disease was caused by mutations in the SOD1 gene. That tiny superoxide dismutase one gene, located on chromosome twenty-one, controlled her fate.

Insomnia had plagued her in the lead-up to her testing, and the doctor's clinical facts had been terrifying as they echoed through her head: people with the faulty gene had a high chance of developing MND in later life, or could develop symptoms in their twenties.

Like her.

She'd worried herself sick for days after the test, and even though it had come back clear—she didn't carry the mutated gene—she'd never fully shaken the feeling that she had a swinging axe grazing the back of her neck, despite the doc's convincing argument that many people *with* the faulty gene didn't go on to develop MND.

Then the worry had given way to guilt. Guilt that she was the lucky one in her family.

During this time the support group had been invaluable. Artie had been there, just as frustrated, just as angry. He'd lost his wife of forty years.

They'd bonded over espresso and biscotti, gradually revealing their bone-deep resentment and helpless fury at a disease that had no cure. Those weekly meetings had led to an invitation to Rivera's, a place that had instantly become home.

She loved the worn, pockmarked wooden floor, the rich mahogany bar that ran the breadth of the back wall, the maroon velvet embossed wallpaper that created a cosy ambience beckoning patrons to linger over delicious tapas and decadent sangria.

This was where she'd started to thaw, where the deliberate numbness enclosing her aching heart at the injustice of what her mum faced had melted.

This was where she'd come to eat, to chat and to dance.

She lived for the nights when Artie cleared the tables and chairs, cranked up the music, and taught Spanish dances to anyone eager to learn.

Those nights were the best—when she could forget how her life had changed that momentous day when she'd learned of her mum's diagnosis.

She nodded at familiar faces as she weaved through tables towards the bar, her heart lightening with every step as Artie waved his hands in the air, gesturing at her usual spot.

'You hungry, *querida*?'

Considering the knot of nerves in her stomach, the last thing she felt like doing was eating, but if she didn't Artie would know something was wrong.

And she didn't feel like talking about the cause of her angst. Not when she'd spent the fifteen-minute walk to the bar trying to obliterate Archer from her mind.

'Maybe the daily special?'

Artie winked. 'Coming right up.'

As he spooned marinated octopus, garlic olives, *banderillas*, *calamares fritos* and *huevos relleños de gambas* onto a terracotta platter, she mentally rummaged for a safe topic of conversation—one that wouldn't involve blurting about the blackmailing guy who had once stolen her heart.

He slid the plate in front of her, along with her usual espresso. 'So, are you going to tell me what's wrong before your coffee or after?'

She opened her mouth to brush off his astute observation, but one glance at the shrewd gleam in his eyes stalled her. She knew that look. The look of a father figure who wouldn't quit till he'd dragged the truth out of her.

'It's nothing, really—'

He tut-tutted. '*Querida*, I've known you for more than seven years.' He pointed to his bald pate and wrinkled forehead. 'These may indicate the passage of time, but up here…?' He tapped his temple. 'As sharp as Banderas's sword in *Zorro*.'

She chuckled. If Artie had his way Antonio Banderas would be Spain's president.

He folded his arms and rested them on the bar. 'You know I'm going to stay here until you tell me.'

'What about your customers?'

'That's what I pay the staff for.' He grinned. 'Now, are you going to tell, or do I have to ply you with my finest sangria?'

She held up her hands. 'I'm starting work early tomorrow, so no sangria.'

How tempting it sounded. What she wouldn't give to down a jug of Artie's finest, get blotto, and forget the fact she had to accompany Archer to Torquay tomorrow.

'Fine.' She pushed a few olives around her plate before laying down her fork. 'CJU Designs scored its biggest account ever today.'

Artie straightened and did a funny flamenco pirouette. 'That's brilliant. Well done, *querida*.'

'Yeah, it'll take care of mum's bills for the next year at least, thank goodness.'

Artie's exuberance faded. 'How is Nora?'

'The same. Happy, determined, putting on a brave face.'

Something *she* was finding increasingly hard to do when she visited and saw the signs that her mum's condition was worsening. While Nora coped with her wheelchair, relaxed as if she was lounging in her favourite recliner, Callie watched for hand tremors or lapses in speech or drifting off.

She couldn't relax around her mum any more. The effort of hiding her sadness clamped her throat in a stranglehold, taking its toll. She grew more exhausted after every visit, and while she never for one second regretted spending as much time as possible with her mum, she hated the inevitability of this horrid disease.

Artie patted her hand. 'Give her my best next time you see her.'

'Shall do.'

That was another thing that bugged her about this Torquay trip. She'd have to give all her attention to the account in the early set-up—and to the account's aggravating owner—which meant missing out on seeing her mum for the week before Christmas or long drives to and from the beachside town. Which would lead to Archer poking his nose into her business, asking why she had to visit her mum so often, and she didn't want to divulge her private life to him.

Not now, when things were strictly business.

'If this account has alleviated some of your financial worries, why do you look like this?' Artie's exaggerated frown made her smile.

'Because simple solutions often mask convoluted complications.'

'Cryptic.'

'Not really.' She huffed out a long breath. 'The owner of the company behind this new account is an old friend.'

'Ah...so that's it.'

She didn't like the crafty glint in Artie's eyes much—his knowing smile less.

'This...friend...is he a past *amor*?'

Had she loved Archer? After the awful break-up, and in the following months when she'd returned to Melbourne and preferred reading to dating, she'd wondered if the hollowness in her heart, the constant gripe in her belly and the annoying wanderlust to jump back on a plane and follow him around the world's surfing hotspots was love.

She'd almost done it once, after seeing a snippet of him at the Pipeline in Hawaii three months after she'd returned from Europe. She'd gone as far as logging on, choosing flights, but when it had come to paying the arrow had hovered over 'confirm' for an agonising minute before the memory of their parting had resurfaced and she'd shut the whole thing down.

That moment had been her wake-up call, and she'd deliberately worked like a maniac so she could fall into bed at the end of a day exhausted and hopefully dream-free.

Her mum had been diagnosed four weeks later, and as a distraction from Archer it had been a doozy.

Now here he was, strutting into her life, as confident and charming and gorgeous as ever. And as dangerously seductive as all those years ago. For, no matter how many times she rationalised that their week together would be strictly business, the fact remained that they'd once shared a helluva spark. She'd better pack her fire extinguisher just in case.

Artie held up his hands. 'You don't have to answer. I can see your feelings for this old *amor* written all over your face.'

'I don't love him.'

Artie merely smiled and moved down the bar towards an edgy customer brandishing an empty sangria jug, leaving her to ponder the conviction behind her words.

While Callie would have loved to linger over a sangria or two when the Spanish Flamenco band fired up, she had more important things to do.

Like visiting her mum.

Nora hated it when she fussed, so these days she kept her visits to twice weekly—an arrangement they were both happy with.

The doctors had given her three years. The doctors didn't know what a fighter Nora Umberto was. She'd lasted seven, and while her tremors seemed to increase every time Callie visited the spark of determination in her mum's eyes hadn't waned.

After the life she'd led, no way would Nora go out without a bang. She continued to read to the other residents and direct the kitchen hands to prepare exotic dishes—dishes she'd tried first-hand during her travels around the world, during which she'd met Bruno Umberto.

Callie's dad might not have stuck around long in his first marriage—or any of his subsequent three marriages, for that matter—but thankfully Nora's love of cosmopolitan cuisine had stuck. Callie had grown up on fajitas, ratatouille, korma and Szechuan—a melting pot of tastes to accompany her mum's adventurous stories.

She'd never really known her dad, but Nora had been enough parent and then some. Dedicated to raising her daughter, Nora hadn't dated until after she'd graduated high school and moved out. Even then her relationships had lasted only a scant few months. Callie had always wondered if her mum's exuberance had been too much for middle-aged guys who'd expected Martha Stewart and ended up with Lara Croft.

As she entered the shaded forecourt of Colldon Special Accommodation Home she knew that made it all the harder to accept—the fact her go-get-'em mother had been cut down in her prime by a devastating illness no amount of fighting could conquer.

She signed in, slipped a visitor's lanyard over her neck and headed towards the rear of the sandstone building. As she strolled down the pastel-carpeted corridor she let the peace of the place infuse her: the piped rainforest sounds, the subtle scent of lemon and ginger essential oils being diffused from air vents, the colours on the walls transitioning from muted mauve to sunny daffodil.

Colldon felt more like an upmarket boutique hotel than a special home and Callie would do whatever it took to ensure her mum remained here.

Including shacking up with Archer Flett for a week to work on his precious campaign.

She shook her head, hoping that would dispel the image of her agreeing to his demands. It didn't, and all she could see was his startling aquamarine eyes lighting with a fire she remembered all too well when she'd said yes.

She'd been a fool thinking she had the upper hand: she'd known his identity; he hadn't known the woman behind CJU Designs. However, the element of surprise meant little when he'd been the one who ended up ousting her from her smug comfort zone.

Her neck muscle spasmed and she rubbed it as she entered Nora's room. She didn't knock. No one knocked. Her mum's door was perpetually open to whoever wanted to pop in for a chat.

Vibrant, sassy, alive: three words that summed up Nora Umberto.

But as she caught sight of her mum struggling to zip up her cardigan that last word taunted her.

Alive. For how much longer?

She swallowed the lump of sadness welling in her throat, pasted a smile on her face and strode into the room.

'Hey, Mum, how you doing?'

Nora's brilliant blue eyes narrowed as she gestured at the zip with a shaky hand. 'Great—until some bright spark dressed me in this today.'

Her defiant smile made Callie's heart ache.

'Buttons are a pain, but these plastic zips aren't a whole lot better.'

Need a hand? The words hovered on Callie's lips but she clamped them shut. Nora didn't like being treated like an invalid. She liked accepting help less.

Instead, Callie perched on the armchair opposite and ignored the increasing signs that her mum was struggling.

'I'll be away next week.'

Nora instantly perked up. If Callie had to sit through one more lecture about all work and no play she'd go nuts. Not that she could blame her mum. Nora loved hearing stories of Rivera's and dancing and going out, living vicariously through her.

Callie embellished those tales, making her life sound more glamorous than it was. Her mum had enough to worry about without concern for a daughter who dated only occasionally, went Spanish dancing twice a week, and did little else but work. Work that paid the hefty Colldon bills.

'Holiday?'

Callie shook her head. 'Work. In Torquay.'

She said it casually, as if heading to the beachside town *didn't* evoke visions of sun, surf and sexy guys in wetsuits.

Particularly one sexy guy. Who she'd been lucky enough to see without a wetsuit many years ago on another sun-drenched beach.

'You sure it's work?'

Nora leaned so far forward in her wheelchair she almost toppled forward, and Callie had to fold her arms to stop from reaching out.

'You've got a glow.'

'It's an "I'm frazzled to be going away the week before Christmas" glow.'

Nora sagged, her cheekiness instantly dimming. 'You'll be away for Christmas?'

Callie leaned forward and squeezed her mum's hand, careful not to scratch the tissue-thin skin. 'I'll be back in time for Christmas lunch. You think I'd miss Colldon's cranberry stuffing?'

Nora chuckled. 'You know, I wouldn't mind if you missed Christmas with me if your trip involved a hot young man. But work? That's no excuse.'

Ironic. Her trip involved a hot young man *and* work, and she had a feeling she'd need to escape both after a long week in Torquay.

She stood and bent to kiss her mum's cheek. 'Sorry it's a flying visit, but I need to go home and pack. I'm leaving first thing in the morning.'

To her surprise, Nora snagged her hand as she straightened, holding on with what little strength she had.

'Don't forget to have a little fun amid all that work, Calista.' She squeezed—the barest of pressure. 'You know life's too short.'

Blinking back the sudden sting of tears, Callie nodded. 'Sure thing, Mum. And ring me if you need anything.'

Nora released her hand, managing a feeble wave. 'I'll be fine. Go work, play, have fun.'

Callie intended to work. As for the fun and play, she didn't dare associate those concepts with Archer.

Look what had happened the last time she'd done that.

Archer didn't jerk women around, and after the way Callie had reacted to him yesterday he shouldn't push her buttons. But that was exactly what he'd done in hiring the fire-engine red Roadster for their trip to Torquay.

She'd recognise the significance of the car, but would she call him on it?

By the tiny crease between her brows and her compressed lips as she stalked towards him, he doubted it.

The carefree, teasing girl he'd once known had disappeared behind this uptight, reserved shadow of her former self. What had happened to snuff the spark out?

'Still travelling light?' He held out his hand for her overnight bag.

She flung it onto the back seat in response.

'Oo-kay, then. Guess it's going to be a long trip.'

He glimpsed a flicker of remorse as she slid onto the passenger seat, her rigid back and folded arms indicative of her absolute reluctance to be here. To be anywhere near him.

It ticked him off.

They'd once been all over each other, laughing and chatting and touching, a hand-hold here, a thigh squeeze there. When she'd smiled at him he'd felt a buzz akin to riding the biggest tube.

But you walked away anyway.

That was all he needed. For his voice of reason to give him a kick in the ass too.

But she hadn't been forthcoming during their meeting yesterday, and he'd be damned if he'd put up with her foul mood for the next week.

If he showed up at Trav's wedding with her in this snit his mum would know Callie was a fake date and be inquisitive, effectively ruining his buffer zone.

Yeah, because that was the only reason he minded her mood...

He revved the engine, glanced over his shoulder and pulled into traffic. 'You know it's ninety minutes to Torquay, right?'

'Yeah.'

Her glance barely flicked his way behind Audrey Hepburnesque sunglasses that conveniently covered half her face.

'You planning on maintaining the long face the entire way? Do I need to resort to I-spy and guess the number-plate to get a laugh?'

'I'm here to work—'

'Bull.'

He swerved into a sidestreet, earning momentary whiplash and several honks for his trouble.

'What the heck—?'

He kissed her, pouring all his frustration with her frosty behaviour into the kiss.

She resisted at first, but he wouldn't back off. He might have done this to prove a point, but once his lips touched hers he remembered—in excruciating detail—what it had been like to kiss her.

And he wanted more.

He moved his mouth across hers—light, teasing, taunting her to capitulate.

She remained tight-lipped—until his hand caressed the nape of her neck and slid into her hair, his fingertips brushing her scalp in the way he knew she liked.

She gave a little protesting groan and he sensed the moment of surrender when she placed her palm on his chest and half-heartedly pushed. Her lips softened a second later.

He didn't hesitate, taking advantage of her compliance by deepening the kiss, sweeping his tongue into her mouth to find hers, challenging her to deny them, confident she wouldn't.

For what seemed like a glorious eternity they made out like a besotted couple. Then he eased his hand out of her hair, his lips lingering on hers for a bittersweet second before he sat back.

What he saw shocked him more than the rare times he'd been ragdolled by a gnarly wave.

The old Callie was back.

Her brown eyes sparkled, her lush mouth curved smugly at the corners and she *glowed*.

Hell, he'd wanted to get her to lighten up. He hadn't counted on the winded feeling now making his lungs seize.

Being wiped out by a killer wave was easier than this.

But in the few seconds it took him to come up with something casual to say Callie closed off. Her glow gave way to a frown and shadows effectively cloaked the sparkle.

'Happy you sneaked a kiss for old times' sake? Did you want to prove something?'

He shook his head, still befuddled by the strength of his reaction to a kiss that should have meant nothing.

'I wanted to make a mockery of your "just work" declaration.'

She quirked an elegant brow. 'And did you think one little kiss would do that?'

He hadn't. Been thinking, that was. Like feeling the overwhelming rush he got from riding the perfect set on a huge swell he'd done the spontaneous thing. And now he had to live with the consequences: working alongside Callie for the next seven days while trying to forget how incredible she looked all mussed and vulnerable, and how she tasted—like chocolate and coffee.

'I guess I'm just annoyed by your attitude and I wanted to rattle you.'

As much as it turned out she still rattled *him*.

He expected her to bristle, to retreat behind a mask of cool indifference. He didn't expect her to unravel before his eyes.

'Hell, are you *crying*?'

He reached out to hold her, but stopped when she scooted away.

She dashed a hand across her eyes before turning to stare out of the window, her profile stoic and tugging at his heartstrings.

'It's not you. I'm just juggling some other stuff, and it's taking a toll even though I have a handle on it.'

He'd never heard her sound so soft, so vulnerable, and he clamped down on the urge to haul her into his arms. Mixed messages be damned.

'Anything I can do to help?'

'Keep being a smartass. That should make me laugh.'

The quiver in her voice had him reaching across, gently cupping her chin and turning her towards him.

'I can back off if you're going through stuff. Cut the jokes. No kissing. That kind of thing.'

She managed a watery smile. 'No kissing's a given while we work together. The jokes I can handle.'

As she gnawed on her bottom lip realisation slammed into him as if he was pitching over the falls.

She probably had boyfriend troubles.

'Is it another guy? Because I can kick his ass—'

'Not a guy.'

Her smile morphed into a grin and it was like surfacing for air after being submerged underwater for too long.

She held a hand over her heart. 'I promise to lighten up. I'm just…overworked and tired and grumpy in general.'

'That seventh dwarf had nothing on you,' he mumbled, eliciting the expected chuckle—the first time he'd heard her sound remotely light-hearted since yesterday. 'Maybe you should thank me for kissing you. Because you've had an epiphany and—'

'Don't push your luck,' she said, tempering her growl with a wink, catapulting him back to Capri, where she'd winked at him in a tiny dinghy the moment before they'd entered the Blue Grotto, warning him to be careful because the cave was renowned for proposals and he might succumb.

She'd been teasing, but it had been the beginning of the end for them: no matter how carefree their fling, he'd wondered if Callie secretly harboured hopes for more.

And Archer had already learnt that the price paid for loving wasn't one he was willing to pay.

'Okay, so if kissing's off the agenda, work it is,' he said, holding her gaze for several long, loaded moments, daring her to disagree, hoping she would.

'Just work,' she echoed, before elbowing him and pointing at the road. 'If we ever get to Torquay, that is.'

As he reversed out of the sidestreet he knew he should be glad he'd cracked Callie's brittle, reserved outer shell.

But now he'd seen the woman beneath—the same warm, lush woman who'd almost snared his heart eight years ago—he wondered if he should be glad or scared.

CHAPTER FOUR

OKAY, so Callie hadn't been thinking straight since Archer had strolled into her office yesterday.

She'd been caught off guard by the gorgeous familiarity of him, by his outlandish suggestion to live with him for a week while they work, by his demand to agree or lose the account.

She'd also been worried about leaving Nora for the seven days before Christmas once she'd given in to secure the campaign—a worry that hadn't eased despite seeing her mum yesterday.

Her head had been filled with *stuff*. That was the only explanation for why she hadn't seen that kiss coming.

He'd done it out of frustration. She could see that now. He'd wanted to snap her out of her funk, to prove a point.

So what was the rationale behind her responding?

She'd assumed she could handle their cosy living arrangements for business's sake.

She hadn't counted on *this*. This slightly manic, out-of-control feeling because despite her vow to remain platonic he could undermine her with one itty-bitty kiss.

Damn.

She'd been silent for most of the trip, jotting fake notes for the campaign, needing to concentrate on something

other than her tingling lips. Thankfully he'd respected her
need for silence until about twenty miles out of Torquay.

They'd arrived, and she hadn't been able to believe her
eyes.

As he'd steered up the winding, secluded street and
pulled up outside Archer had called it his beach shack.

Massive understatement. *Huge.* Considering she now
stood in a glass-enclosed lounge room as big as her entire
apartment, with floor-to-ceiling glass and three-hundred-
and-sixty-degree views of the Tasman Sea.

This place was no shack.

The pale blue rugs on gleaming ash floorboards, the
sand-coloured suede sofas, the modern glass coffee tables—all screamed class, and were nothing like the mismatched furniture in the log cabin *shack* she'd imagined.

Archer had never been into material things when they'd
first met. It looked as if being a world pro five years running changed a guy.

'I put your bags in the first guest room on the right,'
he said, his bare feet barely making a sound as he padded
up behind her.

Another thing she remembered: his dislike for footwear.
It hadn't mattered much in Capri, when they'd spent many
hours on the beach, and she'd hidden a smile as he'd unlocked the door here, dumped their bags inside and slipped
off his loafers.

She liked him barefoot. He had sexy feet. They matched
the rest of him.

'Thanks.'

He wiggled his eyebrows. 'Right next to my room, in
case you were wondering.'

'I wasn't.' Her heart gave a betraying kick.

'Liar,' he said, snagging a strand of hair and winding
it around his finger, tugging gently.

She knew what he was doing—flirting to keep her smiling. But she *sooo* wasn't going to play this game. Not after that dangerous kiss in the car.

'You still feel the buzz.' His gaze strayed to her lips and she could have sworn they tingled in remembrance.

The smart thing to do would be to lie, but she'd never been any good at it. That was how they'd hooked up in the first place—because of her complete inability to deny how incredibly hot she'd found the laid-back surfer.

He'd romanced her and she'd let him, fully aware that their week in Capri was nothing more than a holiday fling. Pity her impressionable heart hadn't caught up with logic and she'd fallen for him anyway. Her feelings had made it so much harder to get over him—especially after the way he'd ended it.

She'd do well to remember their break-up, not how his kiss had zapped her synapses in the car and reawakened a host of dormant memories she'd be better off forgetting.

'As I recall, didn't we have a conversation in the car about focussing on work?'

His finger brushed her scalp as he wound the strand all the way and she suppressed a tidal wave of yearning.

'You didn't answer my question.' His finger trailed along her hairline, skirting her temple, around her ear, lingering on the soft skin beneath it and she held her breath.

He'd kissed her there many times, until she'd been mindless with wanting him.

'That kiss you sprung on me in the car? Out of line. Business as usual this week. That's it.'

'Protesting much?'

'Archer, don't—'

'Go on, admit it. We still share a spark.'

His mouth eased into a wicked grin and she held up a

hand to ward him off. 'Doesn't mean we'll be doing any-thing about it.'

She expected him to ask why. She expected him to undermine her rationale with charm. Instead he stopped touching her, a shadow skating across his eyes before he nodded.

'You're right; we've got a ton of work to do. Best we don't get distracted.'

'Sounds like a plan,' she said, struggling to keep the disappointment out of her voice.

But something must have alerted him to the raging in-decisive battle she waged inside—flee or fling—because he added, 'But once work is out of the way who knows what we'll get up to?'

She rolled her eyes, not dignifying him with a response, and his chuckles taunted her as she headed for the sanc-tity of her room.

She needed space. She needed time out. She needed to remember why getting involved with a nomad charmer again was a bad idea.

Because right now she was in danger of forgetting.

After what he'd been through with his family, Archer hated dishonesty.

Which made what he was doing with Callie highly un-palatable. He needed to tell her about being his date for the wedding pronto.

They'd arrived at the house three hours ago, and she'd made herself scarce on the pretext of unpacking and doing some last-minute research.

He knew better.

That impulsive kiss in the car might have been to prove a point but somewhere along the way it had morphed into something bigger than both of them.

He'd been so damn angry at her perpetual iciness he'd wanted to shock the truth out of her: the spark was still there.

Oh, it was there all right, and interestingly his little experiment had gone awry. He'd been shocked too.

He'd asked her to accompany him here for work—and the wedding. Nothing more, nothing less.

That kiss? Major reality check.

For there was something between them—something latent and simmering, just waiting to ignite.

Hell.

Way to go with complicating matters.

Best to take a step back and simplify—starting with divulging his addendum to her week-long stay.

He knocked twice at her bedroom door. 'Lunch is ready.'

The door creaked open and she stuck her head around it. What did she think? He'd catch sight of the bed and want to ravish her on the spot?

Hmmm…good point.

'Raincheck?'

He exhaled in exasperation. 'I need my marketing manager in peak form, which means no skipping meals—no matter how distasteful you find my company.'

'It's not that.' She blushed. 'I tend to grab snatched meals whenever I remember, so I don't do a sit-down lunch very often.'

'Lucky for you we're not sitting down.' He snagged her hand, meeting the expected resistance when she pulled back. He tugged harder. 'It's no big deal, Cal. Fish and chips on the beach. You can have your head buried behind your computer again in thirty minutes.'

Her expression softened. 'Give me five minutes and I'll meet you outside.'

'Is this a ploy so I have to release your hand and you'll abscond?'

She chuckled, a welcome, happy sound after her apparent snit. 'It's a ploy to use the bathroom.' She held up her hands. 'No other ulterior motives or escape plans in the works—promise.'

'In that case I'll see you down there.' He squeezed her hand before releasing it. 'But more than five minutes and I get the best piece of fish.'

'You're on.'

Thankfully she only kept him waiting three, and he'd barely had time to spread the picnic blanket on the sand before she hit the beach running.

His breath caught as he watched her scuffing sand and snagging her hair into a loose knot at the nape of her neck. The actions were so reminiscent of their time in Capri he wanted to run half way to meet her.

Not liking how fast she'd got under his skin, he busied himself with unwrapping the paper and setting out the lemon wedges and salt sachets alongside the chips and grilled fish. Anything to keep his hands busy and resisting the urge to sweep her into his arms when she got close enough.

'That smells amazing,' she said, flopping down on the blanket next to him. 'But you said no sitting down.'

'Trivialities.' He pushed the paper towards her. 'Eat.'

And they did, making short work of the meal in companionable silence. He hadn't aimed for romance but there was a certain implied intimacy that had more to do with their shared past than any concerted effort now.

The comfortableness surprised him. Considering her reservations about heading to Torquay with him in the first place, and then her absentee act all morning, he'd expected awkwardness.

This relaxed ambience was good. All the better to spring his surprise.

'I need to ask you a favour.'

She licked the last grains of salt off her fingers—an innocuous, innocent gesture that shot straight to his groin.

'What is it?'

Now or never. 'My youngest brother Travis is getting married Christmas Eve and I'd like you to be my date.'

She stared at him in open-mouthed shock, her soda can paused halfway to her lips.

'You're asking me to be your *date*?'

She made it sound as if he'd asked her to swim naked in a sea full of ravenous sharks.

'We're not heading back 'til Christmas Day, and it doesn't make sense for you to spend Christmas Eve alone when you could come to what'll basically be a whoop-up party, so I thought you might like to come.'

'I don't have anything to wear,' she blurted, her horror-stricken expression not waning.

So much for that spark he'd imagined when they'd kissed.

'There are a couple of local boutiques, but honestly it'll be a pretty casual affair.'

'Well, you've thought of everything, haven't you?'

Her eyes narrowed, and he braced for the obvious question.

'Why didn't you ask me before we got here?'

Several lame-ass excuses sprang to mind, but he knew nothing but honesty would work now.

'Because I knew you wouldn't come.'

Her fingers clenched so hard she dented the soda can. 'So the business thing was an excuse?'

'No way. I need this surf school campaign to fly and

you're the best.' He tried an endearing grin. 'I just figured we could kill two birds with one stone.'

'I could kill *you*,' she muttered, placing her soda can on the sand and hugging her knees to her chest. 'I don't like being taken for a fool.'

'You know that's not how I see you.'

She rested her cheek on her knees, her sidelong glance oddly vulnerable. 'How do I know? It's been eight years since I've seen you.'

Hating the certainty pinging through him that he'd majorly stuffed this up, he scooted closer and draped an arm across her shoulders, surprised when she didn't shrug it off.

'Honestly? I wanted to tell you, but I was pretty thrown at your office, and you weren't exactly welcoming so I took the easy way out and focussed on the business side of things. Forgive me?'

'I'll think about it,' she said, her tone underlined by a hint of ice as the corners of her mouth were easing upwards.

'Is it that much of a hardship to be my date for an evening?'

'Considering I don't know you any more, yeah.'

'Easily rectified.'

Before he could second-guess the impulse he leaned across and kissed her.

It was nothing like his reckless prove-a-point kiss in the car. This time it just felt *right*.

She fought him initially, trying to pull away, but his hand slid around the back of her head, anchoring her, and he sensed the second she gave in.

Her lips softened and she moaned, the barest of sounds but enough for him to deepen the kiss, until the roaring in his ears matched the pounding of the surf crashing metres from their feet.

He had no idea how long the kiss lasted. A few seconds. An eternity. But when it ended he wished it hadn't.

'You've gotta stop doing that.' She shoved him away—hard.

'Sorry,' he said, not meaning it, and by her raised eyebrow she knew it.

'Hollow apologies after the fact don't cut it.' She jabbed a finger at his chest. 'And neither do those kisses. Quit it, okay?'

'Hey, I'm an impulsive guy. You can't blame me—'

'You want me to be your date for the wedding?'

'Yeah.'

'Then no more funny business.' Her gaze dropped to his lips, lingered, and he could have sworn he glimpsed longing. 'This campaign means a lot to both of us, so let's keep our minds on the job, okay?'

'Okay.'

He wanted to lighten the mood, end on a frivolous note. 'Maybe I wanted that kiss to prove it won't be so far-fetched for you to pretend to be a devoted date at the wedding—'

'You're impossible,' she said, leaping to her feet and dusting the sand off her butt—but not before he'd seen a glimmer of a grin.

'Nothing's impossible,' he murmured to her retreating back as she marched off in a semi-huff.

He'd got her to agree to manage the biggest campaign of his career—and the one that meant the most. He'd also coerced her into staying with him for a week, and to be his date for the wedding.

Considering how he'd ended things between them all those years ago, he hadn't just pulled off the impossible he'd pulled off a miracle.

* * *

Archer didn't want his family getting wind of his house-guest just yet.

The Christmas Eve wedding would be bad enough without the Flett hordes descending on his place to check her out.

He'd twigged pretty fast that despite Callie being a Melbourne girl she was vastly different from his usual choice of date. She didn't need a truckload of make-up before being seen in the morning, she didn't need a hair-straightener or the name of the nearest manicurist, and she didn't wrinkle her nose at walking on the beach in case her pedicure got chipped.

Maybe he'd made a mistake asking her to be his date for the wedding, because from where he was sitting, staring at the distant dot strolling on the beach, her hair streaming in a dark cloud behind her, he wondered if she'd be enough of a safeguard.

Callie was naturally warm and vibrant, not aloof and standoffish, the way he wanted his women to be when he visited home.

He *liked* that his folks disapproved of his dates and kept their distance. That was the whole point. What if they were drawn to Callie like he was and his plan to keep them at arm's length came crashing down?

He had to keep the Fletts away for as long as possible until the wedding, just in case.

He'd managed to fly under the radar so far. Last night had been spent poring over Callie's ideas for the surf school website, thrashing out slogans and content, working late over homemade pizzas and beer.

It scared him, how comfortable it was having her around. He'd never had a woman stay at his place, let alone lived with anyone. It was his sanctuary, away from the surf crowd, the fans, the media.

No one knew he owned this place except his family.

Some of whom were belting down his door at this very minute.

Damn. So much for keeping their distance.

Cursing under his breath, he yanked the door open and glared at Trav and Tom, ignoring the familiar squeeze his heart gave when he glimpsed Izzy, his six-year-old niece, peering up at him from behind her dad's legs.

He hated how out of all the Fletts she was the one guaranteed to make him feel the worst for staying away. The kid was too young to realise what was going on, but she managed to lay a guilt trip on him every visit.

At three, she'd stuck her tongue out at his date every chance she got and bugged him to teach her how to surf. He'd begged off with his usual excuse—only staying for two days, maybe next time.

At four, she'd placed stick insects in his date's handbag and a hermit crab in her designer shoe, while pestering him for the elusive surf lesson.

At five, she'd verbally flayed his date for her 'too yellow' hair and 'too red' lipstick, and had given up asking him to surf.

He should have been glad. Instead it had ripped him in two when he'd said goodbye to her around this time last year.

It wasn't Izzy's fault he had issues with the rest of his family, but he was scared. Getting close to Izzy might let the rest of them in again, which made him angsty. What if he let them into his heart again only to have it handed back to him like eight years ago?

Every trip home it was the same. Initial tension between him and his brothers soon easing into general ribbing and guy-chat, his mum fussing around him, and prolonged stilted awkwardness with his dad. He still wanted the security of Callie as his buffer zone, but maybe this time he'd swallow his pride and make the first move.

He'd wanted to in the past, but every time he made the decision to broach the gap he'd realise two days weren't long enough to make up for the years apart.

This year he was staying for a week. No excuse.

He squatted down to her level. 'Hey, Iz, long time no see.'

She frowned, but it didn't detract from the curious sparkle in her big blue eyes.

The expression in those eyes—guileless, genuine, trusting—slugged him anew. A guy couldn't hide for long from those eyes. They saw too much, knew too much—including the fact he was acting like a recalcitrant jerk in not welcoming his brothers into his home.

He opened his arms, saw the indecision on her face before she slowly stepped out from behind Tom's legs. She hesitated and his gut squelched with sadness.

It shouldn't be like this—his own niece treating him like a stranger. *He'd* done this, with his stubborn pride. He needed to get over the past. For the longer it took the harder it became to pretend nothing had happened and go back to the way it had been before: a close-knit family who supported each other through everything.

Archer waited, eyeballing Izzy, hoping she could see how much he wanted to squeeze her tight.

After another interminable second that felt like sixty, she flung herself into his arms. He exhaled in relief as he hugged her hard, ignoring the flutter in his chest he got every time this kid wrapped her arms around his neck and hung on as if she'd never let go.

'Where've you been?' She released him, stepped back and crossed her arms as he stood. 'You never come see me any more.'

Practically squirming under the interrogation, Archer floundered for words that wouldn't sound like a trite excuse.

Tom placed a hand on his daughter's shoulder. 'You know your uncle travels a lot, honey. We're lucky to see him when he has time.'

Ouch. Tom's barb slugged him like the punches they'd traded as kids, wrestling at the water's edge to see who'd get the long board for the day.

'At least he always brings me a gift,' Izzy said, pushing her way past him and bounding to the chessboard set up in a far corner, her natural exuberance replacing the reticence that sliced him up inside.

'Manners, Iz,' Tom said, following his daughter into the room and looking around in a not too subtle attempt at sussing out Callie's whereabouts.

'Couldn't keep your big mouth shut, huh?' Archer elbowed Trav as he brought up the rear. 'When we surfed the other day you said you'd keep your lips zipped about me being back early.'

His youngest brother grinned. 'Tom threatened me with bodily harm, and considering he's around a lot more than you, I caved.'

Great—another dig at his absenteeism. Closely following Izzy's reluctant treatment, it made him feel like a heel.

'So where is she?' Tom stuck his hands in his pockets and looked around.

'Who?'

'This mystery woman, of course.' Tom eyeballed him. 'When you make it home for your obligatory Christmas visit your date stays in town. So the fact she's staying here speaks volumes.'

Tom jerked a thumb in Trav's direction. 'We want to check her out, make sure she hasn't got two heads, 'cos that's the only kind of woman who'd be crazy enough to stay here with you.'

Despite another dig from Tom about his obligatory visits, Archer felt his tension fade at his brother's jocularity. 'Wanna beer?'

'Sure.'

Ideally Archer didn't want them hanging around long enough to meet Callie, who'd gone for a walk on the beach to clear her head after a marathon morning brainstorming. But Tom was right; he barely saw his brothers any more and, even though they'd been complicit in his dad's decision to keep the truth secret, he missed the camaraderie they'd once shared.

'I bring a date home every year. This one's no different.' Archer's heart gave a betraying buck at the lie.

'So you're letting some plastic, fake, stick-thin bimbo share your secret hideaway?' Tom snorted. 'Not bloody likely.'

Archer wanted to defend those poor women his brother had just disparaged, but sadly he happened to agree. The women he'd brought home in the past had been exactly as Tom described and not a patch on Callie.

'She's not real, is she? You've made her up so Mum won't go into her speed-dating frenzy in an effort to have you settle for a local girl rather than *those city girls*.'

Archer chuckled at Tom's imitation of their mum, who made *those city girls* sound as if he was dating a brothel's inhabitants.

Tom had followed him into the kitchen, and Archer handed him a beer while uncapping another for Trav and popping an orange soda tab for Izzy.

'She's real. And you'll get to meet her at the wedding like everyone else.'

He held up his beer bottle and Tom clinked it. 'Sure she hasn't got two heads?'

Archer smirked. 'Trust me, Callie's pretty great—'

'Callie? *The* Callie?'

Tom lowered his beer and stared at him with blatant curiosity as Archer silently cursed his slip of the tongue.

He'd had no intention of telling anyone her name until the wedding—let alone Tom, the only Flett who knew how close he'd come to giving up his dream for her.

He'd blurted it out after Tom's divorce had been final-ised, sitting on his deck four years ago. That had been one hell of a night. Tom had been miserable, Trav had been blind drunk and clueless how to handle the situation, and Archer had felt like an outcast. The three of them had been in a foul mood and it had almost come to blows. Archer had tussled with Tom and that release of steam and tes-tosterone had opened up a narrow pathway to the truth.

Tom and Trav had told him about dad then—how he'd sworn them to secrecy, how they'd hated keeping it from him but hadn't wanted to stress the seriously ill Frank.

He guessed he understood their logic—who knew? He might have done the same—but it didn't make it any eas-ier to handle when he still didn't know why he'd been the odd man out.

With the air somewhat cleared between them, talk had moved on to Tom's divorce, and Archer had sunk beers in commiseration, alternating between being outraged and bitter on behalf of his brother, who'd done the right thing by marrying the girl he'd got pregnant and yet got screwed over anyway, and determination never to end up like him.

Tom had been morose, berating himself for losing his head over a woman, and Archer had made the mistake of opening up about Callie to make him feel better.

'You're not the only one. We all get sucked in by a memorable female now and then.'

That confession under the onslaught of too many lagers had now come back to bite him on the butt.

He forced a laugh, aiming for casual. 'Turns out my on-line marketing manager is Callie. Had no idea 'til we met in Melbourne to tee up the surf school campaign. She's here to work for the week—made sense she came to the wedding as my date. Nothing more to it.'

Archer took a slug of beer after his spiel, wondering who he was trying to convince—himself or Tom.

Yesterday had been tough. Hell, it had been sheer torture, watching Callie come alive as she sketched out ideas, seeing her glow as he approved an early pro forma, seeing glimpses of the vibrant woman he'd once lost his head over many years ago.

Sadly she reserved her enthusiasm for work only. Following that impulsive kiss on the beach she'd reverted to coolly polite and casually friendly.

She might have ditched her initial antagonism, but an invisible barrier between them was still there—one he had no hope of breaching considering how things had ended between them.

Correction: how *he'd* ended things between them.

He didn't blame her for being wary. But late last night, with the woman he'd once been crazy for sleeping in the room next door and insomnia plaguing him, he'd wished they could recapture half the easy-going camaraderie they'd once shared.

He only had a week to get this surf school campaign up and running before he flew out to Hawaii for Christmas Day, so realistically he couldn't afford to stuff around.

He knew what he was doing. Flirting with her as a deliberate tactic to distract himself from the stress of being home and having to deal with his family. It was a distancing technique he'd honed with other dates before her. But none had affected him as much as Callie.

He'd deliberately kept things between them light-hearted and work-focussed, but what would happen if he ratcheted up the heat? Would she release some of that new reserve she carried around like an invisible cloak and resurrect the passion they'd once shared?

Tom pointed his beer in Archer's direction. 'The fact she's the first woman you've ever brought here speaks volumes.'

'It was convenient for work, that's all.'

'Yeah, keep telling yourself that.'

Or course Callie chose that moment to hustle through the back door, wind-tousled and pink-cheeked and utterly delectable.

'Hey, Arch, there's a car out front—' She caught sight of Tom and stopped, her eyes widening, before she crossed the kitchen and held out her hand. 'You're a much better-looking version of Archer, so you must be a Flett too.'

Tom laughed as he shook her hand. 'I like her already,' he said, while Archer shot him a filthy look.

'Callie, meet my older brother, Tom.'

A playful smile teased the corners of her mouth as she glanced up at Tom—a smile she hadn't shot *him* once since they'd arrived.

'Pleased to meet you.'

Something painful twisted in his chest at the way she lit up in the way she'd once used to light up around him.

'Come meet his daughter—and Trav, the groom.'

Tom's goofy grin proved what he already knew: he sounded like an uptight ass.

'You have a little girl? That's great,' Callie said, falling into step beside Tom while Archer brought up the rear, hating himself for feeling petty and out of sorts that Callie had lightened up for the first time since yesterday because of his brother.

'Hey, another girl. Awesome.'

Izzy flew at Callie and a strange, unidentifiable feeling swamped him as he watched his niece hug her, spontaneously and without reserve, the way he'd wished Iz had hugged *him* when he'd first opened the door.

Unfazed, Callie led Izzy back to the chessboard, where she shook hands with Trav, whose goofy grin matched Tom's.

Great—two Flett males she'd slayed. He couldn't wait until she met his dad.

Three.

The number popped into his head.

Three Flett males she'd slayed, including him. No matter how many times he denied it, the fact remained: Callie was the kind of woman who could have an impact on a guy.

An unforgettable impact, considering the schmuck he turned into around her.

When he finally tore his gaze away from the captivating sight of Callie giggling alongside Izzy, Tom's smug smirk greeted him.

'So tell me. What did an amazing woman like that see in a putz like you? And why the hell did you let her go?'

Did.

Past tense.

Having his brother verbalise what he'd been wondering himself since reconnecting with her ticked him off more than the uncertainty plaguing him.

This week was about work and familial obligation, before he fled back to the life he liked. If a little light-hearted flirtation with Callie made it more bearable, so be it.

He hadn't banked on this restlessness, this annoying

feeling that he was missing out on something by making the lifestyle choices he had. Worse, having his brother articulate it.

'Leave it alone,' he muttered under his breath, garnering a broader grin from Tom.

'You know I'm the last person to believe in all that romance crap, considering the number Tracy did on me, but have you ever considered this coincidence of her coming back into your life might mean something?'

Archer stared at his brother in amazement. Tom had given up his dreams to turn pro for Tracy, a local surf groupie who'd deliberately got pregnant to snare her man. Tom had foregone his dream to marry Tracy, stay in Torquay and raise Izzy.

Ironically, Tracy had been the one to take off a year into the marriage, leaving Tom with a toddler and a nagging bitterness.

Tom didn't believe in happily-ever-afters, so the fact he'd mentioned the word *romance* and alluded to fate alerted Archer to how badly he must be making a fool of himself.

'You've been spending too much time reading Izzy's fairytales, mate.' His gruff response came out as a snarl, and he immediately realised his reaction had increased rather than eased Tom's suspicions.

Tom held up his hands. 'Just voicing an impartial opinion. No need to get your tether rope in a knot.'

Callie pumped her fists in the air and shimmied her shoulders as Trav made a disastrous move with his queen. Izzy cheered and Callie joined in, her vivacity flooring him in a way he'd never expected.

She'd been so focussed yesterday, concentrating on business and little else. He'd forgotten she could be like this: funny and vibrant and cute.

Well, not forgotten exactly; the memories had been deliberately shoved to a far recess of his mind and ignored. It wouldn't be good for him to recall how good they'd been together for that brief time in Capri. It would only end in tears.

Archer glared at Tom. 'You breathe one word of her staying here to the folks and you're dead.'

A cunning glint lit Tom's eyes. 'Tell you what. I'll keep my mouth shut if you admit you still want her.'

In response, Archer got him in a headlock. He could never stay detached with Trav or Tom for long. Each year when he returned his initial aloofness disappeared a little quicker.

Besides, he didn't really blame them for withholding stuff he should have been privy to. That had been his dad's doing and, while he loved the stubborn old coot, he couldn't forget. Forgive? Yeah, he'd done that a few years back. Now he just had to pluck up the courage to let Frank know, rather than punishing him because he couldn't get the words out to make it all better.

As he tussled with Tom, Izzy joined in the fun by leaping on her dad's back. Her squeals of laughter didn't distract him from the truth.

Denying any semblance of feeling for Callie was useless.

She'd wheedled her way under his skin.

Again.

And there wasn't one damn thing he could do about it.

CHAPTER FIVE

'PEACE at last.' Archer slid Callie a coffee as she lounged on the balcony.

'Your brothers are cool and Izzy's adorable,' Callie said, adding an extra spoon of sugar to her espresso.

She needed the hit, still reeling from seeing Archer in a family environment. The guy she'd known had never talked about family. He had been the quintessential loner who breezed through life without a care in the world. The guy who didn't commit to anything or anyone beyond his beloved surfing.

So to see him interacting with his brothers had thrown her. He'd been reserved at first, as if he didn't want them in his home—which made no sense after the rough-housing she'd seen once he'd lightened up.

When she'd strolled into the kitchen after her walk it had been like walking smack-bang into an invisible glass wall. The tension had been that thick. She'd glimpsed the circumspection in his eyes and the fact she'd recognised it, could get a read on his feelings after all this time, had irked.

She'd masked her discomfort by being bright and bubbly and a little gushing with his brothers and niece. Which had seemed to annoy Archer further.

What was wrong with the guy? As his date for the wedding, didn't he want her to act naturally around his family? *Sheesh*.

And that was another thing that had thrown her: his obvious attachment to his niece. He'd never struck her as the type to like kids. Not with his lifestyle. But he'd been smitten with Izzy, and seeing the two of them together, their heads bent close as they mulled over a jigsaw puzzle, had unlocked a host of feelings she'd rather not deal with.

She didn't want to remember how attentive and caring he'd been in Capri. And she sure as hell didn't want to acknowledge his consistent flirting, slowly chipping away at her necessary resistance.

She wouldn't give in—not when she knew his overt displays of charm came as naturally to him as catching a wave. She'd been sucked in by it once, and had been let down beyond belief.

She knew that feeling well. Bruno Umberto had made an art form of building up hopes only to let down his daughter.

As for the rare glimpses of unguarded admiration— first when she'd been playing chess with Trav, then when she'd made lemonade for Izzy—she didn't like that at all.

He'd used to look at her like that in Capri, as if she were the only woman in the world, and to see the same look seriously perturbed her. She couldn't afford to get involved with Archer again—not when her emotions were already bruised and fragile from the rollercoaster ride with her mum.

Living life in the moment was one thing. Setting herself up for another dose of heartbreak was another.

She'd given in to his request to be his wedding date for one reason only: to keep the peace between them so they could get the surf school business done and dusted this week.

That kiss on the beach had been just like the one in the car on the way down here yesterday morning. Archer being Archer. Impulsive. Rash. Selfish. Doing what he wanted regardless of the consequences.

Harsh? Maybe, but all the kisses in the world couldn't turn back time and erase the way he'd ended things between them, and that was what she had to focus on if she were to keep any residual feelings at bay.

And doing that was imperative. She couldn't afford to acknowledge how incredible his kisses were, how alive they made her feel.

Uh-uh. She needed to focus on the one reason she was here: business.

'Yeah, Izzy's the best.' Archer held up a hand, wavered it. 'Tom and Trav? Not so much.'

'Your mum must've had a handful with three boys.'

He stiffened, as if she'd asked an intensely personal question rather than making conversation. 'Yeah, we kept her on her toes.'

She wanted to ask about his parents, about his childhood, but she couldn't get a read on his mood.

They were sprawled on comfy cushioned sofas—she'd studiously avoided the love-seat—on the glass-enclosed balcony, overlooking an amazing ocean tinged with sunset. It reeked of intimacy, yet Archer's perfunctory answers and shuttered expression weren't encouraging.

'Do you want kids?'

And then he went and floored her with a question like that. A question far surpassing intimacy and heading straight for uncomfortable.

'Not sure.'

She cradled her coffee cup, hoping some if its warmth would melt the icy tentacles of unease squeezing her heart.

After the genetic testing, when it had been proved she

didn't have the mutated gene that sounded a death knell for her mum, she'd undergone counselling to get a grip on her rioting emotions: relief, guilt, happiness, fear. Yet for all these years, deep down where she hid her innermost fears, she hadn't been able to shake the irrational dread that somehow those doctors had made a mistake and she'd contract the disease after all.

Crazy and illogical. The odds were in her favour to have perfectly healthy kids. But why tempt fate when it had dealt her such a rough hand so far?

'The opportunity hasn't come up?'

Surprised by his line of questioning, she eyeballed him. 'If you're asking if I've been in a serious relationship since Capri, no. I've dated. That's about it.'

She half expected him to flinch at her bluntness in bringing up the past, but to his credit he didn't look away.

'Why?'

'What is this? Pry into Callie's soul day?'

She placed her coffee on the nearest table and her hands unexpectedly shook.

'Callie, I—'

'Sorry for snapping your head off, but if you're hoping to hear I've been pining for you all these years, and that's why I'm not involved in a serious relationship, you're delusional.'

His eyes widened in horror. 'Hell, that's not what I want.' He rubbed the back of his neck in a familiar gesture that added to the poignancy of the moment. 'I just feel like we've been doing this avoidance dance, concentrating on work, making polite small talk, retreating to our rooms. Then I saw how you were with Izzy and it got me thinking...'

She shouldn't ask. She really shouldn't. 'About?'

Yep, she was asking for it.

'About why the beautiful, vibrant woman I met in Capri hasn't been snapped up by some smart guy?'

A guy smarter than you? she wanted to say, but silently counted to five before she blurted it out.

'Maybe I don't want to be snapped up? Maybe I'm happy with my life the way it is?'

'Are you?'

She stiffened as he reached out and traced a fingertip between her brows, eliciting a shiver.

'Because you've got this little dent here that tells me otherwise.'

Touched he'd noticed, annoyed at his intuitiveness, she swatted his hand away. 'How did you get so perceptive?'

'Honestly?'

She picked up her coffee cup, cradled it, hiding behind it as she took a deep sip and nodded.

'The way you lit up around Izzy was the same way you used to be in Capri. Carefree. Quick to laugh. Like nothing fazed you.' He paused, as if searching her face for approval to continue. 'At first I thought it was me and the way I treated you in the past that was bugging you. But it's something else—something that runs deeper.'

He snaffled her hand and squeezed it before she could protest.

'You know you can tell me, right?'

Uh-oh. Callie could handle teasing, charming Archer. She couldn't handle this newer, sensitive version, who'd honed in on the emotional load she carried daily like an invisible yoke.

'We should finish off the home page of the website—'

He gripped her hand tighter. 'Tell me.'

'Wow, you're bossy.' She blew out a long, slow breath, not wanting to do this but knowing he'd keep badgering until she did.

He'd been like that in Capri: badgering her to have dinner with him that first night; badgering her to stroll along the moonlit beach afterwards; badgering her with his loaded stares and sexy smiles and wicked ways.

Now, like then, she was powerless to resist.

'It's my mum. She has motor neurone disease.'

Shock widened his eyes and sadness twisted his mouth. 'Aw, honey, I'm sorry.'

'Me too,' she said, gnawing on her bottom lip and willing the sudden sting of tears away.

She'd cried enough to fill the Tasman Sea but it didn't change the facts. The horrid disease was eating away at her mum's nervous system one neurone at a time.

'There's nothing they can do?'

She shook her head, grateful for the strong hold he had on her hand. She would have bolted for the sanctity of her room otherwise and not come out for the next few days.

'They initially gave her three years. She's lasted seven.'

Quick as ever he did the math, and understanding flickered in those aquamarine depths. 'Did you find out soon after you got home from Europe?'

She nodded, remembering the far-reaching consequences of that diagnosis.

Despite the way they'd ended, would she have booked a flight to join Archer if her mum hadn't fallen ill? Would her life have been filled with sunshine and sand and surf rather than a rented box-like office space? Would she have been blissfully unaware of the potential gene landmine pumping through her veins and had Archer's kids?

Stupid thinking, considering Archer hadn't wanted her back then, let alone a commitment that could lead to kids.

'So she's undergoing the usual rounds of physiotherapy and occupational therapy to keep her as mobile as possible?'

'Yeah, though her muscle wastage is advancing pretty rapidly.'

How many times had she gently massaged those muscles in the hope they'd somehow miraculously regenerate? Too many. The sight of Nora wasting away before her eyes broke her heart.

'She's confined to a wheelchair, though the special home where she lives is fabulous in taking care of her.'

'The staff in those facilities deserve a medal, considering the range of healthcare they provide.'

'How come you know so much about it?'

'I sponsored a charity benefit for Lou Gehrig's disease in LA. Thought I'd better know something about it before rocking up to the shindig.'

Callie eyed him speculatively. Sportsmen around the world attended charity benefits, but she doubted many of them cared enough to delve into the details of the fundraiser's disease.

'Is there anything I can do?'

Touched he'd offered, she shook her head. 'Thanks, but I've got it covered.'

At least she would have once she got paid for this surf school campaign. Which meant getting back to work, despite the urge to linger in this intimate cocoon where the guy she'd once loved seriously cared.

'We should get back to work—'

'Tomorrow,' he said, scooting alongside her and draping an arm across her shoulders before she had a chance to move. 'We've been pushing it pretty hard since we arrived yesterday. Let's just chill tonight.'

Chilling sounded good, but sadly there was nothing cool about being snuggled in the crook of Archer's shoulder. The opposite, with her body warming from the inside out until it felt as if her skin blistered.

She should move, should head inside and collate a few more ideas for the website's link page. Instead she found herself slowly relaxing into him, wanting to savour this moment.

The irony of being cradled in Archer's arms after she'd rammed home the fact that this week was just about business wasn't lost on her. It felt good. Great, in fact. But temporary—a comforting hug from an ex. An ex who'd ended their all-too-brief relationship in no uncertain terms.

She wouldn't get used to it, but for now, with his solid warmth seeping through her, she couldn't help but wonder what it would be like if she made the most of their remaining time together.

Was she a glutton for punishment to contemplate another short-term fling? Heck, yeah. But considering the road ahead—the uncertainty of her mum's illness, her lifespan, and the ensuing pain when the inevitable happened—would it be so bad to take a little bit of happiness while she could?

Logically, she'd be an idiot to contemplate it.

Emotionally, her heart strained towards him, eager for affection, knowing how sensational they could be together even for a scant week.

He kissed the top of her head and she sighed, appreciating his sensitivity in not pushing her to talk any more.

Besides, she'd said enough. She hadn't told any of her past dates about her mum—hadn't let them get close enough. Yet in two days she'd let Archer march back into her life—and a little corner of her heart if she were completely honest—and trusted him enough to divulge the truth about her mum.

At least she hadn't told him all of it. Some things were best left unsaid.

The memory of her genetic testing sent a shiver through

her and he tightened his hold, conveying strength in silence.

Yeah, she could do worse than have some fun for a change over the next week.

In the lead-up to Christmas surely she'd been a good girl all year and Santa owed her big-time?

The next morning Callie had to admit spending the week in Torquay had been a stroke of genius on Archer's part.

She'd worked uninterrupted for the last three hours, perched on his balcony, enjoying the sea air and the view, inspired in a way she hadn't been for a long time.

She didn't know if it was being away from the office for the first time in years that had sparked her creativity, but she'd added some amazing touches to the surf school website today. Ideas to build on when he gave her the grand tour this afternoon.

It helped that he'd made himself scarce since dawn this morning. She hadn't been looking forward to having him hover over her workspace after her confession last night.

Sure, it had seemed as if telling him about her mum had been the right thing to do at the time, while they were relaxed and cosy at dusk, but in the harsh light of day, after a sleepless night spent second-guessing herself, she hadn't wanted to face him.

Shared confidences bred intimacy, and that was one thing she couldn't afford with Archer. She'd been foolish enough in testing herself by being here this week. For while he'd demanded she come to Torquay to secure the campaign she probably could have weaselled her way out of it if she'd tried.

But the moment he'd strutted into her office, spouting his terms, she'd wanted to prove to herself once and for all that she was over him, that he had no hold over her de-spite spending seven days in her company.

She'd been doing a good job of it too—those kisses he'd sprung on her notwithstanding—until last night.

Following their break-up, she'd tarred Archer with the same brush as her dad: selfish, self-absorbed, a man who followed his whims without regard to anyone else. It had been a coping mechanism, labelling him so harshly.

Yet last night—the way he'd comforted her, the way he'd been attuned to her mood and content to sit in silence—had seriously undermined her lowly opinion of him and made her seem childish in lashing out in the past because she'd been foolish enough to feel more than he had.

Laughter drifted up from the beach and she sheltered her eyes with her hand to focus on the group by the wa-ter's edge.

A bunch of teenagers surrounded Archer, their boards stuck vertically in the sand like sentinels. He stood in the centre, gesturing towards the ocean, demonstrating a few moves, while the teens jostled and elbowed for prime po-sition in front of their idol.

Embarrassment twanged her heart. A selfish guy wouldn't give up his precious school-set-up time to hang with a bunch of kids. Just as a selfish guy wouldn't have taken the time to comfort her last night.

Feeling increasingly guilty, she shut down the webpage program she'd been tweaking, scooped up her paperwork and dumped the lot inside.

Another bonus of working here. She could take a head-clearing walk along the beach any time. And right now, remorseful, she wanted to let Archer know he wasn't so bad after all.

Not that she had any intention of confessing such a thing to him, but she'd been pretty remote, deliberately maintaining an invisible distance between them. Considering how great he'd been with her last night, it wouldn't hurt for her to lighten up a tad.

She slipped off her sandals at the bottom of the steps, loving the gritty sand squelching between her toes as she strolled towards him.

The closer she got, the more she could see the rapt expressions on the teens' faces, and hear Archer giving a pep talk. The guy was usually a livewire, but she'd never seen him so animated. Which made her wonder why he'd been so reticent with his brothers when he was obviously a people person.

The pep talk must have worked because the teens let out a rousing cheer before grabbing their boards and heading for the surf.

Archer's eyes glowed with pride and satisfaction as he waved her over.

'Did you see that?'

She smiled and nodded. 'Those kids think you're a surf god.'

'I just gave them a few pointers. But the way they responded...' He shook his head, staring at the wetsuited blobs bobbing in the ocean. 'They were blown away to hear about the surf school and asked a million questions. They're going to tell their mates.'

He pumped his fist. 'I'm stoked.'

'You did good.' She touched his arm, an impulsive gesture to convey her approval, but one she regretted when he snagged her hand and tugged her close.

'Your approval means a lot.'

'Why?' She eased away, needing to put a little distance between them, overwhelmed by his closeness.

'Because I hate to have you think badly of me.'

Still wrestling with her recent revelation as to his true

character, she aimed for levity. 'Come this time next week it won't matter what I think. You'll be hanging loose in Hawaii or Bali, and I'll be doing an amazing job maintaining your surf school website.'

'You're wrong.'

She pretended to misunderstand. 'No, really, I'll be working like a maniac on your website—'

'Your opinion matters.'

She glanced away, unable to fathom his steady stare, almost daring her to—what? Argue? Agree? Analyse?

'Aren't you going to ask me why?'

She bit down on her bottom lip. No, she didn't want to hear any of the deep and meaningful reasons he'd concocted. However much she regretted misjudging him all these years, she didn't want anything from this week beyond a successful campaign.

'Fine. I'll tell you anyway.' He released her arm, only to capture her chin, leaving her no option but to look at him. 'You're the only woman I've ever known who gets me. And, while it scares the hell out of me, I kinda think it's cool.'

Oh, heck. Trapped beneath the intensity of his stare, with his praise like a soft caress, she felt the inevitable pull between them flare to life.

She couldn't look away, couldn't resist as their lips inched towards each other, couldn't think of a rational reason why she shouldn't kiss an old flame on a pristine beach.

Old flame… Those two words penetrated her dazed fog.

What the heck was she doing? She could blame his first two kisses on impulse, but this? This was something else entirely.

If her opinion mattered to him, his praise mattered to

her. She basked under his admiration, but letting it go to her head would be beyond foolhardy.

She couldn't do this. Fall under his spell. *Again.*

She wasn't the same naïve girl any more. This time she had no doubt if they had another fling it would end the same way.

All the whispered words in the world wouldn't change the facts: Archer lived for his freedom; she lived for making Nora's lifespan—what was left of it—as comfortable as possible.

Their goals were worlds apart.

With their lips almost touching, she wrenched out of his grasp and took a few backward steps.

'Callie—'

She couldn't bear the confusion warring with something deeper in his eyes, so she did the only thing possible.

She turned and ran.

CHAPTER SIX

'WHAT do you think?'

Callie stared at Archer's 'little' surf school, not quite comprehending how the plans and architectural impressionist photos she'd used for the pre-website had morphed into this sprawling complex perched on a sheltered bluff metres from the ocean.

'It's absolutely breathtaking,' she said, doing a three-sixty, taking in the whitewashed main building, the dorms with bright blue doors, the storeroom large enough to house her apartment three times over, and the supplies shop tucked to the left of the entrance.

'You designed all this?'

His mouth quirked. 'Don't sound so incredulous. I'm not just a pretty face.'

She grimaced at his lame line. He laughed. 'Come on, I'll give you the grand tour.'

He snagged her hand as if it was the most natural thing in the world, and she clamped down on her first urge to ease it away.

She'd done some hard thinking after she'd bolted from the beach earlier. Confiding in Archer about her mum's illness last night, allowing him to hold her, welcoming his comfort, followed by their closeness on the beach that morning, had solidified what she'd already known deep down.

That spending time with him, albeit for work, had the potential to crack open the protective wall she'd erected around her heart.

The fissures had appeared with his kisses, and they'd well and truly fractured last night, when they'd sat on that damned deck until the sun set. Throw in that *moment* on the beach today and…trouble.

That was another thing. He'd been quiet last night, attuned to her need for silence while still holding her. He hadn't prattled on with small talk designed to distract. He'd just held her, his arm wrapped solidly around her waist, his cheek resting lightly on the top of her head.

He thought she *got* him? The feeling was entirely mutual and that was scarier than any reawakening feelings she might be experiencing.

He'd been like that in Capri—attuned to her moods and desires after only just meeting. It was as if they'd fitted. She didn't believe in love at first sight, or great loves, or romantic kismet—her pragmatic mum and selfish dad had ensured that—but her connection with Archer eight years earlier had defied logic.

He'd anticipated what she'd wanted back then—more Chianti, a cotton shawl for their evening walk, another swim—but his intuition beyond the physical had impressed her the most.

He'd tuned in to her emotionally, on some deeper level that had made her truly comfortable with him in a way she'd never been with another guy. They'd talked for hours. Usually about inconsequential stuff, childhood anecdotes, secret dreams, and she'd never recaptured that magic with any date.

It had made their break up all the harder.

They'd both had open-ended travel tickets and hadn't discussed moving on. While the end of their holiday idyll had been inevitable, she'd expected to stay in contact. And a small part of her had hoped they'd reconnect in Melbourne one day.

But all that had ended when he'd told her the blunt truth: she'd read too much into a holiday fling. What they'd shared was nothing more than a bit of fun and she needed to lighten up before she scared off more guys.

His harsh words had hurt. Devastated her, in fact, and she'd never understood how the guy she'd grown so close to in such a short space of time could shut down emotionally and walk away without looking back.

She'd do well to remember the past before those cracks and fissures around her heart disintegrated completely.

Thankfully he hadn't mentioned her bolt up the beach after their almost-kiss, and she'd been working double time to pretend everything was fine.

She'd finish out this week without him knowing how he still affected her if it killed her.

She pointed at a sign with her free hand. 'I still can't believe you called it Winki Pop Surf School. Sounds like something out of a kid's fairytale.'

He feigned indignation. 'I'll have you know Winki Pop is one of the best surf breaks around here.' He chuckled. 'Besides, it has a better ring to it than some of the other breaks around here.'

'Like?'

'Southside. Centreside. Rincon.'

'I see your point. It does have a certain charm.'

''Course it would, with me as the owner.' He winked. 'Mr Winki, that's me.'

She groaned at his terrible joke, his carefree laughter

reminding her of another time they'd swapped banter like this, a time she'd treasured before reality set in.

She listened closely as they toured the school, taking mental notes. The smart thing to do would be take out her iPhone and dictate ideas, or pull out the trusty notepad she kept in her bag.

But both activities would involve releasing Archer's hand, and for now her blasé act depended on it. Easing her hand out of his would probably have him asking what was wrong, and if it was connected to earlier on the beach, and yada, yada, yada. She just didn't want to go there.

When they reached the store shed he unlocked the door and flung it open. 'Ready to put the master touch on the online forums you suggested?'

Confused, she glanced inside the shed lined with surf-boards and wetsuits of all shapes and sizes. 'Not sure what you mean.'

His wicked grin alerted her to an incoming suggestion she wouldn't like.

'If you're going to be the moderator of the school's on-line forums, you need to know what it feels like to surf.'

The incoming missile detonated and left her reeling. 'Me? On a surfboard? Out *there*?' Her voice ended on a squeak as she pointed to the expanse of ocean a short stroll away.

'Yeah. And no better time to start than now.'

Like hell. She loved swimming, loved the ocean, but no way would she klutz around like a floundering whale in front of him. Learning to surf had always been on her life's 'to do' list, but here, now, with *him*?

No flipping way.

She snapped her fingers. 'Sorry, no bathers. Maybe next time—'

'I'm sure we stock your size.'

His gaze roved her body, assessing, warming, zinging every nerve-ending along the way.

Before she could protest further he placed a hand in the small of her back and propelled her forward.

'Come on. You said surfing was on your bucket list. No time like the present to tick it off while getting first-hand experience for work.'

Stunned he'd remembered her bucket list, she allowed him to lead her into the dim interior.

A pungent blend of new fibreglass, rubber and coconut-scented wax tickled her nose, but through all that she could smell the potent male beside her: sunshine and sea air and pure Archer.

He was right, of course. Knowing what learning to surf entailed would give her more credibility when she manned the surf school online forums, so technically this classified as work.

But the part where he sized up her body, his glance as intimate as a lover's caress, went beyond work. Way beyond.

Her skin grew clammy as he flicked through the suits on a rack before unhooking a black wetsuit with a fuchsia zig-zag and handing it to her.

'Here—this should fit.'

A little tremor of excitement shot through her as her fingertips brushed the rubber. How long since she'd done something spontaneous and fun and just for her? Too long. And as he handed her a practical navy one-piece, she suddenly couldn't wait to get out there.

He jerked a thumb over his shoulder. 'Changing rooms back there. But first let's get you set up with a board.'

'Whatever you choose will be fine.'

He folded his arms, making his biceps bulge beneath the

trendily frayed ends of his designer teal T-shirt. 'Don't you want to get a feel for the board in here before we head out?'

Feeling one hundred percent novice, she wrinkled her nose. 'Um, I'm guessing I'm supposed to say yes?'

'Yeah. You need to connect with your board.'

'Oh, brother,' she muttered, rolling her eyes as they moved across to the other side of the shed, where boards stood vertically in racks. 'Next you'll be making that hand sign and telling me to hang loose.'

He smirked. 'The *shaka* sign is part of surf culture.'

She extended her thumb and little finger while keeping the middle fingers curled. 'So does this make me cool?'

'Nah. You have to stay on a board longer than thirty seconds for that.'

She laughed, watching him run his hands over the boards, sliding down the smooth surfaces, his rapt expression almost making her jealous.

He'd once looked at her like that.

Before he bolted without a backward glance.

She'd do well to remember that rather than wishing she were a surfboard right about now.

'This one.' He slid a monstrous cream board etched in ochre swirls from the rack. 'This is your board.'

'Did the fibreglass speak to you?'

His eyes narrowed in indignation. 'Are you mocking me?'

'A little.'

'Let's see who mocks who when you're face-planting the waves,' he said, beckoning her closer. 'Here, you hold it.'

The thing weighed a tonne, but she managed to hold it upright—just. 'Feels like this thing's made of stone.'

'The best epoxy resin, actually, which makes it stronger

and lighter than traditional boards.' He took hold of her hand and ran it down the board. 'This is called the deck.'

He edged her hand towards the side of the board in a long, slow sweep that made her bite her lip to stop groaning out loud.

There was something so sensual about having him stand close, his body radiating heat, warming her back, his arms outstretched and inadvertently wrapping around her, his large fingers splayed across hers as they'd once splayed across her belly.

She swallowed and prayed he didn't expect an answer, for there wasn't a hope she could speak with her throat constricted.

Her heart pounded like a jackhammer, the blood coursed through her body like liquid wildfire.

The heat suffocated her, making breathing difficult, making thinking impossible, making her crave the insane...him shoving the board aside, ripping off her clothes, and taking her right here, right now, on the sandy floor.

'The back is the tail, the forward tip is the nose, and the side edges are the rails.' He guided her hand back to the middle and she swayed a little. 'The concave surface from nose to tail is the rocker.'

He moved the board side to side and she almost whimpered.

She must have made some giveaway sound, because he wrapped his arms around her from behind, making holding the board steady impossible.

She could feel his heat, feel how much he wanted her pressed up against her, and she'd never felt the urge to forget sanity as much as she did at that moment.

Correction. She'd experienced the same insanity the first night they'd met—the night he'd romanced her and charmed her and convinced her that tumbling into bed in the early hours of the morning, with the Capri moonlight spilling over them and accentuating the beautiful craziness of the night, was the only possible thing she wanted.

Which begged the question...what did she want now?

While her mind tussled with the dilemma, her body gave a resounding response by leaning back into him.

She heard his sharp intake of breath, felt his arms stiffen.

She had no idea how long they stayed like that, suspended for an incredibly tension-fraught moment in time, and if it hadn't for the beep of her darn phone indicating she had a message she had a fair idea of what might have happened.

'Better get that in case it's about Mum,' she said, instantly missing his warmth as he released her and stepped away, managing to hold the board upright and disentangle herself from her simultaneously.

'I'll meet you outside when you're done,' he said, his voice husky and laced with the same passion pumping through her veins as he picked up the boards as if they weighed nothing and marched outside.

With a sigh of regret she shook her head to clear it, fished her phone out of her pocket and checked it. The message from a client could have waited.

This all-consuming yearning, making her want to run after Archer and drag him back to the sanctity of this shed to finish what they'd started, was not so patient.

Torn between wanting to indulge her newly awakened cravings and wanting to slap herself upside the head, she marched over to the change rooms.

The sooner she got back behind the safety of her computer screen and away from sexy surfer, the better.

* * *

Archer jammed the surfboards into the sand and took off for the ocean at a run.

He needed the clarity only the sea could bring. And the chill to ease his inexorable desire.

He'd had a close call back there. So close to giving in to the relentless drive to possess Callie again, to see if the resurfacing memories were half as good as he remembered.

Who was he trying to kid? Those hazy memories were becoming sharper by the day. Even the most trivial things, like watching Callie snag her hair into a ponytail or jot down notes, would resurrect memories of how she'd done the same thing years ago, and he'd be catapulted back to a time when they'd had no responsibilities, no pressures, and were free to indulge their passion.

A time he'd deliberately screwed up to avoid feeling the same way he had when he'd discovered his family had withheld the truth about his dad: as if he wasn't good enough.

He'd trusted his family and they'd let him down, seriously interfering with his ability to trust anyone.

If he couldn't trust them, who could he trust?

Walking away from Callie back then had been inevitable. Early days in a burgeoning career taking him straight to the top. So when she'd got too close, when he'd started to think beyond Capri, when those trust issues had raised their ugly head, it had been easier to sabotage and run without looking back.

That didn't stop him wanting to have that time again. *Now.*

The waves broke around his ankles as he sprinted into the sea and dived through the break, the invigorating brace of cold water slicing through his musings but doing little to obliterate his need for her.

He should have known this blasé flirting as a ploy to distract himself from the impending catch-up with his folks would morph into something more.

He had a feeling nothing would dull this ache for Callie. Nothing less than indulging in a mind-blowing physical encounter designed to slake his thirst and get this thing out of his system.

He could have damped down his need, could have kept things friendly and continued on his casual flirting way, if she hadn't blown his mind in the shed.

She wanted this too.

She'd had a choice and she'd made it, leaning back into him, pressing against him, showing him she felt the buzz too.

He'd been stunned, considering the way she'd aborted their kiss a few hours ago. This time, why had *he* bolted?

As he sliced through the water, free-styling as if he had a shark on his tail, he knew.

Last night, when she'd divulged all that heavy stuff about her mum and he'd held her for ages comforting her, he'd started to feel something. He'd felt that sitting on the deck of his home for ages, with a woman he seriously cared about, content to just sit and not talk, was kind of nice.

It was the first time he'd ever been in Torquay and felt like staying. And that terrified him more than any Great White. He wasn't a stayer. Even for a woman with doe eyes and a soft touch.

He rolled onto his back, letting the swell take him. He closed his eyes, savouring the sun warming his body.

This was where he felt at home. In the ocean, with all the time in the world to float, far from people he'd trusted who hadn't returned the favour.

This was where he belonged.

Then why the urgent pull, like a rip dragging him where he didn't want to go, that said belonging to Callie mightn't be so bad after all?

Callie felt like a trussed-up turkey in the wetsuit. She hated the way the rubber stuck to her skin. She hated the way it moulded and delineated every incriminating bump, and she particularly hated how it made her feel.

Like a novice floundering way out of her depth.

She didn't like floundering. She liked staying in control and staying on top and staying in charge.

She'd lost control once before. And the reason was staring at her with blatant appreciation as she trudged towards him.

'By your foul expression, I'm guessing a wisecrack about rubber and being protected isn't in my best interests?'

She glared at him. 'I'm here under sufferance and you damn well know it.'

She could have sworn he muttered, 'You weren't suffering in the shed,' but didn't want to call him on it.

She didn't need a reminder of the heat they'd generated in the shed. Not if she wanted to stay upright on this stupid piece of fibreglass for more than two seconds.

Errant, erotic thoughts of Archer were guaranteed wipe-out material.

She yelped as something brushed her ankle—only to discover Archer grinning up at her.

'How about a crack about keeping a wild woman on a leash?'

She let him fasten the cord attached to the board around her ankle before nudging him away with her foot. 'How about I crack you over the head with one of those boards?'

He laughed, straightened, and unkinked his back.

'Just trying to get you to loosen up.' He added a few side stretches. 'The looser you are, the easier it'll be to get the feel of balancing on the board.'

'I'm loose.'

She took a step and tripped over the leash in the process. His hand shot out to grab her, and even through the rubber his touch sent a lick of heat through her.

'You okay?'

An embarrassed blush flushed her cheeks. 'Let's do this.'

Concern tinged his glance before determination hardened his mouth, and she wondered if this was his game face—the one he used pre-competition. If so, she wasn't surprised he'd won the world championship five times.

He pointed towards the sea. 'We're in luck. Surf's up today and the waves are off the hook.' She raised an eyebrow and he winced. 'Habit. Surf-speak for the waves being a good size and shape.'

'Gnarly dude,' she muttered, earning a rueful grin.

'We'll concentrate on the basics today, and see if we can catch a wave or two.'

Basics sounded good to her. Basics wouldn't involve tubes or rips or drowning, right?

'I'll break it down into steps and you copy, okay?'

She nodded and he dropped down on the board on his front, leaving her with a pretty great view of a rubber-moulded butt.

'You'll need to be in this position to paddle out.'

Got it, she thought. *Paddling...butt...*

'Cal? You planning on joining me down here?'

With an exasperated grunt at her attention span—not entirely her fault, considering the distraction on offer—she lowered herself onto the board and imitated paddling.

'Nice action,' he said, and her head snapped up to check for the slightest hint of condescension.

Instead she caught him staring in the same vicinity she'd been looking at a moment ago, and a thrill of womanly pride shot through her.

'Next is the pop-up.' He demonstrated going from lying on his board to standing, all in one jump. 'And gaining your balance.'

He held his arms out to his sides, looking so perfectly natural on the board it was as if it was an extension of his feet.

'Now you try.'

And try she did. Over and over again. Until her arms, knees and back ached from her lousy pop-ups and her pride absolutely smarted.

Though she had to hand it to him. Archer was a patient teacher. He praised and cajoled and criticised when needed, eventually getting her from the sand into the water. Where the fun really began.

'Don't worry if you get caught inside,' he said, paddling alongside her.

'Huh?' she mouthed, concentrating on keeping her belly on the board so she didn't slip off as the swell buffeted.

'It's when a surfer paddles out and can't get past the breaking surf to the calmer part of the ocean to catch a wave.'

'Right.' She tried a salute and almost fell off the board.

'If you do, you can try to duck-dive by pushing the nose of the board under the oncoming wave, but it's probably easier just to coast back into shore and we'll try again later.'

She nodded, knowing there wouldn't be a 'later'. She reckoned she had enough first-hand experience now to facilitate the online forums. Perching on top of a wave wouldn't give her much more beyond a momentary rush of adrenalin.

'Follow me.'

And she did. Until she got caught inside, just as he'd predicted, and ended up paddling back to shore, where she gratefully dragged the board onto firm sand, plonked her butt, and watched Archer strut his stuff.

The guy was seriously good—cresting waves, twisting and turning on his board with precision, looking like the poster boy for surfing that he was.

She could have watched him for hours, but a few minutes later he coasted into shore, picked up his board, tucked it under his arm and jogged towards her.

For some inexplicable reason she felt compelled to get up and run to meet him halfway. Last night when he'd comforted her might have been the catalyst, or maybe his admission on the beach earlier today, but whatever it was she felt she wanted to be close to him.

As he drew near the urge intensified, and when he smiled at her, with tiny rivulets of sea water running down that impossibly handsome face, her heart twisted like one of the fancy manoeuvres he'd pulled out there.

She wanted him.

With a desperation that clawed at all her well-formulated, highly logical reasons why she shouldn't, shredding them beyond repair.

'You're looking at me like I'm Red Riding Hood and you're the big bad wolf.' He laid the board down and sat beside her. 'My showy moves impress you?'

'*You* impress me,' she said, sucking in a deep breath and covering his hand with hers.

His questioning stare snagged hers, and with her heart pounding loud enough to drown out the breaking surf she leaned across and did what she should have had the guts to do earlier that morning.

She kissed him.

Archer had pulled some pretty fancy moves out there. Show-pony stunts: fins out, a sharp turn where the fins slide off the top of the wave; soul arch, arching his back to demonstrate his casual confidence; switch-foot, changing from right to left foot forward, and hang-ten, putting ten toes over the nose of his long board.

Usually when he hit the waves he surfed for himself, for the sheer pleasure it brought him. It was that enjoyment that gave him the edge in competitions, for he concentrated on fun and not his opponents.

Not today. Today he'd surfed to impress Callie.

By that lip-lock she'd just given him it had worked. And how.

If he'd known that was all it would take he would have hit the waves the first day they'd arrived.

'You're grinning like an idiot,' she said, nudging him with her elbow.

'It's not every day a guy gets a kiss like that for balancing on a few waves.'

She rolled her eyes. 'Give me a break. You get smooches from bikini babes every time you win a tournament.'

'Congratulatory kisses.' He traced her lower lip with his fingertip, exploring the contour, feeling the faintest wobble. 'Nothing compared to that lip-smacker you just planted on me.'

She blushed, but to her credit didn't look away. 'You wanted a date for the wedding. I'm just trying to make it look authentic.'

'How authentic do you want to get?' He puckered up in a ludicrous parody and she chuckled.

'How important is it for you to convince them I'm the real deal?'

His smile faltered as her innocent question hit unerringly close to home. 'Hold my hand, gaze adoringly into my eyes, smooch a little. Well, actually, a lot. That should do the trick.'

'So why would you need a date to your brother's wedding anyway?'

He'd been waiting for her to ask that for days, but she'd been so hell-bent on burying her nose in business and avoiding him that they hadn't strayed into personal territory. It looked as if last night had well and truly changed all that.

'Things with my folks are a little tense when I come home for flying visits. It's awkward.'

He waited for the inevitable *why* but she surprised him, tilting her head to one side as if studying him. 'I'm surprised a tough guy like you can't handle a little *awkward*.'

He should have known she wouldn't buy his trite answer. But how could he tell her the rest without having to answer a whole lot of other questions he'd rather left unsaid?

'It's easier this way.' He snagged her hand and pressed a kiss to her palm, enjoying the flare of heat in her eyes. 'And much more enjoyable with a date I actually like.'

Her nose crinkled adorably. 'You *like* me? What are you? In fifth grade?'

'You'll be pleased to know I'm a lot more experienced than I was in fifth grade,' he said, tugging on her hand until she almost straddled his lap. 'I like you, Callie. You know that. And I'd like nothing more than to spend the next few days showing you how much.'

He expected her to bolt again. To revert back to business mode. To resurrect the invisible wall she'd steadfastly maintained since they'd arrived.

Instead, she surprised him.

She captured his face between her hands and gently bridged the distance, whispering against the side of his mouth, 'Then what are we waiting for?'

Callie didn't want time to second guess her impulse.

She wanted Archer.

Now.

'Let's get cleaned up, grab some dinner, then head home—'

'No.' It almost sounded like a desperate yell, and she laughed to cover her nervousness. 'I—I want this to be like in Capri.'

His eyes widened at the implication.

He remembered. Remembered that hedonistic time in a sheltered alcove on a deserted beach. Remembered the frantic hands and straining mouths and incredible eroticism of it.

'You sure?'

'Never been surer of anything in my life.'

And then she promptly made a mockery of her brave declaration by stumbling as she tried to stand.

He steadied her, his gaze never leaving hers. 'Cal, do we need to talk about afterwards? Because nothing will change. Our lives are separate—'

'Since when did you talk so much?'

She silenced him with a kiss—a hot, open-mouthed kiss designed to distract and titillate and eradicate any lingering doubts they might harbour.

When they finally came up for air, he held her hand as if he'd never let go. 'There's a bunch of deserted dunes just over that hill.'

She liked how he didn't spell it out, how he left the option up to her with his silent challenge.

Tilting her head to meet his heated gaze, she tried her best sexy smile and hoped it didn't come out a grimace. 'Lead the way.'

After making a detour to the sheds, where they struggled out of their wetsuits and Archer snagged his wallet and a throw rug, they ran, their feet squeaking on the clean sand, their soft panting in rhythm with her pounding heart.

When they crested the hill and she saw the pristine dunes stretched out before them tears stung her eyes.

It was so beautiful. A perfect place to resurrect incredible memories and to create new ones.

They didn't speak as he led her by the hand to a secluded spot sheltered by an overhanging rock, laid out the rug, and knelt.

She'd never felt so worshipped as she did at that moment, with the guy she'd once had serious feelings for kneeling at her feet and staring up at her in blatant adoration.

When he tugged on her hand she joined him on the rug and in a flurry of whispered endearments, sensual caresses, and mind-blowing passion they came together.

Afterwards, as Archer cradled her in his arms and she stared at the seagulls wheeling overhead, Callie wondered one thing.

What the hell have I done?

CHAPTER SEVEN

'SHOULD'VE known you two bozos couldn't keep your big traps shut.'

Archer glared at Trav and Tom, who merely grinned and raised their beer bottles in his direction.

'What do you mean? This barbecue's in lieu of Trav's rehearsal dinner. You had to come.' Tom smirked and gave a less than subtle head-jerk in Callie's direction. 'And you couldn't leave your wedding date at home. That just wouldn't be right.'

Archer punched him on the arm. 'I had to tolerate Mum's interrogation on the phone for thirty minutes this arvo, and I've spent the last hour dodging her since we arrived, thanks to you.'

Tom raised his beer. 'You can thank me properly when she's presiding over *your* wedding.'

'Like hell,' Archer muttered, the thought of marriage making his chest burn like he'd scoffed a double-pepperoni pizza.

'It happens to the best of us, bro.' Trav nudged him and Archer frowned. 'You lot are a poor example to bachelors the world over.'

'Hey, *I'm* a bachelor.' Tom thrust his chest out and beat it with his fists like a gorilla and they laughed.

'With behaviour like that I'm not surprised,' Trav said,

pointing at a group of his fiancée's friends clustered around the chocolate fountain. 'Shelly has loads of nice single friends. Why don't you go chat up one of them?'

Tom shrugged, his nonchalance undermined by the way his fingers gripped his beer. 'Not interested.'

'Not every woman's like—'

'Trav, Shelly's calling you,' Archer said, earning a grateful glance from Tom.

'Think about it. Izzy needs a mum.'

Archer stiffened, expecting Tom to fire a broadside at Travis, but he merely muttered 'Punk' under his breath as Trav headed for his bride-to-be with the swagger of a young guy in love.

'At the risk of being bashed over the head with that bottle, maybe Trav's right.'

As expected, Tom bristled. 'Izzy and I are doing just fine.'

'I know you are, mate, but she's growing up.'

He glanced at his niece, her blonde pigtails streaming behind her as she raced across the lawn in pursuit of a rabbit. 'She's six going on sixty, and one day soon you'll find her asking a bunch of questions you'd rather not answer.'

To his surprise, Tom seemed to deflate before his eyes. 'She's an amazing kid.' He dragged a hand across his eyes, blinking as if he'd just woken up. 'She's my world.'

'Then maybe you should think about joining the land of the living again?' Archer hoped to lighten the sombre mood. 'When's the last time you had a date anyway?'

Old hurts darkened Tom's mood and his usually jovial brother frowned. Archer felt like a jerk for probing his wounds but Trav was right. Tom needed to start dating again—for his own sake as well as Izzy's.

Not that he had a right to butt in where his niece was concerned, considering his deliberate distancing over the years. But this visit was different. Seeing Callie interact with his family made him appreciate them in a whole new light. And made him feel like a first class jerk.

How long would he keep his own old hurts locked away inside where they festered? How long would he let wounded pride get in the way?

Tom's turbulent gaze focussed on his daughter as he placed his bottle on a nearby table and folded his arms. 'You ever wish you had a different life?'

Never. Discounting the hash of a relationship he now had with his family.

Archer loved his life: the freedom, the buzz, the adrenalin. He liked being his own boss, and valued his independence as much as his trophies. Though he'd be lying if he didn't admit to wondering more and more these days why he was so hell-bent on the single life.

At the start it had been about striving for success and not needing ties to hamper him. Emotional ties that ended up causing pain.

His family might not know it, but in their decision to ostracise him from his dad's illness and not trust him enough to cope they'd solidified his life choices.

Better for him not to connect emotionally with anyone, to enjoy his lack of responsibility and savour the single life. No strings attached; a motto that had served him well over the years.

Callie's laughter floated on the breeze and something in his gut clenched.

No, he didn't regret a thing, but for a moment he wondered how different his life would have been if he'd put his trust issues aside and taken a risk on their relationship.

'No use wondering about maybes, mate. All we can do is make the best of what we've got.'

Pensive, Tom nodded. 'I don't regret marrying Tracy for

the sake of Izzy, that's for sure. But sticking around here with its same-old, same-old has its moments.'

Tom wouldn't get any arguments from him. The monotony of living in the small town he'd grown up in would've driven him nuts.

'What about surfing?'

Tom's frown deepened. 'What about it?'

'Do you resent not going pro?'

'Hell, no.' Tom guffawed. 'I was never as driven as you, squirt. No way would I have spent years traipsing the world chasing the next big wave.'

'It was all you talked about growing up. I think it's half the reason I wanted to go pro—because you did.'

Tom shook his head. 'You always wanted it more than me. I couldn't hack all the training and moving around.'

'But I thought…'

'What?'

'That you gave it all up when Trace deliberately got pregnant. That she trapped you and you hated it and that's what eventually led to the marriage falling apart.'

Tom slapped him on the back. 'Not that it matters now, but to set the record straight—yeah, Tracy fell pregnant on purpose, but she didn't trap me. I didn't have to propose. I wanted to, because I was young and dumb and idealistic.'

He glanced towards their folks, toasting each other with champagne at a quiet table at the rear of the marquee, oblivious to the family bedlam around them. 'I guess I secretly wanted what they had.'

A familiar sadness enveloped Archer when he glanced at his folks. The Fletts had always been a close family, and his folks seemed more devoted now, following the health scare that had so shocked him when he'd eventually found out.

He envied them that closeness. It was like standing on the outside looking in at an exclusive club.

Tom's mouth twisted into a wry smile. 'I'd give an arm and a leg to have a relationship like that. A woman who adores me, who's content to be with me and doesn't need all the fancy trappings of a big city.'

Liking the fragile bond of reconnecting with Tom on a deeper level than mock-wrestling, Archer delved further. 'Is that why Tracy left? Because she wanted the high life?'

''Course. Once she had Izzy it was all she talked about. I wanted a future that focussed on building a stable environment for our child to grow in, and she couldn't leave fast enough.'

Archer rubbed the back of his neck, wondering if Santa would make an appearance to dispel any other myths he'd once believed in.

'Wow, I didn't know.'

'Because some things are best left unsaid. Besides, I don't want Iz hearing bad stuff about her mum, just in case Trace grows a conscience one day and wants to see her daughter.'

'Where is she?'

'Sydney, last I heard but who knows? She sends the obligatory birthday and Christmas gifts. That's about it.'

While Tom's tone didn't hold an ounce of censure, guilt niggled at Archer.

Was that how the Fletts talked about *him* when he wasn't around? Saying that he should *grow a conscience* rather than sending *obligatory* birthday gifts and making an *obligatory* Christmas visit during which he couldn't wait to escape back to his life?

Considering how he'd withdrawn from them, he couldn't blame them.

He *wanted* to forgive and move on.

He *wanted* to shelve his pride and bring the whole thing out into the open.

But every single time he wanted to broach the painful subject of how he'd felt at being shut out, and how their rebuttal of his overture had hurt, one image stuck in his mind.

His dad, elbows braced on his precious piano, head in his hands, crying. Big, brusque Frank Flett never cried, and to see his father so broken had left a lasting legacy.

It had been just after they'd finally told him the truth— a year after his dad had been given the all-clear. Twelve freaking months, on top of the six months Frank had battled the disease that could have claimed his life, when his family had shut him out because they didn't want to distract him, or thought he couldn't handle it, or some such rot.

He'd been livid, and seeing his father's tears had reinforced what they thought of him as nothing else could.

If his dad could still cry when he was cancer-free, how bad must it have been during the long battle of surgery, chemo and the rest?

A battle *he'd* been excluded from because they'd deemed him not responsible enough to handle it.

His hands unconsciously clenched into fists and he inhaled, forcing himself to calm down before any of his bitterness spilled out.

'What's wrong?' Tom's perceptive stare bored into him and he glanced away.

'Nothing.'

'Like hell.' Tom paused, made an exasperated sound. 'Is that why you keep running? Because you think I got trapped, gave up a dream, and you don't want the same to happen to you?'

Archer's tension eased as he saw Callie strolling towards the bar, her pale lemon floral dress swishing around her calves, making her look ethereal and pretty and all too ravishing.

What could he say?

The truth?

That he didn't dare trust an incredible woman like Callie? That even now, after the incredible reconnection they'd shared last night, first at the beach and later at his house, he was absolutely terrified of giving in to the feelings she evoked?

He settled for a partial truth. 'You know I wanted out of Torquay, and surfing was my ticket out. No harm in following your dreams.'

'Unless it interferes with what you really want.'

Archer glared at his brother, not liking the direction this conversation was taking.

'How would you know what I really want?'

'Because I see the way you look at Callie.'

He hated Tom's condescending smirk as much as his homing in on his innermost fears.

'And I'd hate to see you throw away a chance at real happiness because you're stuck on some warped idea that being in a relationship means giving up your freedom.'

That was not the only thing being in a relationship meant. Reliance, trust, love, they were all a part of it too, and those were the things or, more to the point, the loss of those things that ensured he'd never let Callie get too close.

She'd almost made him slip once before.

Not this time.

'You've been watching too many chick-flicks after Izzy's in bed,' he said, wanting to wipe the infuriating, know-all expression off Tom's face. 'I *like* my life. I'm doing what I want to do, so lay off.'

'Truth hurts, huh?'

Archer swore. 'How about you concentrate on getting your own love-life in order and leave me the hell alone?'

He stalked off a few paces. Not far enough to escape Tom's taunt.

'Who said anything about love?'

He strode faster. He might be able to outrun his brother's annoying chuckles, but he couldn't shake the insistent little voice in his head that focussed on that one little L-word and its disastrous implications.

Callie's head ached.

Bad enough she'd spent the last twenty-four hours over-analysing her impulsiveness in tumbling into a physical relationship with Archer—now she'd inadvertently joined the unofficial Archer Flett Fan Club.

Ever since she'd arrived at the party she'd been bombarded with glowing recommendations from every female family member. And the interrogation from the Flett females was truly frightening.

They wanted to know *everything.*

And she didn't know what to tell them. What could she say? That she'd handed Archer her heart eight years ago, he'd trampled it, and now she'd foolishly come back for more?

Uh-uh. So she'd glossed over her relationship with Archer as being old friends catching up while he was in Melbourne. Interestingly, Shelly had revealed what a refreshing change she was from Archer's usual dates, '*snobby, plastic, citified bimbos*', who wouldn't mingle let alone talk to his family.

She'd wanted to pry, but Archer's mum had shot Shelly a warning look and she'd clammed up. Not that Callie wanted to acknowledge the twinge of jealousy, but considering how warm and welcoming Archer's family had been towards *her*, she was surprised he'd bring that type of woman home.

That was another thing. His interaction with his family. Something was definitely *off*.

He'd been nervous about attending this party. She'd seen it back at his place, subtle signs that his usual confidence was rattled: pacing the balcony while she'd been getting ready, sculling caffeine drinks, absentmindedly changing TV channels without watching any show.

When she'd asked him about it he'd laughed it off, but she'd known there was more to it when he'd taken his sweet time getting out of the car when they'd arrived and then remained on the outskirts the entire party.

She'd seen him talking to his brothers, but beyond a perfunctory greeting for his parents he'd kept his distance from them.

Which begged the question *why*?

She'd ask later—add it to the million other questions buzzing around her brain. Questions she should have asked before falling in lust with him all over again.

One thing was for sure: Archer's family wanted him to stick around for a change. No way would she break the news to them that there was more chance of her winning the next surf pro classic than Archer Flett putting down roots.

He was a confirmed nomad, and in a way it added to his charm. His impulsiveness, his spontaneity, his live-for-the-moment attitude. What they'd done on the beach…the memory had her running a chilled glass across her forehead. It did little to cool the scorching images replaying like a naughty film.

Archer peeling off her swimsuit, exploring every inch of her body with strong, sure hands, kissing her everywhere…

'You can get arrested for looking like that.'

Archer's whisper fanned her ear, sending little pin-wheels of sensation ricocheting through her as his arm slid around her waist, anchoring her to him.

As if she'd want to run. Her surname wasn't Flett. More was the pity.

'Like what?'

He growled at her *faux* innocence. 'Like you've spent the day in bed and you can't wait to get back there.'

She glanced up at him from beneath her lashes. 'Who said anything about a bed? As I recall, the beach served us just fine—'

'Stop, you're killing me.'

His grip tightened as he swung her around, protecting her from prying eyes and backing her towards the rear of the marquee.

'Like you haven't been thinking about it,' she said, challenging him to open up a tad.

They hadn't talked much since the beach, and had fallen into a physical relationship as easily as they'd tumbled in Capri. It had suited her yesterday, not discussing much beyond the present. She'd been on a high, wallowing in the decadence of being in Archer's arms again.

But today reality had set in.

Considering their proximity, living together, it had been all too easy—almost inevitable—sliding back into a physical relationship with the underlying attraction still sizzling between them.

It shouldn't mean anything. Sadly for her it did.

Getting physical with Archer had thrust her right back to the same place she'd been eight years earlier: knowing there'd be an expiration date and not liking it.

She also didn't like being vulnerable to him, and that

was exactly what she'd made herself in opening herself to him again.

Incredibly foolish, considering Archer hadn't fundamentally changed. Footloose, fancy-free and loving it.

The situation reminded her of the many times she'd taken a chance on her dad, when he'd blown into her life, swept her off her feet with gifts and empty promises, only to forget her when he left.

It had been such a buzz being around him. But later the let-down and disappointment and devastation had sucked.

With Archer in Capri she'd made the mistake of masking her feelings, pretending a fling was no big deal. This time she wouldn't be so stupid.

At the start of this week they might have agreed that spending time together in Torquay was about work and being his date in exchange for the surf school campaign, but getting physical had changed the boundaries.

Their futures weren't intersecting, but this time she deserved more. She deserved answers.

Why had he really asked her to be his date for the wedding? How could he be so caring with her, especially about her mum, and shut down around his family?

What were his plans? Because from all accounts the guys at the surf school she'd spoken to had collectively mentioned that Archer would be around more often. What could that potentially mean for them?

Because she wouldn't let him walk away this time. Not without a fight.

She wasn't the same idealistic, naïve girl she'd been in Capri. Life was short—too short—and second chances were rare, so if she and Archer had a remote shot at making some kind of relationship work she'd take it.

She didn't want deep and meaningful, but something

casual and fun to lighten her days in the tough time ahead with her mum. She was all for that.

Ironic how she'd changed in a few days. She'd initially thought Archer wasn't a keeper, wasn't the kind of guy who'd support her when the going got tough.

Maybe he still wouldn't, but the more she saw him interact with his brothers, Izzy and the teenage surf crew, the more he held her and talked to her about her mum's illness and what he could do to raise awareness of her horrid disease, the more she realised she'd misjudged him.

He might have broken her heart eight years ago, but she'd changed. Why couldn't she believe he had too?

Only one way to find out.

Ask the hard questions.

Archer nuzzled her neck. 'I've been thinking of getting you naked again ever since we got here, but there are children present.'

Those questions she needed to ask were momentarily put on hold. 'Stop. People might see.'

'Let them,' he said, his lips trailing down her neck towards her collarbone, nipping along the way.

Her skin rippled with sensation as she arched towards him, wanting whatever he could give.

A low wolf-whistle signalled the arrival of company and Archer swore as they disentangled. 'If that's Tom I'm going to kill him,' he said as Callie readjusted her skewed dress straps.

'Sorry to interrupt, but we're doing speeches.' Travis grinned, not sorry in the least.

Archer shot him a death glare. 'Can't you leave that boring stuff until the wedding?'

'Why? Got better things to do?'

The corners of Archer's mouth curved up and Callie's

heart gave a little kick. She loved that half-smile, as if he was genuinely amused and loving life.

'Yeah, and if you had any sense you'd be doing the same thing rather than getting caught up in all this wedding nonsense.'

'Hey, why not add to the Christmas festivities with a rousing Flett shindig? Keeps the folks sweet, that's for sure.'

'It's a sad day when a Flett male turns into a romantic sap,' he said. An odd expression Callie couldn't fathom flitted across Archer's face as he released her waist to snag her hand.

'We'll be there in a sec,' he added.

A little frown creased Travis's brow but he merely nodded and walked away, leaving her the perfect opportunity to discover what it was about his family that made Archer tense up.

'I've ordered a whole lot of online gift cards for your family for Christmas. Think that'll be okay?'

'Fine,' he said. But clearly it wasn't. That little exchange with his brother had left Archer edgy and reticent and standoffish.

She preferred him laid-back and happy, but she wanted answers and there was only one way to get them.

'Why do you do that?'

He shot her a confused glance. 'What?'

'Close off around your family.'

His brow instantly furrowed. 'That's bull—'

'Is it?'

His lips compressed as he stared at his parents, in deep conversation with Tom on the other side of the marquee.

When he didn't answer, she continued. 'When your brothers showed up at your house and I walked into the kitchen I could feel the tension. Since then you've spent all your time either working or surfing and haven't visited your folks.'

The slash between his brows deepened.

'And tonight, rocking up to this party seems like the last thing you wanted to do.' She blew out a long breath. He was still here, listening. She took it as a good sign. 'Your family can't speak highly enough of you, so I don't get it. Maybe—'

'Maybe you should butt out.'

Hurt slashed her hopes. Hope he'd changed, hope he'd trust her with the truth, hope they had a future.

She tugged on her hand, but rather than releasing it as she'd expected he held on tighter and swore under his breath. When he finally looked at her, the pain in his eyes made her breath catch.

'Sorry for snapping at you.' He gestured towards his family with his free hand. 'None of this is your fault.'

'Want to talk about it?'

'Not really.'

But he did. She could see the turbulent conflict tearing him up inside as his wild gaze swung between Tom, Trav, his folks and Izzy.

It was as if he waged some great inner battle before his stare softened, fixed on Izzy.

'I'm not around much any more. I feel like a stranger.'

He said it so softly she had to lean into him to hear, and the underlying sadness in his reluctant admission tore at her heart.

'My fault, not theirs,' he added, his hand gripping hers as if he'd never let go. 'It's like once I hit the surf circuit I didn't belong here any more.'

Silence stretched as she tried to come up with something to say that didn't sound trite.

'Your lives are so different. Maybe having less in common made you feel like that?'

'It's not that,' he said, his eyes bleak as he tore his gaze away from his family and refocussed on her. 'They kept something from me. It changed everything.'

Oh, heck. She could see it was big from his shattered expression. She'd wanted answers; she hadn't wanted to cause him this much pain.

'What happened?'

He sucked in a deep breath and blew it out in a long stream.

'Dad had prostate cancer. They didn't tell me for eighteen months.'

Stunned, she stared at him in disbelief. She couldn't comprehend the enormity of how betrayed she'd feel if her mum hadn't told her the truth about her disease. And in that moment she understood everything: Archer's discomfort around his family, his unwillingness to get too close.

'I'm so sorry,' she said, pulling him in for a comforting hug that didn't convey half of what she wanted to say.

'It sucked.' He disengaged, the slight catch in his voice underscoring his vulnerability. 'Apparently he was diagnosed around the time I first started making a name for myself on the pro circuit. A couple of years before we first met.'

His gaze swung back to his family.

'They didn't want to burden me with something I could do little about. They waited to tell me once he'd got the all-clear so I would follow my dream.' He dragged a hand through his hair. 'Damn it, do you have any idea how shallow that makes me sound?'

Wishing she could do something to ease his pain, she captured his chin and made him look at her.

'Don't judge them too harshly. I've been where they are,

sitting around helpless and frustrated, waiting for results. It's a relentless, mundane task that eats away at you, and there isn't one damn thing you can do about any of it.' She released him, shaken by the vehemence of her response. 'I know how hurt you must've been at being shut out, but did you stop to think they did it because they love you?'

Confusion clouded his eyes and she continued. 'You told me in Capri that all you'd ever wanted growing up was to be the best surfer in the world. You said that every night you poured into getting your degree part-time was because you wanted to *be* something. Something beyond a local Torquay guy with big dreams and little else.'

She grabbed his arms and gave him a little shake. 'You wanted it so badly I envied you that certainty of what you wanted and how far you'd go to get it. If I picked up on that in a week, don't you think your family knew how much your dream meant to you?'

He opened his mouth to respond and she placed a fingertip under his chin and gently closed it. 'Think about this. If you'd known and given up everything to be with your dad, would you have ended up resenting your family because of it?'

''Course not. I should've been here, supporting them.'

She shook her head. 'You're telling me the independent, driven, determined guy I know would've been happy giving up his dream to stay in Torquay?'

His frown was back. 'It was my decision to make, and they didn't give me a choice.'

His hurt was audible and she cupped his cheek. 'They love you, Arch, and your dad's fine. That's all that matters. Don't waste time on regrets, because life's too short.'

She saw the moment some of his load eased. His confusion cleared and clarity shone through.

'Is that why you gave me a second chance?'

His question came out of left field and stunned her a little. Of course her 'seize the day' mentality had a lot to do with her mum's illness and her approach to life, but him being intuitive enough to pick up on it—and call her on it—really surprised her.

He slid his arms around her waist and rested his forehead against hers. 'I'm sorry for the way things ended.'

Her heart stalled. There was so much she wanted to say, so much more she wanted to ask, but she'd made great inroads in getting him to open up about his family—who were now gathering for speeches and sending curious glances their way. The rest would have to wait until later.

'Me too,' she said, easing away, needing to lighten the mood before she started bawling. 'You know, the faster we get the speeches over with, the faster we can get out of here.'

'I like the way you think,' he said, dropping a quick kiss on her lips.

CHAPTER EIGHT

ARCHER'S guts griped the way they had the time he'd eaten too many jalapeños in Mexico. Sadly, what ailed him this time wouldn't be fixed with a dose of alka selzer.

This was what opening up did to a guy: it made him feel as if he'd be sick at any moment.

How the hell had Callie done that? Wormed some of the truth out of him? He hadn't told anyone about his dad's illness for fear it would paint him in a bad light. Not that he'd been deliberately uncaring. He just hadn't been given the chance to care.

But having Callie articulate his family's possible motivation in keeping such a momentous thing from him had gone some way to assuaging the pain.

Maybe it was time to swallow his damn pride and try to start building a few bridges again?

'Come with me.' His grip tightened on Callie's hand, and as she smiled up at him a new pang twisted his gut.

This one had nothing to do with old regrets and everything to do with a new realisation.

That Callie meant more to him than he'd like to admit.

'Sure. Though if I have to listen to one more anecdote about you guys terrorising Torquay by running around naked as kids I'm bailing.'

'I don't hear you complaining about seeing me naked

now,' he said, his low voice making her eyes widen. The molten depths urged him to head home with her right this very minute, bridges be damned.

'I'm assuming we're heading over to your family to say goodbye?'

He grinned at her cool delivery, spoiled by her healthy blush.

'You assume right.' He ducked down to whisper in her ear. 'The sooner I get you naked the better.'

Her blush intensified and he was chuckling, as Izzy bowled up to him and careened into his legs, almost up-ending both of them.

'Hey, Iz, where's the fire?'

'You're leaving,' she said, hanging off his leg in a similar way he'd seen her do to her dad. 'And I don't want you to go.'

Hell.

Intuitive as usual, Callie squeezed his hand and released it so he could squat down to Izzy's level. She transferred her death grip from his leg to his arm.

'I'm not going far, Iz, just up the road.'

Her blue eyes narrowed, pinning him with the retribution of a child he'd let down too many times in the past. 'You sure you're coming to the wedding on Christmas Eve and everything?'

'I'm sure.'

Her wariness didn't ease, and he half expected her to give him a kick in the shins for all those times he'd side-stepped her too-astute questions about his early departure.

'Okay, then,' she said, but she didn't let go, and as she stared at him with wide-eyed suspicion it hit him.

Izzy didn't believe him.

And that more than anything Callie had said or his family could say got through to him. He needed to stop thinking about making amends and actually start doing something about it.

'Hey, Iz, I know things are kinda busy around here, with everyone getting ready for Uncle Trav's wedding, but if it's okay with your dad why don't I take you surfing tomorrow?'

She stared at him in disbelief for a good five seconds before an ear-splitting grin indicated he'd done the right thing.

With a loud screech that had every guest in the place looking their way, she released him and ran towards Tom, about six feet away, yelling loud enough to be heard in Melbourne. 'Uncle Arch is taking me surfing! Yay, yay, *yay*!'

His family stared at him in unison.

Tom's warning glare spoke volumes: *You'd better not let my kid down this time.*

Trav was giving him a thumbs-up of encouragement.

His mum's soft smile was warm and appreciative and hopeful.

His dad gave a brief nod of approval before he glanced away, unable to look him in the eye as usual.

Well, he'd *make* Frank Flett look him in the eye before he left this time. If the surf school didn't show his dad he was worthy and responsible he'd face this situation head-on regardless.

Callie's pep talk had got him thinking. He'd spent too many years being an outcast in his own family—his choosing. Time to discover the truth about what had happened during his dad's illness, and why they hadn't deemed him fit to know at the time.

And he had Callie to thank for giving him the push he needed.

'Thanks.' He caressed her cheek with his fingertips, a

fleeting gesture he hoped conveyed even half of what he was thinking.

'For what?'

'Everything,' he said, pulling her in for a quick hug to the sound of embarrassing applause from his family.

She laughed as they disengaged, and as he took in her flushed cheeks and sparkling eyes and smiling mouth he realised how much he'd given up in walking away from her all those years ago.

And he'd end up doing it again.

He didn't want to lose her, but he didn't trust himself to make her happy. He'd analysed it at length: if his family didn't trust him when the going got rough, was it *him*?

Was it because he didn't inspire trust in people? And if his own family didn't trust him, how could he connect emotionally with a woman like Callie?

Where did that leave them?

Damned if he knew.

While Izzy alternated between dancing around Tom and tearing towards him, he grabbed Callie's hand and tugged her towards his family.

He made arrangements with Tom to pick up Izzy in the morning, slapped Trav on the back and hugged his mum.

When it came to Frank, the inevitable questions bubbled to the forefront of his mind.

Why didn't you tell me, Dad?

Why didn't you let me be there for you?

Why did you trust the others and not me?

He didn't ask. Now wasn't the time. But before he left this trip he'd discover the truth behind all the pain.

They stood there, self-conscious and ill at ease. Archer wanted to say so much, yet he was plagued by the same discomfort that inevitably occurred around his dad these days. When Frank tried a tentative grin Archer shook his hand and mumbled something about seeing him at the wedding. He wanted answers, but right now he was plain exhausted.

This emotional re-bonding took it out of a guy, and hot on the heels of his realisation that he didn't want to lose Callie...well, Archer knew he had some serious thinking to do.

When Archer had invited Izzy to surf he'd envisaged the two of them having a little uncle-niece bonding time.

What he *hadn't* imagined was the entire Flett clan descending on the beach for an impromptu picnic. Izzy loved the attention and the mayhem and the laughter. Him—not so much.

As he watched Trav elbow their dad and share a laugh with him on the foreshore, regret strengthened his resolve to put the past behind him and move on.

Regret that he'd missed out on being there for his dad when he'd needed him most.

Regret that he'd missed out on so much with his family because of his deliberate withdrawal.

Regret that he hadn't confronted the issue sooner because of his damned pride.

'Hey, you're not watching me!' Izzy's yell refocussed his attention on where it should be: refining her pop up technique.

'I am now, squirt.'

As she sprang from her knees to a standing position, arms stretched out sideways, her grin wide and proud, some of his residual tension whenever his family were around eased.

He'd wasted enough time hanging onto old hurts, and he had missed out on spending time with Izzy as a result.

No more.

'You're a natural,' he said, sweeping her into his arms and tickling her until she squealed.

'I wanna go in the water,' she said, grabbing both his ears and twisting until he released her.

Rubbing them, he tried to frown and failed, his mouth twitching with suppressed laughter instead. 'Ow, Iz, that hurt.'

'Wuss,' she said, poking out her tongue, mischief sparking in blue eyes the colour of the ocean behind her.

'That's it. Lesson's over.'

She giggled and ran into the shallows, kicking water at him as he followed. They dodged and weaved and splashed until he tackled her, scooped her in his arms and made for deeper water.

'My daddy will get cross at you for taking me out so far.' She pouted, but there was no denying the mischievous twinkle in her eyes or mistaking the devious machinations of an intelligent, conniving child who'd say anything to avoid a good old-fashioned dunking.

'Your daddy's laughing as hard as Nan and Pop,' he said, laughing when she glanced towards shore and saw he spoke the truth.

'Put me down,' she said, pummelling his shoulders, so he obliged, chuckling as a wave swamped them and Iz resurfaced, a wide-eyed, bedraggled imp with a grin as wide as the stretch of beach.

Archer lost track of how long they frolicked in the waves—duck-diving, playing tag—and he didn't care. The longer he stayed out here with Izzy, in the one place he felt truly at home, the easier it became to let go of the past.

He'd recaptured some of the magic with his niece and he'd be damned if he lost it again.

Now if only he could do the same with his dad.

'I'm hungry,' Izzy said, flinging her arms around his neck and hanging on tight. 'And thirsty.'

'Okay, kiddo, let's go attack that mountain of food your nan brought along.'

As he waded into shore with Izzy in his arms and strode towards his family their collective expressions gave him hope for the future. Approval, warmth, relief and optimism—the latter on his dad's weather-lined face as admiration lit his smile.

Yeah, it was definitely time to put the past behind him, and he owed it all to Callie.

As if on cue she popped out from the main office of the surf school, where she'd been putting a few finishing touches to the website.

He saw her glance towards his family, sprawled across a picnic blanket on the sand in casual unanimity, and back to him, as if unsure whether to join them or not.

Later. For now he had to thank her.

He lowered Izzy until her feet hit sand, savouring her hesitation to let him go. 'Save me a Vegemite sandwich, kiddo, I'll be there in a sec.'

'But I get the last brownie,' she flung over her shoulder, already racing towards the Fletts, where she flung herself into Tom's arms.

Archer had never envisaged himself settling down, let alone having kids, but watching his brother and niece rub noses in an affectionate greeting he damn well wanted what they had.

'You did a good thing today.'

Callie touched his arm, and the immediate lick of heat made him wish he could drag her back to their sand dune for a repeat performance of that time earlier in the week.

'What? Take my niece surfing?' He shook his head. 'I should've done it a long time ago.'

'It's never too late,' she said, and the barely audible quiver in her voice reminded him that for her, for her mum, one day it *would* be too late.

'Thanks.' He rested his hands on her waist, enjoying the way they seemed to belong there.

'For?'

'For giving me the kick up the ass I needed.'

Her gaze darted towards his family and a small, satisfied smile curved her lips. 'It's hard when you're too close to a situation. Sometimes all it takes is a little objectivity to help clear through the fluff.'

He chuckled. 'The fluff?'

Her gaze met his and it was as if he'd been dumped beneath a massive wave and couldn't catch his breath.

'The extra stuff that weighs us down and clouds our vision and makes us go a little crazy.'

She was something else.

Her beauty, her warmth, her wisdom.

And he'd let her go.

'I think I had some of that fluff clouding my judgement in Capri.'

Understanding sparked in her eyes and she opened her mouth to respond just as Izzy bowled into them like an out-of-control dervish.

'I've saved a sandwich for you, Uncle Arch. Come and get it.'

'Now, how can you refuse an offer like that?' Callie said as she ruffled Izzy's damp curls.

Izzy's nose crinkled in consternation. 'I don't think there's any more Vegemite ones for you, Callie, but I reckon you can have a piece of my fairy bread.'

'Sugar sprinkles? My favourite.' Callie slipped out of his grasp to hold Izzy's hand, but he snagged her arm before she could leave.

'You're amazing.'

He ducked down for a swift kiss, which resulted in a blush from Callie, an excited whoop from Izzy, and cheers from his family.

Yeah, he definitely had some talking to do later—with his dad and with Callie.

Christmas this year wasn't looking so bad after all.

'This place is awesome, dude.' Trav slapped Archer on the back as they entered the supply store at the end of the tour.

He'd been hyped, taking his family around the surf school while Callie entertained Izzy—who was demanding sandcastles—on the beach.

The Fletts' opinion of this place mattered.

He wanted them to like it. He wanted them to tell him he'd done good. Most of all he wanted them to realise he had a lot to give and was a guy of substance—not the flake they'd wrongly presumed.

'Great job, bro.' Tom shook his hand. 'Torquay needs something like this, a place where the kids can hang out.'

'Yeah, that's what I thought.'

They shared a conspiratorial smile, remembering their own tearaway teenage days and some of the mischief bored kids could get up to at the beach.

'I'm so proud of you, son.' His mum enveloped him in a squishy hug, the familiar lavender and fresh bread scent clinging to her so reminiscent of his childhood he felt choked up.

'Thanks, Mum.'

He hugged her tight, saddened by how much he'd missed over the years through the choices he'd made. Distancing himself from his family had probably hurt them, but he'd been the one to suffer the most.

They'd had each other.

He'd had no one.

He planned on changing all that.

When he released his mum, she moved over to the doorway, where Tom and Trav were deep in conversation. It gave Archer the opportunity to seek out his dad, who'd been hanging back during the tour.

While his brothers' and mother's opinion meant everything to him, it was Frank's he prized most.

Over the years they'd fallen into a pattern of mutual gruffness and avoidance that seemed impossible to breach.

Every time he made the slightest effort to reconnect his dad would brush it off as unnecessary in his usual jovial way. And Archer would let him. He never pushed the issue, his pride reiterating that there was only so far he could extend the olive branch and it was up to his dad to grab it.

Frank never had, and he hated the distance between them. He'd once idolised his dad. He'd always reckoned him, Tom and Trav had been super-lucky, having a hands-on dad who took them fishing and camping and hiking. Frank had attended every one of their footy matches, had never missed a training session either.

It made what had happened later all the harder to accept, and made Archer doubt himself as nothing else could.

Tired of second-guessing himself, and buoyed by the shove in the right direction Callie had given him, he had every intention of ensuring the gap between them wasn't irredeemable this time.

'What do you think, Dad?'

He hated having to ask, wished Frank had volunteered some faint praise without prompting, for it signalled that the divide between them was bigger than he'd anticipated.

'Good for Torquay.' Frank glanced around, stuck his hands in his pockets, shuffled his feet as if he couldn't wait to escape. 'Though it's a bit rough putting your name to something around these parts when you're going to be AWOL all the time.'

His dad's aloofness stung, but not as much as the barb behind his words. Frank hadn't acknowledged the good thing he'd done in setting up the school; he'd said it was good for the town.

As for the dig about him being away all the time, it might be true, but why couldn't his dad admit he was proud of him, rather than chastising him for having a school in his name?

'I may be around more often,' Archer said, making it sound blasé when in fact he was hanging on his dad's response.

Frank turned away, but not before he'd seen the scepticism twisting his mouth. 'Uh-huh.'

How two little syllables could hold so much doubt he'd never know.

Archer swallowed his disappointment. His pride in showing his family around and his hope for the future was shattered by his dad's continued standoffishness.

If Frank didn't get why he'd done this, couldn't bring himself to offer one word of positive encouragement, why the hell should he keep busting a gut trying to build bridges between them?

His pride might have kept him from being truly a part of this family all these years, but they'd wronged him first. Was that a childish way to look at it? Yeah, but as years' worth of hurt bubbled up from deep within it obliterated his intention to heal the rift between them.

'Why, Dad?'

Frank stiffened. 'Why what?'

Disgusted, Archer shook his head. 'You know what.'

'Frank, come take a look at this.'

Archer glanced at his mum. Her worried expression was

a dead giveaway that she'd sensed tension and was trying to avoid a messy confrontation.

Uncertain, Frank hesitated.

With disappointment warring with his bitterness, Archer said, 'Go.'

Which was exactly what he intended to do on Christmas Day, as planned.

Go back to his life, far from Torquay and the ghosts of the past haunting him.

'Come back to bed.'

Archer slid his arms around Callie from behind, resting his chin on her head.

'Just let me finish this.' She'd like nothing better than to slip back into his arms, but she had less than a day to get this website done and she didn't want to leave any loose ends.

Once Archer left she wanted a clean break. No contact.

It might be idealistic to hope for a stress-free resumption of their previous working relationship, where they e-mailed each other as needed, but she had a feeling Archer wouldn't mind.

Since Izzy's surf lesson and the impromptu Flett picnic at the beach this morning he'd withdrawn. Nothing overt, but she could tell.

She'd been here before.

In Capri it had been that silly joke she'd made about proposals in the Blue Grotto. Now she had no idea what had prompted his emotional shutdown.

From what she'd seen this morning he'd been closer to his family than he had all week. He'd been demonstrative and open and carefree—in his element.

Something must have happened during the tour of the surf school, because when they'd met up afterwards the tension between him and his dad had been so thick she was surprised it hadn't clouded the sky.

And he refused to discuss what was happening on Christmas Day with his family, despite her subtle prompting this afternoon. She had plans of her own to make, and the least he could do was let her in on what the heck was going on.

The Christmas holidays might not be a big deal for him, considering he lived his life on the road, but his youngest brother was getting married, for goodness' sake—surely this Christmas would be different?

'We've got all tomorrow morning to work on the website.' He ducked down beside her and kissed her cheek. 'Now's the time to play hooky.'

'Won't you have to do last-minute Christmas stuff before the wedding tomorrow night?'

Shadows darkened his eyes to indigo. 'Not really. Like you, I do all my shopping online, so stuff will get delivered direct to the family tomorrow.'

Knowing she was treading a hazardous path, she pushed away from the laptop and swivelled to face him.

'Don't you do other stuff?'

'Like?'

'Help your mum chop veggies for the roast on Christmas Day? Set the table? Fill stockings? That kind of thing?'

He stared at her as if she'd suggested he dress up as Santa and prance around Torquay lugging a sack for the day.

'I don't do that stuff.'

'Why?'

A part of her was dying to know, while the realistic part knew he'd never divulge the truth in a million years.

Guys like him didn't share deep, dark truths. They hid them away beneath a veneer of charm and practised wit.

She should know. Her dad had been the same.

A quick smile and a clever quip for everybody. Loving the world, but not staying put in one place long enough to form any real emotional attachments to anyone.

Including his own daughter.

She'd thought Archer was like that too until she'd seen the way he'd connected with those teenagers on the beach. And Izzy.

He genuinely cared about people, willingly gave of his time expecting nothing in return. That generosity came from within. It wasn't something you could fake; kids—especially teenagers—picked up on that kind of thing. She had with her dad.

Seeing that side of Archer, giving himself freely to those teens on the beach, had opened her eyes to his deeper facets—the ones he kept hidden. And it had made it pretty darn impossible to resist him.

Even with his complicated family history, why didn't he want to show that side of himself to *them*?

'I'm not around enough to warrant that kind of involvement in the rituals,' he said.

His jaw was clenched so hard she was surprised she couldn't hear his teeth grind.

'I fly in each year, stay a few days, then I'm outta here. Why disrupt their routine?'

'Maybe because they want you to?' She kept pushing, her previously undiscovered sadistic side wanting to prod an obvious wound. 'I know it's tough on you, after what you told me at the party, but your family light up when you're around.'

His sceptical glare indicated that he didn't believe her for a second. 'Prodigal son syndrome.'

She touched him on the arm. 'Why do you do that? Pretend your family isn't important to you?'

'That's bull.' He leaped to his feet as if she'd electrocuted him. 'They know how I feel about them.'

'Do they?'

She stood, wanting to see his reaction when she continued peppering him with bombshells. 'From what I've seen, Travis hangs on your every word, Tom looks out for you, and your folks think you walk on water rather than surf it.'

She reached for him, but he stepped away on the pretext of shutting a window, when in fact he was shutting her out.

'It's like they're vying for your attention and you don't want any of it.'

A tiny vein pulsed just below his ear, in the spot she loved to kiss. By his formidable glower, kissing was the last thing on his mind.

'You've met my family only a few times. A few more than any other woman I've known. What gives you the right to judge when you don't know them?'

Or me. The words hung unsaid between them and she resisted the urge to rub her chest where his barb had hit.

Because it was true.

She didn't really know him.

They'd connected for a brief seven days in Capri, but that had been mostly physical—as articulated by the man himself when he'd walked away.

As for their time together here… She'd fallen into the old trap of believing physical closeness implied intimacy, when in fact Archer didn't want to share anything with her. Not the stuff that mattered.

She wanted him to open up to her about what had happened earlier today to make him retreat—wanted him to trust her enough to do it. She'd thought they'd made major inroads in their developing relationship when he'd divulged the truth about his family at the party.

She'd been wrong.

For all she knew nothing had happened with his family during that tour this morning and he was deliberately closing off to *her*.

Maybe she'd been getting too close, and this was his way of cluing her in that come Christmas Day, when he dropped her home, they were finished.

Well, newsflash, surfer boy. She already knew they were over, but this time she wouldn't walk away with a whimper.

'So I'm supposed to be grateful you let me meet your family?' She slow clapped. 'Well done. You took the monumental step of letting a woman get closer than your bathrobe and a kiss on the cheek on her way out the next morning.'

Stricken, he paled, staring at her as if she'd morphed into a monster, and she knew she'd gone too far.

He was so infuriating, standing there in his emotional cocoon, holding everyone at bay when all they wanted to do was love him.

Her included.

Damn, she *loved* him.

Fine time to realise it. Her shock mirrored his.

'Sorry, that was way out of line. I'm just so mad at you for—'

'What, Callie? For walking away from you in Capri? For blackmailing you into being my date for the wedding? For sleeping with you again?' Anger radiated off him like a nuclear cloud. 'You've been mad at me since the day I stepped into your office.'

He jabbed a thumb at his chest. 'You've done such a great job of dumping home truths on *me*, why don't you take a look at yourself?' He took a step towards her, the air crackling with tension. 'Go on—admit it. You're still mad as hell for something that happened eight freaking years ago.'

She shook her head, close to tears. 'It's not that…'

He gripped her upper arms. 'Then tell me why you're so mad.'

She could have lied, could have made up some lame story, but that was what she'd done in Capri. Put on a brave face and lied when he made light of their week together.

Not this time.

'I'm mad at a lot of things, most of them beyond my control, but I'm mostly mad at myself.'

Confusion creased his brow and his grip on her arms eased now he was convinced this crazy woman wouldn't slug him. 'Why?'

'For being a hypocrite. For making light of what we share now, for calling it a fling and pretending I'm happy with it.'

Archer stiffened as she'd expected when she confronted him with the truth.

'I'm mad I let you walk away in Capri belittling what we'd had. I'm mad at you for not trusting me enough to tell me what's going on with you now. And most of all I'm mad as hell you're going to do the same thing this time around.'

Shock slashed his brow. 'I don't know what you want me to say.'

Saddened that even now, when she'd laid it on the line, he couldn't open up, she touched his cheek. 'That's the problem between us, isn't it?'

Fierce determination lit his eyes as he hauled her close. 'Callie, I don't know what you want me to say because I'm clueless here. I've never felt this way about anyone, but I can't change who I am.'

'I'm not asking you to change.'

Though inadvertently she was, and that wasn't fair. She didn't want Archer to give up his life.

She wanted him to love her the way she loved him.

And she couldn't make him love her. Just as she hadn't been able to make her dad love her.

That was when it hit her how alike the two really were. On the surface Archer appeared to be more giving of his time, but only with those not close to him. Why, she had no idea and she wouldn't waste time figuring it out.

How many years had her mum wasted trying to decipher her dad? How much time had Nora spent hoping Bruno would change, that he'd actually commit to something, even if it were only regular visits with his daughter, before being disappointed repeatedly?

She'd hated being second-best in her dad's affections, and no way in hell would she put herself through that with another guy who couldn't commit.

She'd finally told Archer the truth and, while he did care, he could never be the guy she wanted him to be.

So she had two choices.

End things now and spend the next day and the wedding being miserable.

Or make the most of their remaining time together.

Her mother's 'seize the day' attitude flashed through her mind.

'I'm not expecting anything from you.' She stepped into his personal space, almost treading on his toes, to whisper against his mouth. 'But it's Christmas Eve tomorrow and I have a few wishes I need to come true.'

Archer was too smart to buy her excuse completely, but she knew he wouldn't push it. She'd given him an out from the heavy, confrontational stuff and he'd take it. No doubt.

'Want to be my personal elf?' he said, a moment before he kissed her.

She loved this infuriating, emotionally repressed guy, and she'd be anything he wanted for the next twenty-four hours.

For come Christmas morning they'd be saying goodbye, and this time she didn't want to have any regrets.

CHAPTER NINE

ARCHER spent the morning at the surf school.

He'd always done his best thinking at Winki Pop, his go-to place when he'd been a kid. It was like home.

He owned property near Mavericks in Northern California, Pupukea on Oahu's north shore near the Pipeline, and Jeffreys Bay on the Eastern Cape of South Africa. Perfectly nice houses situated near the world's surfing hotspots—houses where he chilled at regular intervals.

But none brought him the peace of Winki Pop.

He'd surfed at dawn, eager to escape the house and Callie's all-seeing eyes.

She'd got close last night, too damn close, homing in on areas of his personal life strictly off-limits.

Hell, he could hardly go there himself.

He didn't get it. One minute he'd been coaxing her to come back to bed, the next she'd seen into his soul.

The thing was, she'd been right about some of it. He knew his family wanted more from him than he was willing to give. He saw it every time he came home—which was why he rarely did.

But this time he'd tried, damn it. Although he'd already made inroads with his brothers, his mum and Izzy, he'd finally done what he'd been yearning to do for years: tried to bridge the gap he'd created with his dad. But the way his dad had reacted at the surf school had demonstrated there was nothing he could say or do to mend metaphorical fences with him.

Because of that he'd been edgy since, and Callie had noticed. She hadn't pushed him and he'd appreciated it—until she'd blown up in his face last night.

When she'd admitted to considering their relationship more than a fling—then and now—he'd wanted to say so much, to lay it on the line: how he was feeling, what he was thinking. But with his dad's rejection fresh from the morning he hadn't been able to do it. Hadn't been able to take another chance with his jumbled, messed-up feelings.

Until he sorted out his options for the future, what would that mean for Callie? A casual relationship with benefits whenever he happened to be in town?

He doubted she'd put up with an arrangement like that, and he wouldn't want her to. She deserved more. More than he could give.

But for one infinitesimal moment, as he stared at the surfers bobbing like buoys on the ocean, he wondered what it would be like to have Callie on a permanent basis.

A woman to come home to.

A woman to love.

Shrugging off the terrifying thought, he resumed his final inspection.

As far as he could see the surf school was in tip top shape and ready for business.

Which was more than he could say for himself.

He was in lousy shape, and considering he not only had to face Christmas Eve but a Flett wedding too things could only go downhill.

Callie dressed with particular care.

She wanted to make this a night to remember.

She'd bought a knockout dress for the wedding from a local boutique expecting to show Archer what he was missing out on. Considering what they'd been up to the last few days, the strapless maroon chiffon cocktail dress with its flared skirt had become redundant.

Archer hadn't been missing out on anything.

Except the one thing she could never give him.

Her heart.

The realisation that she loved him shouldn't have come as any great surprise. She'd fallen hard during their week in Capri all those years ago—had only been saved from pining by her mum's diagnosis. But this time around it had hit her harder, and the constant slightly breathless feeling she had when he was near was beyond annoying.

She knew the score: there'd be no romantic proposals under the mistletoe for her this Christmas.

They were leaving first thing in the morning, apparently. Considering how his family had shut him out during his father's cancer battle she shouldn't be surprised he didn't want to spend Christmas Day with them.

She understood what it felt like when family let you down. She'd put up with it from her dad for too long, until she'd wised up and learned to expect nothing from the selfish, self-absorbed guy who valued his carefree lifestyle more than his only kid.

But from what she'd seen the Fletts were a close-knit, loving bunch. His parents had been married for yonks and still held hands, his youngest brother believed enough in romance to get married on Christmas Eve, and even Tom, who should be disillusioned after his wife had run off after less than twelve months of marriage, was keen to settle down again, according to Travis.

But, despite professing a wish to build bridges with his folks, Archer was still refusing to commit to them.

And her.

Foolish to think that way. Once he'd crept under her guard again and they'd fallen into a physical relationship she'd gone into it with her eyes wide open. In it for a short, good time, not a long time. A self-indulgent fling filled with amazing memories to sustain her through the tough times ahead.

In that respect getting involved with Archer again had exceeded her expectations. Every kiss, every touch, every whispered endearment had been imprinted on her brain to resurrect on a cold winter's night, when she was huddled over her computer working at midnight with a cooling coffee and a bowl of chocolate almonds for company.

Archer had been attentive, charming and altogether gorgeous over the last few days. Little wonder she'd fallen in love.

Her diaphragm gave a little spasm and she dragged in a deep breath and rubbed under her ribs. It didn't ease the stitch that grabbed her every time she associated the words 'love' and 'Archer' in the same thought.

She might be a realist, but the thought of spending the evening at a romantic wedding, the night in his arms and waking up together on Christmas morning made her want to bawl.

She had every intention to farewell him tomorrow, but it wouldn't be easy. Now she finally understood why her mum had secretly pined for Bruno's love all those years ago. *'We always want what we can't have,'* Nora had once said, in relation to Callie's pony request one Christmas, but by the tears in Nora's eyes Callie had known there was more to it.

Nora had led a full life, the epitome of a single mum who was loving it, but as a child Callie remembered hear-

ing muffled sobs late at night, and seeing the way Nora lit
up when Bruno returned home for a rare visit.

Callie empathised with her mum, but she didn't want
to be that person. She didn't want to cry over lost love.
She wanted to remember the good times and celebrate the
second chance she'd had with Archer—even if it ended in
tears like the first.

Snatching a tissue from the dresser, she dabbed under
her eyes, absorbing the seepage. No way would she cry.
Archer would be knocking on her bedroom door any moment and she wanted to wow him—not send him back to
the surf school where he'd hidden out all day.

On the pretext of work, of course. A final inspection or
some such guff. But she knew better.

He'd opened up a little last night and then emotionally
closed down a lot. To the point where, when she'd shut
down the program she'd been working on and backed up
her work, he'd been asleep when she'd returned to bed.
Or pretended to be.

She'd been too drained to care, but when she'd woken
this morning to find a terse note and no Archer she'd had
her answer to any silent questions she might have been
contemplating.

Questions like had the last few days meant anything to
him beyond a fling?

Did he feel their connection on a deeper level?

Would he walk away again without a backward glance?

Pointless questions, really, for even if he came up with
the answers she wanted to hear it wouldn't change a thing.
Her life was in Melbourne for the foreseeable future; his
was traipsing the world. The closest they'd be was in cyber-
space, where she'd contact him on a need-to-know basis.
End of story.

A loud rap sounded on her door and she blinked rapidly, ensuring her eyes were sheen-free.

'Be right there.'

The incongruity of the situation struck her. They'd been intimate, this was *his* house, and yet he wouldn't open the door to her room.

Yeah, the barriers were already up, and the sooner she got used to it the better.

Attending this wedding, pretending she was happy, would be tough. Then again, compared to what she had to face in the future, she could handle it.

She could handle anything. It was what she did. Capable Callie. Canny Callie. No one ever saw lonely, emotionally fragile Callie, a woman who craved love and affection and a foolproof guarantee that she wouldn't end up like her mum.

'Damn,' she muttered, swiping a final slick of lip gloss across her lips and staring wide-eyed at the mirror so she wouldn't cry.

She didn't like feeling edgy, as if she'd snivel at any moment. Considering their impending goodbye she'd have plenty of time for that tomorrow.

Until then...*time to put her game face on.*

Archer held onto Callie's hand through the ceremony, the congratulations, and most of the reception.

He caught her wary glances several times and squeezed her hand in response, as if he never wanted to let go.

The truth was he was absolutely freaking terrified.

Weddings scared him.

The Fletts *en masse* scared him.

Combine the two? Guaranteed scare-fest.

Thankfully, having Callie meet his family at the barbecue and on the beach guaranteed he was safe from his mum's matchmaking for once. But holding onto her hand was more than a gesture, and only he knew it.

She anchored him.

Her ability to socialise with ease, to smile and laugh and be absorbed by his family's mayhem, to make everyone around her feel at ease, was a gift.

Maybe it was all the romantic claptrap in the air? Maybe it was Christmas working its magic? Whatever it was, he found himself strangely reluctant to let her go.

And not just her hand.

Even now, after she'd survived the Flett females' incessant teasing when she caught the bouquet, after dancing with Izzy and the kids until she hobbled, after being ribbed by his brothers, she stood tall, surrounded by the bride, the bridesmaids and his mum, laughing and exuberant and glowing.

She'd never looked so beautiful.

It was more than her brown hair hanging in a sleek curtain down her back, her lush lips slicked in gloss the same colour as her dress, her bare shoulders glittering with a dust of bronze.

It was *her*.

When they'd met in Capri she'd blamed her spontaneity on her Italian heritage and he'd loved her impulsiveness. But it was more than that. She was alive in a way many people weren't. People who dragged their bored butts to work every day, doing a job they hated to pay the bills, returning to equally dead-end relationships at the end of a day.

By the way Callie glowed she'd never had a boring day in her life.

What would it be like to be close to that vitality on a daily basis? Would it rub off?

He loved his life, loved the constant travelling and challenges and business success, but he'd be kidding himself if he didn't admit some of the gloss had worn off lately. Now that he wasn't competing as much he felt jaded, as if his lifestyle wasn't all it was cracked up to be.

Having someone like Callie along for the ride would brighten his days, that was for sure. But with her mum terminally ill would she go for it?

'That's some young lady you've lucked in with.'

His dad sidled up to him and Archer inadvertently braced for another confrontation.

'No such thing as luck, Dad. It's the legendary Flett charm.'

Frank's tentative guffaw sounded as if he had something stuck in his throat. Probably his conscience.

'Whatever it is, she's a keeper.'

'Thanks. I'll take your advice into consideration.'

Archer silently cursed his hint of sarcasm when Frank stiffened, hesitated as if weighing his words.

'Don't let her get away,' he said.

Archer swallowed his annoyance at being given relationship advice from a father who'd deliberately shut him out years ago.

Frank cleared his throat. 'We worry about you, son.'

Yeah, right. His dad was so worried that despite the times he'd made tentative overtures these last few years he'd been brushed off or shut down every time.

'Don't. I'm having the time of my life.' Archer made the *shaka* sign. 'Living the dream.'

Frank's scrutiny almost made him squirm. 'Are you?'

'Hell, yeah.' His response came too quickly, sounded too false. 'I like what I do. It's better than—'

He bit back the rest of what he'd been going to say, on the verge of saying more than he should.

'Better than what?' Frank swept his arm wide. 'Better than being stuck near your family?'

Archer took a steadying breath. Another. 'Do you really want to do this here? Now?'

Frank shook his head, sorrow deepening the creases around his eyes. 'I've only ever wanted what's best for you.'

Archer knew he should walk away now. Make a flippant remark to cover his profound anger and walk away.

But he'd had a crappy day, he was confused about Callie, and he'd had a gutful of being on the outside with his dad for leading the life he did.

'What's best for me is staying true to myself. What about you, Dad? What's best for you?' Years of suppressed anger and pain bubbled up and he couldn't have stopped the questions even if he'd wanted to. 'Having your family around you while you battle a life-threatening illness? Being able to rely on your sons to take care of business while you're juggling chemo? Trusting your family to support you no matter how ill you feel or how bad the diagnosis?'

Frank recoiled as if he'd struck him, but Archer wasn't finished.

'I saw you, Dad, that day you finally told me about being given the all-clear.' He sucked in a breath. The vision of that day was embedded deep, yet so clear. 'Eighteen freaking months too late, you finally deemed me responsible enough to handle the truth about your prostate cancer. After I stormed out you sat at the piano, slid your sheet music into a folder, and you cried. You sobbed like you'd been given a death sentence rather than the all-clear. And right then I knew how big a battle you must've faced, and it acted like a kick in the guts all over again.'

Hating how his voice had clogged, he lowered his tone. 'You should've told me earlier, Dad. I should've been here!'

'You're wrong.' Frank stared at him as if he were a stranger. 'I cried because I knew I'd done the right thing in not telling you, despite how damn furious you were. Even though seeing you hurting almost killed me more than the bloody cancer.'

Stunned at his dad's words, Archer pinched the bridge of his nose. It didn't help ease the headache building behind his eyes.

'You still think you did the right thing in not telling me—?'

'Son, you were a world champion when I finally told you. You'd done it. Followed your dream. Achieved the ultimate. I was so proud of you.'

Frank blinked, and the sight of possible tears tempered Archer's disbelief like nothing else.

'That's what I wanted for you. Success. It kept me going all through the illness: watching your competitions, charting your stats, following every mention on the internet. It gave me focus even when I felt like giving up.'

Frank gripped his arm and gave it a little shake.

'*You* did that. You helped me in ways you can't possibly imagine. And no way in hell would that have happened if you'd known about the cancer.'

Shock peppered every preconception about his dad Archer had ever had, and he couldn't formulate a word in response.

Frank gestured towards the family. 'As much as I love those guys, and the support they gave me, their constant hovering became smothering.' His rueful grin eased the lines bracketing his mouth. 'Some days I'd fake fatigue just so I could get into bed with my laptop and check out what you'd been up to.'

'Hell, Dad.' Archer dragged a hand through his hair, wanting to say so much but still floundering.

'Did you know I could've toured with the Melbourne Symphony Orchestra?'

Whiplashed by the change of topic, all Archer could do was shake his head.

'I would've liked performing to large crowds, living on the road.' Frank squared his shoulders and gazed fondly at his wife. 'But I met your mother and my dreams changed. I ended up teaching local kids and looking forward to your mother's slow-cooked lamb and apple pie and long walks along the beach every night.'

His dad rested his hand on his shoulder.

'While I don't regret staying in Torquay and giving up on my dream, I didn't want you to give up yours, son. I wanted you to have the chance I never had.'

Stunned, Archer stared at his dad—really looked at him for the first time in years. 'That's the real reason you didn't tell me?'

Bashful, Frank nodded. 'I'm sorry for being a jerk at the surf school yesterday. The distance between us over the years has been rough. We both have too much pride for our own good. And the bigger the divide between us the guiltier I felt about what I'd done, and the harder to breach the gap became. Then I saw you re-bonding with everyone and I wanted to do the same, but things were so damn awkward between us all the time. I just didn't know how to express half of what I was thinking.'

'Honestly, Dad, I don't know what to say.' Archer blew out a long breath, knowing he had to exorcise the past and move forward. 'I tried a few times but you always shut me down, pretended nothing was wrong. Now you tell me all this stuff and I'm having a hard time dealing with it.'

'Deal with it. Move on. Life's too short.' Frank nodded towards the dance floor, where the mayor was treading on his mum's toes for the umpteenth time. 'I'm happy with the life choices I've made.'

What about you?

Though his dad didn't say it, the question was there, lurking in his shrewd stare.

Archer had led a charmed life. No regrets.

A peal of laughter floated on the air and he turned, seeing Callie as if in slow motion, with her head thrown back, her hair streaming behind her. Her laughter was loud and boisterous and genuine, and he could have sworn his heart turned over.

He'd lied. He did have one regret in his life. Walking away from this incredibly striking woman.

The real question was, would he make the same mistake twice?

'Settling down isn't all bad.' Frank's genuine smile alleviated the tension between them. 'Happens to the best of us. Just ask your brother.'

Archer winced as he saw Travis doing the Time Warp with his bride. Trav gawky and awkward, Shelly laughing so hard she clutched her sides.

'Think about what I've said, son.' Frank nodded towards Callie, who glanced up at that moment and waved. 'You'd be a fool to let a woman like that slip through your fingers for the sake of a footloose, fancy-free lifestyle. Times change and so do we. We move with them or get left behind.'

As Callie moved towards them, Frank chuckled and nudged him in her direction.

Archer didn't know what to think. His head was spin-

ning with what he'd learned; his heart was reeling from
the possible truth.

Did he dare give up one dream to trust his heart and
follow another?

CHAPTER TEN

'I'VE never had a Christmas like this,' Callie said, staring at the table in amazement.

Covered in crisp white linen, crimson tealights, vases filled with decorative baubles, sparkling crystal, shiny silverware and tiny handmade wreaths sprinkled with silver glitter, it stretched from one end of the marquee to the other.

'Trav and Shelly wanted a combined Christmas-wedding theme, but I think Mum commandeered the decorations.' Archer pointed overhead at the liberal mistletoe hanging from strategically placed hooks. 'She's always gone the whole hog with Christmas. It's the same every year.'

'It's beautiful.' Callie cleared her throat, embarrassed by the sudden surge of emotion making her want to cry. 'You're lucky.'

He must have caught her hint of whimsy and he clasped her hand. 'How do you usually celebrate?'

'Low-key,' she muttered, instantly ashamed of her bitterness.

She'd tried to take her mum on day-trips, especially on special occasions like birthdays and Christmas, but Nora had deteriorated so fast over the last few years it had become easier to stay in.

Her mum had been so distressed last Christmas that she'd made Callie promise not to do it again.

So celebrations these days consisted of snuck-in take-away Thai and luscious chocolate cake from Brunetti's, carols on her iPod and a lot of forced cheerfulness when neither of them really felt like celebrating.

Even their gifts had gone the way of practical rather than indulgent. That hadn't stopped her buying an e-reader Nora could swipe with a fingertip, special organic cream for her crêpe-like skin, and her favourite chocolates this year.

She'd ordered online a few days ago, when she'd been flushed with happiness after her escapades with Archer at the beach.

If she was going to live in the moment, she wanted her mum to also.

Now, with her heart deliberately sealing itself off and her impending departure in the morning, she wondered if she'd been foolish and frivolous.

'Guess it's hard celebrating when your mum's so sick.'

'Yeah.'

He stared at her with blatant curiosity and she wished she'd kept her mouth shut. What better way to ruin their last evening together than to rehash her dysfunctional family's past? Especially in the face of his familial warm and fuzzy perfection.

'You don't want to talk about it?'

She shot him a grateful smile. 'I'd rather focus on this.'

She waved towards the table as the first guests trickled in from the other entry. 'It's really beautiful.' On impulse, she kissed him on the cheek. 'Thanks for coercing me into accompanying you to this wedding.'

He had the grace to look sheepish. 'Sometimes a guy's gotta do what a guy's gotta do.'

That motto applied to girls too, and for tonight she'd drink, dance and be merry. And later, she'd spend an incredible night in Archer's bed, hoarding away memories she'd always cherish.

She hadn't had the opportunity last time, had deliberately banished their time together courtesy of his abrupt break-up. And she'd had more important things to worry about since, like her mum's illness.

Yet for all her reservations about getting involved with him again this week she was glad she'd done it. The last seven days had shown her that the guy she'd thought she'd known in Capri she hadn't known at all. Archer was caring and intuitive, and he had vulnerabilities like the rest of them, and discovering his hidden depths had guaranteed she fell for him.

That was another thing she was glad she'd done: confronting him with her feelings. While she still wished things could have been different, the outcome wasn't unexpected. How could a guy who'd been emotionally shut off from his family for years commit emotionally to her, when realistically they'd known each other for only two weeks eight years apart?

'There is a way you can thank me properly.'

'How?'

He slid an arm around her waist and tugged her close. 'Look up.'

'Beautiful hand-crafted wood beams, red-gum panelling—'

'Mistletoe,' he murmured, a second before he kissed her—a ravishing, soul-reaching melding that left her breathless and clinging to him when he eased away.

It was only then that she registered the hoots and claps of the Fletts.

She blushed, while Archer waved towards the clan,

squared his shoulders and escorted her to pride of place with the rest of the family at the head of the table.

As he pulled out her chair and caressed the back of her neck, a sliver of longing lodged in her shielded heart.

What would it be like to belong to a family like this? To be surrounded by love and laughter? She'd never known it, and she'd never felt her deprivation so acutely as now.

Her dad had done that to her—taken away any semblance of a happy family upbringing—and while she'd given up on him a long time ago it was moments like these when she could easily throttle Bruno Umberto.

She could thank him for her dark hair and eyes, her love of pasta and her quick-fire temper, but there was little else Bruno deserved her gratitude for.

The self-absorbed man who'd now married four times, who lived life on the edge and loved the same way, had breezed in and out of her life like a flitting butterfly.

Since Nora had been diagnosed he hadn't been near them, and the odd e-mail didn't cut it.

The genetic testing had proved she hadn't inherited the mutated gene from her mum. Luckily she hadn't inherited something far more deadly from her father.

His selfishness.

She'd be there for her mum whatever it took, whatever she had to sacrifice, however much it hurt.

'You're kinda spaced out.' He waved a hand in front of her face. 'Everything okay?'

She dredged up a dazzling smile to fool him. 'Fine.'

She'd ensure everything was fine tonight, for come tomorrow their dalliance would be over. But for a fleeting moment she wished she had Bruno's selfish streak and could demand this wasn't the end.

'Hey, surf dude, when are you going to introduce us?' A

tall, broad-shouldered guy who had the Flett blond good-looks sat next to Archer and jostled him.

Archer grinned and elbowed him back. 'Callie, this is my cousin Jonesy.' He draped a proprietorial arm across the back of her chair. 'Jonesy, this is my friend Callie.'

'You're a stunner.' Jonesy reached across Archer and shook her hand vigorously, his smile goofy rather than leery.

'Thanks,' she said, grateful when Jonesy started interrogating Archer about wave conditions for the upcoming season.

Friend.

He'd introduced her as his friend, and while it might be the truth it sounded so distant after what they'd shared.

All her one-on-one pep talks with her voice of reason meant nothing in the face of reality.

Mistletoe kisses, passionate love in the sand dunes and cuddles on the balcony aside, she was right back to where she'd been in Capri.

Wishing for a miracle.

Wishing for him to love her.

After what she'd been through with her mum, she'd given up on miracles a long time ago.

What could be so different now?

But she wouldn't waste her life pining. She'd move on ASAP.

Starting first thing in the morning.

Archer couldn't figure it out. One minute Callie had been kissing him with all the passion and exuberance he'd come to expect from her, the next she'd retreated.

Not that it was obvious to anyone but him. She danced and giggled and ate two pieces of red velvet wedding cake, apparently having a ball.

But he could tell. Every time she glanced his way he saw the shadows. Fleeting, willow-o-the-wisp flickers of... what? Pain? Regret? Disappointment?

He'd wanted to ask what was wrong on their drive home, but she'd been trying hard to fill the awkward silence, chatting non-stop about his family and the ceremony and the exchanging of gifts. And he'd been happy to let her talk, still trying to assimilate the truth behind his dad's secrecy all those years ago.

He'd wanted to thank her for encouraging him to swallow his pride and give his family a go, for making him see beyond his anger and resentment. But she hadn't stopped talking. Anything to avoid silence.

Yeah, there was definitely something wrong. Or maybe she just felt weird about their impending departure tomorrow?

Not that she should. He had it all figured out. Make tonight a night to remember, wake up with her in his arms Christmas morning, then talk to her when they arrived back in Melbourne.

He had a rough plan that he'd come up with over the last few hours.

His dad was right. His pushy brothers were right.

Callie was a keeper.

He'd be a fool to let her go.

He hadn't figured out all the logistics yet. He'd never done a long-distance relationship. Hopefully with a little help from her they'd figure out how this would work.

The thought of having her in his life made him want to ditch the tux, grab his board and head for the beach—but to celebrate, not to escape. He wanted to crest a wave, ride a tube, to see if anything could beat the adrenalin rush of realising he didn't have to lose Callie.

Not this time.

'I know you said no gifts, but I've got you something,' she said, strolling towards him on the balcony before sliding onto the love seat next to him.

He shook his head. 'Should've known you wouldn't listen,' he said, wondering what she'd think of his gift when he presented it to her tomorrow.

He'd arranged it online ten minutes ago, as part of his grand plan, while she'd been 'turning back into a pumpkin'—her words, not his—exchanging her dress and up-do for T-shirt, leggings and a loose ponytail that left tendrils curling around her face.

She looked tousled and tired and casual, and she'd never looked so beautiful.

'It's nothing big. I brought it with me. Didn't want to be caught empty-handed. It's not much.'

She was bordering on babbling, and he covered her hand with his to calm her. 'It's from you. I'll love it.'

Darting a nervous glance at him, she gnawed on her bottom lip, her nerves puzzling. It was only a gift. Then again, considering the yearning he'd glimpsed when his family were handing out gifts after the wedding, and the way she'd clammed up about her family celebrating the Christmas holidays, he figured maybe presents were a big deal for her.

He took his time, tugging on the gold ribbon, fiddling with the knot, sliding his finger under the sticky-tape.

'Hurry up,' she said, practically squirming with impatience.

'I see you're a rip-it-off-in-one-quick-move girl,' he said, putting her out of her misery by tearing the paper in three broad strips to reveal something that snatched his breath with the same surreal, suffocating sensation he'd had being caught in a rip once.

'What—? How—?'

He remembered the day they'd stumbled upon the tiny glassblower's cottage as if it was yesterday. It had been their third day together in Capri—a day filled with swimming in a pristine ocean, sharing grilled calamari and fresh bread for lunch, indulging in a decadent session of afternoon delight, before strolling hand in hand through the cobbled streets.

They'd laughed and jostled and snuggled, typical holiday lovers, and discovering the cottage with exquisitely made glass figurines had made Callie's day. She loved that kind of thing, and he'd indulged her by going in, surprised by the wizened old guy who looked about a hundred creating mini-masterpieces.

The porpoises had caught his attention because he'd seen some during his first major competition, and he'd labelled them his good luck charm ever since.

He'd commissioned a Californian artist to carve a replica of these little glass guys a few years ago, and it took pride of place in the entry hall of his Malibu home.

A home that, like the rest of them, he barely visited.

'You thought it was cool when we went into that glassblowing shop in Capri, so I went back and bought it. I was going to give it to you that last day, but…' She trailed off, not needing to finish.

He'd acted like a jackass, deliberately saying stuff he didn't mean before he let another person get close. Easier to depend on no one and avoid the ultimate let-down.

'Reading too much into a holiday fling…nothing more than a bit of fun…lighten up before you scare off more guys.'

The words came back to haunt him. Come tomorrow he'd make amends and say the words she wanted to hear.

He had all night to work on his delivery. When he wasn't making love to her, that was.

'I was a jerk.'

'Yeah, but you were right.'

He didn't like her emotionless tone, or her shuttered expression as he turned over the delicately intertwined frolicking porpoises.

'I can't believe you've kept them all these years.'

She ran a fingertip along their fins, a soft, wistful sigh escaping her lips. 'I actually forgot I had them. Then, when you showed up and bossed me into coming here, I thought they'd make an okay Christmas gift.'

'An okay gift?' He stared at her in disbelief. Was she being deliberately blasé or did this really not mean anything to her?

She'd kept something so special all these years, something he'd specifically wanted, and she was acting as if she'd given him a pair of woollen socks.

'It's a trinket from the past. Nothing more.'

She shrugged, and the first fingers of doubt crept around his dream of a relationship and strangled it.

'I'm glad this time we had the foresight to know this was a fling and nothing more. No expectations that way. No feelings get hurt. Nice and clean.'

Her brittle laugh set him on edge.

'What did you say back then? A short time and a good time?' She interlaced her fingers through his. 'It's certainly been that, Archer Flett. Consider this a thank-you gift too.'

Gobsmacked, he let her take the porpoises and place them on the glass-topped table beside them before clambering onto his lap. Her arms snaked around his neck, tugging his head towards her, her lips meeting his in an explosion of need.

There was nothing tender about the kiss. It was pure desperation, heat and passion and fear. Fear of the future? Fear of farewell?

Whatever, now wasn't the time to dwell on it. He had a million questions to ask her.

In the morning.

For now he wanted to show her how much she meant to him.

He might not be able to eradicate the immature stuff he'd said in Capri, but he could sure as hell let his actions do all the talking now.

CHAPTER ELEVEN

CALLIE wasn't proud of what she'd done.

She should have told Archer the truth last night. And she shouldn't have snuck away in the early hours. Or made Tom complicit in her deceit.

She had to give him credit for not spilling her secret. She'd half expected Archer to confront her about her plan to abscond once she'd asked Tom for a favour at the wedding.

But Archer hadn't suspected a thing.

She'd had her chance to say goodbye and she'd taken it. Several times during the night, with each erotic encounter surpassing the last.

It had been subliminal, knowing it would be their last time together. She'd imprinted every whispered word, savoured every caress, treasured every touch.

If Archer had been surprised by her wild enthusiasm he hadn't shown it. He'd responded in kind, taking her to heights she'd only ever read about in novels.

And then she'd left, creeping out at 5:00 a.m.

Thankfully Izzy had been asleep in the back of the car, and after a few less than subtle questions Tom had given up interrogating her.

The Fletts were a loyal bunch, for not once had Tom

discredited his brother, apart from saying he was a nong
for letting her get away again.

She'd had to give him something to shut him up, so
she'd settled for a semi-truth. They'd already said their
goodbyes last night. They were happy to resume their respective lives, and she had to get back to her mum on
Christmas Day.

All perfectly respectable, perfectly legitimate reasons…
for running out like a chicken.

The truth was she couldn't face the long car ride back
to Melbourne with Archer—couldn't face the awkwardness of another goodbye.

This way they could resume their old relationship—e-
mailing for business—and avoid any mess.

He was flying out today, so he wouldn't have time to
worry about her early departure anyway. He had things
to do, places to be.

Things and places that didn't include her.

That was why she'd given him the porpoises. She'd
lied about that too, telling him she'd forgotten about them.

As if. She might have banished her memories of their
time in Capri, but every now and then, when her mum had
a particularly bad day and Callie felt lonely, she'd take
them out of their recycled cardboard box, cradle them in
her hand and remember…

Remember that special time in Capri, wishing she could
have one ounce of it again.

Well, now she had, and where had it left her? Worse
than before. Seriously in love with a guy who had no clue.

To his credit, his reaction to her gift had blown her
away. She hadn't expected to see him emotional, and for
a few tense moments beforehand had half expected him
not to remember that day in Capri at all. But he had. And
it had made her wish things could be different all the more.

Instead she'd go back to working on his lucrative cam-
paigns—with the bonus of having Nora's medical bills
taken care of—and he'd hit the surf on some exotic island
far removed from Melbourne and the memories they'd
built.

Memories that would have to last a lifetime.

For now, it has time to get on with her life, starting with
a quick visit to Rivera's to wish Artie a Merry Christmas
and then spending the day with her mum.

The Spanish bar was jumping when she arrived, with
revellers in Santa hats and flashing reindeer noses spilling
out onto the street. Many locals came straight from mass
to get a taste of Artie's special virgin sangria on Christmas
morning, before heading off to their respective hot roast
lunches with family.

It had become a Johnston Street tradition, and one she
enjoyed, because it gave her an all too brief taste of what
a normal Christmas should be.

Not like the understated days she'd had growing up,
where she'd wait for her dad to show up with the pony he'd
promised only to be disappointed yet again.

Or the recent Christmases spent with Nora, forcing
cheer when all she'd felt like doing was holding her mum
fiercely and banishing the disease slowly sapping her life.

She slipped through the crowd and entered the main
door, her despondency lifting when she glimpsed Artie
taking pride of place behind the bar, his costume this year
more outlandish than the last.

He'd gone for monstrous reindeer antlers that threatened
to take a person's eye out when he turned, a big red nose
made from a dyed tennis ball, and a fake white beard that
reached to his belly.

It made her happy to see him enjoying life, a far cry

from the devastated man he'd been following his wife's death.

He caught sight of her and waved, calling her over.

Determined to put on a brave face, she wound her way towards the bar, where he swept her into a bear hug.

'*Hola, querida.* Merry Christmas.'

'Same to you.' When he released her she tweaked his nose. 'How can you breathe with that thing?'

'I can't,' he said, in a fake nasally voice, and she laughed. 'Come. Have some sangria.'

For a moment she wished it was the alcoholic version, despite the hour.

'Tell me about this new business.'

Great. Just what she felt like. Talking about her week in Torquay. *Not.*

He poured her a drink, garnished it with a strawberry, slid it across the bar and winked. 'And tell me more about this old *amor.*'

She remembered contradicting Artie a week ago. *I don't love him.*

This time she didn't have the energy to lie.

'The business is exciting. I've developed an online marketing campaign for his new surf school, including online forums and interactive sessions on his webpage, and a social networking page unlike anything anyone's ever seen.'

'Sounds impressive.' Artie topped up her glass even though she hadn't taken a sip. 'Now, tell me about when you weren't working.'

She blushed and Artie patted her cheek, his smile indulgent.

'You're in love. I can tell.'

'How?'

'You have the look.' He pointed at her eyes. 'You have a

sparkle dampened by sadness.' Artie frowned. 'This *amor*, he broke your heart, *si*?'

'No, nothing like that.'

More like she'd broken her own heart by being foolish enough to fall in love despite knowing the expiration date on their seaside fling, knowing he couldn't emotionally commit, and knowing he had traits of her dad she'd rather forget.

Artie cupped his ear. 'You want to talk about it? I'm a very good listener.'

'Don't I know it?'

Artie had listened to her deepest fears and regrets after their unofficial support group for two had formed. He'd been just as forthcoming in his sorrow, yet strangely this time she didn't want to talk about Archer.

Besides, what was there to say? They were headed in different directions, their lives on different paths, without a hope of colliding.

Artie snapped his fingers. 'I can see you don't want to talk to an old man about your *amor*. I understand.' He shrugged. 'If you do, you know where to find me.'

'Thanks,' she said, making a big show of drinking the refreshing fruit sangria as he was called away, when in fact her favourite Christmas drink had already lost its fizz.

With Artie shooting her concerned glances in between mixing drinks and plying his customers with Christmas cookies, she sculled her sangria and gave him the thumbs-up sign.

She had to leave. Before she took him up on his offer to listen. For she had a feeling once she started talking about her relationship with Archer she wouldn't stop.

* * *

Archer stared at the note in disbelief.

> Sorry to run out but had to get back to Mum.
>
> Tom & Izzy heading to Melbourne to visit Izzy's mum, who unexpectedly dropped into town today so I hitched a ride.
>
> Thanks. Had a lovely time at the wedding.
>
> Will be in touch about the surf school campaign when needed.
>
> Merry Christmas!
>
> Callie

'What the—?' He slammed his palm on the kitchen benchtop, barely registering the pain of hitting marble so vigorously.

His first instinct was to punch something. The second to grab his board and hit the surf.

He settled for pacing. It didn't help. After several laps of the balcony he flung himself onto the soft-cushioned couch where he'd once sat with Callie and uncurled his fingers to reveal her crumpled note.

He reread it, no closer to understanding.

She sounded so cool, so remote, so untouchable after all that had happened over the last week. They'd reconnected on so many levels, to the point where he'd been about to reveal his thoughts for the future to her this morning.

Schmuck.

This was his family all over again.

Trusting someone with his heart, only to have them hand it back with a *Thanks, not this time, maybe another,* and having no clue as to why.

To make matters worse it catapulted him back years, to when his family had first told him the truth. The same insidious doubts were creeping in, making him wonder what the hell was wrong with him that the people he trusted the most with his feelings didn't return the favour.

How could she up and leave without saying goodbye? Leaving a freaking note?

He glared at the offending piece of paper in disgust, bitterness twisting his gut into knots.

Growling in frustration, he shoved it in his pocket and headed for the storage room under the house where he stashed his gear. He had to hit the waves. It was the place he did his best thinking.

However, as he stomped around, grabbing a wetsuit and his favourite board—the one with more dents than a dodgem—a funny thing happened.

Some of his initial anger faded, to be replaced by a clarity that left him shaken.

He paused mid-step, halfway between the storage room and his car.

What the hell was he doing?

It was Christmas morning—a time for warmth and caring and happiness. Emotions he'd been lacking lately, if he were honest with himself.

Not this last week with Callie, but before that.

Riding the tubes hadn't held the same buzz in a long time, crashing in fancy hotel rooms after a competition had lost appeal, and the string of meaningless dates left him feeling faintly empty.

The real reason behind the surf school had been to make his family sit up and take notice, see he was more than a sport-obsessed surfer, to show them they'd done wrong in not trusting him with his dad's illness.

But another underlying reason was that he'd wanted to give something back to the sport that had given him everything, and connecting with the kids at the beach last week had made him feel worthy in a way he hadn't in for ever.

That had been the hardest thing to realise over the years following his dad's cancer disclosure—that somehow he hadn't been worthy. He might now understand his dad's motivation for secrecy, but it would take a while for his old beliefs to ease.

Hanging with the teens had helped with that. Callie had too. He'd felt rejuvenated this last week, had truly felt close to a woman for the first time ever.

She'd made him reassess the way he treated his family, made him see things in a new light. And he'd been happy in a way he hadn't for a long time. So what the hell had happened?

Buoyed by his overture towards his dad, he'd taken another risk and told her he had feelings for her. Why had she run?

After she'd given him that gift last night he'd thought she felt the same way... Well, he'd thought wrong.

The way he saw it, he had two options. Forget about the gift he'd bought her, then head for the surf before boarding that plane this afternoon and heading back to the life he knew.

Or quit running and confront Callie.

He headed for the car, the board tucked under his arm suddenly weighing him down. When he stowed it in the back, the weight didn't shift. Then his gaze landed on the red Roadster he'd driven Callie here in—a replica of the car they'd explored Italy's south coast with.

He remembered the thrill of taking the curves of a spectacular scenic route, laughing and teasing, and later he'd explored *her* sensational curves in minute detail.

He'd wanted to resurrect the past—this car was testament to that—but was he willing to try a different outcome this time?

What would his life be like if he didn't walk away second time round? If he made a full-blown declaration and truly trusted her with his heart?

Terror made his hands shake, and he stuffed them into the pockets of his board shorts.

He had his answer right there.

He'd re-established a bond with his dad and he'd never felt so relieved. Taking a risk on people wasn't all bad. And he wouldn't be feeling this sick unless he really felt something for Callie. Something that went deeper than caring.

The question was, how far was he willing to go to prove it to her?

Callie had put on a brave face for her mum. She'd made a show of savouring the cardboard-tasting turkey and dry Christmas pud, she'd sung the loudest through the residents' carolling, and she'd fake-laughed over each and every corny joke pulled from a cracker.

She'd thought she'd done a pretty good job of pretending there was nothing wrong. Until she wheeled her mum back to her room and Nora snagged her hand, concern deepening the fatigue lines in her sunken cheeks.

'What's wrong?'

Callie opened her mouth to protest but Nora shook her head.

'Do me a favour, sweetheart, and let me be a mum to you in whatever way I can.'

As a guilt trip, it worked. She'd been taking care of her mum for a while now, and she knew it irked the once independent Nora.

Nora had relished her role as a single mum, not once complaining. When a job had needed doing, she'd got on and done it, so to have her mobility and her dignity curtailed by this dreadful disease… Callie couldn't begin to fathom how awful it must be.

'Work pressures. Nothing major,' she said, not wanting to worry her mum—not today.

Nora had always loved Christmas with all the trimmings: roast turkey and stuffing, trifle, pudding—the works. They'd always had a fresh tree and stuffed stockings, and a day made all the more special by a mother who'd do anything for her only child.

It might have been understated and only the two of them, but it had meant a lot to her mum.

Now those Christmases were in the past, but the least Callie could do was not ruin this Christmas for Nora. Not when she'd already ruined her own.

Nora searched her face, as if seeking the truth, and Callie ducked down to give her an impulsive hug. 'Don't worry, Mum, I'm fine.'

And then she glanced over her mum's shoulder and saw Archer hovering in the doorway.

'What the?'

'Callie?'

She straightened and laid a comforting hand on her mum's shoulder, hoping her glare conveyed what she wanted: for Archer to turn around and leave the way he'd come.

Following her line of vision, Nora slowly swivelled until she too faced Archer.

'Can I help you, young man?'

He hesitated a moment, before squaring his shoulders and stepping into the room. 'I sure hope so, Mrs Umberto.' He held out his hand to her. 'I'm Archer Flett, a friend of your daughter's.'

The way he gently shook Nora's hand eased Callie's anger somewhat. Though she couldn't figure out why she was so angry. Was she upset at him showing up here, or upset at herself for wanting to fling herself at him despite a definitive goodbye?

Well, on her part anyway. It looked as if he hadn't taken too kindly to her brief farewell note.

'Sorry to barge in on you like this, but I need to see Callie before I fly out later today.'

Callie frowned but he blithely ignored her, his dazzling smile deliberately taunting.

'Merry Christmas, by the way,' he said.

He produced a box from behind his back, in crimson shiny paper bound by gold ribbon. 'Not very original, I'm afraid, but if you're anything like your daughter I thought you might enjoy a sweet treat.'

'How thoughtful.' Nora's hands shook as she took an eternity to undo the ribbon and rip the paper.

Callie had to stop from reaching out to help. Not from pity for her mum but the desire to see Archer leave.

'Dark mint, my favourite.'

Nora's grateful smile made Callie's heart ache. She hadn't wanted to tell her mum anything about Archer, and now the rat had left her no choice. Nora would want to know all about the nice young man who knew her favourite chocolates and how he knew and…the rest.

She'd kill him before she sent him packing.

'I hate to intrude, but do you mind if I have a quick word with Callie?'

Nora shot her a quick look—a very perceptive look by the mischievous gleam in her eyes.

'Not at all. Go ahead.' Nora rattled the box. 'And thanks for these. I'll enjoy each and every one.'

'My pleasure.'

His smile was genuine, without an ounce of pity, and Callie grudgingly admired him for it.

'We can talk outside,' she said, with a subtle jerk of her

head towards the door. The last thing she needed was for her mum's gossip radar to prick up. Any *more*, that was.

Callie couldn't figure out what Archer was doing here. She'd given him an easy out with that note, and she'd assumed he'd jump at the chance to fly off into the blue yonder and resume his life.

The last thing she'd expected was to see him rock up here. It made her angsty and uncertain and decidedly edgy.

She'd had this all figured out—end fling; resume working relationship—and now he'd messed that up.

She waited until they'd stepped outside Nora's room before jabbing him in the chest. 'How did you find me?'

Her snappish tone only served to make him lean against the wall, arms folded, grin cocky.

'Not all that difficult. You said you'd be spending the day here, so I checked redial on the phone at the beach house for the number, rang it, discovered where your mum was staying.'

'Nice one, Sherlock,' she muttered, still clueless as to why he was here.

'Actually, I'd make a lousy detective, because I have no clue as to why you ran out on me in the middle of the night.'

'It was early morning. Tom and Izzy were heading to Melbourne, so I thought I'd get a head start on spending Christmas with Mum.'

'Bull,' he said, his grin replaced by thinly compressed lips and an unimpressed frown. 'You couldn't have rung Tom at four a.m. on impulse to hitch a ride, which means you must've organised this last night.'

Why couldn't he be all brawn and no brains?

'Tom's wisely not answering his phone, but I have no doubt you coerced him into aiding and abetting your little escape.' For the first time since he'd shown up a flicker

NICOLA MARSH   167

of uncertainty creased his brow. 'I don't get it, Callie. I
thought we had something going—'

'*Had* being the operative word.' She shook her head,
wishing her heart would stop flipping all over the place
and slamming against her ribcage at the thought of him
showing up here because he genuinely cared.

No use wishing for the impossible.

Fact: he was still getting on that plane later today.

Fact: whatever he said wouldn't change a thing. They
led different lives, a world apart.

Fact: she loved him, and seeing him again only drove
the knife in that little bit deeper.

'Look, we had a great time, Arch, but it's over.'

His glare turned mutinous. 'Doesn't have to be.'

He rummaged in his jacket pocket and pulled out a
folded piece of paper.

'Here. This was supposed to be your Christmas present.'

When she made no move to take it, he placed it in her
hand and curled her fingers around it.

'Go on, take a look.'

More than a little curious, she unfolded the paper and
gasped.

A computer printout for an open-ended, first class,
round-the-world air ticket.

In her name.

'We've got a pretty good thing going, Cal, I don't want
it to end. This way you can join me wherever I am. We
can hang out—'

'No.'

She crumpled the paper ticket and let it fall to the floor,
her gut spasming with sorrow.

'Don't you get it? I can't just jet off whenever I feel like
it. I have obligations.' She jerked a thumb over her shoulder. 'I can't leave Mum and you know that.'

His face fell. 'I thought... Well, I hoped you might want to explore...a...relationship—'

'On your terms?'

Pain lanced her resolve, making her waver. Was she being too harsh? Was she annihilating any chance of a possible future of happiness?

She shook her head. 'If you're so keen to explore what we have, why don't you stick around? Stop running? Commit to something for once in your life?'

A flash of anger sparked his eyes. 'I've committed my life to being the best in the water—'

'Yeah, but what about out of it? What about your family? You can't bear to spend longer than a few days with them once a year. How the hell do you expect to maintain a relationship?'

She knew what she was doing: deliberately sabotaging his attempt at a relationship. Fear clogged her throat at the thought of continuing what they had, growing closer, only to discover he hadn't really changed after all and she'd end up pining and waiting for someone she couldn't rely on. Been there, done that, still waiting for her dad to bring her the T-shirt as a present.

She might have foolishly wished for a happily-ever-after with Archer this past week, but at the time she'd recognised her pie-in-the-sky dream for being just that. That was why she'd indulged in another week-long fling, confident of the end date.

She'd never take the risk of a full-blown relationship knowing she was opening herself up to further heartbreak.

'Just go.'

She expected him to run as he always did. The fact that he was still standing there, a vein pulsing in his neck, shoulders rigid, only served to rile her further.

What was he waiting for?

'I'm not the one running scared this time, Callie. You are.'

Sadness seeped through her, making her want to curl up in a corner and sleep for a century. 'Shows how well you know me. I'm not running anywhere. I can't.' She jerked her head towards Nora. 'And the fact you'd give me an air ticket expecting I'd follow you on a whim proves it.'

Tears prickled at the backs of her eyes. She had to drive him away before she collapsed in a wailing heap in his arms.

'You don't know me and you never will.'

When he didn't flinch, didn't move, her mum called out, '*You* should go, dear.'

Callie did the only thing possible.

She fled.

CHAPTER TWELVE

For the second time today Archer wanted to punch something.

Frustration made his head ache as he watched Callie run away from him.

Again.

He should follow her, try to make her understand... His gaze landed on the crumpled plane ticket at his feet and his resolve hardened.

He'd wanted to explore the spark they shared. She'd rejected him.

Best to walk away and not look back.

'Archer? Could you please come in here a minute?'

Great, just what he needed. For her mum to berate him for messing up her daughter's life.

He snatched the ticket off the floor, jammed it into his pocket and entered the room.

'I have a plane to catch—'

'"Later" is what you said.'

The woman before him might have a terminal disease which left her stoop-shouldered and shaky and fragile, but the determination in her intelligent eyes was pure Callie.

He sat on the footstool opposite her wheelchair. 'I'm not comfortable discussing my relationship with Callie.'

'From what I overheard, seems like you're not comfortable with a relationship period.'

'Harsh.'

Nora's eyebrow rose. 'But true?'

When he opened his mouth to protest, she held up a trembling hand.

'This is none of my business, but if you want a chance with my daughter I recommend you listen.'

He remained mute.

'Good. You want to know why Calista refused your offer?'

He nodded.

'She's scared.'

'Of?'

'It's not my place to tell you, but I think you need to ask her if you want a future together.'

He let out a breath he'd been unaware he was holding, his fingers relaxing from where they'd dug into the footstool's leather.

Damn right he'd ask her. If Callie's mum thought he still had a chance, no way would he waste it.

'You might be interested to know that when Calista returned from Europe she was glowing. She had a bounce in her step, she smiled constantly, and she hummed Spanish tunes under her breath. Then I was diagnosed and her exuberance faded.' Tears glittered in her eyes. 'I hate this disease for doing that to my beautiful Callie.'

Archer didn't handle emotion well, tears least of all, and he sat there like an idiot, searching for the right thing to say and coming up empty.

'Interestingly, when Calista came to see me last week, before her trip away with you, she had some of that old spark back. Which leads me to believe you were more responsible for her post-Europe glow than geography.'

If acknowledging emotions wasn't his forte, discussing them sent him into full-blown panic.

'We shared something special.'

The simple truth, and the right thing to say by Nora's nod of approval.

'My advice? If you want to share that same spark again, don't give up. Go after her. Convince her how you feel. Make her trust you. Trust is everything to my little girl.'

He knew the feeling.

To his surprise, a lump wedged in his throat, and no matter how many times he swallowed he couldn't dislodge it.

'As for her fear of leaving me in case I die—don't worry. I'll fix that.' Nora's smile turned wicked. 'If she doesn't spend some of her time on the road with you I'll threaten to live out my time in the smelly nursing home up the road—the one with roaches the size of rodents—and donate the exorbitant fees she pays for me to stay here to the lost dogs' home.'

The lump of emotion in his throat eased, and his admiration for this feisty woman skyrocketed. 'I'm glad you're on my side.'

She pointed a bony finger at him. 'I'm only on your side because I can see you're head over heels in love with my daughter. Hurt her—you die.'

He laughed. 'Got the message, loud and clear.' He stood and ducked down to kiss her cheek. 'Thanks.'

A faint pink stained her cheeks. 'I may not be around much longer, but while I'm here I'm going to be the best damned mother-in-law you could ever wish for.'

It took him a good sixty seconds to process what she'd said, and by then he'd reached his car.

Him? Head over heels in love? What were the chances?

As for a mother-in-law…that involved marriage…

By the time he'd hit Alexander Parade some of the initial shock had worn off and he found himself heading for Johnston Street.

He needed answers.

Only one woman could provide them.

Callie texted her mum an apology as soon as she pulled into a parking spot at home.

She'd cooled off by the time she'd walked through to the foyer, and had headed back to Nora's room. But when she'd got there she'd seen Archer in the room. It had looked as if her mum was telling him off so she'd left. She hoped Nora had flayed him alive.

The guy didn't have a clue, thinking she could traipse around the world while Nora was stuck in that home dying.

Selfish. Unthinking. *Male*.

She thumped the steering wheel. It did little for the resentment simmering like a dormant volcano. She wasn't footloose like him. She couldn't jump on a plane whenever he snapped his fingers. She wasn't impulsive and selfish. She wasn't her father.

But as her anger faded a sliver of clarity glimmered through. Maybe she was looking at this all wrong. Archer had walked away from her once without looking back. This time he wanted to continue seeing her, to explore a relationship. And, while she didn't want to risk her heart again, she'd been harsh. She'd said some pretty nasty stuff at the end, accusing him of being a shallow, emotionless commitment-phobe.

And what had he done? Gone and copped more from her mum. Not many guys would do that. The Archer she'd once known would have headed to the airport without hesitation.

But this older, more mature Archer wasn't the same

guy he'd once been. He was wiser, more responsive, more willing to see past the end of his surfboard.

And the thing was, if a guy like him had taken a monumental risk in tracking her down to lay his heart on the line should she consider taking a risk too?

Was her lack of trust worth a life of misery in losing the love of her life?

She rested her hands on the steering wheel and her head fell forward, her eyes closed.

She couldn't leave Nora, that was a given, but maybe she could compromise in some way? She wouldn't expect him to wait for her, but the thought of having Archer in her life—to support her, to care for her when the dreaded inevitable happened with her mum—was pretty darn appealing.

She knocked her head repeatedly against her forearms.

Yep, she'd been a fool.

The rev of an engine penetrated her misery, punctuated by three short blasts on a familiar horn. She lifted her head, daring to hope, just in time to see Archer kill the engine of the red Roadster, unclip his seatbelt and vault over the door.

He strode towards her, determination lengthening his strides, and she got out of the car, waiting for him to reach her.

'We're going for a ride and I want you to promise me you won't speak the whole way.' He snagged her hand and tugged.

She resisted. No use giving in too easily. 'As an apology, that sucked.'

She bit back a grin at his comical disbelief.

'*Me* owe *you* an apology?' He shook his head. 'Not. Another. Word.'

This time she let him lead her towards the Roadster,

open the door and buckle her in. His familiar fresh air and sunshine scent wrapped around her like a comforting hug.

She gritted her teeth to stop herself from nuzzling his neck, and curled her fingers into her palm to stop herself reaching for him.

He took a deliberately long time, taunting her, and she almost capitulated. Almost. He straightened, his grin smug, and she wanted to smack that smugness off his face.

As they wound through the heavy Christmas Day traffic she snuck glances at him, her heart giving an extra kick when they locked stares for a long, loaded moment at some traffic lights.

All her mental pep talks to get over him, all her determination to move on, vanished in that one look. The sizzle of heat was invisible yet unmistakable.

She'd never been more thankful when the lights turned green.

Ten minutes later he'd pulled into a rare parking spot in Lygon Street and his intention hit her.

He'd brought her to Melbourne's Little Italy. Was he aiming to soften her up by resurrecting memories of Capri?

They were so past Capri it wasn't funny, and she fully intended to tell him so. But the hint of vulnerability in his questioning gaze caught her completely off guard and she bit back a smartass remark.

She saved it for when they were seated in a tiny trattoria so reminiscent of their favourite place in Capri she half expected Luigi, the owner, to come strutting out to welcome them.

'Can I talk yet—?'

'No.' He made a zipping motion over his lips and proceeded to order: linguine marinara, fresh bread, Chianti.

Their meal.

Yep, he was trying to schmooze his way into getting her

to change her mind. As if a fabulous Italian meal would do that.

She had obligations.

She had responsibilities.

He snuck his fingers across the table, snagged her hand, lifted it to his lips and kissed her knuckles.

She had it bad.

He released her hand and she reluctantly, perversely, snatched it away.

'You can talk soon, but only after you listen first.' She rolled her eyes and he chuckled. 'I had a plan. Wake up next to you Christmas morning, make all your Christmases come at once—' she winced at his corny pun '—and then tell you how I feel.'

Her pulse stuttered, before pounding like a jackhammer.

'But you robbed me of that opportunity and I wanted to run. I was all set to head to the airport early 'til I realised something.'

His gaze dropped to her hands, clasped on the table, before slowly raising to eyeball her, and what she saw snatched her breath.

Adoration? Hope? Dared she think it...*love*?

'I figured this time I wanted to run *towards* something and not away from it.'

Some of her resentment melted as she gnawed on her bottom lip, wanting to speak, afraid of saying too much.

'That airline ticket was my lousy way of saying I want to be with you.' He cleared his throat. 'I can't lose you, Cal. Not this time.'

The silence stretched between them and she took it as her cue to speak.

'I can't traipse around the world after you, even if Mum says it's okay.'

He nodded. 'I know. I was thinking maybe I should

stick around for a while—teach classes at the surf school, give back to my home town and the sport that's given me everything.'

Shock ripped apart her carefully constructed defences.

'You're staying in Torquay?'

'If you make it worth my while.' His mouth kicked up at the corners in a cheeky dare, and she could have sworn her heart kicked right back.

Wow.

Renowned nomad and confirmed gypsy Archer Flett was willing to put down roots. For her.

It was what she'd dreamed of—what she would have traded anything for eight years ago. But despite the urge to be selfish for once in her life, grab what she wanted and damn the consequences, she couldn't do it.

Archer was willing to stick around now, but for how long? What about when the going got tough with her mum? What about when they had to live apart for months because of his work commitments and her emotional ones?

Constant pressures on a relationship would wear it down and she'd be right back where she started. Loving Archer, her trust shattered.

'So what do you say? Think you can handle having me in your life?'

Her heart wanted to yell, *Hell, yeah.*

Her mind froze with the implications of losing him. This time around it would be so much worse, because he was willing to give it all up for her.

And she had to push him away.

'I—I can't. I'm sorry.'

She had a second to register his open-mouthed shock before she bolted from the restaurant, dodging a family of boisterous children brandishing crackers and a bedraggled Santa who looked as if he'd been doing overtime all week.

She couldn't head for the car, and both sides of the road were lined with outdoor chairs and tables filled to overflowing with Christmas revellers.

Her hesitation cost her dearly. A hand clamped around her upper arm.

'I've asked the waiter to hold our meal until we've had a little chat. In private.'

She could have struggled, but with people casting concerned glances their way and reaching for their mobile phones she acquiesced to him leading her to the car, where she slouched in the front seat like a recalcitrant child.

'Nora told me you have trust issues and that you'd tell me the rest. Is that what this is about?'

Way to go, Mum, she thought. *Traitor.*

She folded her arms and glared. 'Maybe I'm just not that into you?'

He laughed. 'Not buying it. Try again.'

She clamped her lips shut in the hope that he'd tire of the silent treatment and give up.

'She said you were scared. Has some guy done a number on you? Because I can emasculate him if that'll help.'

The corners of her mouth curved upwards before she could stop them.

'You know I'll keep throwing out outlandish suggestions 'til you tell me the truth, right?'

And he would. If the guy had been determined enough to win the World Championship five times, odds were he wouldn't let up.

She took a deep breath, blew it out. 'My dad let me down repeatedly. Rarely followed through on promises. Popped in when he felt like it. Paid more attention to his next three wives than he did to Mum and me. Then when Mum was diagnosed he stopped contact altogether.'

Archer swore.

'Yeah, I think I've used that expletive a few times my-self.' She shrugged, hoping he'd back off and she wouldn't have to divulge the rest—the real reason why she was pet-rified of a relationship with Archer. 'Guess I'm reluctant to trust people because of that.'

'There's more.'

She should've known he'd be too smart to let this go.

'Cal, look at me.'

But she couldn't. Couldn't risk him seeing her real fear.

'Your dad sounds like a selfish jerk, but that's not what has you so scared.'

When she still wouldn't eyeball him, he swore again. 'Thanks to you, I sorted things out with my family. I stashed my damn pride and took the first step in rebuild-ing the gap I created.' He jabbed a thumb at his chest. 'I've got trust issues too, because they didn't trust me enough to confide in when they should've. I often wonder if it's me, something about me that made them do that. But I'm not wasting time second-guessing myself any more, Cal. It's not worth it. I'm going out on a limb here because it's *you*. I'm scared like you are, so there has to be more.'

Damn him for being so intuitive.

'Is this about the motor neurone disease? Are you scared you'll inherit it?'

Her gaze snapped to his, and in that instant she gave away her final fear.

'Because it's natural to be scared, but whatever hap-pens in the future we'll face it together.'

'Are you crazy? You saw my mum. And she's only going to get worse. You think I want you to…?' She trailed off in horror, tears blurring her eyes at how close she'd come to blurting the truth.

'Tell me.'

He placed a fingertip under her chin and gently tipped it up so she had no option but to look at him.

She wanted to fob him off, to lie, but the love blazing from his intent stare was her undoing.

'You think I want you to be stuck with something like that? For you to give up your freedom for me?' She shook her head, dislodging his touch. 'If the disease didn't kill me, the guilt would.' A great sob tore from her chest. 'I want more for you.'

'*You're* all I want—'

He broke off, and for one horrifying moment she thought he might cry.

'Look, I'm new to this emotional stuff. I don't know what to do or say to prove I love you.'

He dropped his head into his hands, his defeatist posture so far removed from the confident guy she knew it got through to her as nothing else could.

He loved her.

He wanted to be with her.

How many people got a second chance at their first love?

Tentative, she reached out and laid a hand on his shoulder. 'Genetic testing says I don't carry the mutated gene, but that doesn't mean I can't get it. My chances are still elevated.'

He lifted his head, his bleak expression tearing at her inside. 'Life's full of risks, Cal. I take risks every day. Sharks. Rips. Getting on a plane. In a car. If we don't take risks we're half dead anyway. And that's not you. The woman I remember in Capri was vivacious and bold and lived life to the max. I've seen glimpses of that woman the last week and she's magnificent.'

She couldn't speak if she wanted to. Her throat was constricted with emotion.

'I won't pre-empt your mum, but she's going to tell you the same thing I just did. She wants you to make the most of your life, to embrace it, not run from it for fear of losing it one nebulous day that may never come.'

'I don't want you to give up who you are for me. I won't be that selfish, like Dad—'

'He's a callous bastard and you're nothing like him. You're standing by your mum. You're doing everything in your power to show her how much she means to you. As for your trust issues because of him, I can deal with them.' He jabbed a hand through his blond spikes. 'I can deal with anything as long as I have you by my side.'

When it came down to it, that was what convinced her to give their relationship a go.

Having Archer by her side, through good and bad, was a pretty potent attraction.

'What about kids? I'm not sure I could take the risk. They may inherit—'

'Enough. You're reaching for excuses, probably terrified to commit like me.'

Damn straight she was.

He tapped his chest. 'If you're feeling half as vulnerable and open wide in here as I am, you're grasping at whatever you can to avoid taking a risk.'

He was good. He'd homed in on exactly how she was feeling: raw and vulnerable and shell-shocked.

And downright petrified.

He was right. She was grabbing at any old excuse, hiding her fear behind it.

But in opening her heart to him a second time around hadn't she already taken the biggest risk of all?

He snagged her hand, squeezed it. 'You're worrying about the future when we need to live in the present.'

When her mum had been diagnosed, and later when

Callie had been given the all-clear following genetic testing, she'd made it her mission to make the most of every opportunity.

Archer had proved how much he loved her by his willingness to give up what he treasured most: his freedom.

He wanted to be with her for ever. It was the greatest opportunity of a lifetime.

What was she waiting for?

He enveloped her in his arms and she finally let go, her emotion spilling out in torrents of tears as she drenched his shirt.

'Kids, marriage, the works, we'll face it. Together,' he murmured, smoothing her hair, stroking her back until her sobs subsided.

Stunned that this incredible man was willing to give up so much to be with her, she eased back and gazed into his eyes.

'I love you. I always have.'

He kissed her, long and slow.

By the time they made it back to the restaurant their Christmas dinner was cold.

EPILOGUE

'WE SHOULD HAVE eloped to Hawaii,' Archer murmured in Callie's ear after the umpteenth back-slap and congratulatory kiss.

Callie elbowed her new husband. 'And miss out on sharing another Flett Christmas Eve wedding with our families? No way.'

'You're such a romantic sap,' he said, sliding an arm around her waist and holding her close.

'So sue me.' She sighed and snuggled into him. 'Thank you.'

'For?'

'This.'

She waved towards the festivities in full swing on the beach foreshore in front of the Winki Pop Surf School.

Artie, resplendent in tux and Santa hat, was mixing up another batch of his secret sangria.

Izzy, too cute in an eclectic Christmas elf-fairy costume, was racing around Tom in a demented version of Ring-a-Rosie. Travis and Shelly were canoodling, and Archer's folks were sitting hand in hand alongside Nora, watching the fun with benign smiles.

Even the recalcitrant Bruno had made a rare appearance, resurfacing from the Middle East *sans* wife, and trying to make it up to Nora and his daughter.

Let him keep trying. Callie wasn't buying it, even if she'd generously agreed to let him come to the wedding and to Christmas lunch tomorrow.

The wedding ceremony on the beach had been incredible, but it had been earlier, when Archer had carried Nora in his arms and gently deposited her in a front row seat, that Callie had lost it.

He'd wiped away her tears to a chorus of sniffles from their small crowd of guests and she'd managed to hold it together for the vows. Just.

The fact that she'd married her first love, her only love, was so surreal she kept smoothing her strapless calf-length ivory silk wedding dress to ensure it was real.

Lucky for her, Archer rarely released her hand, and his solid presence was all the reassurance she needed.

His gaze followed hers. 'You sure your mum's going to be okay while we honeymoon in Capri? Because I'm happy to stay here—'

'She'll be fine.'

Callie had had a long talk with her mum when she'd almost lost Archer twelve months ago, resulting in her letting go of her residual fears and starting to live life in the moment.

Sure, watching her mum deteriorate a little every day sliced her in two, but Nora was making the most of the time she had left. The least Callie could do was the same.

It was what Nora had wanted—to see Callie happy—and they'd brought the wedding forward for that very reason.

Not that she or Archer minded. They'd been living together anyway, spending Monday to Friday in Melbourne and the weekends in Torquay.

He didn't mind the commute, and she didn't mind a sexy surfer crowding her space. They hadn't decided on permanent living arrangements yet. Time enough when they returned from Capri.

She couldn't believe they were returning to the beautiful town where they'd met, where this amazing guy had wooed her with wine and moonlight and sea.

'What are you thinking?'

She glanced into her husband's deep blue eyes and smiled. 'I'm thinking about old memories of Capri.'

'Well, I'm thinking about creating new ones.'

His exaggerated eyebrow-wiggle made her laugh.

'You know we're going to have an amazing life together, right?' He cradled her face in his hands, his thumbs caressing her cheeks.

'You bet.'

For whatever they faced in the future she'd do it with her incredible husband by her side.

Life didn't get any better than this.

He lowered his head and kissed her, a soft, tender melding of lips that quickly escalated into heat and passion and need.

Maybe it did…

* * * * *

MILLS & BOON®
The Billionaires Collection!

This fabulous 6 book collection features stories from some of our talented writers. Feel the temperature rise with our ultra-sexy and powerful billionaires. Don't miss this great offer – buy the collection today to get two books free!

Order yours at
www.millsandboon.co.uk
/billionaires

**Fall under the spell of *New York Times*
bestselling author**

Nora Roberts

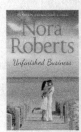
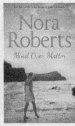
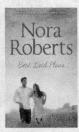
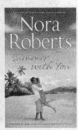

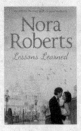
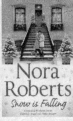
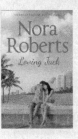

**450 million of her books in
print worldwide**

www.millsandboon.co.uk